81

82

83

140

15

VICTORIA FOUR-THIRTY

THE MACMILLAN COMPANY
NEW YORK · BOSTON · CHICAGO · DALLAS
ATLANTA · SAN FRANCISCO

VICTORIA
FOUR-THIRTY

BY
CECIL ROBERTS

NEW YORK
THE MACMILLAN COMPANY
1938

CONTENTS

BOOK I. THEY SET OUT

vi CONTENTS

BOOK I

THEY SET OUT

CHAPTER I

JAMES BROWN, OF VICTORIA

"YOU'D better 'urry up!" called his mother, at the head of the stairs.

"Righto!" shouted back Jim, bent over the kitchen sink. He rinsed his head and neck, washed the lather off his chest, dipped his face again, spluttered, raised his dripping head from the wash-basin, and squeezed the water out of his thick chestnut curls. Then, taking a towel off the hook on the kitchen door, he began to rub himself until his red cheeks shone, and his smooth flesh glowed under the friction.

He gave a glance at himself in the little square mirror over the sink, and saw his youthful figure, naked from the waist up. He set back his strong young shoulders, and braced himself, observing his developed biceps and pectoral muscles with brief satisfaction. He had every reason to be so fit, for he was carrying bags and swinging parcels about all day, and even before he became a porter at Victoria Station he had been the best boxer at the Lads' Club. He was broad in the shoulders, and tapered triangularly to a narrow waist, and slim flanks. His white, hairless stomach was a boy's, as also his round face with its merry brown eyes. But, as he noted with satisfaction, his arms and torso were now those of a man.

"Jim, what a mess you do make!" cried his mother, coming down into the kitchen, with dinner dishes in her hands. The lodger upstairs was ill in bed, and was having his meals taken up.

"You can't clean up a mess and not make a mess," retorted the boy, good-humouredly. He had spent a busy and sooty half-hour cleaning out the kitchen flue, of which his mother had long complained.

She looked now at the bucket of soot which he had extracted.

"No wonder it wouldn't draw. That's a good job done!" she said, and then, taking a cloth, proceeded to mop up the pools of water around her son's feet.

He gave her a playful smack on her ample behind, and twisted her round.

" 'Ere, I'll do that," he said, and, laughing, gave her an impulsive, sound kiss on her cheek. For a moment she held his warm young body to hers, and then pushed him away.

"If you don't 'urry up, Jim, you'll be late. Here's your clean shirt," she said, taking off the table near by a blue shirt which she proceeded to unfold for his use. "And do turn up your sleeves! They're something awful. I nearly have to scrub the wrists away to get 'em clean."

He lifted the shirt over his head, wriggled into it, buttoned it at the neck and rapidly tied his tie, then, the tails tucked in and the blue corduroy trousers belted at the waist, he slipped on the dark blue waistcoat and jacket with its bright metal buttons.

A swift combing of his damp curls followed. They snapped back under the comb, a golden cluster above his red ears and pink cheeks. Old Mrs. Brown looked at her son with pride. Forty years ago his father had looked like that. He, too, was a railway servant. It was a pity Jim had never known his father.

"There's one thing about this hovel," said Jim, still comb-ing, "it's on the job!"

"If it's your home you're talking about, you ought to be ashamed of yourself!" declared Mrs. Brown. "It's served us well enough for thirty years."

Jim stopped combing, and made a flourish.

"An oven that won't cook, a basement kitchen, no electric light, a grimy back yard, an outside closet, and the dust-bin goin' out through the parlour! And you've paid enough to buy the place twice over."

"You talk like a Bolshevik!" retorted Mrs. Brown. "You know you love the old place."

"Gawd love a duck!" exclaimed Jim, straightening his jacket, and reaching for his peaked cap. "One day, if I know some-thing, we'll have electric light, an indoor closet and bathroom, electric cooking——"

"An' a Rolls-Royce. Get off with you. All you'll get is the sack!" said Mrs. Brown, putting dishes in the sink.

Jim stuck on his cap at a jaunty angle, one curl escaping at the side, and, approaching his mother from behind, put his arms round her wide waist, and planted a kiss on her cheek. Then, playfully, he bit the lobe of her ear.

Mrs. Brown stopped rinsing, laughed, and asked, "Is that what you do to Lizzie?"

"Yes, and she don't half like it!" replied Jim to this allu-sion to Lizzie, with whom he was walking out.

"Well, if that's what you do, an' looking at you, girls have strange tastes these days," said Mrs. Brown, playfully.

He gave her another hug and kissed her.

"Bye-bye, Ma!" he said.

"Bye-bye," she answered.

She heard him go up the area steps, whistling, saw him

pause for a moment, feet level with the top of the window, give her a mock salute, and then disappear. Jim was her treasure. It seemed only yesterday he was a small boy, carrying up the tray to the lodgers' rooms. And now he was twenty-two, a porter like his dad before him, at Victoria Station.

She glanced at the clock. Lor', he'd be late. It was five-and-twenty minutes past two. They were working like niggers just now with all the folks off on their August holidays. Jim wouldn't see Lizzie to-night. She liked Lizzie, a nice steady girl, working in a Lyons' restaurant. But . . . they would want to marry one day, and she just couldn't imagine life without her son Jim, although Nellie, her daughter, was the best of girls. But Jim, with his sunny smile and good-natured ways, was . . . Well, well, why worry about that yet?

> The King of Love my Shepherd is
> Whose goodness faileth never—

sang Mrs. Brown, busy with the dishcloth.

Jim Brown walked along the smoky little Pimlico street that lay immediately behind Victoria Station. That station, whose wide glass roof he could now see over the high brick wall and the long line of dingy houses that backed on to the shunting area, symbolized the barrier between two styles of life. On the other side of the lines running into Victoria lay the land of "the toffs," select Belgravia with Eaton Square, which was not a square, and Belgrave Square, and the well-kept streets and secret houses that lay north towards Knightsbridge and Hyde Park.

Sometimes in the evening, with Lizzie, he walked over into that rich territory. There was always discreet entertainment to be found in its streets. In Belgrave Square they would hear jazz music coming out of an upper window; and on the street level, before the huge portico entrance, there would be a striped awning. On the pavement there was often a crimson drugget to keep the dirt off the dancing slippers of the smart young women who came out of the great chauffeured cars that glided up.

Standing in the crowd, he watched these fortunate children of Society pass into the footmen-haunted hall, and there was a wonderful occasion when a dazzlingly pretty girl, accompanied by a thin young man, had looked straight at Jim and given him a warm, friendly smile.

"Well now, did you ever!" exclaimed Lizzie, hanging on his arm.

"She knows a man when she sees one," said Jim, with a smile. "Poor girl, fancy dragging that around."

Through the bright doorway "that" disappeared, a weedy young man, drooping like a question mark as he hung over his dazzling companion.

"The conceit of you!" retorted Lizzie, with a proud, possessive look.

And looking up at those stone balconies with their great windows all shining, out of which flowed the dance music, they often saw elegant young couples standing in the warm summer night, their happy voices mingling with the thumping rhythm of the dance music.

There was also the entertainment of the smaller houses, houses in narrow streets which had once held servants, grooms, small tradesmen and people in the service of the great mansions in the squares. Now all these little houses, with flat fronts, and areas and basement kitchens, were brightly painted. Their windows had expensive curtains, and expensive cars waited outside them. These houses were no better in size and design than the grimy houses on the other side of Victoria Station, but they were four times the rent, and the leases, sold by the Duke of Westminster, fetched fantastic prices.

In these little houses lived the well-to-do "hard-ups," explained Jim. Many of them were little aristocratic old ladies with one maid, very reserved and proud. Their rich relations came to visit them from time to time, in Rolls-Royces, with chauffeurs in blue uniforms, with gloves, waiting at the wheel.

"Hard-up indeed!" remarked Lizzie, as they passed one of these little houses which hummed with voices. There was a cocktail party being given and the street was lined with cars.

"They spend as much in a day as you and I spend in a month!"

"If you've had five thousand a year and you've only now got one, you're poor," said Jim. "And if you've been used to a butler and footmen, and going away to the Riviera in winter, and you've got to stay at home, and have only an odd-job woman to help, you'd feel the pinch. I see a lot of 'em at the station— goin' away third-class when they used to go first, 'cause their money's shrunk, and as nice as ever to you, with a good tip and a thank you. Not like a lot of these haughty jump-ups with crocodile leather luggage and a sixpenny tip!"

"You always did like toffs, Jim," said Lizzie.

"And Ma says I'm a Bolshevik! So which is it? No, I only want to be fair. Live and let live—that's my motto," answered Jim.

But there were moments when the plan of life seemed a jig-saw puzzle to Jim. How did those elegant young men come to be driving up to those big houses, with their expensive cars and their beautiful girls? They were well educated, they had an easy air, they felt sure of themselves. But money had done all that,

and it wasn't money they had earned, but money their fathers
had paid for them. By an accident they'd been born in a front
bedroom on the north side of Victoria Station, instead of in a
Pimlico street on the south side.

One need not be a Bolshevik to wonder at this freakish chance
in things whereby you went either to Eton College in a top hat or
to the Council School in patched pants. And it seemed to Jim
you weren't necessarily any happier whichever side of Victoria
Station you were born on. What a lot of miserable objects he
carried luggage for—sleek, soft-voiced young men trailing behind old aunts, bored to death because they were travelling
abroad! Why, the very labels excited him: Paris, Milan, Rome,
Geneva, Vienna, Bucharest, Athens, Cairo, Baghdad. If his bag
ever had one of those labels on it he'd run all the way down the
platform instead of drawling—"Aw portah!" or "How frightfully crowded!" or "Really, my dear, it's preposterous!"

Lots of things were preposterous, but not having your luggage carried down the platform, with a Venice label on it, and
a first-class seat to lounge in, and a first-class restaurant to eat in,
and nothing to do but sit and glide away out of smoke into sunshine.

To-day there was little smoke and much sunshine. It seemed
hard to spend the golden August day under the grey old roof of
the station, to be endlessly trundling other people's luggage from
taxi to train, from train to taxi, to fight with the crush of passengers, all clamouring, fussy over their right train, their reserved seat, their luggage in the van, their luggage on the rack.
And there were dogs to deal with, cushions and rugs and sticks
and hampers, and people who thought he should know everything, and people who were sure he knew nothing, and people
who wanted him to take sixpence out of a ten-shilling note just
as the train was moving off, and people who thought he could

run with a trunk and somehow carry eight packages with two hands.

Yes, he saw life, but all this scramble was for other people's pleasure, and sometimes he wished he could change places. He would never see these cities over the Channel, these Ritz hotels, the Miramar, the Grand Hotel Boromeo, the Dunapolota, Lido Excelsior, the Schweizerhof, the Du Lac, Bellevue, Splendid, Europa, Winter Palace and Bristol, whose vivid labels with setting suns, tall palms, gondolas, ski jumps, mountains, lakes, bathing-pools and terraces illustrated the gay life of the rich at play.

He was not envious, but he was still young enough to dream. In a crazy moment he had sworn to Lizzie that they should spend their honeymoon at Lugano, where they would have a bedroom with a balcony, high up on the mountain side, overlooking a blue lake and a range of snow-capped mountains, exactly as the hotel label promised. Lizzie had laughed at him. Of course it was a fantastic promise, but he could not suppress the idea. It seemed possible for so many he carried luggage for, so why not himself?

Well, somebody must stay at home and sweep platforms and carry luggage and stick on labels. And millions were content with Brighton and Bournemouth and Blackpool.

Still whistling, he emerged into the Wilton Road. There was a queue of taxis entering the Continental Bay. Another busy afternoon lay before him. He looked up as he reached the porters' room and clocked in. It was just two-thirty. He was on duty on the Boat Train platform. Trundling a truck he went out to the Continental passengers' bay where the taxis were already arriving for the three o'clock Dover-Ostend-Bâle-Rome train. There was one virtue in all this mad fight to get out of England—the tips were coming in, this was the golden month.

It might, with luck, prove golden enough for him to put a bit away and give Lizzie the shock of her life when she found herself one day a blushing bride, Lugano-bound.

"Nah then! Whoer-yer a-shoving?" asked a colleague, sweating under two portmanteaux. "Get 'old of that suit-case, and take this gent to get it registered through to Lucerne."

"Righto!" responded Jim, cheerily, swinging the case up on his truck. "Follow me, sir!"

CHAPTER II

HERR FRIEDRICH GOLLWITZER, OF VIENNA

HERR FRIEDRICH GOLLWITZER came out of the Carlton Hotel, having cut short his lunch, and crossed the road to the Cook Wagon-Lits Agency in Pall Mall. He always liked London, but this time he would be glad to get out of it. He had lingered for a week after getting off the liner at Southampton, on his return from America where he had conducted a series of concerts that had been greeted with delirious acclaim. Next Friday he was conducting at Salzburg, at the Festival, and he could not delay his departure any longer.

It was distressing to be without the indispensable Hans, his valet-secretary, who did everything, and was an inseparable part of his life. Last Monday the light-hearted Hans had suddenly felt terrible pains in his stomach, and by eight o'clock in the evening he was being operated on for appendicitis, in a London nursing home. Thus had come to an abrupt end Hans' ambitious plan for them to visit Scotland and see the famous moors when the grouse shooting began. Hans had always had a passion for shooting, which had been gratified in his boyhood in Carinthia, where he had lived on his father's farm.

Hans was progressing well, said the surgeon, but there could be no question of moving him for two or three weeks. When he had visited him this morning in the Wimpole Street nursing home, Herr Gollwitzer had found Hans as bright as ever, his pink boyish face beaming. His one worry was that his em-

12

ployer had to travel alone, and Herr Gollwitzer was as helpless as a baby in the mundane affairs of life.

"You have your ticket all ready?" asked Hans, from the pillow.

"Yes—you mustn't talk, Hans," answered Herr Gollwitzer.

"You can register your luggage through to Salzburg. Send a telegram to Herr Geicher and he'll meet you at the station, and your——"

"Ssh! Hans! I promised you should not talk too much," warned Herr Gollwitzer.

"I'm all right—your rooms are reserved at the Bristol—the corner suite looking over the Dollfuss Platz."

"Thank you, lieber Hans—and now I must go. I've had five minutes. *Auf Wiedersehen,* dear boy—get better. I'll wait for you in Vienna."

He held Hans' hand for a few moments. He hated leaving the boy who had given him such faithful service for four years. Friends wondered at his devotion to Hans, but those who did not like to acknowledge it could pass out of his life. He knew the faithful heart of this engaging boy, his intense loyalty, his ceaseless vigilance, his forethought in everything that affected his comfort or his work. "If you want to do anything with old Gollwitzer get the right side of Hans," said those who knew. "Gollwitzer's under the thumb of his valet—a Carinthian peasant lad!" exclaimed a concert director,—"it's preposterous!" His friend laughed. "It's better than having the Maestro under the thumb of a termagant mistress. That little Hans wet-nurses him."

Oh yes, Gollwitzer knew all that they thought, and sometimes said. But he had suffered so much, experienced so many humiliations at the hands of those he had trusted, that now he had found unswerving loyalty, and an affection that had not an atom of avarice in it, he valued Hans, and clung to him in the teeth of gossip and criticism.

Four years ago he had so nearly gone to pieces when this lad of eighteen, nervous, awkward, and certainly underfed, had come round from the Agency to which Gollwitzer had telephoned in despair. His housekeeper and her rascally husband had disappeared with all his linen and silver. He had arrived home from a South American tour to find the house in a state of indescribable filth, as though it had been the scene of a debauch, with all his treasured carpets stained, his precious china broken, even his beloved piano burnt with cigarette ends.

In one day, with an apron round his waist, Hans had produced order out of chaos, and an excellent meal out of the kitchen. Within a week he was indispensable; within a month he had detected Gollwitzer's agent in embezzlement of fees, and taken the professional business into his own hands. In gratitude Gollwitzer would have given him the status of private secretary and agent. "No—let me stay as I am, your valet, Herr Gollwitzer. I am a peasant. I could not sit at table with your friends. I will not be patronized. It is enough to be just Hans."

So just Hans he remained, though in Gollwitzer's intimate life Hans often sat at his table and travelled with him in the train. He was skilled at fading out tactfully. Everyone knew Hans was there, but no one could point to a single act that presumed on his position. That Gollwitzer entrusted to him all the details of his life, all his acquaintances knew, hence the care that everyone took to keep on the right side of Hans.

This was the first time in four years they had been separated, the world-famous conductor of sixty, the peasant lad of twenty-two. Herr Gollwitzer felt lost, but he tried hard just now, for Hans' sake, to appear calm and confident.

"You'll want a new hot-water bottle, the other's perished. You must get it to-day before you start," said Hans, still holding Herr Gollwitzer's hand.

"*Ja.* I will get it."

"You promise?"

"*Ja.*"

The hot-water bottle was essential to Herr Gollwitzer's health. For years, after the fatigue of rehearsals, or when the concert ended, he fell a prey to nervous exhaustion and suffered excruciating pains in the stomach; it was Hans who had discovered that a hot-water bottle warded off the colic. The rubber bottle was never missing from the Gollwitzer baggage.

There was a moment's pause. Hans had no further instructions. He lay there smiling at his employer.

"*Gute Reise!*" he said, softly.

"*Danke, mein lieber Hans. Auf Wiedersehen.*"

"*Auf Wiedersehen, mein Herr!*"

Outside in the corridor he met the fresh-complexioned nurse. Herr Gollwitzer was frightened of all nursing homes although he had never been an inmate of one, *Gott sei Dank.* He stood aside to let her pass, peering at her, short-sightedly, through his glasses.

"Herr Gollwitzer," said the nurse, stopping, "may I speak to you a moment?"

Herr Gollwitzer's heart gave a flutter. It was about Hans. There was something wrong.

"Ach—vat ees eet, please?" he asked.

"There's a young lady—very ill. She's heard you were here —and she's begged me to ask for your autograph."

"Ach! Das ees all? So!" ejaculated the conductor, beaming on her. "Wid pleasure!"

The nurse produced the album. After much searching through his pockets Herr Gollwitzer found the fountain-pen which Hans filled with ink every morning.

"Wid goot wishes for recovery—ees that correct?" asked Herr Gollwitzer.

"Oh, that would be splendid!" exclaimed the nurse.

Slowly the conductor wrote the words, in his heavy level style, and signed his name. The nurse thanked him and followed him to the stairs. But at the bottom he was not to escape, for it happened that Sir Henry Blore, the surgeon who had operated on Hans, came in as the porter opened the street door.

"Ah, Herr Gollwitzer!" said the surgeon, cheerily.

"He ees goot patient?" asked the conductor after an exchange of greetings. "Eet all goes vell?"

"Excellent! Excellent, Herr Gollwitzer. The boy's doing splendidly, a nice, clean operation, no complications. Good nursing, that's all now. Leave him to us—he's in good hands," cried Sir Henry, putting down his hat. "I'm just going up to see him."

The old fellow seemed inclined to talk, but Sir Henry was in a hurry.

"Oh—this afternoon you leave? Well, well. A pleasant journey, Herr Gollwitzer!" said Sir Henry, shaking his hand.

The conductor went slowly down the steps, the door closed. Mounting the stairs Sir Henry reflected that Herr Gollwitzer must be a good-hearted fellow. He had paid a hundred pounds for the operation, and the nursing-home fees were three guineas a day. Most servants would have been sent to a hospital.

On his way back to the Carlton Hotel Herr Gollwitzer remembered Hans' injunction, and bought a rubber hot-water bottle. But he had told a little lie when he said he had got his ticket; the hotel clerk had ordered it for him. Thus it was that, at a little after two o'clock, Herr Gollwitzer, having had a brief lunch, was crossing the road to the Cook Wagon-Lits Agency in Pall Mall, to collect and pay for the ticket and wagon-lit that were to take him through to Salzburg, in order that he might conduct Mozart's *Don Juan* on Friday evening next.

He soon found the renowned Messrs. Cook, and was directed to the Continental Section, but when he arrived he was dismayed to find a crowd pressing against the counter, and four harassed clerks making out tickets, checking time-tables, and answering ceaseless questions. For a few moments he stood hopelessly on the verge of this crowd of holiday-makers. He had forgotten that it was August in England, when all Englishmen with any money seemed impelled to cross the Channel and travel in countries whose language they could seldom speak.

"But I wanted third-class as far as Bâle!" protested a shrill female voice.

"There's no third-class on that train, madam," replied the patient clerk.

"But you don't know your own business. I told you——"

Herr Gollwitzer was wondering why the clerk did not bang the time-table on the woman's head, when a voice beside him quietly said:

"Will you please come this way, Herr Gollwitzer? I have your ticket ready."

At the mention of his name several members of the crowd lost their anxiety temporarily, and turned to look at the world-famous conductor. Yes, that undoubtedly was the great Gollwitzer, the wizard with the baton, who had no living rival. That thick-set body, the full clean-shaven face, with the eyes peering through spectacles, and the broad-brimmed black felt hat, were familiar the world over. He looked like a heavy German professor, but when his delicate hand lifted the baton in the hushed hall everyone forgot that heavy body in the pure spirit which he drew from the hypnotized orchestra.

Herr Gollwitzer started at the mention of his name, and then meekly followed the young man down the long office until he came to a small private section. Here he was offered a chair, which he sank into heavily. The day was warm and he usually dozed after lunch. He looked at the pleasant young clerk, surprise visible on his face, and the young man, discerning, said:

"The hotel telephoned to say you were coming across, Herr Gollwitzer. We could have brought you the ticket but the clerk said you were coming in."

"*Ja.* Best thanks. Eet is all ready?"

"Everything, I think. Here is your ticket. London-Folkestone. Folkestone-Boulogne. Boulogne-Bâle. Zurich-Buchs. Buchs-Innsbruck-Salzburg. Here is the ticket for the sleeper, which you will enter at Boulogne. I have a Pullman seat reserved for you from London to Folkestone."

The young man smiled, took from a drawer a green folder with an elastic band, and put the ticket in it. "You would like your time-table, Herr Gollwitzer?"

"I tink I know it vell," said the conductor, smiling.

"I've no doubt, sir, you know all the trains in Europe better than us."

"Victoria four-thirty, Boulogne twenty-fifteen, Bâle five-five, Buchs eight-ten, Innsbruck eleven-twenty, Salzburg fifteen-twenty," said Gollwitzer, reeling off the times.

"Ah—I see you know it well, sir. Here is your ticket, sir, with Pullman supplement and wagon-lit—would you like to insure your luggage?"

"Tank you, no. I have travelled for thirty years and never have lost eet."

"You are one of the lucky ones, sir! Life has been very kind to you in every way, sir," observed the affable young man.

"Eh—vy do you say that?" asked Gollwitzer, peering into the frank young face before him.

"You are very famous, sir, you've travelled all over the world, you do the thing you most want to do, follow the art you love."

Herr Gollwitzer stared hard at this engaging young fellow for a few moments. He was a typical fresh-faced English boy, well-groomed, with his neat shiny hair and spotless stiff white collar. Twenty-four perhaps.

"And do you tink all that is happiness?" he asked after a pause.

"No, sir—but it all helps, doesn't it, sir?"

"Are you happy? You look very happy."

"Yes, sir, I am!" laughed the young man. Inwardly he thought: 'Who would imagine I should be talking like this with Friedrich Gollwitzer—but how human he is!'

"So—vy?"

The young man gave an embarrassed laugh.

"Well, sir—early this morning my wife had a baby."

"Ach! You are married?"

"Yes, sir."

"Und the baby—ees it boy or girl?"

"A boy, sir, a splendid little fellow the doctor says," responded the young man.

"I congratulate you. You are very young?" asked Gollwitzer, taking out his wallet to pay for the ticket.

"Twenty-two, sir. Too young, they said, but I don't regret it a moment."

"Und vat ees to pay?" asked Gollwitzer.

The young man became business-like at once.

"Here is the voucher, sir. Ticket London-Salzburg, single

first class, ten pounds twelve, wagon-lit four pounds ten, Pullman supplement Victoria-Folkestone three and six. Total, fifteen pounds five shillings and sixpence, if you please."

Herr Gollwitzer counted out four five-pound notes. The clerk
gave him the change. Then, taking another five-pound note
from his wallet, the conductor smiled and said:

"Vill you please me?"

"Yes, sir?" asked the young clerk.

"I vant to geeve your baby a present. Buy someting or save
eet for him," said Gollwitzer, proffering the note.

"But, sir—I—I really—" began the embarrassed young man.

"Please—take eet. You make me happy to hear such a ting.
I like many leetle Eenglish boys. The Eenglish are a great, goot
people and ve want more and more. Be happy wid your wife
and your boy."

"Oh, thank you, sir," said the young man, now red in the
face and neck.

"Goot day to you. I must go. Eet ees not long for my leaving," said Gollwitzer, rising.

"No, sir. Victoria, four-thirty—and thank you, sir," said the
clerk, escorting him down the office.

Herr Gollwitzer disappeared through the revolving door,
leaving a rather breathless young man behind him.

Outside on the pavement, in the bright August afternoon,
Herr Gollwitzer watched the traffic awhile before attempting to
cross to his hotel. And as he waited he murmured to himself,
"Twenty-two and happily married, and a son. And I am sixty
and have been unhappily married, and have no son. And the
whole world thinks I'm a success. *Das Leben ist eine Kunst. Ja*,
and I have never learned it. Yes, Friedrich Gollwitzer, Life is
an Art, and you've been a fumbler at it all your years."

Still ruminating on life, he crossed the road, missed a taxi by a hair's breadth, plodded on unconscious of the Cockney curse that followed the broad-brimmed hat, and reached the hotel. Even the slim, diminutive page-boy that took him up in the lift to his room emphasized the unkindness of Fate. That boy was somebody's son. It would have been something if out of the wreckage of his marriage there had been one child to offset the bankruptcy of these lonely years.

He reached his room, sat down, and looked at his watch. It was three o'clock. He could have half an hour's doze. He rang the bell for the valet, who in place of Hans had packed his bags, tipped him and said, "Be sure you call me at half-past three o'clock. I must catch the four-thirty at Victoria."

"Yes, sir," said the valet, and closed the door.

Herr Gollwitzer put up his feet, and dozed.

CHAPTER III

MRS. DOROTHY BLAKE, OF BELGRAVIA

I

SHE must have awakened just after dawn, for as she lay in bed the light was still dim in her room. Then she dozed again, and, later, awoke. It was still early. Down in the hall the clock struck seven. She counted the strokes one by one. How silly of her to wake so early, for she had a long day before her, and to-night she would get very little sleep in the train.

Wednesday, August the tenth. There had been other Wednesdays in other Augusts, but this was *the* Wednesday, the most important day in all her life. There were only two other days that might be as important. There was the day she was born, of which she had no recollection, and the day she would die, of which she had no knowledge. But this day was the greatest day, her happiest day, the one in which she would be at the peak of her life. It was the day on which she was marrying Derek Beddington Blake, who, at this moment, was quite unconscious of the great day, being fast asleep in the Grosvenor Hotel, scarcely half a mile away, where he had arrived yesterday, with his father, mother, two brothers and three sisters, from their home in Leicestershire, to be ready for the wedding.

This morning, reflected the bride, she was Dorothy Sewell. Soon after two o'clock to-day she would be Dorothy Blake. Mrs. Dorothy Blake, with a gold ring on her finger, placed there by her darling Derek.

And then, in the midst of her happiness at the thought, there

22

was a stab of pain, for this was her last day in England. This afternoon, with her husband, she was leaving for Kitzbühel, in Austria, and after three weeks' honeymoon, they were going on to Burma, where Derek was employed by an oil company. He had been home a month on leave, and although a wedding in August found many people away there seemed no alternative. Even so, it was surprising how many people were coming. The church would be full with her family's relations and friends and with his.

Her thoughts turned to her father. There were moments when she felt quite wicked at being so happy. Her two sisters were married, her brother was with his regiment in India. She was the last to leave the nest. Four years ago, when her mother had died, she remembered how she had flung herself upon her poor father and cried, "Oh, Daddy, Daddy, I will never, never leave you!" And now she was going to leave him, quite alone in this much too large London house, and it would be fully two years before she would see him again, unless he could be persuaded to make the long journey to Burma.

What a little thing altered the course of one's life! Two years ago she did not know that such a person as Derek Beddington Blake existed. One day, while visiting some relations in Leicestershire, their car had broken down and they were stranded, when a young man had come up and proffered help. After twenty minutes unsuccessful work the young man confessed himself defeated.

"Well, if you wouldn't mind taking us to Walley Manor, a couple of miles from here, where we're lunching, we could then get somebody to come and fetch the car—that is, if it's not causing you too much trouble," said Dorothy's uncle.

"Not at all—only too glad," replied the affable young man. So Uncle John and Cousin Gladys sat in the back of the car, and she sat near to their rescuer. The first things she noticed about him were his lovely grey eyes and long lashes, the next, his hands as they gripped the steering-wheel.

"Tell your man there's a perished connection to the autovac and she's not getting petrol," shouted the young man over his shoulder, to Uncle John.

"Thank you. You appear to understand cars. They're bonneted mysteries to me!" confessed Uncle John.

"I ought to! I'm an engineer," laughed the young man.

So that accounted for the powerful hands, not quite the hands one expected of a gentleman. Dorothy looked covertly at his face. It was a pleasant one, with a good line to the jaw, a firm neck, a well-poised head. His voice, too, gave her pleasure.

"You live in these parts?" asked Uncle John, affably.

"A little—I'm just home from South America. Now I'm in England for a year. Next year I go to Burma."

"It must be lovely to travel like that," ventured Dorothy.

He gave her a smile, his grey eyes regarding hers momentarily.

"Yes—I'm a bit of a rolling stone. Fortunately my company likes that kind," he answered.

"Here we are," said Uncle John, pointing to some gates with a drive.

"The Ascotes, yes, I know them," said the young man, as he turned in.

In a few moments they drew up to the entrance. The young man got out and opened the saloon door.

"I'm sure we're much obliged to you," said Uncle John.

"It's a pleasure," replied the young man. As he removed his hat Dorothy noticed the crisp black hair on a neat head. He re-entered the car, and just as the servant came to the door he drove off.

"I wonder who he is—silly not to have asked his name," said Uncle John, stepping in.

"Oh, wasn't he nice!" exclaimed Gladys, frankly.

Happily that was not their last sight of the young man. They went to the Ascotes to dine, a few days later, and there he was, Mr. Derek Blake, the son of Colonel and Mrs. Beddington Blake, their host's neighbours.

That was how it all began. He called, on invitation, at their house in Chester Square when he came to London a month later. He called again, and again. And when there seemed no excuse for calling, he still called, until a point came when Mr. Sewell began to wonder about these attentions.

"I suppose you've guessed, sir. I want to marry Dorothy," said Blake one day.

"And when I asked him whether he'd spoken to you," reported her father, "he said, 'No—not yet;' which showed a consideration for fathers which they don't get these days."

Darling Derek. She tried at this moment to imagine his dark head on the white pillow. After to-day she would see that beloved head on first waking in the morning. How strange, how wonderful, and, oh, just a little frightening.

Dorothy looked round the room. She really could not sleep any more. It was full daylight now. The birds were cheeping in the trees of Chester Square. She threw back the bedclothes, put her feet into blue satin slippers, and went across to the window. Then, drawing the curtain, she looked out, over the central garden in the Square, with its great plane trees, green turf, and black railings.

It was a radiant morning. They faced south, but the sun had not reached them yet. She could just see the spire of St. Michael's where, at two o'clock, she was to be married. It was so near that it seemed stupid to have to drive to church, but of course there was her train to consider.

The sunlight fell on the leaves of the trees. Next door the maid was washing the steps, and a young man from the dairy came up from the area, having left the milk. He went across to a small pony-cart belonging to the dairy company, entered something in a small book, and then moved on with his cart. Dorothy felt tempted to shout to him. She could not, of course, but she wanted to call,—"Do you know I'm getting married to-day at two o'clock, and this is the last time I shall get up in this house, and see you and your pony delivering the milk?" The young man would have been so very surprised. But everything that was to happen to-day was almost unbelievable. She was going to cherish and obey. Oh, yes, she wanted to cherish and obey, for all the modern nonsense, and he was going to answer "I will" when asked to take her for his lawful wife.

She left the window and glanced round the dear, familiar room. Stretched on the back of a chair was the priceless silk net veil which old Lady Mannering had lent her for the wedding. And although it was very silly, she had to open the wardrobe door and have another look at the wedding-gown which Friar, the parlourmaid, had hung up yesterday with such expressions of admiration. It was a most lovely gown, of pearl-tinted satin with long sleeves and a high neckline, embroidered with pearls and diamanté. The train was cut in one with the skirt, and little Hugh, her five-year-old nephew, was to carry it.

In the corner of the room was a small writing bureau. In the middle of the pigeon-holes there was a cupboard which she kept locked. Taking a key out of her handbag she unlocked the little mahogany door and took out a bundle of letters tied up with a blue ribbon, under which was tucked a card, "Letters from

Derek" inscribed on it. The last had been written from Rangoon, Burma. The first—she opened it again to look at it—had come in a handwriting then strange to her. It had been written from his Leicestershire home and ran—"Dear Miss Sewell, I shall be in London next Tuesday. May I call to see you on Wednesday afternoon? Unless I hear to the contrary I will come at four o'clock. Yours sincerely, Derek Blake."

How ludicrously formal! Dear Miss Sewell—yours sincerely, Derek Blake. She laughed, and catching sight of her face in the mirror, said to it, in a solemn voice: "To-day, at two o'clock at St. Michael's, Chester Square, the marriage will be solemnized of Mr. Derek Beddington Blake, youngest son of Colonel and Mrs. Beddington Blake, of Windyates, Market Harborough, and Miss Dorothy Agnes Sewell, youngest daughter of Mr. Geoffrey Sewell, of Chester Square, S.W. Yes, believe it or not—me!" declared Dorothy, and then burst into laughter at her foolishness.

She tied up the bundle of letters, put them back in the bureau, and locked it. Daddy had said this was to remain her bedroom until such time as she and Derek had a home in England.

The door opened and Friar appeared with morning tea.

"Goodness gracious, Miss Dorothy, are you up already!" exclaimed the parlourmaid.

"Oh, Friar, I'm terribly, terribly excited!"

"Of course you are, miss. I remember how I was myself," confessed Friar, putting down the tray on the bedside table.

Dorothy remembered with a shock that Friar, who never had any prefix to her name, was Mrs. Friar. But the marriage had not been a success, and Friar never talked of it.

"Were you up very early on your wedding morning?" asked Dorothy.

"I 'ad to be, Miss Dorothy, to go to my work. I 'ad to get married in my lunch hour—I was in a tea-shop then—at a Registry Office, but I remember how I shook all the morning."

"I've never said so, Friar, but I'm sorry it was not a happy marriage," said Dorothy, sympathetically.

"Thank you, miss, we never talk about it—and, do you know, I've forgotten almost everything about it. I brought it on myself. I was getting anxious, and just snatched 'im, although I knew in my 'eart of 'earts he wasn't much good. That's twelve years ago, and I 'aven't seen 'im for ten. For all I know I'm a widow."

Friar crossed to the windows and pulled back the velours curtains.

"It's a glorious day for you, miss. Will you have your bath now, or will you go back to bed a bit? You'll be awfully tired before the day's over," said the kind Friar.

"Oh, I couldn't go back to bed! I'll have my bath, and I'll breakfast with Daddy."

"Very well, miss. I'll run it now," said Friar, retiring.

II

Mr. Sewell was surprised to see his daughter come into the dining-room. He was standing by the window, opening *The Times*, and he peered at her over the top of his pince-nez.

"Well now—how's this? I thought you'd keep in bed and rest for a bit."

"Daddy, I can't. I'm too excited."

She put her arms round his neck and kissed him. For a few moments he held her, then he looked at her, and said nothing. She, too, was silent. She knew how thin was the wall between their emotions. This was their last breakfast together.

Dorothy went to the table and sat down before the teapot. Her father liked the first cup without sugar, the second with one lump. He stood now, by the sideboard, lifted the lid of the salver and helped her to a rasher of bacon and an egg.

"Oh, Daddy—I can't eat all that—please," she protested.

"Come now, you've got a great"—he almost said 'ordeal,' but felt somehow the word was not quite suitable, and repeated—"a great day in front of you. Look at the sunshine! And a smooth crossing, says *The Times.*"

She smiled. Poor Daddy, he was trying so hard to be normal, and underneath it all they were both feeling the strain of this last occasion. He told her the news in the paper. There was a letter from Uncle John, who was arriving in London, with Gladys, at eleven o'clock. They would come straight on to the house. Gladys was one of the bridesmaids.

Their conversation was interrupted by a commotion at the front door.

"What was that?" asked Mr. Sewell, when the second parlourmaid came into the room with more hot water.

"It's the men, sir, they're arrived with the awning. They're putting it up," she replied.

"Oughtn't they to have a glass of wine after, Daddy?" asked Dorothy.

"H'm, I suppose it's the thing—but I'll bet they'd prefer beer."

Mr. Sewell turned to the parlourmaid.

"Tell cook to give 'em a glass of wine—or beer, if they prefer it," he said, and added with a chuckle, "I'm not going to open the champagne yet!"

At ten o'clock Dorothy, packing with the aid of Friar, heard the telephone in her room tinkle. She went to it.

"Oh, Derek!" she exclaimed, and, turning, said to Friar, "Come back in a moment." Friar retreated.

"Who's there? I want you alone," asked Derek.

"Only Friar. She's gone."

"Very happy, darling?"

"Terribly, Derek darling."

"I want to see you—I don't feel I can wait until two o'clock."

"But, Derek, you must!"

"I know, my pet. You will come, won't you?"

"Come?" echoed Dorothy.

"To the altar, darling. You won't take sudden fright, and run away. Some brides do."

"Silly darling, how could I!"

"I shall be all pins and needles until I see you come in at the far end."

"I won't be late, Derek dear."

"And, my sweet, don't walk up the aisle too fast. I want 'em all to see you. I'm so proud of you. I know you'll be ravishing."

"Silly boy. I'll be so proud of you—and we'll walk out still slower."

"Oh, I don't know. I'll look a mess. My trousers won't hang properly, and my tie'll slip up over my collar, and they'll whisper and say, 'How could she marry that man!' "

"Derek, we'll be the handsomest couple in London."

"Yes, darling, we will, and the happiest."

"I'm rather trembly, Derek, are you?"

"Just a weeny bit—do you want to call it off?"

"Silly darling—do you?"

"I say—have any more presents arrived?"

"Two—late last night. Another coffee-pot——"

"O God!"

". . . and a gorgeous rose bowl, from the Ascotes."

"We've done very well, darling."

"Marvellously!"

"And there'll be some in Burma. I say, how awful of us!"

"Awful, darling!"

There was a pause.

"Darling!"

"Yes, Derek?"

"I believe my bath water's running over."

"Aren't you dressed yet?"

"No, I'm still in pyjamas, messing about—last time as a bachelor. Listen, darling, one thing more."

"Yes?"

"Do you love me enough to risk it?"

"Darling—there isn't any risk. I couldn't just live without you."

"Good-bye, my precious. Listen."

The sound of a kiss came over the wire. Then she heard the telephone ring off.

Dorothy rose with a flushed face, and saw herself in the mirror.

"Just idiots! And in a year from now— No, Mrs. Blake!" she said firmly, to her face—"Ten, twenty, thirty years from now you'll know this was the luckiest day of your life."

Ten minutes later Friar reappeared.

"Look, miss, it's come—isn't it just lovely!"

She opened the box. It contained a large sheaf of Madonna lilies, from Derek. Dorothy lifted them out and gazed, entranced.

"Hold it a moment, Friar," she said, excitedly, thrusting the bouquet into the maid's hands. Then, picking up the silk net veil, she threw it over her head, and from the dressing-table took up a wreath of mother-of-pearl orange-blossom, which she placed over the veil.

"Now the bouquet," she called, and took it from the maid. "Do I look nice, Friar?"

"You look simply wonderful!"

"Pom-pom-te-rom-pom-pom-pom!
Pom-tiddle-om, tiddle-om-pom!"

she sang, slowly walking round the room to Mendelssohn's *Wedding March*.

"And not too eager, Friar?"

"Oh, miss—simply lovely!"

"Of course," said Dorothy, laying down the bouquet and taking off the bridal wreath, "I shan't look a bit like that. I shall look like death."

"Oh, no you won't, miss. When you see him waiting for you there, you'll go up to him like a princess."

"Friar, you old dear," said Dorothy, kissing her cheek, "you're just as silly as I am!"

III

There was a very early lunch, and then, accompanied by Gladys, and her married sister Ann, Dorothy went up to her room to dress for the great event. But passing the drawing-room she looked in to see the unusual sight it presented. Down one side of the long room was a table with all the presents displayed. Across by the double windows overlooking the Square there was a long buffet laden with every kind of confection. A side table was stacked with champagne bottles. Towering over everything in the middle of the long buffet rose the wedding cake. A hired butler and three waiters were already there. The butler, very professional in his evening dress, bowed gravely and asked "The bride, miss?"

"Yes," answered Dorothy.

"Our very best wishes for you, miss, on this great day."

"Oh, thank you—everything looks lovely," answered Dorothy, beaming, and then withdrew. She mounted with her escort to her bedroom. The faithful Friar was waiting.

"Everything's packed, miss. All your going away things are laid out on the bed," she said. "And Mr. Blake's things have come."

"Mr. Blake's—what things?"

"His going away things, miss. He'll change in the master's room."

"Oh, of course!" said Dorothy.

She had quite forgotten that Derek also would have to rush up and change after the reception. He couldn't go away in a tail coat and top hat.

With the help of Gladys and Ann, and with Friar in the background, she began to dress. She slipped out of her morning things, and, sylph-like, stood before the mirror, thinking,— "When next I undress this body won't wholly be my own. The hands of my lover will touch it. How terrible if I am not as lovely as he expects. I shall know at once by the look in his eyes. You silly, you know you are quite beautiful; in fact clothes have never been quite fair to you, and you're so much better than your face. It's unreasonable what an advantage a pretty face has. Men are captivated by it when the rest, body and soul, are quite awful. Derek's got a first-class body, I've seen him swimming. I simply couldn't marry a man with bandy legs, or a flat chest, no matter how handsome his head was. I should laugh or squeal if he made love to me. I'm so proud of my body. I'm fit for Derek."

And as if to echo these wild thoughts, flitting through her head, she heard Ann's voice say, "I always envied Dot. She's the prettiest figure of the lot of us."

With that, Ann slipped the pale blue silk vest over her sister's head. She had blue silk knickers, and long blue silk stockings,

with dark blue rosette garters that matched her egg-shell blue
shoes. And now, with much arm lifting and wriggling, assisted
by Gladys and Ann, she struggled into her frock, and while
Gladys hooked it down, Ann pulled out the train across the
carpet.

"Now you must go and dress yourselves!" said Dorothy. "I'm
quite all right. Friar will look after me. I'm going to walk this
train a bit."

They went out. A few minutes later, in the midst of Friar's
ecstasies, there was another tap on the door.

"Yes?" called the bride.

"It's me, Auntie Dorothy," cried a small voice.

"Hugh, my lamb, come in!"

The door opened and a tiny boy entered, with a serious face,
in his page's dress, a jade green velvet jacket with long white
satin trousers.

"Oh, darling, you look heavenly!" cried Dorothy, dropping
to her knees in great peril, and hugging him to her.

"They're very thin," complained Hugh, "and I mustn't get
dirty."

"Of course not—not yet, darling. Look, here's my train for
you to hold."

Hugh looked doubtfully at the long folds of satin.

"Is it very heavy?" he asked.

"No, darling, feel," said Dorothy, putting it into his hands.
"Now let's walk a few yards. Ready? Go!"

> "Pom-pom-te-pom-pom-pom,
> Pom-tiddle-om-tiddle-om-pom."

"That's right! That's right!" exclaimed Friar. "Oh, you both
look wonderful, miss."

Another tap, and the under-parlourmaid appeared.

"I've come for Master Hugh, miss. His mother wants him. Oh, miss, you do look beautiful, if I may say so."

"Thank you, Mabel. Go along, Hugh dear," said Dorothy.

"Auntie, why can't I ride in the carriage with you?" asked Hugh, on his way out.

"Because I'm the bride, and must be taken by Daddy."

"But I'm holding your train!"

"Yes, Hugh—but you'll join the other pages and the bridesmaids at the church first, and wait for me."

"Yes?" he said, doubtfully, and went out in the charge of Mabel.

In a few minutes Gladys and Ann were back, wearing Empire frocks of jade green velvet, with short sleeves trimmed with fur, girdles of narrow gold cord, and wreaths of gold leaves in their hair.

"Oh, darlings, how lovely you look!" exclaimed Dorothy.

Gladys contemplated herself in the mirror.

"I feel rather like Madame Récamier," she said, after a pause, "and Ann's Josephine!"

Friar had gone to the window.

"The cars have come, miss," she said.

"But it isn't time yet—my veil and wreath!" exclaimed Dorothy.

"Come along, come along—the car for the bridesmaids," said a voice at the door.

"Daddy—oh, Daddy, come in and look at me!" cried Dorothy.

Mr. Sewell appeared, in tail coat and striped trousers, with spats, grey waistcoat, cravat and pearl pin, his silver grey hair contrasting with his ruddy complexion. He tried not to feel excited, but his heart was beating too fast, and when he saw his daughter standing there, so virginal, so radiant on this day of days when he was going to lose her, he had to fight a mist in his eyes, and shout a little to make sure his voice came through.

"Lovely, my dear, perfectly lovely," he said.

The bridesmaids disappeared. Dorothy linked her arm in her father's, while Friar arranged her veil. The wreath felt a little unsteady.

"I'll give it a pin, miss!" said the breathless Friar.

Dorothy smiled at her father as they fronted the mirror.

"We do look nice, Daddy."

"Lovely, my dear, lovely. All right? Not—not dizzy—or—" He faltered.

"Oh, no. Just deliciously happy! And you?"

"Oh—me? Oh, I'm all right, of course," he answered.

But she knew he was not. When her hand had slipped over his she found it ice-cold.

"I think we ought to go down, my dear," said Mr. Sewell.

Friar gathered up the train. Dorothy followed her father down the stairs. At the foot, lined along the hall, there was a small audience. Out in the street there was a gathering of spectators, black against the sunlight. The drugget glowed red up to the waiting car. The gathering at the foot of the stairs consisted of the cook, two parlourmaids, a scullery maid, Henry, the odd-job youth, and the hired butler and waiters. They all smiled at her. Then cook suddenly spoke.

"God bless you, Miss Dorothy, and may you ever be happy—and that's the wish of all!" she said, tearful with emotion.

"Thank you, cookie. Thank you all," replied Dorothy, smiling, and passed on.

They were in the car now. They were off. No—the car hesitated. Gracious, they had forgotten the bouquet! Friar came running out with it. And now.

It was really only a minute or two to the church. She held her father's hand, and felt the pressure of his. He kept clearing his throat, but he said nothing, until they drew up at the church door.

"Bless me, there's a crowd!" he said, as he helped her out.

Faces, faces, faces, then darkness. Then she saw her bridesmaids, and the four pages, with Hugh at their head. The procession formed. The organ began to play. The congregation rose. At the far end of the aisle she briefly saw two young men, and a clergyman in a white surplice.

"Ready?" asked her father, as she took his arm.

"Yes, Daddy."

Slowly the procession made its way to the chancel, while the solemn music filled the dim church.

IV

It was all over at last. The whole service, the signing of the register, the kisses, the congratulations, the return journey down the aisle, on Derek's arm, the delirious swift journey home again, with Derek holding her hand and saying, "Oh, darling—darling. I can't believe it's me! You are unbelievably lovely!"

Instantly the hall door was open, and there was Friar, and the butler. They went at once to the landing by the drawing-room door, and took up their positions for the reception. In the drawing-room the waiters were ranged behind the buffet. They heard cars draw up. Mr. Sewell, the bridesmaids and pages were here. And now the guests.

"Ready, Mrs. Blake?" asked Derek, as the advance guard swept up the staircase.

V

And at last, at last they were together, together as they would remain for the rest of their lives. As the car bore them away from Chester Square, Dorothy sank back.

"Tired, darling?" asked Derek, and then he saw tears well up in her eyes, and trickle down her cheeks.

"Oh, my darling—don't be unhappy. I'll take care of you," he said, drawing her to him.

She looked up into his face, a smile battling with her emotion.

"Derek, I'm so, so happy. It's poor daddy—he——"

That last look as Mr. Sewell had peered in at the window, his voice as it called "Bless you both—good-bye!" before he turned to join the guests, waving from the steps, she could not dismiss this memory at once. And Derek, knowing all that this meant to his wife, and what he had taken out of a father's life, could say nothing. He simply held his bride, raising her hand to kiss.

"There. I'm better now," said Dorothy, sitting up. "Sorry!"

"My darling!" he exclaimed.

"We're in time?"

"Plenty—it's four-fifteen, and it doesn't go till four-thirty."

"We'd look so silly if we missed it!"

"We shan't," he answered, and he surveyed her possessively, from head to foot.

"You like my going-away dress?" she asked.

"You look marvellous—such a naughty little hat!"

"And a naughty little wife!"

"My angel!"

"Shall we always be as silly as this?"

"Why not?" asked Derek.

"We couldn't go on like this, or we'd pop."

"Then let's, till we do!" answered Derek. "Hullo, here's Victoria. Darling, we're on our honeymoon! Can you believe it?"

"Hardly."

The car drew up to the curb. A porter appeared. Derek helped out his wife.

"The four-thirty Folkestone-Boulogne boat train," he said to the young porter.

"Yes, sir. Have you reserved seats?"

"Yes—Pullman, here they are. The registered luggage is already here. These two suit-cases—and the dressing-case—that's all."

"Very good, sir."

The young porter piled the cases on his truck. As he turned and followed the young couple another porter looked at him and grinned. " 'E's done well for 'isself!" he said.

"Not 'arf!" agreed Jim. "Some folks has all the luck."

He caught up the pair at the barrier, where their tickets and passport were briefly examined. Yes, they were newly-weds all right. He had a brand-new passport for both. Jim wondered where they were going for the honeymoon. A label hanging from the dressing-case satisfied his curiosity. Mrs. D. Blake, passenger to Hotel Anton, Kitzbühel, Austria.

Well, for himself, he'd choose Lugano.

CHAPTER IV

NIKOLAS METAXA, OF ATHENS

I

IT was the habit of M. Gregoropoulos, proprietor of the Restaurant Phaleron, Soho, to stand at the foot of the stairs and greet the clients of the famous Greek restaurant as they came in. Standing there, he could intercept them whether they went upstairs to dine or stayed on the street level. For the ladies he had a special greeting. At his side was a large basket of roses, carnations, or, at times, even orchids, from which he would select a flower, and, with the courtliest bow, present to the lady. Very stout, his black oily hair plastered down over his low broad forehead, with red neck visible between double chins and bullock shoulders, it was not difficult to believe that many years earlier, as a young man, he had first come to London as a redoubtable catch-as-catch-can wrestler, at a time when the Russian lion, Hackenschmidt, had made that sport highly fashionable.

A broken arm and a twice dislocated shoulder were the results of that calling, and when, after an unlucky encounter with a fellow known as The Terrible Turk, he was carried half-dead from the ring, Apollo Gregoropoulos thought it was time he changed his calling. Having begun life as a waiter in a Paris restaurant, he resumed the trade of his youth, but this time as his own master. He was still a waiter, but a head waiter, since there were now seventeen under him, and a fat Cypriote cooking in the kitchen. But no waiter ever worked so hard or so willingly, for he was also the proprietor of the Restaurant Phaleron.

40

That was how it started. M. Gregoropoulos had prospered through the years. The Restaurant Phaleron had pushed itself out across the back yard, eating up a saddler's workshop in the way. It then expanded sideways, evicting a hairdresser on the right and a greengrocer on the left. The new premises did not accommodate the growing clientele for long. The Restaurant Phaleron began to grow upwards. It engulfed the first floor, pushing into the street a surgical instrument maker whose business boasted of being established since 1830.

In five more years, the clientele still growing, such was the fame of the Phaleron cuisine, and the tact and flattery of Gregoropoulos of the roses, more space was urgently required. The Phaleron could not grow sideways or backwards any more, for implacable leaseholders barred the way. There was only one way it could grow, and that was upwards. With characteristic enterprise M. Gregoropoulos took off the roof, built another floor, and put on another roof. The new floor was a triumphant enterprise. Along the great wall a scenic artist painted a panorama of Phaleron Bay. On the end wall rose the Acropolis. In the panels there were excellent plaster replicas from the Elgin marbles. The room was suitable for banquets.

But success, as Apollo Gregoropoulos realized from the start, lay in the kitchen and not in the decorations. Please the stomach of man, make him aglow with content, and he would not cavil over the bill, though the bill, considering the perfect service, was never immoderate.

M. Greporopoulos did all his own marketing. He trusted no one, not even Madame, a neat-figured robust Cretan lady who had blessed him with six black-eyed children in the intervals between roasting ducks, dressing crabs and frying scampi, Madame Gregoropoulos's three specialties.

Every morning at half-past six, with a small basket on his arm for purchases of such quality or delicacy as he would not entrust the merchant to send, M. Gregoropoulos walked across from his restaurant to Covent Garden. Everyone knew him, no one would dream of cheating him, an impossible achievement, and his verdict was not to be disputed. He looked, he smelt, he pinched. He had the eye of a connoisseur among the vegetables. At a glance he knew his article, and he bought craftily. Picking up the worst lettuce in the bunch, he would expose its yellow centre marred by a worm. Put on his mettle, the vendor would produce his finest lettuce, which Gregoropoulos regarded critically. "No —the inside's mushy and slippery—it's not fresh."

"Not fresh! Not fresh!" exclaimed the outraged greengrocer. "It's only been here half an hour from a Kent garden!"

"Nonsense—you couldn't sell it yesterday—I'm sorry for you. But don't souse them in water and pretend they're new. I know lettuces that have been cut from their stalks and have gone stale. Look at that!"

The greengrocer looked, unwillingly.

"You give me some very fine stuff. But these lettuces are despicable," went on M. Gregoropoulos. "Now these savoys—" he said, turning to a new hamper.

Oh yes, he knew. Slowly picking his way down the avenue he distributed his slips of paper, with the order neatly written on them. He was happiest among cases of apples, peaches and oranges. He could smell out an apple like a witch doctor. The one proffered him looked perfect. It shone with health, its complexion was flawless. M. Gregoropoulos raised it to his nose, delicately tapping it at the same time. The greengrocer gave a smile of complete assurance. The next moment the Greek had slipped a penknife from his pocket and cut the apple in two.

"Ha! I thought so!" he exclaimed, exposing a slightly discoloured core, to the amazement of the dealer. "Now don't be surprised—haven't you noticed the marvellous complexions of consumptives?"

Oranges with rust or red spider scale never got past him. "But it's only the peel!" protested the dealer.

"Perhaps—but an orange for my customers must look as good as its contents, not better, not worse."

Big cauliflowers, likely to catch the eye of any housewife, were objects of immediate suspicion. M. Gregoropoulos knew their complaint. They were soft and no longer fit for the table. The "flower," carefully examined, had started a second growth, it was no longer a clear white, tinged with the yellowish undergrowth. Asparagus, too, if not freshly cut, betrayed itself. It should be pinky-white, and the green tip should be firm and tightly packed.

And in the fish market, too, M. Gregoropoulos walked with the renown of a connoisseur. His fish had to have bright eyes and moist mouths. He would pick up a fish by its tail, waggling it to and fro. Then he would try to bend it, and if the tail slipped from his fingers he would buy it. "Don't buy a tomato that doesn't smell a yard, don't buy a fish that does" was one of his axioms. He had a disconcerting habit of rapping oysters together. If they sounded like stones, he bought them. If they rang hollow he dropped them. Live shellfish kept their shells tight, dead ones had opened and the air gave them a hollow sound.

With all this "finickiness," as the market called it, M. Gregoropoulos was hard to please, but he paid high prices if the wares were of the finest. There were some days when he made no purchases rather than fall back on the second-rate. Customers of the Phaleron declared the cooking was marvellous. "Half the secret lies before," would say the swarthy Greek, adding—"and after," for at any moment M. Gregoropoulos, in spotless black tails and dress front, might be seen in the kitchen going from pan to pan, spoon in hand. "No!" he would suddenly bellow, pointing with his spoon at the pan, and he would stand, an outraged figure, until a pale chef had borne the offending pan out of sight.

"You waste too much, Apollo," his wife once ventured to protest.

He turned on her like the ex-wrestler he was.

"Waste, woman, waste!" he exclaimed. "Have you ever gone hungry or wanted a dress? Do I pay bad wages or owe bills? Are my tables empty? I'll have no mean cook here!"

Never again did Madame Gregoropoulos criticize her husband in his own kingdom.

II

It was therefore a great school in which young Nikolas Metaxa received his training. Born at Pedoulas, a mountain village in Cyprus, an orphan, he had reached Athens at the age of twelve in the capacity of mule boy. Various adventures, which often entailed hunger and sleeping out, had led, at sixteen, to his being dressed in his first pair of black trousers, with a white apron round his middle, in the capacity of junior waiter in a struggling establishment off Constitution Square.

This restaurant went bankrupt at the end of the tourist season, when Nikolas found himself not only unemployed but even without the black trousers, which were seized as part of the assets. So back into rags he went, with a month's wages due to him that were never paid. He slept for a month in an attic over a greengrocer's shop, where the greengrocer's fat middle-aged wife gave him lodging, not wholly out of pity for she levied tribute from this lusty boy of seventeen. Discovery one day resulted in uproar and his being pushed out into the street with his shins all bruised from the greengrocer's boots.

Nikolas felt aggrieved. He had been kissed to death, and twice a day, in return for an abominable meal, he had hawked the greengrocer's basket, bawling *"Seeka freska! Seeka freska!"* in a vain attempt to sell figs to the Athenians.

One asset his attic room possessed, and it was not until later years passed in exile that he realized how much he treasured it. The small window looked on to one of the greatest jewels of civilization, the stupendous Parthenon cutting the sky, high upon the rock of the Acropolis. By craning his neck he could just see the side of the Temple of Nike, perched against the steep ascent to the Propylæa. At dawn and sunset he would watch the lovely light waxing and waning, unconsciously absorbing the beauty of the scene. A Greek, it was his inheritance, and in exile his heart ached for one evening when the violet light lay on the slopes of green-girdled Lycabettus, and the columns of the Parthenon were silhouetted against the departing sun.

After his forceful eviction from the greengrocer's he slept out for a week, was faint with hunger, and existed by standing outside the Hôtel Grande Bretagne and pretending he had procured the taxis that came up for the guests. This involved a long battle with the incensed hotel doorman, but it resulted in a few drachmæ; also, more cigarette-ends seemed dropped about that doorway than anywhere else.

Nikolas possessed an engaging smile, and the classic features which tourists so seldom find in Greece. He discovered that certain of them were quite excited by his distinct resemblance to the Hermes of Praxiteles, as a stout pursuing German had once informed him, and he hung about Constitution Square securing odd commissions from various tourists attracted by his solicitous eye and Greek grace.

For a whole week he lived with a full stomach. An American hired him to carry his cinema camera, tripod and impedimenta. He tasted power for that wonderful week, when he commandeered taxis, suggested excursions and restaurants, and dispersed the army of touts that bore down upon them. When the American left, Nikolas possessed a new suit, shoes, a straw hat, and had money in his pocket. He went down to the Piræus and wept copiously as the liner bore his patron away.

Nikolas now saw his chance. He walked straight to the best restaurant in Athens, saw the head cook, and the next day began work as kitchen boy. The menial position cost him one thousand drachmæ, two-thirds of his American legacy. It was a wise investment, the tourist season was coming to an end, and he had to dig in for the winter.

Nikolas was a hard worker, and intelligent. He established himself firmly in the kitchen, and watched with his quick dark eyes the chef at work. He was promoted from dish-washer and general scullery-hand to the vegetable larder. But this seemed a dead end, and he adroitly wriggled his way back into the cooking part of the establishment. At last he became one of the chef's trusted assistants. The embers of ambition began to smoulder. At night in his tiny room he studied French from a book picked up for a few drachmæ. A friendly waiter who had lived in Paris helped him.

He had been six months at the restaurant, fatter in body and now in the full bloom of young manhood, when something happened that transfigured his world. He fell in love.

Her name was Xenia. She was seventeen, a black-haired, white-faced young woman with smouldering eyes. Her father was a cobbler, originally from Cos, who had married a native woman, and Xenia maintained the reputation of that island for producing beautiful women. She was graceful in all her movements, with a cat-like ability to subside into repose, to sprawl, or to suddenly spring into alert movement: there were those who thought her flighty, but she was the kind of young woman who generated ardour in the masculine breast without any visible overtures on her part. Clearly Nikolas, from the moment she saw him, was the most favoured one. She first saw him early one morning when he came into the dim untidy shop with a pair of the chef's shoes for repairing. Her father was absent for a few minutes and Nikolas, having given the order, lingered to talk with the cobbler's daughter.

Her smile dazzled him, her dark eyes burnt like a flame, he had a strange sensation of giddiness, of incredible happiness. He must have walked out of that shop on his feet, but had he been told he achieved his exit by levitation he would not have thought it fantastic. All day he saw nothing, his eyes were so dazzled. At half-past nine, when at last he was free, he went round to the cobbler's shop, merely to stand on the opposite side of the road and watch the door. For a whole hour he stood there. No one came in or out. Somehow he must speak with the cobbler's daughter again. He did not even know her name.

Two days later he saw her in the street and she stopped and laughed at him. She told him her name was Xenia. She was the only child of the cobbler and his wife. When Nikolas told her how he had come and watched the shop in the hope of seeing her, she laughed again, and looked a little shy. He had never seen such beautiful teeth, or such soft dark eyes as this girl possessed. And although so young, her figure was developed. Her low bodice half revealed the swelling breasts. Her arms were plump. Her black hair was drawn tightly up from the nape of her neck, and he noticed her exquisite ears, so small and pink, with little pearls hanging in the pierced lobes.

She worked, she told him, in a café down Stadium Street, and she was free in the mornings till eleven, and in the evening only after midnight.

"I shall come to-night, after midnight, and take you home," he said at once. "Yes?"

She laughed again, and made no answer. Then, suddenly like a bird, she darted off with a flash of her dark eyes and white teeth. Nikolas took a deep breath. That day at noon he was soundly rated by the chef for absent-mindedness at his work. Somehow he lived until nine o'clock, when he was free. Then he rushed to his room, changed his clothes, and hurried down to the Café Lycabettus in Stadium Street. There she was, going in and out of the swing doors that divided the café from the kitchen behind. There were two other girls, and the fat proprietor, an odious-looking man of fifty. Nikolas noticed the patrons were all very familiar with the waitresses. They put their arms round their waists, pinched them, and one young lout, rising to go, held one of the girls from the back while he gave her a playful bite on the shoulder. She gave him a slap, but it was obvious she liked the attention. The proprietor leered. Nikolas was glad it was not Xenia who had been so treated. He would have got up and stabbed the lout.

After a time he began to notice that the clients of the café were all of the same class, and young. Later, he learned they were chiefly waiters from the Grande Bretagne, who came in when they were off duty, to sit and play cards. There was a roulette wheel at the end of the room. Obviously there was gambling. Nikolas got up and went to watch, but he did not put any money on the wheel. He disapproved of gambling. Already he had tasted a little of the power of money. It had got him his start in the restaurant. He was saving. The germ of ambition was growing. One day he would have his own restaurant. Xenia would sit at the desk. No. He would keep Xenia in the kitchen at the back. He would not have his customers being familiar with his wife.

At midnight Xenia was free. In order not to expose himself to the proprietor and the customers, Nikolas left the café a few minutes before twelve and went and stood in the shadow on the opposite side of the street. In the still night his heart seemed to shake him. It was a warm May night with a new moon among the fleecy clouds. When at last she came out of the café, and, seeing him, crossed the road, he could not refrain from catching her hand and kissing it. Without speaking a word they set off down the silent moonlit street. Soon they came to Constitution Square. The long façade of the Royal Palace shone in the white light. They crossed by the ornamental gardens, and mounted to the terrace where the two Evzones in their fustanellas were on sentry duty. Nikolas and Xenia stood for a moment in front of the war memorial plaque and watched the sentries pass, a little like ballet dancers with their short pleated petticoats and stockinged legs.

"Must you go home at once?" asked Nikolas.

"Oh no—not for a while," answered Xenia.

For a long moment they stood looking at each other. Nikolas wore only a shirt and dark blue trousers. His brown throat showed at the open neck, and the thin cotton shirt lay moulded on his muscular chest. In that moment Xenia became aware of her lover, and his suppressed passion communicated itself. Already many men had courted her, but never with this intense restraint. An emotion stirred in her, evoked by something other than his physical puissance.

"Let's go up to the Acropolis," he said, quietly.

"So late?"

"It's quiet there—and beautiful."

She made no answer, but walked with him, wondering a little

at his words. There were dancing places still open in the town. No other youth had ever suggested climbing up to the Acropolis at midnight because it was quiet and beautiful. The oddness of his suggestion gave her a sensation of adventure. He was not like other Greek lads. When he looked at her there was something strange in his eyes, a devotion that made her slightly uncomfortable. If only he would make love to her instead of being so reverential.

Slowly they took the winding way up to the Acropolis, the sacred way trodden by the feet of the ancient Athenians. The town with its radiating lights glittered below them. A grey mass of mountains rose like a wall under a haze of moonlight. They passed the Areopagus where Paul of Tarsus had preached to the supercilious Athenians and named their unknown God. In the daytime the place to which they now came was littered with touts, vendors of beads, post-cards and stationery. It was the level where the taxis and charabancs stopped, and the eager tourists began the last steep ascent to the massive columned entrance of the Propylæa. But to-night there was not a soul. All was silent except the suppressed murmur of the living city below, the occasional hooting of a taxi, and nearer, in one of the cafés under the hill, someone playing a concertina, only audible when a departing customer opened a door.

They sat on a fallen fragment of marble beneath the steep bastion on which the Temple of the Wingless Victory, so exquisite in its small dimensions, jutted out from the Acropolis. Immediately below them, in a fold of the hillside lay the ruined theatre of Herodius Atticus, and a little round the bend, white in the moonlight, rose the tiers of the theatre of Dionysus, hushed, as if at any moment the young Æschylus might dance in the chorus before the solemn Elders and Ephors of the Athenian Republic, or suddenly alive with laughter, as the rapier wit

of Aristophanes made a wicked thrust at some local politi-
cian.

But Xenia and Nikolas knew little and cared little of history's melancholy pageant spread here around them. The vic-
tories, defeats, exultations and agonies of a dead people who had
held the torch of civilization flaming against the dark clouds of
Time were unknown to them. Yet they were still the playthings
of the same creative instinct and passion. Their blood pulsed as
it had pulsed for Daphnis and Chloe.

Nikolas trembled a little with the wonder of this girl sitting at
his side. Xenia's hand lay in his, and the magic of this hour
lay under a spell of silence. The night was warm, and tranquil.
The moon had begun to set, and already its rim touched the edge
of the mountains. The lights of the city rimmed its boulevards
out to the suburbs.

Nikolas now found tongue and began to tell her about his
life at the restaurant.

"One day I shall have a restaurant of my own. I'm saving
now. And you'll work in it with me."

"I?"

"Yes—I shall open it in Korai Street and I shall cater specially
for the Americans and the English. They don't mind what they
pay if they can get what they want," said Nikolas. "I wish I
could go to New York or London. I want to learn more English
and study their habits. And after that I'd like to be in Paris and
Vienna."

"You'll never come home again," interrupted Xenia. "No
one ever comes home again from Paris. I shouldn't!"

Nikolas did not speak for a moment, and gazed out over the
city.

"I should have to come back," he said, quietly.

"But why? One's always poor here."

"I'd come back for you, Xenia."

She laughed, and then seeing his face so serious, his dark eyes solemnly scanning her face, she ceased laughing and looked at this strange youth. The next instant he had roughly crushed her against his hard chest, and as her head fell back and she looked up into his face, unresisting in his embrace, her soft body yielding to his passion, he kissed her, his mouth pressing hers in his impetuous ardour. Finally, breathless, she pushed him away, and he looked at her a little dazed and frightened.

They talked very little after that. He did not attempt to kiss her again, a little to her disappointment, although she leaned up against him when they had reached the street where she lived and he said good night in the shadow. But he had arranged to take her out again the next night.

Soon, he expected, she would go out with him every night, when she left the café at midnight, but she made an effort to retain her freedom. On Sunday afternoons he took her for excursions. There was an idyllic day at Daphni, where they picnicked in the pinewoods, and lay among the asphodel, looking down on the old church with its white cupola among the dark cypresses. At the end of a month he had established a claim to her, but there was as yet no formal betrothal.

Xenia was both excited and disappointed. He was ardent, and had moments of intense passion, but always, just as he had induced in her a mood of complete surrender, he repressed himself. It was thrilling to be so passionately adored, but there were moments when she wished to be treated less as a goddess and more as a human being. What she could not understand was that his passion, physical in its manifestation, was spiritual in its source. There was a dissonance in their natures, which neither quite understood.

At the end of two months of this intense courtship, Nikolas

bought Xenia a ring. It cost him three months' savings. Although nothing was said, their betrothal was implied by her acceptance. He was made miserable twice by her omission to wear it. He had noticed she never wore it at the café, on the very few occasions that he went into the place. Xenia explained that the proprietor would not let his waitresses wear engagement rings. His customers liked to think the girls were free.

"You must leave," said Nikolas. "I hate that man."

"Oh no—he pays good wages. It's the best place I ever had."

"Most of the customers are waiters. They're no good," protested Nikolas. "Trash!"

"But you're a waiter, Nikolas," answered Xenia.

He tapped his chest. His eyes glared with indignation.

"I? I'm a chef. Waiters! Fools!" he exclaimed. "I know waiters. Waiters are vagabonds!"

Xenia laughed. At times Nikolas was so intense.

"You are funny!" she said. "Find me a better place, and I'll go."

There was no answer to that. Xenia earned more money than he did. She was able to buy anything she wanted. Her clothes were beautiful. She was generous, and he always had a battle to prevent her paying for things, which humiliated him. Between his passion for saving for that day when he would buy his own restaurant, and his desire to frustrate Xenia in her readiness to pay for their excursions, he was made miserable. He noticed with dismay that she had no idea of thrift. Money was for one purpose only, to spend, to command a good time.

"Don't you save anything yourself?" he asked.

"Save! What could I save?" demanded Xenia.

He wanted to tell her he was sure she could save a lot, if she had less expensive clothes, spent less on her hair. Why, she

had paid one hundred drachmæ for a bottle of scent! But he did
not say what he would have liked to say, that if she saved the
sooner they could marry and have their restaurant. His pride
would not let him say that, and also he did not like reproving
her. She was easily made unhappy, the tears came so quickly.
She was so gay, so bird-like, so ready to sing and laugh, and dis-
play her beautiful clothes in the sunshine.

III

The summer passed, a young lover's summer of enchantment, momentary despair, intoxicated happiness. Then, in October, the great blow fell. The restaurant was not prospering.
The tourists gone, strict economies were essential. The staff
was cut down. Among them Nikolas found himself dismissed,
with a good recommendation and a promise of reinstalment
when business improved.

The winter that followed was a nightmare. He could find no
work, his savings dwindled. Xenia would cheerfully have
helped him, but his pride would not let him accept. He was living now in a miserable room with no heating. Athens at Christmas was intensely cold. He lay in bed, with newspapers as a supplement to the thin counterpane. Much of his time was spent in
studying English. He earned a few drachmæ by going in the
evenings to assist a friend of his, servant to a member of the
English Legation. The large bright flat with its beautiful furniture and books seemed like a new world after his own grim
little room over a fish shop.

Nikolas was employed at the Englishman's when there was
a dinner-party, and he put on his white jacket and black trousers
to serve at the table. Even more welcome than the money he
earned on these occasions was the opportunity to hear English
spoken. The owner of the flat was a very elegant young bache-

lor, who knew all the smartest women in Athens. He played the
piano wonderfully and his flat was full of English books and
papers. Two Oxford undergraduates came to stay with him at
Christmas, and one of them took a lot of notice of Nikolas and
employed him as a valet and general messenger. The young man
must have been very rich, for he had the most astonishing wardrobe, and when he left, Nikolas, who went to the aerodrome in
the second taxi, counted five portmanteaux.

But what delighted Nikolas most was the conversation, some
of which he could now understand. There was an occasion when
they actually discussed him before his face, little knowing he
was listening as he moved about the room in which the three
young men and their ladies were dining.

"Have you noticed this boy's head?—it's classically perfect.
It's like having the god Hermes to valet one," said his young
patron, called Teddy.

"Yes," laughed the host. "It's a pity that isn't his name. Last
year our kitchen boy was called Ganymede!"

"He's such beautiful hands—where did you find him?" asked
one of the ladies, a young Frenchwoman, who had drunk five
cocktails, and beckoned Nikolas for a sixth. He dare hardly look
at her, so beautiful were her cold frank eyes as she surveyed
him.

"Oh, he comes in to help—he's an out-of-work waiter," answered the host. "Teddy's Hermes gives me an awful thought!"

"What?" asked Teddy.

"The gods probably ate garlic."

There was a shout of laughter. Nikolas turned away. He felt
the blood rush up his neck and into his cheeks. For the rest of
the evening, humiliated, he kept his head turned away. They
might look at his hands. They should not smell his breath. So,
with the English garlic was taboo.

Sometimes when helping in the kitchen after dinner, Aleko, his friend, purposely left the sitting-room door open so that they could hear the wireless. The radio was often tuned in to London, and Nikolas heard the news.

His English improved every day. He had now one master passion, to get to England. When Mr. Teddy left he astounded Nikolas by giving him an English five-pound note. It was the first he had ever seen, and he could hardly believe the flimsy bit of white paper was worth nearly three thousand drachmæ.

"That's for keeping your hands so nicely—I hate dirty hands. Good-bye and good luck, Nikolas!" said the astonishing Mr. Teddy.

The five leather portmanteaux followed the young gentleman on to the plane. Mr. Teddy kissed all the four young ladies gathered to see him off, shook his host's hand and said, "S'long, old thing!" A few moments later he soared out of sight.

So that was how the amazing English took leave of each other after a month's visit. A cool handshake and "S'long, old thing." He could not forget Mr. Teddy, his cheerful voice, his kind smile, his five-pound note. Nor would he ever forget about eating garlic, or that he had beautiful hands.

IV

January passed, February passed. Xenia would not let him despair. Then one day she had a perfect plan for his future. It was so bold that he shook his head, but Xenia wore down his opposition. The idea made his heart beat so fast that he felt dizzy. It was this—he should leave at once for London where she had a cousin working in a restaurant, the Phaleron. Her cousin would help him to find a job.

"Will you write to him?" asked Nikolas, unable to believe that any such wonderful thing could happen to him.

"No!" replied Xenia, with a twinkle in her eyes.

"No!" he echoed, his heart sinking. "Why do you laugh at me?"

She brushed his cheek with her lips, and her dark eyes mocked him.

"You are stupid, Nikolas," she said. "If I write to my cousin and ask him to get you a place, he will write, 'Don't come. It's impossible.' But if you arrive, it's different. You are there. You cannot come all the way back again. He must help you. Now, do you see?" she asked.

But he was not sure. It would cost such a lot of money; more than he had. Also the English would not let him go to work there. He knew so many who had tried to get into England.

"You were born in Cyprus?" asked Xenia.

"Yes."

"Then you can get a British passport. You are British," said Xenia.

Dumbfounded, he stared at Xenia. She was right. He had left Cyprus so long ago, as a boy on a tramp steamer bringing mules to Athens, that he had forgotten he was a British subject.

"But the money, Xenia—it costs a terrible sum to go to England."

"Leave it to me. You must go to London. They earn big wages there. My cousin has become rich. One day he will come back, and buy a farm and be a great man, he tells me when he writes. He is now the second chef and he takes his wife for rides in his own motor-car. He has sent me a photograph of it."

Nikolas began to feel more hopeful. If only he could get to England all his dreams would come true. He would never be silly enough to buy a motor-car. He would save everything he could, and as soon as he had enough he would come back to Athens, marry Xenia, and open his restaurant. But how could he get to England? Nearly all of that Englishman's five-pound note was spent. His one hope now was to hold out somehow now the spring was coming when the tourists began to arrive and the restaurant might want him back.

But Xenia had bold plans. She had enough money to buy his ticket. Aleko's employer at the English Legation must be asked to help in the matter of the passport.

Two weeks later, with the resourceful Xenia to spur him on, he found himself, a little fearful, on the eve of departure for England. He was travelling on a Greek boat, sailing from the Piræus with a cargo of sultanas and sponges.

The day before the departure Xenia took a day off from the café, and they made an excursion to their favourite Daphni, along the Sacred Way where they picnicked in the early spring woods. Nikolas was on the verge of tears, but Xenia was very happy and laughed at him. He had wanted to marry her before going, but she pointed out how stupid that would be, as she would lose her job at the café. In four years he would be home again, or he could send for her.

It was a lovely spring day, and already the sun was powerful. They gathered some flowers, and in the Convent church, down in the hollow, with its high cupola, Norman arches, and Byzantine mosaics, they knelt before the little altar, with its primitive triptych. Nikolas, devout, said a little prayer, and bought four candles for the Christos in a niche by the door. Then into the woods they went again. They lay down on a slope, in the warm flower-scented air, and Nikolas played for the last time with Xenia's black tresses which she let fall down over her shoulders and began to divide and plait. Two of the plaits were so long he tied them round his throat, and they almost went to sleep like that in the drowsy April afternoon. Then a shepherd playing on a pipe went by, and his sheep came running all over the hillside. The lovers sat up and saw the sun was beginning to burn through the dark pinewoods. It was time to go. Nikolas never forgot that sad enchanted afternoon in the woods of Daphni, with the mingled odour of pine and thyme, and the clusters of asphodel, and the shepherd piping down the hillside, and the old Convent church lying in the hollow where the Sacred Way wound to ancient Eleusis.

v

Could all that really be five years ago, wondered Nikolas Metaxa as for the last time he slammed together the doors of the refrigerator in the Restaurant Phaleron. Only a few minutes before, upstairs in the little office, he had said good-bye to M. Gregoropoulos. He had always been afraid of M. Gregoro-poulos. He would blow through the kitchen like a tornado when something went wrong. Yet he was a good employer, and all that Nikolas knew had been learned in his kitchens. For five years, from his beginning as humble pantry-boy to his proud position as second chef, he had closely watched M. Gregoro-poulos. In his own restaurant he would bestow flowers on his fair customers with just that grand manner so famous throughout Soho.

The great man himself had shown emotion at their parting a few minutes ago. At three o'clock, Nikolas, his chef's white hat and apron sadly discarded, had said good-bye to his em-ployer, who always retired at that hour for his sleep until five o'clock. "Good luck, Nikolas. You will get on. You're a worker, and you've brains. But don't let your ambition run away with you. There's no money in Athens, I warn you. Well, well! Athens—ah——"

M. Gregoropoulos sighed.

"Thirty years ago I said I'd go back. Twenty years ago, I still said it, and ten years ago, and—well, I still play with the idea. You can't have everything, Nikolas, and England's been very good to me."

M. Gregoropoulos seemed about to say something more, but instead, he patted the young man on the back, and then, pulling a pearl pin out of his tie, fastened it in Nikolas's.

"There—a little token, Nikolas. Don't forget us, my boy. Good-bye. Good luck!"

Outside the office again, with a choking feeling, Nikolas stumbled down the stairs, returned to the kitchen, slammed the refrigerator doors as a last symbolic act of resignation, and somehow got through the farewell greetings of all his colleagues. Some of them he would see again in an hour or so. Oh yes, they would come and see him off at Victoria.

He went round to his tiny lodging in Greek Street. He dare hardly look at all the shops, the doors, the signs he knew so well. Sentimental, he nourished his heartache through this last day of his life in London. His one modest bag was already packed.

He looked at the small room, with its grim outlook, its broken grate and discoloured wallpaper, where he had lodged for the last three years, making his own bed and doing his own cleaning, according to the rigid plan of economy from which he had never departed. He picked up his bag, locked the door, and went down the stairs. He said good-bye to the grocer and his wife, and gave them the key. Yes, he would send them a card from Athens. They regarded him as a young man going to the other side of the earth.

Outside, reaching Shaftesbury Avenue, for a moment he had

an outrageous fancy to take a taxi, in celebration of the great occasion, but he crushed the reckless inclination, and took a bus. It was half-past three. There was plenty of time. The train left Victoria at four-thirty. For Athens, for Athens, for Athens, his mind repeated. Moreover, he was departing in great style. He was travelling second class on the Arlberg-Orient Express. He had been extravagant in going second class, but the third-class train was too slow, he was impatient at every hour's delay. To-day was Wednesday. Thursday, Friday, Saturday. On Saturday morning at ten-thirty-six he would be in Athens, holding Xenia in his arms. The fairy-tale had come true. The penniless lad who had left Athens five years ago was now returning a man, with six hundred pounds in the bank. He had wanted Xenia to come to London and marry him, and settle there, but she would not leave Athens. Moreover, she had an ambitious scheme for them to open a café-restaurant. That was a year ago. He had added one more year to his exile, for it was these last years in which he could save money.

The bus arrived at the end of Victoria Street, near the station. He got off, carrying his bag, and crossing the road gave a farewell glance to London's traffic. How frightened he had been on his first arrival in London, with the tremendous surge of traffic, the vast buildings, endless grey streets, and millions of strange faces! Now he felt exhilarated by the scene. He had made a nest for himself in this immense tree of humanity, he knew many of its inhabitants, he could hold up his head, for he had fulfilled his ambition.

Strange, but if it were not for Xenia his ambition would have been greatly changed, he would have continued at the Phaleron until he was in a position to open a restaurant of his own in London. Homesick as he was at the thought of the Greek city, and the hot sun, he had come to love this good-natured, vivacious capital. Perhaps when he told Xenia about London, his life here, the great possibilities for a hard-working pair like themselves, she would change her mind. But for the present he must dismiss the idea. Back in Athens, no doubt, he would wonder how he could live anywhere else.

Nikolas clung to his bag, despite the porters, found the platform and the ticket barrier. Hot, excited, he fumbled for his ticket and passport. He had bought a bowler hat, which was a little too tight, and his black tie had slipped sideways, and a pair of new shoes pinched him. While he was searching through his pocket for the ticket, so safely put away that he did not know where it was, he heard someone shouting behind him. He turned and frowned for a moment. Six of his friends from the Phaleron were there: three waiters, a waitress, a girl from the kitchen and an assistant chef. They were inclined to make a scene, and he disliked being the centre of any demonstration.

"You bought a ticket, eh, Nikolas?"

"You've not eaten it, Nikolas?"

"Have you packed it with your pyjamas?"

They fired questions at him, laughing uproariously at their own banter. Very superior people passing the barrier ignored them.

" 'Ere, 'ere, let the lady pass!" shouted the ticket inspector, to the little group all talking Greek, a bunch of excited foreigners.

They moved for a very elegant lady to go through followed by a parcel-laden porter. At last Nikolas found his ticket, and in another pocket he discovered his passport. They let him through the barrier. He turned to say good-bye to his friends, but they all had platform tickets. The Greek delegation was seeing him off. He wished they would not talk so loud and be so

excited, people were staring at him. Also he felt slightly ridiculous in his bowler hat. It would look odd when he arrived in
Athens, but it was too clumsy to pack.

Nikolas had some difficulty in finding a seat. The train was
crowded. But at last he found a corner, and two of the waiters
had a brief squabble for the honour of putting his bag on the
rack. Nikolas marked his seat with the bowler hat and joined
the others on the platform. Suddenly the kitchen girl, the only
English one among them, flung her arms around Nikolas's neck
and began to sob. He blushed with embarrassment and stood
paralysed. The waitress tried to comfort the girl.

"Take her with you, Nikolas," chaffed Giorgios, the waiter.

"I knew she was going to cry," said the little waiter from
the second floor.

The porters were slamming doors, somewhere a whistle blew,
people were shouting, and waving, and getting into the train.
There was a sudden scrimmage around Nikolas and in a burst
of emotion they all soundly kissed him in turn. He scrambled
from them and boarded the train, which was moving. Like a
flock of shrill blackbirds, his Phaleron colleagues began to run
with the train, shouting messages in Greek. Then, when they
could no longer run, they stood waving to him as he leaned out
of the window and waved back.

The last sight was of the kitchen girl sobbing in the waitress's
arms. He felt sorry for her. He had been nice to her, and had
kissed her sometimes, but he had never meant anything serious.
Now, if it had been Maria, the waitress, the tears would not have
been surprising. Maria loved him madly. A week before he
left she had implored him to stay. She had three hundred pounds
of her own and they could buy a nice little business in Soho.

Nikolas entered his carriage, removed the bowler hat, and

sat down, mopping his face. His black curls had fallen over his damp brow. He felt very self-conscious now in this carriage of prim people, and when he nervously glanced round no one took the slightest notice, as if he had grossly misbehaved. They were all well dressed, with expensive-looking luggage stacked up on the rack. Nikolas felt ashamed of his old fibre portmanteau with a battered end.

Goodness gracious, someone was smiling at him.

"What a wonderful send-off from your friends!" said a middle-aged woman, dressed in a grey tweed costume.

Nikolas smiled back, but felt too shy to speak.

The other passengers looked curiously at him and at the middle-aged woman. They were all pretending to read, but he knew they were watching. He wished now he had spoken, for the kind-looking lady perhaps thought him unsociable. She, too, was now reading. Furtively Nikolas discovered it was Baedeker's *Central Europe*.

The train, gathering speed, slipped through the suburbs of London. Nikolas looked out over a sea of tiles and chimney-pots shining in the afternoon sun. Then he glanced at his hands. They were still beautiful, but no longer brown. He had once received five pounds for keeping his hands so nicely. He wondered now where in London or England was the astonishing Mr. Teddy. He had never seen him again, and that was his only disappointment in London. For five years he had hoped to see him come into the Restaurant Phaleron one day.

An attendant came along the corridor asking for tea orders. Nikolas was the only one in the carriage not taking tea. He felt very conspicuous, but rigid economy had to be maintained. He glanced up at his bag. A third of its contents were packets and tins of food to be consumed on the journey. Meals on

trains were only for rich people. Also in his bag there were two
hundred and forty-one letters, all written to him by Xenia.
She had never missed a week in five years, except this last week,
when probably she had not written since she knew he was coming
home. Home, Athens, with six hundred pounds in the bank,
and Xenia waiting for him. He was a lucky fellow, and he owed
it all to Xenia.

CHAPTER V

PRINCE "SIXPENNY," OF SLAVONIA

I

"SIXPENNY! Sixpenny! Where are you?" shouted Gerry Hamilton, walking down the orchard.

There was no answer. At the end of the orchard, where the reddening apples gleamed in the sun that broke through the haze of the August morning, there was a large paddock in which grazed the ponies ridden by Gerry and his friend Sixpenny. Gerry looked across the paddock, but there was no one there.

"Hey! Hey!" shouted a voice from somewhere.

Gerry looked around puzzled.

"Sixpenny! Sixpenny! You must come at once, you're wanted!" shouted Gerry.

"Hello! Hello!" called the voice.

It was then that Gerry saw his friend. In one corner of the paddock stood an ancient dovecote, a round tower built of flint and mortar, with a conical tile top. It was at least five hundred years old, a legacy of the monks who had once lived at the Abbey, and with pigeon flesh and pigeon eggs had tided over the meatless winters. It was out of the top of this dovecote that the body of the small boy known as Sixpenny now appeared. He had gained this height by climbing the swinging ladder inside the dovecote, by which the monks had once collected eggs from the tiers of nests cut into the wall.

"I say, you must come down! We've been looking for you everywhere!" cried Gerry, flushed with excitement. "There's two fat men arrived in a big car—foreigners—and they want you at once."

"Want me?" asked the small boy in the dovecote roof, still panting from exertion.

"Yes—do come down, Sixpenny. Daddy's in a great state about you."

Gerry went inside the dovecote and watched his school friend descend. They had been home a week now from their preparatory school, where Gerry had been asked to keep an eye upon this foreign boy, aged thirteen and therefore a year his junior. His father, Dr. Hamilton, had been in charge of a field hospital with the Slavonian army in the Great War. In this way he became the friend of Sixpenny's father.

"I say, you do look a mess," said Gerry, surveying the dishevelled Sixpenny. One stocking was half down his leg. His shorts were covered with whitewash, his face and hands were grimy. No one would have believed this dirty little boy was the heir to the throne of Slavonia. For Sixpenny was not his true name. Less than a year ago he had arrived at school in England very frightened and shy, where Gerry Hamilton had taken him under his wing. The other boys had not taken much notice of this dark-eyed little boy, who spoke only a little English learned from his governess. One morning, under the school shower-bath, where he felt overwhelmed with shame at standing naked with half a dozen other boys, one bold spirit had addressed him.

"I say, your Royal Lowness, how much a year do you get for being a prince?" he asked, grinning.

And Prince Paul, aged thirteen, feeling very naked and humble, had replied, "Please, I am allowed sixpence a week."

For some reason this truthful answer was received with a yell of delight. Ever after that he was dubbed Prince Sixpenny.

Gerry helped to bat down the dishevelled Sixpenny.

"They're not going to take me away?" asked the smaller boy, apprehensively. There was another week of this marvellous freedom ahead of him. When he went home Gerry was going with him.

"I don't know—they're a dismal-looking pair," answered Gerry. "Come along!"

The two boys hurried back to the house. Sixpenny wanted to go and look at the Angora rabbit Gerry had given him yesterday. "Can't I go and feed it first?" he pleaded.

"No. Mummy and Daddy seem in an awful state. Come on!" replied Gerry, firmly.

They reached the house. Mrs. Hamilton met them in the hall.

"Paul—come in, my dear, there's——" she began, and then seemed unable to speak.

Bewildered, Paul followed her into the drawing-room, where Dr. Hamilton was talking French to two gentlemen. One, Paul recognized at once. He was M'sieur Stanovich of the Legation in London, who had been to see him at school. The other, a burly bearded man, he did not know.

"Ah, Paul!" said Dr. Hamilton, kindly, as he entered the drawing-room. "This is very sad for us—you have to leave at once; these gentlemen have come for you."

M'sieur Stanovich presented his companion, Colonel Tetrovich, the Military Attaché. He explained they were instructed to take him back to Nish at once.

"But why?" asked Paul, dismayed.

"It is our instructions, your Royal Highness. Madame Hamilton is having your things packed. We must leave in half an hour for London."

They saw the small boy was on the verge of tears.

"Come along, Paul, my dear—Gerry and I will help you to go through your things."

Mrs. Hamilton led the unhappy little boy out of the room. How much longer could he be kept in ignorance of the dreadful truth, she wondered. They had kept all the newspapers carefully out of sight, following the telephoned instructions yesterday evening that on no account was the boy to learn the truth. Already three pressmen had traced the boy and been repulsed. The morning papers were full of the ghastly assassination of the King of Slavonia.

Poor little boy. Mrs. Hamilton wanted to take him into her arms and comfort him. She acted desperately. She lied boldly when Paul asked, "There's nothing very wrong, is there? I shall come back to England?"

In half an hour everything was ready. The moment came when Dr. Hamilton said good-bye to him, and Mrs. Hamilton, slipping to one knee, held him a moment and kissed him. A tear trickled down her cheek.

"Mrs. Hamilton—why are you crying? Why am I going?" he asked.

"Am I crying, my dear?" asked Mrs. Hamilton, forcing a smile to her face. "Well, we don't like losing you, Paul."

"But I shall come back," said Paul. "I want to come back."

After that he was taken out to the large saloon car waiting at the door. It was just then that Gerry dashed up with a wooden box and a small brown paper parcel.

"Here's your rabbit, Sixpenny—and here's a lettuce," said Gerry, thrusting the parcel into his hand. "If you'll give him some water he'll last the journey."

The two gentlemen from the Legation looked very surprised. The Doctor frowned, but Mrs. Hamilton laughed. Clutching the box, Paul got into the car.

After that events moved rapidly. He was back again at the Legation in London, where he had briefly stayed when he had first come to London. M'sieur Georgeovitch, the Minister, whom he liked, talked to him very kindly and said how sorry he was that such a hurried journey had to be made. "And I've got a friend for you, to travel with you," said the Minister, smiling. He rang a bell, and to Paul's delight who should be ushered in but Miss Wilson, his English governess, who had brought him from Nish. He rushed into her arms.

She held him to her for a time, and then Paul was certain something was wrong. The Minister had slipped out of the room.

"Please, please, Miss Wilson, why am I going?"

And Miss Wilson said very quietly:

"Paul—something has happened—they will call you 'Your Majesty' now."

"But that's Daddy!" he answered, and then, Miss Wilson's face solved the mystery for him. He flung himself on her, sobbing.

II

There was a miserable lunch at which Miss Wilson had tried almost in vain to make him eat. They were leaving London at four-thirty, and they would be on the train two nights, and not arrive in Nish until Friday morning.

"Your mother will meet you," said M'sieur Stanovich.

"Everything will be done to make Your Majesty's journey comfortable," said Colonel Tetrovich, who could not help being pompous.

"I don't like those men," whispered Paul to his governess when they were out of the room.

"But Paul, dear, be nice to them. They've come to take you home. They're a little frightened."

"Frightened? Of me?"

"No, dear—of everything, I expect," said Miss Wilson, and quickly changed the conversation.

She pulled out a pocket handkerchief, and wiped Paul's face. The poor child's eyes were red with crying. For half an hour he had been inconsolable, and again and again he asked, "But why did Daddy die?" And Miss Wilson, a poor liar, evaded the awkward question by saying, piously, "When God summons us, my dear, we must go dutifully. He is the King of Kings."

Just before they left the Legation Paul went to the window. There was a small crowd outside, surrounding the waiting car. There were men with cameras. One of them had climbed up a lamp-post and sat on the bracket, calmly smoking a cigarette.

"What do they all want?" asked Paul. "To see me?"

"Come away from the window, Paul," cried Miss Wilson. "It's really disgusting—have they no sense of decency?" she protested, addressing the Minister.

"I can't think how they know he's here—we've kept it so secret," he replied.

M'sieur Stanovich and Colonel Tetrovich came into the room. They were in morning coats and carried silk top hats. They said something to the Minister.

"Yes," he said, glancing at his watch.

Miss Wilson took Paul's hand.

"Walk quietly with me, my dear, and look straight ahead," she said.

There was an awkward moment: Colonel Tetrovich blocked the doorway with his huge figure. Then he almost leapt aside. Miss Wilson stepped firmly forward with her charge. Down the stairs they went. Paul was dimly aware of a small group in the hall, of a butler holding open a door, revealing a patch of sunshine, an English policeman, a double line of solemn faces.

Paul was dazzled for a moment by the brilliant sunshine. He

shrank back when a young man thrust a camera forward, and heard Miss Wilson say "Really!" in a voice of mingled protest and contempt. Paul was the first in the car, propelled into a corner seat. Then in got the Minister, M'sieur Stanovich and the Colonel. To Paul's dismay, Miss Wilson disappeared, and as he leaned forward to peer out of the half-open window a woman came forward and cried, as she thrust a bunch of flowers into the carriage, "You poor darling!"

Paul had a glimpse of a middle-aged woman, with a fat good-natured face, being pulled back by the policeman. And as he watched this episode he felt someone nudging him, and whispering "Salute, salute, Your Majesty!" It was Colonel Tetrovich.

"Oh no, no. Don't bother the poor boy yet," protested the Minister.

"He will have to do it. He should begin now," retorted the Colonel, testily.

Paul stared at his flabby face with its pouchy eyes, and hated the man. There were long black hairs on the back of his hands, which glittered with rings.

"Please, I want Miss Wilson," cried Paul, in panic.

M'sieur Stanovich, sitting opposite, patted his shoulder.

"There—there. Miss Wilson is in the next car," he said, re-assuringly.

"I hope there's no crowd at Victoria, I've asked the authorities to get us through as quietly as possible," said the Minister.

The car glided through the sunny streets. Paul remembered how, the last time he had ridden through these streets, he had felt very miserable, for he was on his way to a strange school, to live with boys who were foreigners. Now he was going home, but he was not at all happy. His father had died.

He remembered the last time he had seen him. He had been taken into his father's study by one of the aides-de-camp, a young officer who had taught him to ride, and his father was standing by the window giving nuts to his favourite marmoset, Tinga. Outside in the Palace grounds they were changing the guard. Nish lay below with its river, its slim minarets, and the buildings along the banks of the Nishava. They loved this summer palace and his father was always happy there.

"Well, Tinga, here's Paul come to say good-bye to you. He's going to school in England," said his father. And Tinga had capered and screeched as though it were a matter for rejoicing. Paul scratched him behind the ear. The tears were very nearly welling over, but he tried hard to keep them back.

His father stooped to kiss him, and, catching his hand, thrust it into his blue uniform jacket. Paul felt something hard, and when he pulled it out of his father's pocket it was a wonderful gold watch, engraved with the Royal arms of Slavonia on the back and his own initial P. under the eagle. It was his father's parting gift. He flung his arms round his neck in excited gratitude, and the bitterness of parting had been lessened somewhat by this fulfilment of his ambition to possess a watch. Miss Wilson, waiting outside in the corridor, had been the first to be shown his father's gift.

Paul felt the watch now, and took it out. It was ten minutes past four.

Suddenly Paul remembered something. He sat up, with nervous excitement.

"My rabbit! My rabbit! Please, M'sieur Stanovich, where is my box with the rabbit?" cried Paul.

"Rabbit? Rabbit?" repeated Colonel Tetrovich, astonished at the small boy. "Whatever does Your Majesty mean? This is no time for rabbits!" he added, testily.

"Oh, but it is. Please, I can't go without the rabbit Gerry gave me. I want my rabbit."

"I expect it's quite safe with the luggage in the car behind," said M'sieur Stanovich, reassuringly.

"We'll see about it at the station," promised the Minister, smiling at Paul.

They arrived a few minutes later. There was a crowd, but it was not large, with four policemen on duty. A gentleman in a top hat and frock coat was waiting by the curb as the car drew up. He removed his hat and bowed as Paul got out. The crowd stared but made no sound.

"Who's that?" whispered Paul to the Minister, as the frock-coated figure, with top hat in hand, led the way.

"The station-master. On the platform there will be a gentleman from the British Foreign Office. You will shake hands with him, and when he has spoken, say 'Thank you very much.' I shall present him to you."

Preceded by the gentleman in the frock coat they reached a reserved carriage. As foretold, an English gentleman, also with a top hat, was presented to him. Was he going to see nothing but gentlemen with top hats, all very solemn and yet wishing to be kind? The Englishman presented his wife, a pretty lady, who gave him a small packet and said, with a lovely smile for him, "I hope Your Majesty likes chocolates."

He had hardly thanked her when he was propelled into the compartment, with four seats reserved for them. To Paul's relief, there was Miss Wilson. The Minister and M'sieur Stanovich remained on the platform talking with the English gentleman and his wife. The Colonel seated himself at Paul's side, opposite the governess.

"Miss Wilson!" whispered Paul.

"Yes, my dear?"

"Where is my rabbit? It's in a wooden box with a wire top —Gerry gave it to me just as we left."

"His Majesty seems very worried about his rabbit," said the Colonel. "I've no doubt it's among the luggage."

"I'll go and see," said Miss Wilson, rising.

She left the carriage. In a minute or so doors were slammed. They were going. M'sieur Stanovich got in, the Minister, the Englishman and his wife grouped themselves in a line before the window. A whistle blew. Agitated, Paul wondered whether Miss Wilson would miss the train while looking for the rabbit. He felt wretched, and was on the verge of tears.

"Stand up and bow!" said the Colonel, getting behind him.

Paul stood up. The gentlemen on the platform removed their hats. Paul bowed. A man with a camera rushed up and snapped him through the window. The train began to move. They were going.

Dismayed, Paul turned to his seat, and then his heart gave a bound and his face had the first happy smile on it for five hours. For there was his dear Miss Wilson triumphantly standing in the doorway with the rabbit box in one hand and the bag with the lettuce in the other!

CHAPTER VI

MR. HENRY FANNING, OF CHELSEA

I

"My boy, you're finished!" said Henry Fanning, looking into the mirror as he began shaving. "You knew quite well this day would come—and it's come!"

A door opened and a woman between fifty and sixty, in a green dressing-gown, stood and looked at her husband as he gazed in the mirror, his pyjama-clad back towards her.

"Daddy—were you talking to me?" she asked.

"No—no," answered her husband, abruptly.

Mrs. Fanning paused. She knew he had been talking. She had heard him distinctly in her own room next door. Of late Henry had been a source of great anxiety, and she was watching him acutely. He had always been highly strung, but for the last twelve months his nerves had been in a dreadful state.

"It's going to be a lovely day," said Mrs. Fanning.

"Yes, Alice," he replied, intent on his shaving.

Mrs. Fanning paused in the doorway. Then she withdrew. Henry was busy shaving, and uncommunicative.

When the door closed, Henry looked round. He must really stop this growing habit of talking to himself, of telling himself that he was finished. By the irony of Fate there had been a package of Press cuttings among the letters brought up with his morning tea. Most of the cuttings assured him that he had never written with more power and freshness of imagination than in

76

his new novel just published and already high in the best-selling class in which he had been for quite the last twelve years.

But what his large, faithful public did not know, nor the reviewers, was that he was a completely finished man, at the end of his tether. That novel they acclaimed, published last week, had been written quite fourteen months ago. Since then he had been unable to write a line. He had made three forced starts, after some nine months of agonizing idleness. But each start, as he knew, was a false one. He had no faith in his beginning, the characters were logs, the plot too indefinite, and inspiration was missing. He abandoned the wretched efforts.

He had never written in that fashion, forcing himself to his desk. All his other books had demanded to be written, his fecund mind had created the characters, and they were so spontaneously vivid that he wondered where they had come from. For although he had been writing for some thirty years, and had written a score of highly successful novels as well as two plays and some biographical studies, he had always been astonished by himself. His books had somehow come out of the air, and after each was completed, he had always felt he could never do it again. Every book had been his last book. He had "dried up" for good.

Alice, who had heard this cry for the last fifteen years, laughed at him. She had too often heard him declare that he was finished, seen him mope and hang around, the picture of misery. Then one morning he had disappeared into his den, and was extracted late for lunch, with his eyes shining, and his manner elated. "I believe I've got it," he would say, and would soon disappear again. For two or three months this furtive industry would continue, and then the book was finished.

"I shall never write another," she always heard Henry say. And, as ever, she laughed and said, "Oh, Daddy!" Then after three or four months of restlessness and depression, the process would begin again.

But this time the restlessness and despair had continued for over twelve months, a record, and even Alice Fanning herself began to feel alarmed, although she would allow her husband to see nothing of her anxiety. "Don't worry, Daddy, it'll come," she kept repeating.

Henry Fanning, shaving at eight o'clock on this August morning, looked at himself critically. Fifty-five years of age, his thin æsthetic face might have been that of a judge or a successful doctor. His appearance was always described as distinguished. Tall, fine-featured, with greying hair nicely wavy over the broad brow with its deep-set solemn eyes, he looked as his readers generally expected him to look, a man of serious mien, whose delicate and philosophical treatment of human nature placed him among the foremost imaginative writers of the day. He had always been, perhaps, a little too solemn, too sensitive in his assessment of character, with a sweet melancholy in his judgment that put him in the rank of the sorrowing pessimists who can never quite reconcile the cruelty of life with the many manifestations of beauty that surround it. And because he quietly despaired, all his hope, and his faith, was placed with youth, who should build a nobler world than the one they inherited from their warped and sapless elders.

Holding this belief, his own personal hope centred upon his five-year-old grandson, Roger. He loved the child, lived for it, determined his way because of it, and generally worshipped it with a quiet passion that was only checked by apprehensive fear at the thought of how he could be smitten by any mishap to the child.

It was young Roger who was at the bottom of his misery this morning. He was being sent away, and for two or three months he would not be able to run round to the nursery in his son's house, on that daily visit, always with some small gift in his hand. It was the richest hour in his day. Not even that rare joy of the artist, the consciousness of the creative spirit working triumphantly, equalled the happiness he found in his grandson's affection, responsive to his own.

"You're finished, and they're sending you away, in the attempt to make you believe that fresh scenes will inspire you. But you've been everywhere, you can't get new enthusiasms at fifty-five, you really have no desire to write any more. And you'll not see Roger for weeks."

This was what ran in Henry Fanning's mind as he shaved at the mirror, but this time he did not utter the words. He turned and ran the bath-water, and glanced out of the window.

Their flat, high up on the fifth floor, overlooked the sports field of the Chelsea Barracks. The big green square of turf was surrounded by plane trees in thick leaf. Away to the west lay the roofs and chimneys of Chelsea. On the left, its light stone coping glinting in the morning sun, was the long façade of the Chelsea Royal Hospital, with its clock tower and cupola and flat Wren windows. Henry Fanning liked this view from his study. It was familiar and cheerful. London lay at his feet, and high above trees and chimney pots he sat at a desk in the window and worked.

He used to sit and work. Now he just sat at his desk, and then got up, prowled up and down the room, and finally put on his hat and went round to play with Roger, or chat at his club, hoping that to-morrow an idea would come. And so the months had gone by.

"You're tired, Daddy, give your mind a rest, lie fallow!" said his wife. Not that Alice Fanning ever took her own advice. She was tireless. At forty-eight, when her son and two daughters had

gone out of the family nest, to settle in their own, she had suddenly developed a passion for mineralogy. She enrolled herself
among the students, and set forth every morning in a taxi to the
classrooms. In due time she qualified for her B.Sc. and she
turned her industry towards laboratory work, and laboured with
zest among learned gentlemen in the Department of Mineralogy.
All this was achieved without the slightest diminution of her
care for Henry, so helpless in the ordinary domestic details. She
tied his tie, made him buy a new hat, order a new suit, and pro-
hibited his going out in a shirt with a rent at the neck. In return
he offered her a childlike obedience and affection.

Henry went into the bathroom, after gazing disconsolately out
of his bedroom window. To-morrow morning he could not have
a bath. He would be cooped up in an expensive cell called a
"wagon-lit," pressing a tap and getting a little hot water that
swayed in the basin with the motion of the train. For to-day,
in obedience to his family, he was leaving Victoria at four-thirty,
for Vienna—at least he was going to Vienna first, and then he
would wander.

Why had he not been firm and refused to go? "Daddy, you
want a change of scene, you must get out of yourself," said
Alice. "Daddy, you've brooded so long that you've developed a
complex," said his eldest daughter, "You've persuaded yourself
you're finished and you're paralysing yourself." And the cheerful Henry junior, happy father of Roger, said: "Hop about a
bit, Dad. Go gay! The world isn't coming to an end, even if
there's a jolly old war. Have a bottle of fizz and a bust at
Sacher's, and get a glad eye in the Prater!"

Henry junior's vision of his father getting "a glad eye" made
his mother laugh. An archangel would have been more responsive to a Viennese lady. In the end they bullied him into making
a trip abroad. He wanted to take Alice with him, but she was

adamant. "Women have to travel with boxes, and know where they're going to get their hair done decently. You'll do much better alone, just nosing about," she said. So alone he must go. He hated being alone, except when he was working.

He put a foot into the bath, and took it out again quickly. The water was too hot. Why had he chosen Vienna, he pondered, as he ran in some cold water. Vienna in August would be empty, with everybody holidaying in the Salzkammergut. He had thought of Salzburg, but it would be full of English, some of whom he was certain to know—which meant just gossiping and sitting around, and hearing incessant talk about music, mostly devastating criticism by supercilious amateurs. Vienna suggested itself, he must confess, because it had an air of pathetic gaiety these days, and the ghosts of history lurked in its streets. In Vienna he might get an idea for the new book, if ever there was to be a new book.

Henry Fanning got into the bath and sat down. There was no doubt he was getting thin with worry about this book. Vienna, of course, was an old love. Alice and he had spent their honeymoon there, in the great days of Francis Joseph, when the daily life of the capital provided a pageant with its uniforms and carriages and horses. So naturally, Vienna, his first love and most enduring among the cities of the Continent, had suggested itself.

Yet it was not a wise choice, reflected Henry, reaching for the sponge. His first real success had been a novel about Vienna, long before this post-war vogue of Austria in fiction, promoted by *The White Horse Inn's* success on the stage. The public had been surfeited with lovers on the balconies of Tyrolean chalets, with gay lads in leather shorts slapping their thighs and uttering wild whoops in the *Schuhplattlertanz*. He should really keep out of Austria. He ought to go further afield, to the Balkans perhaps. No. There had been far too many Ruritanian novels.

Really how difficult it was, thought Fanning. The fact was everything had already been written about and there were far too many novels. Why worry about a new one? He had written a score. He could exist, somehow. He had saved enough to live very quietly. His son was getting on nicely on the Stock Exchange, his daughters were well settled. He could give up this ridiculously expensive flat and retreat to their old cottage in Hampshire, which he loved, and where he liked to potter about.

No, that was not quite true, reflected Fanning. After a few weeks of pottering he grew restless, and began to worry about getting back to the writing-desk. The fact was he was tense with nervous strain when writing, and sick with worry when he was not. Besides, there was his long career to consider. He had been so long before the public, had tasted so much success. It was not easy to retire when one was still physically untired and when the last book had shown no shrinkage of the affection and number of his readers.

And, after all, it was something to be Henry Fanning, though he had no great opinion of himself. Years ago he had got over the elation of seeing himself in print, of seeing his name in the largest type of his publisher's advertisements, of being asked to speak, or to lecture, or to attend prominent functions, and eat enormous dinners provided by societies whose extravagance always made him feel slightly ashamed when he thought of all the hungry people in the world. And when he was being lionized he always had a humbling idea that he was being used. There were thousands of quite decent and unimportant people who had a passion for associating with "names," though what pleasure they could derive from an "Oh yes" or "Thank you very much" or "Oh really, how interesting" with which the lion responded to their attempts at association, feeble reminiscence, or suggested affinity of tastes, he could never discover. He supposed it was the case of the moth to the candle, though as a candle he often felt he was rather a feeble flicker.

But Fame, whatever the degree, seemed to increase the blood pressure of the respectably obscure. Even the concierge, who saw him come in and out of the flat several times a day, could not resist the glamour. "You're driving Mr. Henry Fanning," he would whisper to the taxi-man, and all their scoldings could not cure the fellow. Fanning purposely had his name omitted from the board in the hall. Yet within two days of their coming to the flat three occupants of the block, well-bred and normally reserved people, had rung his bell and forced themselves upon him by the most trivial subterfuges.

It was annoying, it wasted his life, and subjected him to bores whom he was too weak to cast out resolutely. Annoying, yes—but would he really enjoy fading into complete obscurity, which was what would happen if he did not continue writing successfully? No, he would not. It was pleasant to be known as a successful man, whatever one did, to move, if not as an equal then as an honoured companion among the men who were making history in their various spheres. With a mere pen he had won a very comfortable competence for twenty years, and moved in the most interesting circles of his fellow men, his fame a passport through two continents. All this would vanish if he failed to write a new book, to maintain his reputation. But where was he to——

"Daddy—are you still in that bath?" said a voice the other side of the door. "There's somebody named Lessing wants to speak to you on the telephone. She says she knows you. Shall I tell her to ring again?"

"Oh, Lord," cried Fanning, rising out of his bath. "Lessing? I don't remember anybody named Lessing. How has she got our number?"

"How do they get our number?" complained Mrs. Fanning.

"I'm coming in a minute—tell her to hang on," said Fanning.

He roughly dried himself, and slipped on a dressing-gown and slippers. It was really no use not having your name in the telephone directory. It was less than useless, for when someone did ring you it probably was a friend or someone who knew your number quite legitimately. Lessing—he really could not think of anyone he knew named Lessing.

He slithered along the passage into the study and picked up the telephone.

"Hello?" he said, a little warily.

"Is that Mr. Henry Fanning?"

"Yes?"

"Oh, Mr. Fanning, perhaps you won't remember me. I'm Mrs. Arthur Lessing—I sat opposite you last week at the Empire Society's dinner and you talked so interestingly about the alarming conditions in the Balkans where you——"

"Oh, yes?" said Fanning, suppressing a groan.

"Well, I felt I had to ring you up. I happened to be in Cook's yesterday, and I saw a folder with your name on it, so I asked the young man if by chance you were going to Austria. And it happens you are, on the same train as my daughter——"

"Oh yes?" said Fanning. Damn Cook's, and could he cut her off soon? How had she got his number? Lord, yes, he gave it to Cook's—and she'd probably seen it on the folder. He couldn't really blame that most obliging young fellow at Cook's. He had never bargained for the lynx-eyed Mrs. Lessing.

"She so much admires your books, Mr. Fanning. And I couldn't resist asking, as a favour, as you're both on the same train and going to Vienna, if she might make your acquaintance. She's going out to her husband in Vienna—a most sad case. He——"

No, this had to be stopped.

"Thank you. I don't expect our seats are anywhere near each other. But if we do meet I'll remember what you've told me. I'm afraid I must ring off now as I'm——"

He hesitated. He could not tell the woman he was just out of a bath, inadequately clad and dried.

"Thank you so much! I knew you would be kind about it," continued Mrs. Lessing, enthusiastically. "It's so nice to think she will not be quite alone on that long journey. Good-bye, Mr. Fanning."

"Good-bye," he replied, replacing the telephone, and, when it was on its rest, "Well, I'm dashed!" he exclaimed.

He went back to his bedroom and dressed, wondering what he should wear. Whatever he put on Alice was sure to say it was unsuitable for travelling. When he was ready he went into the dining-room, but his wife was not there. He found her seated at his desk in the study opening a pile of letters. There must have been fifty. He groaned.

"Whenever I'm inclined to feel sorry for myself as the wife of a famous author I try to think what the wife of a film star feels like, with a thousand adoring women writing to her husband," said Mrs. Fanning, cutting open envelopes.

"But you really enjoy it, my dear," he replied.

"Come along, breakfast," she said, rising and leading the way. "The Colonials are heavy this morning, with America well behind."

He knew what she meant. Two-thirds of his correspondents appeared to be lonely women living in the wilds of Australia, New Zealand, South Africa and the United States. They wrote to him with astonishing intimacy and at great length. The trouble was he could not treat the daily burden casually, although it sapped his energy, and absorbed his time. Some of the letter-writers seemed to think he could enter into long discussion on the points they brought up, some of them felt he understood them as no one else in the world, and others wrote letters that really moved him with their warmth of spirit, or their simple charm.

They all invariably opened with the declaration that it was the first time they had written to an author. Had he been a hard-headed, hard-hearted man he would have glanced at these letters and thrown them into the waste-paper basket. Sometimes he did and then took them out again, conscience-smitten at his callous behaviour. These letters had been written under the stress of emotion he had evoked. Most of them were expressions of grati-tude, though verbose and autobiographical. And most of them were from lonely souls shut off from their fellows, from what they imagined to be the intoxicating pleasures of life lived in a great city, in the company of the famous. How little did they know that he was often just as lonely as they were, as full of tribu-lations and apprehensions, as now, for instance, when he knew he was finished.

So the letters he decided not to answer were put on one side, and the pile grew and intimidated him, and got mixed with those he knew he must answer. Finally, no space being available in the folder on his desk, he sat down and worked through them, a brief acknowledgment on a card, a few words in reply, and some-times a letter where the writer had touched a responsive chord.

And there the pile was, now twenty or thirty cards and letters, with himself feeling completely exhausted. All that writing, and yet no real writing done. The new book was not begun.

"Daddy, you are incorrigible," his wife would exclaim, com-ing in and finding him exhausted before the massed correspond-ence. "Why should you answer them? You didn't ask them to write."

"Oh, I must, it seems so rude, particularly when they've been so personal about themselves," he replied, weakly.

"Most of them are merely after your autograph."

"Alice, you mustn't be so cynical. I'm sure most of them write out of sheer niceness."

"You mustn't be so sentimental. They don't realize how it exhausts you."

"Well, I'll stop after this."

But he never would stop, he knew. As it was, he often felt guilty because he let some of the letters slip. He remembered how, as a boy, when very ambitious to become a great author, he had summoned up courage to write to a famous literary figure. Day after day, in a fervour of excitement he had awaited the postman's knock and rushed into the hall to examine the letters. But no answer ever came. For months he felt dreadfully humiliated. Even now it smarted a little. And not replying he, too, might be hurting some over-sensitive youngster who had made a great effort to express himself in a desire for sympathy. But Alice was ruthless in the matter. "Daddy, you fritter away your vitality. I'm going to order you some printed acknowledgments," she said.

"Oh, no, no—that's too cold-blooded!" he protested.

And now again, as they were seated at breakfast, she frightened him a little by saying:

"You know, I'm not going to send on any of these letters from readers."

"But there'll be a dreadful pile when I come back," he said.

"Oh, no, there won't!"

"No, Alice—you must send them on."

"I'll send the really necessary ones."

He made no reply. He helped himself to the marmalade, and he thought how he would soon begin to pine for an English breakfast. He could never develop the English tourist's sudden enthusiasm for coffee and rolls, thick coffee in little metal pots, and balls of bread with sad centres. Still, in Vienna, the coffee and rolls were good, and if he wished he could go out and breakfast at one of those pleasant cafés on the Ringstrasse, and watch the world walk by. He had always found it exciting to sit outside the Hotel Bristol and see all the different nationalities of Europe go by. He had found the idea for one of his best stories in something he had seen while sitting on that leafy boulevard.

"Who is Mrs. Lessing—and what did she want?" asked Alice, pouring him his third cup of tea.

"She met me once somewhere, and as her daughter's travelling on the same train she thought it would be nice for me to chaperon her, or for her to chaperon me, I'm not sure which," answered Henry.

Alice looked at her husband sadly.

"I know what'll happen. Some dismal female will fasten herself on to you, and you'll pay for all her meals, and worry about her luggage, and you'll become an unpaid courier. Daddy, you must flatly refuse to meet this creature. When Miss Lessing bears down upon you tell her you've got brain fag and mustn't talk."

"It's not a Miss Lessing—she's married and going out to join her husband in Vienna—and it's a sad case, so Mrs. Lessing said. I'll dodge her somehow."

"You won't. She'll track you down. Look at that woman who saw the label on your portmanteau and followed us into the dining-car, and in half an hour had made you promise to go and speak for her Poor Gentlewomen's Holiday Fund."

"Alice, you make anybody think I'm incapable of looking after myself," protested Henry, nibbling a piece of toast.

"You are," said his wife, at once.

"Very well. That's an excellent reason for my not going abroad. I'll stay at home," said Henry, feeling he had scored.

"Daddy, I shall put you on the train. It's no use trying to wriggle out of it that way," retorted Alice, rising. "And now I'm going to put out your things for packing."

II

He went into the study and looked at his desk. Now that he was going he wanted to sit down at it and write. The most exhilarating moments of his life had been lived at that flat-topped desk. He told everyone he disliked writing, which was true and yet was not true. When the work was going well, when his characters took shape and had vitality, when the dialogue ran crisply, and situations developed, far surpassing in intensity anything he had forethought, how wonderful it was, to achieve expression, to create with a God-like mastery over men's lives!

And best of all was that sense of gathering momentum as the book ran towards its finale. The fear that the task would never be completed was gone; out of the air had come forth those creatures of his story who were now so much a part of him that they had become more real than the living men and women who shared his daily life. In the earlier years of struggle, when he had to prove to the world that he could write, there had been no scarcity of characters springing to life in his fertile mind. Now, when he commanded a large audience by virtue of his previous performances, he had nothing to say. Was old age creeping over him, was this the customary condition of all creative artists? Surely not. He called to mind a dozen men older than himself, all prolific still.

'You know you've got a "fixation"—as young Henry says. It's ridiculous that you should ever dry up. Your mind is as alert as ever, life is an endless pageant, of infinite variations. Good heavens, man, you're at the top of your power.'

So he said to himself at this moment, contemplating his desk, his indented chair, the edge of the mahogany desk polished by

the movement of his wrist for twenty years. He had played with
the idea of going to a psycho-analyst, but a sturdy contempt for
what he regarded as witch-doctoring could not be overcome.

As he contemplated he became aware of the pile of opened
letters on his desk. Despite his grumbling he liked receiving
letters. He had never lost a feeling of excitement on picking up
an unopened envelope. His curiosity was highly developed, and
he could not repress it. If the telephone rang he had to go to it,
or learn who it was. People who called at the flat always apolo-
gized for disturbing him, and thought how nice he was about it,
but actually he liked leaving his desk, they made an excuse for
breaking off his labour, and, like a schoolboy in Form, any diver-
sion from the work in hand was welcome. Alice had tried to shut
him off from all disturbing influences, but his ears were sharp.
He always knew if the telephone rang or someone had called at
the flat. It was all wrong, it did not go with the picture of the
obsessed genius feverishly transferring ideas to paper. But, of
course, he was not a genius. He was rather pleasant to live with,
he hoped, and he had no ruthlessness.

He picked up a few of the letters on the pile, and began to read
them. A lady in South Africa, very friendly and complimentary,
begged him not to indulge in any more unhappy endings. It was
false to life. False? Yes, insisted the lady. "We are exactly what
we think ourselves to be—and man is the master of thought.
We control our destiny." But do we, dear lady, questioned Fanning. He wanted to stay at home and get the idea for a new book.
And he was being sent abroad, in the wild hope that something
would come to him.

He put down the letter with a sigh, glanced at a few others,
and browsed until one correspondent touched him on a raw
nerve; he was greatly looking forward to reading the next book.
Optimist. There was not going to be a next.

Dropping the letter, he saw that Alice had made a smaller pile that required immediate attention. He looked through them; requests to lecture, requests to propose a toast, to respond to one, to take part in a discussion, to join a committee. Then a letter with a familiar heading, from his publishers. He knew before he read it what it was about.

"We do not wish to bother you, but we feel we should not delay any longer the announcement of your new novel. We should be very glad also if you could give us a brief synopsis of the story. As you are aware, our book list, particularly in the Colonies, has to be well ahead of publication, and if it is your intention to publish next summer, as it is our hope, we ought to make an announcement now. We are sorry to bother you again in this matter, but it is now rather urgent."

There was no answer to that letter, except a truthful one, and he knew that Mr. Gerald, the buoyant, hearty chairman of his publishing company, would never believe him. "Don't believe it, my boy—you've said that before! You'll write the best book you've ever written! Now, when's it coming along?"

He had a great affection for Mr. Gerald, but his confidence crushed him in his present plight. Alice would have to telephone to-morrow and say he had gone abroad, but would be giving them what they wanted soon.

"Daddy!"

It was Alice calling him. He had been Daddy for the past twenty years, and remained so now when the girls and the boy had married. He went into the passage, and through the open bedroom door saw his wife laying out his travelling equipment. He always felt ashamed of the unremitting care she took of him.

"If you're going round to see Roger you must go now—they're all going out this afternoon, and we're lunching with the Fergusons at one o'clock," said Alice.

"Oh yes—and I must go to Cook's," he answered.

"Daddy!" cried his wife, reproachfully, "you've surely got your ticket—haven't you booked your wagon-lit? What a man you are! Really, Henry, if I don't——"

"Oh yes—I've got it all done. But I hadn't my cheque-book when I was there on Monday. I said I'd call for the ticket."

"They know you well enough to let you have it, and you could have posted the cheque," said Alice.

"Oh—I wouldn't ask them to do that. They get some funny people, you know."

Mrs. Fanning looked pathetically at her husband.

"They do indeed!" she said, putting out a dress shirt.

"I shan't need that, Alice."

"How do you know? You'll meet someone—a Prime Minister or an Ambassador, or a lady with a *salon* may annex you and ask you to dine."

"But I'm looking for a plot!"

"You're as likely to find it at a good dinner-table as in a cheap restaurant. Daddy, don't be parsimonious. Do yourself well, and go to the best hotels. You can afford it!"

"Yes," agreed Fanning, but without conviction. His youth had been a hard one. He was forty before he had more than a month's income in hand. While he had been writing books, good books which the critics and the public took no notice of, Alice had been making the children's clothes. One of those unremunerative books would now augment his fame, and earn what in those days would have been a staggering fortune. Even now, with no financial anxieties, he often walked home from his club through the rain rather than take a taxi, which seemed very extravagant. Young Henry, just down from Cambridge, regarded taxis as he regarded buses, he just jumped in and out of them.

"Well, I'll go along to see Roger," said Fanning. "You know, there's no need for you to do that, my dear. I can do it when I come back after lunch."

Mrs. Fanning smiled, and gave him a kiss on the cheek.

"Go along, Daddy, you're in the way. Tell Phyllis I'll come in to tea to-morrow, but if she's going out it doesn't matter."

Walking down the street towards King's Road, Henry Fanning, for all his troubles, reflected how lucky he had been in Life's lottery. He had drawn, at twenty-one, the best woman in the world. They had married almost at once, on nothing, for within a week of his marriage the newspaper on which he was a sub-editor had failed. "Henry, you've got to have your own business, under your own hat!" said Alice. "What do you mean?" he asked. "You're a born novelist, you must begin at once," she replied.

And he had begun at once. It had been a long, hard business, but Alice had never wavered in her faith. His three children were all that a proud parent could desire, healthy, good-looking, and happy. The two girls had married well. Young Henry took life with both hands. He had married a girl with a little money, produced a son, and was making money in the City. He lived on a scale that frightened his cautious father. Well, Roger was going to have a first-class education. He was down for Winchester. He was a really exceptional child—though of course every grandfather imagined his grandson was: in this case he undoubtedly was. It was the thought of Roger that made him miserable at leaving England. Every morning he walked round to say How-do-you-do to Roger.

In the King's Road, just round the corner of his street, there was a confectioner's shop. He went in. The young woman behind the counter knew him well. She smiled at him now.

"Good morning, Mr. Fanning. The usual?" she asked.

"The usual, please," he said, and put a shilling on the counter. She took down a tin of "humbugs" and wrapped it up.

"It's a lovely day, isn't it? Everybody's going away. I wish I could," she said.

"Er, yes," agreed Fanning. "Good morning!"

"Good morning. Thank you."

He had felt like disagreeing with the young woman. He would not be going into that shop again to buy young Roger his humbugs for at least a month. But that would mean nothing to her, and had he said he was leaving for Vienna this afternoon she would have thought him one of earth's lucky mortals.

III

"There's quite a crowd, and the police," said Alice Fanning, looking out as the taxi drew up at the station. "It must be someone important going away."

"Perhaps it's for me," said Henry, feeling like a condemned man joking on the scaffold.

A porter took Fanning's luggage, two small portmanteaux and a typewriter. The last was a symbol of hope. He had a seat reserved in the Pullman coach.

"Why, there's Lamond of the Foreign Office. And look at the drugget. Must be some foreign big-wig travelling," said Fanning to his wife.

As he spoke three men, with the station-master and an escort of porters, came along the platform. It was not until they were level with Fanning that he saw a sad-looking little boy in their midst. Behind him came a robust woman, English, unlike the others. She had the stamp of the governess.

"Why, you know who that is, Daddy!" exclaimed Alice Fanning. "It's that little Crown Prince of Slavonia who's at school here."

"Poor little beggar—I expect he's got his name on a bomb. What a life he's going to have," said Fanning.

"I don't suppose they've told him the real truth yet?"

"I should hope not. Fancy, his father blown to atoms."

Fanning entered the Pullman.

"Well, I'll have my last decent cup of tea, anyhow," he said, surveying the teacups on the small table.

"Daddy, don't be such a pessimist," replied his wife.

She stopped and read the name on the reserved seat opposite.

"Mr. Gollwitzer. Well, it's not Mrs. Lessing's daughter, as I expected. She'll get you later. She'll wait till I'm off the train."

"Alice, don't be ridiculous!"

Mrs. Fanning laughed.

"You know quite well, Daddy, it's you they want. Mr. Fanning's wife has to be asked as well, but she's a nuisance."

"You know I hate going anywhere without you."

"I know you do, Daddy—and I have to impress on you the fact that I'm more popular missing. They want the lion alone. And it suits me, I couldn't keep as amiable as you do. Now, have you any papers to read? Here's the boy."

She bought him a couple of evening papers. They were filled with more detailed accounts of the King of Slavonia's assassination. A student had thrown the bomb after the ceremony of opening the new University. There were portraits of the little Crown Prince, one of his preparatory school, and one of his host's house in Surrey, where he had been holidaying with a school friend.

"Surely they'll keep the papers away from him," said Fanning.

"He'll find out everything sooner or later, poor little chap," observed Mrs. Fanning.

"I say, look—why, this must be Friedrich Gollwitzer's seat," said Fanning, looking out of the window as Herr Gollwitzer bought a paper. "Whatever is he doing in London?"

"Well, now you've somebody interesting to talk to."

"I shan't talk to him. I don't know him."

"Daddy, don't be so terribly English. Pass him the sugar, and ask him if he's going to the Salzburg Festival—I should think that's where he's going."

A whistle blew. Doors were being shut.

Mrs. Fanning kissed her husband.

"Good-bye, Daddy."

"Good-bye, Alice darling."

She left the car and stood on the platform, watching him through the window. And now the train began to move.

She waved until he was gone, and then walked down the platform. She had kept a cheerful face and laughed at his fears, but she was worried about him. He had never gone as long as this without finding a new idea. There had been other desperate occasions, but this was quite the worst.

CHAPTER VII

HERR EMIL GERHARDT, OF BERLIN

I

"IT really was a wonderful party!" said Rex, from his corner in the taxi.

"Everybody came—it was a triumphant send-off!" agreed Daphne, wedged in between the two young men.

"I can never, never forget last night—it was *wunderbar!*" exclaimed Emil, with an unusual lapse into his native tongue. "And now it is Good-bye, London, Good-bye, my kind English friends."

"Don't, Emil, or I shall cry—of course you're coming back," said Daphne.

"Sometime—yes," replied Emil, sadly.

Daphne looked at him. It was hard not to look at Emil with his incredibly beautiful head, his blue German eyes and blond hair, so naturally wavy that it embarrassed him with the suspicions it evoked. Here, in England, he was so much the perfect German type that he attracted attention everywhere.

"Who's your Siegfried friend?" was the question Daphne was always asked. Now, as she glanced at Emil, the light blue eyes were misty. He was on the verge of tears. He forced a smile to his face, and said, "It's so good of you to see me off."

"We couldn't let you sneak out of London, Emil," said Rex. "I really don't know why you're going. Do you, Daphne?" he asked, addressing his sister.

"*Ach,* you are too kind. I must go. I must find work. It will

97

not do to accept so much of your kindness," replied Emil. "I am too unhappy knowing I cannot do anything!"

"You will get something, Emil. They can't go on being so silly for long—it's only a temporary madness," said Daphne.

"*Ach*, I don't know. It is all changed. My country is—I cannot say how. It is all *verrückt*."

He made a despairing gesture with his hands, and sank back in gloomy silence.

Verrückt. Crazy. Yes, that was the word. Two years ago Emil was the most admired, most envied young fellow in Berlin. When Rex, a music student, had met him there, Emil Gerhardt's name was on everybody's lips. You saw that singular head staring at you from every hoarding. His name flared on the electric signs down the Kurfürsten-Damm. Crowds collected around his great Mercedes car as it waited outside the Eden Hotel. The *première* of a film in which he was featured was always a great social event, with all of Berlin's smart set in the stalls. Emil Gerhardt's clothes, his ties, the toothpaste he used, the car he drove, the cigarettes he smoked, everything was noticed and advertised to an imitative world.

At twenty-two he seemed the most spoilt, vain, successful and handsome young man in all Germany. The glittering smile, with the perfect teeth, the blond hair crowning the Goethe-like Teutonic head with its smiling blue eyes and sensuous mouth, the athlete's body, broad-shouldered, narrow-hipped, the lean hands, the face at once so charming and alive with nervous health, how known were all these characteristics of the Fatherland's most typical son. In a short time he had won for himself an unchallengeable position as the prototype of the new German youth, zealous, aflame with patriotism, expressive in every phase of that renaissance surging through a nation rising from the aftermath of defeat.

Lucky in his hour, Emil Gerhardt began to crystallize the ideal product of this youthful generation, tempered by adversity and intoxicated by a new doctrine blended of hope, defiance and mass assertion. When the Führer spoke, in his blazing perorations, of the splendid young German who offered a superb body, a dedicated soul, and an unbreakable spirit to the service of the Fatherland, many of his listeners among the younger generation immediately visualized a figure like Emil Gerhardt. Every new film created to embody the new spirit pervading the Fatherland chose Emil Gerhardt for the leading rôle.

Rex Charnwood, studying the pianoforte in Berlin, was soon aware of Berlin's idol. The godlike creature was so much publicized in magazines and on placards that Rex began to dislike this spoilt darling, and wished to plant his fist in the exquisite face of this Teutonic sissy. When informed that the handsome Emil was a good athlete, that he ran and dived, as endless photographs of Adonis in skin-tight tank costumes and abbreviated shorts advertised to the world, Rex laughed derisively. "We've plenty of those at home," he said, "Oh, my dear, how too, too divine!"

Rex had been three months in Berlin when an occasion arose that caused him to dismiss his prejudices and revise his opinion of the handsome film star. He went one evening to a cocktail party in a crowded flat off the Kurfürsten-Damm. After half an hour in an airless room, buzzing with conversation, he began to make his way out, when all heads turned towards someone bowing low and kissing the hand of their hostess. In a moment, as the young man raised himself, shaking back his hair, Rex knew it was Emil Gerhardt.

He looked hard at him, anxious to find out how much reality coincided with legend. The beggar was incredibly handsome, there was no denying that. Moreover, he was masculine and exuded health, unlike so many of the film world's exotic exquisites. Just then the god spoke and smiled dazzlingly at the group that soon hemmed him in. His voice was pleasant and resonant. He seemed perfectly at ease, and yet avoided a sense of studied self-production. He was not, Rex saw on closer inspection, as insipid as his photographs often suggested, and he was so much less theatrical than one expected after witnessing his heroic rôles on the films. He must be, of course, as vain as a peacock. No youth who attracted so much attention could be otherwise. All the girls were now mobbing him and hanging on his words.

"No, you're not going—you haven't met Emil!" exclaimed his hostess, a newly married girl who had been at a Lausanne school with his sister. "Stay a little longer and I'll get hold of him."

Rex could not say outright he had not the slightest desire to meet the film star, that he was, in fact, antipathetic towards that kind of fellow. Instead he said, politely, "Oh, thank you," and getting behind his hostess, awaited an opportunity to slip away unseen. But he was not to escape, for Frau Hollweg suddenly cut her way through the admiring throng and brought Gerhardt straight over to where he stood, wedged against a bookcase.

"Emil, I want to introduce you to Mr. Charnwood. I was at school with his sister—Rex is here studying music," said Frau Hollweg.

The two young men bowed to each other and shook hands. Gerhardt smiled the famous smile, and then said:

"Frau Hollweg has told me what a wonderful pianist you are. I have a passion for the piano."

Rex murmured, "Oh, no," wondering why Louise Hollweg had told him such a thing.

"I play a little—but I have no time for practice," went on Gerhardt. "You are staying long in Berlin?"

"Four more months, I expect."

"*Ach so!* Then perhaps we may meet again? If you are not too busy will you dine with me one evening, quietly, at my apartment?"

Surprised, Rex answered, "Oh, thank you, I should like to."

The film star took out a wallet, bound in gold at the edges. He extracted a card, and with a gold pencil scribbled something on it.

"Please—this is my address, and this my telephone number. I am always home at six. I hope you will ring me, and we can arrange a time."

Rex took the card, astonished by this sudden friendliness, and unable to suppress a little pride at Gerhardt's attention.

"And may I say I have a piano?" added Gerhardt, with the dazzling smile. "*Auf Wiedersehen!*"

The young man bowed and turned away. Rex looked for his hostess. She was across the room. He made his way to her to take his leave.

"Isn't Emil charming?—not a bit spoilt," she said. "I wanted you to meet."

"Why?" Rex could not resist asking. "What interest can I be to him?"

Louise Hollweg looked at him with her mischievous eyes.

"You're his type," she said.

"Type?"

"Yes—he likes solid people, if you know what I mean— *glaubwürdig.* He's a lonely boy."

"Lonely!" repeated Rex, incredulous. He had a conception of Gerhardt living in the midst of an applauding crowd.

"He's a strange, lovable person. I've known him since he was a little boy. But he's terribly introspective and has a fear of Fate."

"That's odd. Fate's been very kind to him."

"Yes and no," said Frau Hollweg. "He lost his mother, whom

he adored, just as he was winning success, and he feels everything far too much."

"Love affairs?" asked Rex, smiling.

Frau Hollweg laughed and shrugged her shoulders.

"I don't know—but with a face like his!" she said.

"He may have a Narcissus complex, he may be egocentric."

"You're getting too subtle for me! *Auf Wiedersehen!*"

II

Three days later, on the spur of the moment he rang up Gerhardt's flat in Marburg Strasse. The film actor answered. Why, of course he remembered! Wouldn't he come round and have a drink, and if he had no engagement perhaps they could dine somewhere? So Rex went round.

Now, he thought, as he rang the bell, I shall really know something about him. Most people gave themselves away with their interior decoration. Rex expected something luxurious and ultra-modern. To his surprise the place was very impersonal and rather dowdy. An old woman answered the door and ushered him into the sitting-room, where Emil Gerhardt rose to meet him.

"This is very nice of you," said Gerhardt, genuine pleasure showing on his face. "I had just come in from the studio when you rang."

For a time they discussed his new film. He was very tired, he said, of playing one kind of character. "I can't get out of this pretty German boy part—always so frightfully patriotic these days!"

He shook a cocktail and filled Rex's glass. Watching him, Rex saw how naturally graceful he was in all his actions. It was not remarkable he was kept to rôles expressive of German youth. He had the slightly sad romantic air of one of Schiller's heroes, when in repose, but in conversation a vivacious temperament showed itself. In half an hour Rex had fallen under the spell of Emil Gerhardt. His laughter was infectious, he talked interestingly, and seemed interested in everything.

Towards eight o'clock Gerhardt glanced at his watch. He suggested they should go out and dine. "And then I would like to be very selfish. I would like to sit and hear you play."

Rex had no music with him, so he suggested Gerhardt should go back to his apartment. Gerhardt agreed at once. They dined quietly at a little restaurant near by, and took a taxi to Rex's place.

"How charming!" exclaimed Gerhardt, on entering. "I'm afraid my rooms seemed very dismal. I've not changed them since my mother died—I've even kept her old servant, which is very sentimental and silly, I suppose, but I hate breaking with the old things."

He slipped down into an easy-chair by the stove, in which Rex put some fresh wood, for it was a cold November day, and with one leg tucked under him, his head thrown back on the cushion, he looked about nineteen.

"How old are you, Gerhardt?" asked Rex.

"Twenty-two."

"Good heavens, am I only one year your senior!"

"Won't you call me Emil? Can I call you Rex? Why Rex? Rex means king?"

"In this case it's short for Reginald. What shall I play?"

"Can we have the lights out—do you like Brahms?"

Rex turned out all lights except one on the piano. He sat silent for a few moments, wondering what to play. Then he began.

"Ah—the *Sonata in F minor*. Gorgeous!" exclaimed Emil.

He drew himself up in the chair and closed his eyes. When Rex finished he called *"Schön! Schön!"*

Rex went on to play. "You won't know this," he said.

Emil listened for a few bars, then he shouted, impulsively, "*The Goldfish* by Berners!"

"However do you know that?" asked Rex, pausing, astonished.

"I can play his *Three Little Funeral Marches—For a Statesman, For a Canary, For a Rich Aunt,*" he answered.

"Play them," asked Rex, rising from the stool.

Emil seated himself, fastidiously adjusting the stool. Then he played. At once Rex knew he was listening to a skilled executant, with fine feeling. He made him play on.

To their great surprise it was soon eleven o'clock. Emil said he must go. He went out riding every morning at seven.

"It has been so delightful. Can I come again? I like you very much. I hope you like me."

Rex murmured some response, a little embarrassed. When his visitor had gone he felt both astonished and elated. Emil Gerhardt was an extraordinary creature. So volatile, so transparent, with an undercurrent of melancholy.

They met again within three days. Within a week they were saying *"du"* to each other. Soon, hardly a day passed in which they failed to meet. Two months, broken by Rex's journey home for Christmas, swiftly passed. Emil began to be troubled by Rex's impending departure for London in April.

It was in their last fortnight that, out of the sky, the blow fell. Rex came back to his studio one evening to find Emil pacing up and down, a flushed, agitated figure.

"I'm ruined!" he blurted out, the moment Rex entered.

"Goodness gracious—have you been gambling on the Exchange?" asked Rex, playfully.

To his amazement Emil, who tried to reply, suddenly turned away, flung himself on the lounge, and broke into uncontrollable sobbing. Bewildered for a few moments, Rex stared at his friend. Then he went and sat down by him, putting an arm across his shoulders.

"Emil! Emil, old boy! Whatever's the matter?" he asked.

After a time Emil spoke. At three o'clock that afternoon, when he was on location, the Director had sent for him. A little surprised by this interruption in the midst of his work—a new naval propaganda film in which he had the rôle of a young sub-marine officer—he went to the Director's room, where he was re-ceived by a worried man who showed him a letter. It was from the N.S.D.A.P. headquarters. Information had been given that Herr Emil Gerhardt had Jewish blood, and was not a suitable person, therefore, to be employed in the rôle of German youth. The company must not employ any actor who was not a pure Aryan.

"Have you Jewish blood?" asked Rex, surprised.

"A little. My paternal grandmother was a Jewess. I had even forgotten the fact."

"But you don't mean to tell me they're as silly as that? Why, it's preposterous! You, of all people! You're the most German thing that ever sang *Deutschland über Alles!*" exclaimed Rex.

Emil held his head between his hands. There was a few mo-ments silence. Then he stood up.

"I wonder if I am dreaming! Everything I have achieved is to be ruined by this—this rabble of adventurers who——"

Emil checked himself.

"No—I must not say that. The Führer has done great things for Germany. We are a new people, we've recovered our pride. But there are dreadful creatures around him. This Herr Streicher, with his foul paper. My stomach revolts whenever I see his post-ers with their obscene cartoons. I am disgusted, as every decent German must be—and it isn't the Jewish blood in me that revolts against this creature and his propaganda. Why, Rex, do you know it's never occurred to me that I, Emil Gerhardt, could be classed a Jew! I've never thought about it. My father was a good German bourgeois—an official in the Staats-Bibliothek, a Christian married to a Christian. Do I look a Jew? Have I any of a Jew's characteristics? *Mein Gott!*"

He threw back his head, his eyes bright with indignation.

"And Rex—what if I were a Jew! What if I were! Aren't they human beings? Haven't they given Germany some of her greatest men—in literature, science, philosophy, music, medicine, finance, chemistry, mathematics, the stage? Why, it's preposterous for us Germans, of all people, to stigmatize the Jews. I don't like Jews, I can't understand their oriental mind, I dislike their internationalism—Isaac in Frankfort always has a cousin in Paris, or a brother or a nephew in Rome, or Vienna, or Madrid, or Moscow—but that's because they've been driven all over the earth, poor devils, and they've learnt to cling anywhere, and burrow in. They're clever, they've given the world many of its greatest discoveries and its masterpieces. There's Russia, I know —but who created Bolshevism? Not a pack of miserable Jews, but the weak Romanoffs, the profligate, loose-living aristocrats, absentee landlords most of them, fornicating in Paris on the money sucked from an illiterate peasantry—that was the ground-soil of Bolshevism! *Gott in Himmel,* when I hear these half-wits talking, these cobblers' apprentices in brown shirts, these pimps turned into martyrs because they were shot up in a street scuffle——"

"I hope you've not been saying these things in public," interrupted Rex.

"This is the first time I've said them—I've indulged in a cowardly reticence," replied Emil. "Like most of us, we've swallowed rhetorical rubbish because in our despair for Germany we could not stop to analyse the mixed elements behind the Führer.

He made us a nation again, when we were a rabble. And now—
I can't see clearly what will happen—the fanatics are running
away with us."

He made a gesture of despair, and stood toying with a Nym-
phenburg figure on the bookcase.

"Did your Director suggest anything about the future?" asked
Rex. "Surely he won't let some petty jack-in-office dictate to
him? After all, it's a powerful company."

Emil shook his head.

"You've no idea how terrified our biggest men are by a mere
hint. They're quite powerless before some anonymous bully in
office. What's happened with me is this—some jealous little
actor, hating my success, saw a chance to remove me. By some
means he's dug out the old Jewish grandmother—whom I never
saw—and has run to some fellow at N.S.D.A.P. headquarters."

"But your Director will say you're necessary to the present
film, to its success and the success of others. Besides, look at your
propaganda assets—to take a Nazi view. You're the living embodiment of young Germany to-day," argued Rex.

"My Director will say nothing. He dare not. If he insisted on
carrying me he would find the picture censored, or the houses
closed to him, or his funds would mysteriously freeze—if not
worse. Poor man, he was stunned, as I was, but he knows he can
do nothing."

"And the film is stopped?"

"Yes. They've shot thirty thousand feet. It's all no use.
They'll have to find a new juvenile lead. I'm not going on the set
to-morrow—or the day after—or the——"

He broke off, and stood still, his face quivering, one hand
twisting his wrist-watch round and round.

There was a silence. Rex could find nothing to say. He had

his own view of the Nazi revolution, its manipulators of mob
psychology, and the whole racket of demagogy beating the patriotic drum, but as a foreigner he was careful never to let a word
of criticism escape him. He had seen the virus working in the
blood of some of his most reasonable German friends. They
were like people in a religious frenzy. They had heard the
Prophet, and their faith was implicit. In England they were distributing League of Nations Union pamphlets and passing reso-
lutions of universal good will. Here they were distributing gas
masks as passports to their new kingdom on earth. Seven-year-
old children going to bombing practice marched with a mission-
ary zeal, a hymn of patriotism on their lips. And with it all, new
roads, new bridges, new buildings, a new nation of superb phy-
sique, marshalled in the unity of self-negation for the Führer.
It was at once magnificent and immoral, regenerative and de-
structive. But whatever he thought of the mental confusion of
this formula of salvation by herd-instinct, and microphonic
hypnotism allied with terror in the air and retreats underground,
Rex allowed no expression of doubt to pass his lips. Emil himself
breathed the name of Adolf Hitler like an *Ave Maria.*

"I think you'll find they'll be sending for you to-morrow," said
Rex, after a heavy silence in which Emil stood with his back
towards him, his hands playing with the china figures on the
bookcase. But he had no real belief in his expressed hope.
Through all these months in Berlin he had seen one person after
another suddenly fall under the ban of the Nazi organization. In
the musical circle in which he moved, particularly with its large
percentage of Jews, there had been wholesale dismissals, vetoes
on the holding of professional offices, and, in some cases, without warning or notification, the victims had disappeared into concentration camps. His own professor, a mild little Jew with
twenty years' service at the Hochschule, had been summarily cast

out. After a struggle to continue private tuition, he had ended his misery by throwing himself under an electric train.

Strange that a people so kind, so patient and industrious, with so much innate cleverness, should hand over their liberty without a protest, and acquiesce in a rule oddly compounded of tyranny, energy, public spirit, self-denial, and mass hysteria! A new Germany was arising, self-disciplined, reliant and healthy, but at what a price of spiritual servitude!

"Rex, I know, and surely you know," said Emil, turning and facing him, keen-eyed, "that I am finished. My company will not dare to let me pass its doors again. If I did, some sneak, some second-rater jealous of me, will run to headquarters, and the Director will find himself called up and lectured like a schoolboy —if not worse. And God alone knows what they might do to me."

"But you're a public figure!" protested Rex.

"That counts for nothing these days. Far greater characters in our public life had not been proof against Jew-baiting. There's Einstein, Bruno Walter, Arthur Schnabel, Emil Ludwig, Feuchtwanger—I could go on. They've been driven out of public life, out of Germany. No, I am ruined. There is no life for me here."

"Well, there's America—or England," said Rex.

"I'm thinking of America. I can go to Hollywood, but you know what these film people are. If they want you they'll pay anything, if they don't want you they can't even say so civilly. You see, mine's a peculiarly national fame. I am Young Germany, the Hitler Jugend, if you like. I've specialized all this time in the rôle of the renaissance of German youth under the Hitler régime, or, if assigned to ordinary domestic parts, then I'm handsome Fritz, heroic Hans, the great boy who defeats the bad man and wins the love of the beautiful *Mädchen*. All Germany knows my smile, my voice, the colour of my hair and eyes. I am Deutsch *par excellence*. In Hollywood I'll have to build up a new personality entirely, if given the chance. All what I am here means little to them. Besides, there's my accent, my English is not good."

"Others have got over that—Jannings—Garbo———"

"Yes—yes. One can master it in time. But—" Emil paused, and made a gesture of futility.

"But what?" asked Rex.

"Rex, I'm German! I love my country, I like to be famous among my own people," cried Emil. "Don't think me too vain, but it's nice to be recognized everywhere you go, to see people turn to look at you, nudge each other and whisper who it is. I'm twenty-two and it's all intoxicating, apart from the fun of having all the money one wants. All of Berlin is my audience, I'm the friend of everybody. The small boys worship me, the young girls adore me, the young men envy me—don't you see what it means?"

Rex put his hand on Emil's shoulder and smiled.

"My dear Emil, of course I see. It's been champagne all the time. But we're looking for ways out, sad though it is. And Hollywood seems the only way."

Emil did not answer for a moment or two. Then he looked at Rex, and his friend saw a new misery in his face. There was something he seemed unable to voice.

"What is it now?" asked Rex, sympathetically.

Emil laughed, bitterly, and looked down at the carpet.

"I've something to confess to you," he said, quietly.

"Yes?"

"I've a girl."

"A girl—you've never mentioned her to me," said Rex, astonished.

"No—I didn't care to."

"My dear fellow!" said Rex, smiling. "Don't you know me better than that? It's nothing to me that you've a mistress. I'm not my brother's keeper, nor my friend's."

"Mistress? Oh no, Rex—I don't mean that. I've a girl—we're in love, and we are announcing the engagement next week."

"Why ever didn't you tell me this before?"

Emil looked at Rex curiously. Their eyes met and there was an air of hesitancy about Emil.

"You may not understand," he said, slowly, his eyes fixed on Rex's, "but I didn't feel my love for Hilda should come into—into—what there is between us," he finished quietly.

Rex, hearing, stared at this young German, baffled, yet half comprehending something he had never analysed underlying Emil's steady cultivation of friendship since that first meeting at Frau Hollweg's. The mixture of romanticism and idealism, the complexes so patiently analysed in the psychological processes of the German mind were something Rex had never wholly understood, though he was not derisive or antagonistic. His friendship for Emil had grown quickly, and was based on various factors, his ingeniousness, his physical and mental attributes, and, though less in proportion than many would believe, the glamour inseparable from a figure so famous in its chosen world. Now, hearing this hesitant confession, he was not curious to probe what underlay it. He only smiled a little at Emil, looking so anxiously at him, and said:

"Well—you didn't imagine I should be jealous, did you? I see, now, there's another reason for your not wishing to break with everything here. Wouldn't she—Hilda, follow you?"

"Yes—we'd marry at once, and go out. But it's a lot to ask her," answered Emil. "Her family is here, all her friends. She's very happy in her life."

The clock struck eight.

"Good heavens, we must go out and eat. You'll dine with me, Emil?"

"Thank you—I would like to."

They picked up their hats and coats, and switching off the lights, descended into the streets, just lit in the soft spring evening. They had not gone a hundred yards when a huge poster of Emil in his latest rôle shone under the electric battens on the hoarding.

"I wonder for how many more nights those lights will shine on me," said Emil, grimly.

Rex slipped his arm through Emil's.

"I think this is an occasion that calls for an extra good dinner and a bottle of the best Rüdesheimer—and no more defeatism," said Rex. "Good Lord, the world can't come to an end for a young genius of twenty-two, Herr Streicher or no Herr Streicher. And now we'll change the subject, and think only of our tummies, my dear Emil," he added, summoning a taxi.

He was already heavily out on his month's allowance, but this situation called for a bright face on a dark business.

For the next two hours he forced his good spirits, and succeeded in keeping Emil from brooding.

III

All this had happened in the March of the previous year. At the end of April Rex, his Berlin studies finished, had returned to London. Emil had already arrived in Hollywood, and had sent him two hopeful letters. He was not unknown in Hollywood, he found, and there was talk of work.

For two months there was silence, then at last Emil wrote again. After heartbreaking delays and unfulfilled promises, he had obtained a small rôle in a film, which was the beginning of bigger things.

Another two months elapsed, and then he wrote to say that he had not received any further work yet, he was very lonely and unhappy and life was alarmingly expensive. Then, in October, without any warning, Rex was called up one evening on the telephone. It was Emil's voice speaking. He had arrived in London from America, and was staying at the Dorchester Hotel. When could he see Rex? At once, replied Rex, who went round to the Dorchester.

He found Emil in a rather sumptuous two-room suite. He looked a little thinner but was as astonishingly striking as ever, in his Teutonic style.

"My word, you look prosperous!" exclaimed Rex, after a joyous greeting.

"Prosperous! Do you know I've not earned a cent for four months, and I've only enough to last me a month here? Then I'm done," said Emil.

"Then why all this?"

"You've got to do it to impress these people. I've failed completely in Hollywood. I can tell you the truth, Rex. Here, of course, I've left Hollywood in triumph. I did two pictures; one was awful, the other, in which I was good, was a shocking production and isn't yet released. After that, for four months I had nothing—nothing! I'm too German, too blond and blue-eyed and damned pretty, to use their words. And Rex, I wasn't happy, I didn't do myself justice. So I decided to make a jump here. British production is rising. The field's less crowded. There's a vogue for Austrian films. So I've risked it. I can hold out a month, then I'm quite done."

"But surely you've plenty of money—you saved when you were in Germany?" asked Rex.

"Not much—what's left I can't get out of Germany. And now I can never go back there," he said, with a sigh.

"Why not?"

"When I was in Hollywood there was a Nazi group, quite unofficial but there all the same, and despite the fact that they call themselves American citizens. One day they were saying pretty libellous things about old Einstein. I couldn't hold myself in any longer—I just let everything I felt come out. Some press fellow there thought it was a fine study and wrote up a couple of columns, featuring my attack on the American-German. A month later I got a furious letter from my married brother. He couldn't think how I could be so un-German as to defame the Führer and the magnificent work the N.S.D.A.P. had achieved for the rehabilitation of the Fatherland. I ought to be ashamed, etc., etc., and besides, it brought him into grave disrepute with the authorities. He had been called up and questioned about me, and was sent home thoroughly scared. I should ruin him and his family, he said. We had a Jewish grandmother. We must be careful. Rex, it's incredible what my own people think of it all. Even Hilda wrote about being 'pained' and said if I only saw the splendid new Germany, growing stronger day by day, I should be proud of my country and its great leaders. Hilda, who knows how they've stripped me of everything! But don't let us talk any more of this. One day I shall wake up and find it was all a nightmare. It's so good to see you, Rex, to be here in England. It's perhaps strange to you, but I think every German longs to visit England. You are the least strange people to us; we like each other. I shall be happy here. And you, is everything well?"

His mood had changed in a couple of sentences. In his excitement at a new experience he had become the old volatile Emil, with glowing eyes and superabundant vitality. He picked up a photograph in a leather frame.

"Did you ever see Hilda—no, of course not. *Ach, sie ist wirklich wunderschön!*" he said, breaking into German, and impulsively kissing the photograph before he showed it to Rex. "I keep sane because of her."

His tribute did not exaggerate her beauty. She was a typical blonde type, with a good brow, rather solid features, and very beautiful eyes. Emil produced other photographs: of himself in his American picture, of his many rôles in Germany. He had four letters of introduction to directors in England. He was full of hope, and, considering his somewhat desperate situation, very buoyant and sanguine.

Rex took Emil to dine at his club, and, as ever, before the evening was through, his personality attracted everybody to whom Rex introduced him in the smoking-room after dinner. He left the club with a number of invitations to dine.

"Oh, how I like this London! It excites me," he exclaimed as they walked up St. James's Street. "I am to be happy here."

IV

Emil soon found work, small parts it is true, but work nevertheless. He gave up his expensive suite and moved to a small hotel in Mayfair. Two months passed, during which Rex saw him frequently. He quickly established himself among all his friends. Rex's mother and sister really loved him, for his handsome appearance and charming manners. At the end of two months there was a period when he was out of work again, and he was worried over the fact that the authorities might not renew his permission to stay in England. Money began to worry him also. He had spent his surplus. He moved to a small bed-sitting-room in South Kensington.

Outwardly he maintained his gay spirits. He never lacked invitations to cocktail parties. He was so handsome, he played the piano and mimicked so well, and there was ever the attraction of a foreign personality speaking English with an odd accent. He might easily have had his head turned by adoring women, but having survived that test in the time of his popularity in Berlin, he was proof against it in London.

Gradually Emil became aware of the same difficulty affecting his career as in Hollywood. He was so very German that the rôles in which he could be cast were few and infrequent. There was no disguising the blond-haired, blue-eyed German youth, and when disguise was attempted he could not realize himself.

The weeks passed and no work came. His money was exhausted. He talked one night of suicide, and Rex laughed at him. Plainly he was becoming neurasthenic. A conference between Rex and his mother and sister resulted in Emil being almost forcibly abducted from his bed-sitting-room and brought to their flat. In the family circle he regained some of his spirits; also, as Rex had suspected, Emil had been economizing on his food. A comradeship sprang up between him and Daphne. To keep him from brooding she made him escort her to friends' houses, where he was instantly popular.

"I can't think why your sister isn't madly in love with Emil Gerhardt," said one of Rex's girl friends. "I think he's too fascinating for words."

Rex laughed. He wondered himself. If Daphne was in love with him she wore a mask that few could penetrate. Not even Emil.

Spring came. The promise of a part was dangled before his nose, then it vanished. He was plunged into despair and they all tried to cheer him. By some subterranean means he continued to get a small sum owing to him out of Germany, via Holland. He at once insisted on returning to independence, and took a small room in the next street. He could not impose on them any more.

How much money had he got? He was mysterious. He became a hermit, and had to be fetched out of his room, which was cheerless.

"I don't believe he gets enough to eat," said Rex. "Something must be done."

A dozen friends would have volunteered to help him, but the problem was how to induce him to accept. He was fiercely independent and his pride was stirred when any suggestion was made that he ate inadequately. Another month passed. Then one day Rex noticed Emil's gold watch was missing from his wrist. He knew without asking what had happened. A discreet inquiry elicited the information from the landlady that Herr Gerhardt had cleared up some weeks' arrears. "Poor young gentleman, I'm so sorry for him. He's dreadfully worried. I sometimes hear him talking to himself in his room."

One morning, soon after breakfast, when Rex had gone to his studio at the bottom of the garden, where he practised on his Bechstein, there was a tap on the door and Emil appeared. The unusual hour for this appearance made Rex fear that something had happened, but Emil was in a light mood and talked cheerfully. No reason for this early visit was mentioned. After a time Emil lay down on the divan in the corner of the lounge and begged Rex to play.

"Very well, I'll get on with my work. I'm memorizing the old Rachmaninoff *Concerto*," said Rex, and began to play. He had almost finished the first movement when he was conscious of an unusual sound coming from the divan. Stopping, he turned. All he could see was Emil's back, as he lay with his face to the wall. But there was no doubt what was happening. Emil was quietly sobbing.

Quickly Rex left the piano and went over to him. For a time Emil ignored him, inarticulate in his grief. At last the paroxysm subsided. He sat up and wiped his eyes. Slowly the story came out.

Last night, by the evening mail, a letter had come from Hilda, in Berlin. It had only one possible meaning. The situation was so difficult. Their separation, the improbability of his early return, and the objection which her parents had developed to their engagement, made it impossible to continue. Still thinking fondly of him, she returned her *Verlobungsring*.

"My poor, poor Hilda. They have driven her to this. You see, the blood taint again!" said Emil, bitterly, wringing his hands as he sat on the lounge. "And so—the end of my Germany. Never, never again will I tread its accursed soil!"

"Oh, come, come, Emil," said Rex. "You can't turn down your country because a girl's been bullied into breaking her engagement."

"My country! My country!" exclaimed Emil, with passion. "What has it done for me but hounded me to poverty, separated me from my friends, my work, my fortune, and now, my fiancée?"

He rose and walked up and down the studio, running his hands through his thick blond hair. Rex did not speak. His mood must exhaust itself, and there was so little he could say.

In half an hour, Emil, calmer, said he must go. But Rex had made up his mind. He would not let Emil return to the loneliness of that small room. He insisted then and there that his friend move back into their home.

They kept Emil for two more months. He was quietly fretting and his moods alternated between boisterous gaiety and brooding despair. He no longer canvassed the film offices. By sheer irony one of his "star" pictures of Berlin days was shown in the West End, during a Press discussion on Germany's organization of its youth in connection with re-militarization. For a fortnight

Emil appeared as the personification of the German renaissance, a young patriot burning with sacrificial zeal for the Fatherland.

At the end of July he had a sudden resolution. An Austrian company was being formed for the production of Austrian films. He had a friend who was one of the directors, a Jew, a brilliant scenario editor who had been one of the most highly paid men in Germany before the anti-Jewish campaign. Emil was certain he could get work with this company. For the first time he asked Rex for a loan, for the cost of the journey.

And now, to the regret of all the friends he had made, charming, boyish Emil Gerhardt was leaving England. Mrs. Charnwood was in tears. Daphne, though hard hit, was borne up by hope for Emil for whom a door had opened at last. She and Rex arranged forthwith to be in Vienna in September at the close of a Hungarian holiday.

The final night of Emil's sojourn in England was devoted to a large cocktail party given in his honour in Rex's studio. A mob filled the place, and as no one seemed inclined to go home the party developed into a dance that went on until midnight.

Emil's popularity, and an excess of sentiment over this *Auf Wiedersehen*, transformed a farewell party into something of the nature of a triumphant send-off to a friend about to achieve the greatest success of his career. In the convivial and kindly air that filled the studio Emil for a short time tasted his former popularity as the film public's hero. So that when, the following afternoon, in the taxi taking Emil to Victoria Station, Rex observed, "It really was a wonderful party," not only did he feel pride as a host, but also he was happy that Emil had had such a send-off.

"The train's sure to be crowded," said Daphne. "People are still going away. You'll find Vienna full of English, Emil. They

twitter like sparrows at the Café Schwarzenberg, and we used to
fight for a seat at the open-air restaurant up at Kobenzl."

"It's lucky for Vienna—for all the Viennese are out of it in
August. But I don't want to go at all," sighed Emil.

Daphne was about to reply "Then don't," but that would have
been foolish for many reasons. Poor Emil, she was in love with
him, but, then, so was every girl. He was a German, he was
frantically poor, and his girl had thrown him over. He was compelled to run all over the earth in the hope of earning a living.
Wherever he went he made friends, and with so much attention
paid to him, because of his striking appearance and his engaging
disposition, how was it possible he should see that she had begun
to live for him?

She could not imagine her life now without their daily excursions, or without the sound of his voice in the house. She liked
to be seen with him, for he was not only distinctive, but he
dressed well, his former lavish wardrobe holding out through
this financial drought. She would be happier with him, she
knew, in the proverbial garret than in her own extremely comfortable home. She was not blind to his faults. He was highly
temperamental, and had developed a tendency to find crises in
situations that could be dealt with by cool judgment. There was
a touch of the Narcissus in his anxiety to preserve his looks, but
this was forgivable since he lived by his face and it won him
prominence wherever he went. "A little bit of a prima-donna,"
had once said Rex, rather unkindly, being made angry by something that had happened.

But what were these faults when weighed against his infectious gaiety, his real physical beauty, and his affectionate and
spontaneous nature? Had he been less self-centred—and if artists were not self-centred, she knew they could not be artists—he
would have discerned the growth of her love for him. When the

Hilda break had happened there had been a sudden, ridiculous hope. He was free. But the difficulties were too great. He did not see her as anything but a good friend and a nice companion, and as Rex's sister.

As Daphne had foretold, the train was crowded. Emil's expensive-looking luggage was piled up on the porter's barrow. Daphne wondered whether Emil felt humiliated going second-class. Hitherto he had always travelled *en prince*. He would not accept a loan larger than was necessary for a second-class ticket. Perhaps he would come back in luxury. Acting for the films was a form of gambling with the public favour that sometimes brought fortune overnight. He had touched the zenith of success once. Why not again? And in that case, Daphne asked herself, would he ever come back to England?

She felt Rex nudge her as they walked down the platform, and it jerked her out of her reverie. She gave him an inquiring look.

"They're a honeymoon pair, I'll bet," said Rex, indicating a young couple walking before them.

Daphne looked at the girl's new tailor-made costume. It was charming, and as she hurried by she looked covertly at the bride, and saw she was a girl with, of course, the happiest expression. The young man looked vigorous and kindly. She would have liked to wish them good luck.

"Lord—not in there, with a bunch of Greek waiters, I hope!" exclaimed Rex, as Emil paused. But no, his reserved seat was not in that carriage at whose door a swarthy group was standing. The porter appeared farther down the corridor.

Emil's portmanteaux were stacked up on the rack. He removed his hat and stood out on the platform with Rex and Daphne. "Of course he knows all about his hair!" a girl friend had said. Silly creature! How could he not? He attracted attention now, so very blond and heroic, so much Siegfried of *Der Ring des Nibelungen.* If only she and Emil had been going away on their honeymoon, like the other couple, thought Daphne.

This waiting was rather trying. Emil had turned silent. He was attempting to look cheerful, but anyone could see he was depressed. They talked trivialities. Yes, he would write at once. For a week at least the address of a friend, Rudolph Steyer, would find him, but he would not stay longer there, as his flat was so tiny. Rudolph was a struggling medical student walking the wards of the *Allegemeines Krankenhaus.*

The whistle was blowing. Emil shook Rex's hand, but he could not say what he wanted to say. Choking, he turned to Daphne.

"I am coming back," he said, huskily.

"Of course—in triumph!"

"Thank you—yes, in triumph. Then I will say—I will come back to tell you——"

"Come on, old boy—hop in!" said Rex, for Emil was the last on the platform. The train had begun to move.

With a smile, the old Berlin poster smile, Emil leapt into the carriage. For a few moments they did not see him, the door window being blocked with travellers shouting farewells, but at last the blond head appeared over the English heads. He put out a hand and waved it, in a familiar gesture. His white teeth and blue eyes shone in the shadow of the receding train. He waved and waved, and at last he was gone.

"Poor old Emil," said Rex, in the taxi, returning home. "If his luck doesn't turn soon he'll break. He's getting terribly jumpy. He actually asked me last night, as he went to bed, if I thought he looked Jewy! He'd been studying his nostrils, he said, and they were developing a Hebraic curve! Did you ever bear such nonsense? You know, that damnable Nazi persecution's preying on his mind day and night. He'll soon be unfit for work."

"But he's so gay, Rex," said Daphne, looking out of the window, as they came to Eaton Square.

"Yes—but there's hysteria underneath. If you'd seen how—"

He broke off and looked at his sister, who was holding a handkerchief to her face.

"Hello, what's—Daphne, old thing, I'm sorry," he said, sympathetically. His hand covered hers in her lap.

"I'm a little fool," said Daphne, wiping her eyes. "I'm better, Rex. You were saying?"

"Nothing of importance."

He smiled at his sister, and suddenly he wondered how he could have been so stupid.

"Daphne—are you just sorry for Emil, or are you——"

He did not finish the sentence. Daphne was looking straight into his eyes, and he read in her own the answer.

"My God—why didn't I—why didn't Emil—heavens, what a mess—no, I don't mean a mess, Daphne," stammered Rex.

"A mess—that's what it is, Rex," answered Daphne. "It's just one of those things that shouldn't happen and do."

"Why ever not?" exclaimed Rex.

"Well, the woman's in a pretty hopeless position," said Daphne, bitterly, "and it's not helped by Emil being a foreigner, and out of luck. I've my own income, we could scrape along on that till his luck changes—and I'd gladly take the risk—but I couldn't tell him that, and I don't know whether I've ever existed for him in this way. Now I'm worrying myself with what he was going to tell me, when the train began to go, when——"

She was going to say 'When you shouted, "Come on, old boy, hop in!" at a moment when I was idiot enough to hope he was going to blurt out that he would come back and marry me," but she checked the words, feeling the rebuke was ungenerous, as Rex had been in no way to blame.

"—when Emil said, 'I will come back to tell you'—and didn't finish," she added.

"Because I pushed him in the train. Good God!" exclaimed Rex. "Sorry, Daphne!"

"It was probably nothing."

He did not answer. He felt it might have been anything. Women were at such an unfair disadvantage. They'd got to wait on the man's move. Did Emil care for Daphne in the deeper sense? There had been no indication, but Emil, though he wore his heart on his sleeve so much, might possess for it a very deep pocket. Hilda was no longer in his scheme of things. Her defection had been a heavy blow, but, a realist, despite his temperament, he had dismissed her from his mind, contemptuous of her weakness in surrendering to political pressure. What, indeed, was Emil about to say when he had urged him into the train?

For the rest of the day he worried over that question. The revelation of his sister's love for Emil made him unhappy. He would not have opposed the match, despite Emil's present position. He had too great an affection for him, and not only affection but respect for his excellent qualities. His mother, too, was devoted to Emil. He would have been welcome in the family where already he had lived on equal terms and in the freest intimacy.

After dinner that evening Rex came to a decision. He would write frankly to Emil and ask him whether there was anything he had wished to say to Daphne.

But seated, later, at the writing-desk, the letter became very difficult to write. He could not, for his sister's sake, appear to be soliciting an overture. Finally, he wrote a cheerful note, saying how different the house seemed without him, and stressed delicately how much his mother missed him, and how depressed Daphne had been after seeing him off at Victoria. "If your hopes are unfulfilled in Vienna, don't hesitate to come back to us. This is now your home," ended Rex.

It was midnight when he finished the letter, and he held it over until the morning for posting.

Chapter VIII

SISTER TERESA, OF TRANSYLVANIA

WHEN she was fifty-two the world lost Lady Ursula Greyne, daughter of the fourth Marquis of Downhouse, and widow of Sir Grahame Greyne, sometime His Britannic Majesty's Ambassador at Washington. Her daughter happily married, her son pursuing a diplomatic career as brilliant as his father's—the younger son had fallen in the War—she found herself with no ties at the age of fifty-two, an active healthy woman, of ample means.

Always devout, it seemed to her that the future would become a round of useless social events unless she found for herself a task. Quietly, but with a firmness of decision that surprised no one who knew her, Lady Ursula visited her daughter, her son, and her friends, and then slipped from the world she had known. She died as Lady Ursula Greyne, with a house in Wilton Place and a manor in Hampshire, and became a Sister of Charity of St. Vincent de Paul.

"Catholics do odd things like that," commented old Lady Derryham, at the bridge table where half her life was spent. "Personally I'm too fond of life to quit it before I'm compelled to. Of course, it's very unselfish of her—gone out to nurse orphans in Roumania, of all places!"

Sister Teresa, as she was now known, had never been conscious of doing anything unselfish. She had merely followed the inclination of a devout nature. She had indeed been greatly rewarded by twenty years of deep happiness. These twenty years

126

through which she now found herself the Sister Superior of the St. Vincent Orphanage at Predeal, in Roumania, had slipped by so quickly in an eventless succession of happy days that only her birthdays marked the count of years. Once in every five years she came home to England, to see her daughter and her grandchildren. She was home now, two years earlier than usual, because her son was in England, during a vacation taken on changing his post. He had just returned from Buenos Aires and shortly was leaving to become the Minister in Copenhagen.

One other reason had brought Sister Teresa home to England. For some time she had been conscious of increasing weakness, and she had noticed the swelling of a gland in the neck. It was nothing alarming, but she thought it prudent to take this opportunity of consulting a doctor in England.

She was preparing to fulfil her appointment with the specialist on this lovely August morning, as she dressed in her cell at the Convent of the Sisters of Charity in Carlyle Place, where she stayed during her London visits. Her family doctor to whom she had gone first seemed a little puzzled by her condition. She had rarely known illness, she was an active, well-preserved woman who passed for sixty, but of late she had had periods of intense weariness.

"I would like you to see Dr. Seeley, in Wimpole Street. Please don't think it is anything alarming," said her old doctor.

"Nothing can be alarming at my age," said Sister Teresa, quietly, her beautiful face framed in the large white cornette of a Sister of Charity. "God has given me a long and tranquil life. It is His to take."

"My dear Sister—please don't take too serious a view. I hope there are yet many years of useful service before you."

The old doctor looked at this patient of forty years. They were old friends. He had seen her children grow up. He had attended her husband in his last illness. She had always been a woman of remarkable qualities. Well-born, the experienced wife of an eminent diplomat who had held the highest posts, she bore an unmistakable air of authority as well as of charm. He had always thought it a pity that she had exiled herself, for over twenty years, in a mountain convent in remote Roumania.

He had called on her there once, some ten years ago when on a visit to Bucharest. He found her in charge of a large convent orphanage, with a group of sisters and two hundred small children all under her charge. The convent was beautifully situated on its thickly wooded mountain ledge, with magnificent vistas over the Transylvanian pine forests, and the valley of the Prahova falling southwards to Bucharest, nearly a hundred miles distant. But how out of the world, and buried among primitive peasants, except for a short season when the tourists came from Bucharest!

A strange choice, thought Dr. Plummer. Nevertheless, she looked happy, and the mention of her name in the local hotel told him that her prestige was as high in this mountain retreat as ever it was when she was the lovely Ambassadress of Paris or Washington.

"You are going back to Predeal?" asked Dr. Plummer, as she took leave of him.

"Of course."

For a moment he seemed to be on the verge of saying something, but he said no more beyond wishing her good-bye.

"Dr. Seeley will communicate with me, and, if necessary, you will see me again?" he said, conducting her into his hall.

"If necessary—but you know I must leave on Wednesday," she answered, with her lovely smile.

He walked out with her to the waiting taxi, her white linen cornette flapping in a puff of wind, her tall thin figure clothed in the simple blue dress of a Sister of Charity. Then, as the taxi moved off, she bowed in response to him.

A specialist. That meant something rather serious. She was not deceived by Dr. Plummer's kindness. What it was she neither pondered over nor experienced anxiety over. Her tranquillity of spirit was innate, not a thing of self-discipline. She had perfect and unchanging faith in the ever-enduring love of God. Did she not wear on her finger the ring of the Bride of Christ? One other bridal ring she had worn, taken at the altar from the hand of young Grahame Greyne. It had been a token of thirty years of felicity, a mortal span closed with Grahame's death. Her present union transcended death and ensured immortal joy. The world had nothing to take from her since she had surrendered it in service.

Now, as she dressed, preparatory to her appointment in Wimpole Street, she wondered how they fared in St. Vincent's Orphanage at Predeal. It was a quarter to nine and the mountain pines would be just emerging from a blanket of mist, and the risen sun would have struck the copper cupola above the Convent. Here, in London, she could faintly hear the noise of traffic coming over the Convent wall from around Victoria, London's incessant voice, so different from the sound of wind in the woods around St. Vincent's, a sigh in springtime, a roar as of the sea in winter.

She was waiting when a Sister told her the taxi was at the door. They had offered to accompany her, but she preferred to go alone. Promptly at ten-thirty she was ushered into Dr. Seeley's waiting-room, communal to the four doctors practising in the house.

A small child, with her Jewish parents, was in tears at the thought of seeing a doctor. The parents spoke to her in a foreign

language, but she refused to be comforted. To their amazement
the elderly Sister in the white cornette talked gently to the child
in her native language. She was a little Roumanian girl, and her
astonishment at being addressed by a stranger in her own tongue
dried up her tears. Sister Teresa was still smiling at this odd inci-
dent when she was shown into Dr. Seeley's consulting-room.

A middle-aged man with iron-grey hair and deep-set eyes, he
listened to her statement after he had asked particulars of her age
and constitution. When he said he would like to make an examination she asked if he had a nurse who could be present. He
summoned one at once. Then, having examined her neck, he
pricked the lobe of her ear, taking a little blood from it.

"Will you wait—or would you like to see me another day?
It will take me about fifteen minutes to complete the blood test,"
asked Dr. Seeley.

"Oh, I'll wait, doctor. You see, I want to leave London to-
morrow," replied Sister Teresa.

"Then, if you will sit here I will be back as soon as possible."

He retired, carrying the small phial of blood with him. What
was the matter, she wondered. Then with a firm resolution not
to worry, she began to talk to the nurse.

When at last Dr. Seeley returned he seated himself at his desk,
and looked kindly at the calm Sister before him.

"I expect you wish me to tell you the whole truth? There are
some to whom one does not tell it, but you, I see, have no fear,"
he began.

"The whole truth, please," said Sister Teresa. But her mouth
was dry; she had anticipated a verdict of cancer. Well, it was
God's will.

"You are suffering from a complaint known as chronic lym-
phoid leukæmia. It is a condition of the blood in which there is
a very great growth of the white corpuscles, which are tremen-

dously in excess of the red corpuscles. It induces a large spleen, and the swelling of the gland you have noticed is one symptom. I cannot say that it can be cured, but its progress might be delayed, with caution. You must take things easily, and rest is essential. For that I should imagine a convent is the very best place," he said.

Sister Teresa smiled at him.

"You mustn't imagine, doctor, that because we are tranquil we are lazy. I rise every morning at half-past five and our whole day is occupied by tasks. There are times of meditation, of course," she said.

"I think you should stay in bed later—until ten or eleven."

"Oh dear—that is almost impossible."

"Well—I advise you to," replied Dr. Seeley, gently.

"What you really mean, doctor, is that I have ceased to be useful. It is the end?"

He tapped the back of his hand with his pince-nez, leaned back in his chair, and looked kindly at this old lady with a saint's face.

"No—with care the condition can be arrested," he replied. "There's one thing, however. You must not live at any great altitude. That does not arise, of course, as you are in London, but if you——"

"Oh, but I do live at an altitude. I'm only visiting the Convent of St. Vincent here. My own convent is in Roumania."

"Roumania!" exclaimed Dr. Seeley, surprised.

"I am the Superior of a convent with a large orphanage attached. We have charge of more than two hundred children, at a place called Predeal, in the Transylvanian mountains, a hundred miles north of Bucharest. I've been there for fourteen years."

"The Transylvanian mountains! What height is your village?"

"Over three thousand feet."

"Sister Teresa, you have come to me for my opinion. I shall give it you, and you will then act on your own responsibility. Any further prolonged stay at so high an altitude would seriously increase your trouble, indeed—it is never my practice to overstate anything—it would endanger your life. You should not go back to that place."

Sister Teresa did not answer for a few moments. Then, raising her head, she looked frankly at the doctor across the desk.

"My life would not be worth anything except at Predeal. Whatever the risk, I must take it," she said, quietly, and then added, with her delightful smile, "You have greatly relieved me, if that is all."

Dr. Seeley looked at her. He had seen many who heard a death sentence. None had shown greater tranquillity than this frail woman.

"I understand—and admire you," he said.

"Oh no—there's nothing to admire. It's just obstinacy—and a complete confidence in whatever befalls. Thank you so much for being so frank and understanding," she said, rising. "May I pay your fee?"

"Three guineas, please."

She opened her purse and paid him. Then she held out her hand.

"Good-bye, doctor."

"Good-bye—I feel I have met a very rare person to-day," he said.

"Rare?"

"One wholly without fear, and wholly happy," he explained.

"I am grateful for my life. God has been very good to me."

But going back in the taxi, her heart sank a little, not in fear but in sadness. Good-byes to those one loved were inevitably sad.

The verdict had one clear meaning. She was going to Predeal for the final time. It would have been presumptuous at her age to think that she would visit London again, and see her children and grandchildren, or sit with the Sisters in the Convent in Carlyle Place, but until this consultation in Wimpole Street there had been no certainty that she would never come again to London.

Her mind passed the early events of her life in review in this England of hers. She had spent her girlhood in their Westmorland home, a rambling stone-built mansion on the shore of Lake Windermere. For two years, in her youth, she had lived with her parents in Rome, in an old villa at the foot of the Pincio, in whose gardens she had spent so many happy afternoons. It was there, at the age of twenty-one, she had first met young Grahame Greyne, still up at Oxford, and spending the Long Vacation with the Colonettis. It was Princess Colonetti who had introduced her to her paying guest, for the impoverished old princess received "foreign" pupils, and Grahame was then studying Italian. How shocked the old lady was when she heard they had had tea together the next day, in a little café that used to be at the foot of the Scala della Trinità, almost opposite the house where Keats had died!

A traffic halt and the noisy passing of a fire engine broke her reverie. To-morrow she left for Bucharest. Only to-day remained to make such final plans as were necessary. Should she tell her daughter Isabel, and her son, the result of this Wimpole Street visit? Why worry them, and let their parting be saddened by the knowledge they would not meet again? No, she would not tell them, she would not tell anyone.

Half-way down Bond Street an idea suddenly possessed her. She looked at her watch. It was just past eleven. It was almost the right time. Did people still go to Gunter's in Berkeley

Square, for their morning coffee? She had not been there for
thirty years, and it was there, fifty years ago, she had made the
most momentous decision of her worldly life. An intense desire
to re-visit the scene overcame her.

She would go. Leaning forward, she tapped on the glass and
told the taxi-man to drive to Gunter's in Berkeley Square.
"Yes'm," he replied. Then it was still there.

Her old heart fluttered as she stepped from the taxi and entered the tea-shop. It had been enlarged, but it was still identifi-
able as the old place of her youth, whereas almost the whole of
Berkeley Square had vulgarly changed into blocks of flats, offices,
clubs, and even shops. In her day there had been only two small
shops, each with an intimate clientele, a little news-agent's, and
the celebrated Gunter's.

Sister Teresa selected a table in the far corner of the first
room. She knew that corner. The fashion had not yet arrived, if
it ever did arrive these days. And what was she doing, the Sister
Superior of the Convent of St. Vincent de Paul, thinking about
the fashion? Her thoughts should be on solemn matters, touching the news she had just heard. Her heart seemed unsteady, as
she quietly ordered a cup of coffee.

The wallpaper and the furniture had changed. The suave, fat
little waiter had given place to a slim, trim girl. That waiter had
probably been dead thirty years. It was improbable anyone then
in the place was alive now. But it was in this corner she had sat
on the morning of May 22nd, fifty years ago. And here at eleven-
thirty, by appointment, had come young Grahame, a little pale,
to propose his bold plan. She had slipped unseen out of her
father's house in Charles Street near by, as she had done on
several occasions to meet Grahame, whom she had known since
that first meeting in Rome in the past summer. They were madly
in love and they had no right to be. They were, it seemed, the

most tortured, ill-fated young lovers in the whole world, for she, Ursula Winchurch, was engaged to her father's Parliamentary secretary, Lord Stephen Tallard, the son of the Marquis of Ebden, who everybody declared was going far.

Brilliant, rich, and aggressive, he was marked for success. He had been considered the catch of the season by the mothers of Mayfair. She was to be married to him on the morrow. This morning, as she had come out of the house, the wedding presents were being laid out on the long table set in the morning-room. So far, since the day she had been pressed into the engagement, despite her misgivings, despite the assurance that she was making a brilliant marriage, she had been unable to believe that the hour would come when she would leave her home as the wife of Stephen Tallard.

It was a nightmare from which she hoped for an awakening. There was nothing she could bring against her bridegroom. He was attentive, he courted her graciously, he consulted her on every point affecting her future, but she had a growing belief that he would show his power the moment she had surrendered her name for his. The love she had tried to cultivate in her heart would not grow. She had smothered doubts when they were engaged, they grew more positive when she came to know Grahame. At a bound he had made her a prisoner of love. It was his voice she heard behind the voice of Stephen Tallard, his face that came first to mind in her waking hour. She loved Grahame Greyne. She was afraid of Stephen Tallard.

Alas, the whole thing had gone too far, and she had been guilty in seeing so much of Grahame, who refused to face the inevitable. To her parents, elated at the match, she preserved a mask. From Grahame she had no need, even had she tried, to withhold the truth.

The night before the eve of her wedding day he had sent her

an urgent message. She must meet him at Gunter's in the morning, at eleven-thirty. It was a matter of life or death to them both. Life or death? What could he mean, she wondered, as she sat in the corner of the café awaiting him on the following morning.

He came, punctually, a little pale, with a suppressed excited air. As soon as the coffee had come, he spoke to her, quickly, decisively.

"Ursula, you have no right to go on with this. You do not love Tallard. You love me. It's wicked to carry on with the thing. You will be miserable all your life. You know he has an ugly side. I love you better than life. Why should we sacrifice ourselves to perpetuate an error? Will you trust yourself to me—do as I tell you?"

"What must I do?" she asked, nervously, looking at the serious young face near hers.

He continued quickly, in a low voice:

"Your passport is in order?"

"Yes."

"This afternoon, without a word to anybody, leave the house, as if you were going for a walk, and take a cab to Victoria Station. Be there at four-fifteen. I shall be waiting, with tickets for Paris."

"Grahame—I can't."

"Ursula, you must. Do you trust me?" he asked.

In answer she put her hand over his, in the shelter of the tablecloth.

"But Grahame, how can I? The terrible shock, the scandal it would be—and Stephen!"

"Ursula, you mustn't consider Stephen. You don't love him, you are dreading to-morrow. It's wicked to marry him, to sacrifice yourself in this way, merely because it's gone on and the pressure's too great now to end it. This is the only way. In Paris we will be married at once by special licence, later we'll have the regular ceremony in church. The first will safeguard us and end any attempt to separate us."

"But Grahame dear, your career—it will ruin you."

"It won't—and what is ruin, what does it mean, if we are together? Ursula, my darling, please, please trust me in this. It will be so simple."

She could not answer. She felt stunned by the boldness of the scheme he proposed. Five hundred guests were coming to the wedding to-morrow. Her friends who were bridesmaids, her father and mother and sisters, Stephen Tallard jilted at the altar—no, it was impossible now.

"Grahame—I can't! Oh, my dear, it isn't that I don't love you, don't trust you," she said, in anguish.

"Ursula, you can, you must! Can you confide in your maid?" he asked, glancing round the café to see they were not being observed.

"I don't know—she would be too excited," she said.

"Very well, leave her, leave everything. My sister is going with us—Kitty will look after you."

"She knows, Grahame?"

"Yes—and approves. We have thought this out thoroughly."

"But I must have clothes."

"If you attempt to take anything out of the house it may arouse suspicion. Go and buy all you need this morning, in Kitty's name, and have it sent at once to us. Do you want money?"

"No—I've plenty. Oh, Grahame, I can't do it. I can't!"

He smiled, the first smile to appear on his serious young face. His hand pressed hers.

"You can—you will. Victoria, four-fifteen. The Paris train leaves at four-thirty. Ursula, we must go—we must not be in view here too much," he said, and beckoned the waiter.

The stout, bald little man came up. Grahame paid the bill.

"If you please, my lady—you are Lady Ursula, aren't you?" asked the little man. "May I wish you both happiness to-morrow."

She threw a startled glance at Grahame. The waiter went on:

"We've had the honour of doing your wedding cake—I've just seen it, it looks beautiful, my lady," said the waiter, his round face wrinkling into smiles.

She recovered herself and thanked him. At the door Grahame left her. She went home. Her father was lunching out. Her elder sister and mother ate with her.

"Have you a headache, Ursula, you look rather pale," said her mother. "Why don't you lie down? You mustn't get too excited."

"How awful if the bride fell ill and couldn't turn up!" exclaimed Alys, her sister. "Stephen would champ! By the way, I saw him in Regent Street this morning."

"Alys, don't be ridiculous, and I don't think it's nice to talk of Stephen in that way," rebuked Lady Downhouse.

"I think I'll go for a walk, mother, I've rather a headache," said Ursula, and went up to her room.

But in the familiar room, where all her intimate things were about her, she felt she could not do this tremendous thing Grahame asked of her. It would be such a terrible blow to her mother, to her friends, and, of course, to Stephen. She felt ashamed that she could feel no real sorrow for Stephen. He was the kind of man who could face anything and keep a set face.

How could she go, and take nothing? For a moment she thought of sending a telegram telling Grahame it was all off.

The things she had bought had been sent to his home for Kitty. They were both believing she would do it.

She caught sight of herself in the mirror, and looked at the image of a slender, pretty girl of twenty-two. She, a runaway bride, running away from the bridegroom, almost at the altar. How innocent she looked!

Turning to her boudoir table she saw a note had been propped up on it which must have come before lunch. It was addressed to her, unstamped, in Stephen's hand. She tore open the envelope in agitation and read the short note written on Travellers' Club paper:

MY DEAREST,

I have just run into Alys, who told me your mother has given you a turquoise clasp for your bridal veil. Please do not wear it. I am not superstitious, but turquoises are unlucky in my family.

Yours,
STEPHEN T.

She crushed the note in her hand with an impatient cry. He was really impossible. Please do not wear it! That was a command. It annoyed her that he should be so silly, apart from the fact that it was insulting to her mother. And how she disliked his habit of signing himself "Stephen T."! He was so very royal. Even his kindness seemed to congeal her blood, and he never was able to dismiss his great future and to laugh at life.

"Very well, Stephen, I shall not wear my turquoise clasp—nor my bridal veil," she said to herself.

Her hat, her gloves, her bag. Yes, she would take her personal jewels. In a moment she had emptied them into her handbag. A note to her mother? No, that would be dangerous. Yes, she had an idea. Seating herself at her desk she hastily scribbled a note to her mother, saying she would write later from abroad. She knew she was doing the only right thing. Later they would forgive her, she hoped.

The note written, she went into her bedroom adjoining and placed it on the pillow under the sheet. When the chamber-maid came in at eight o'clock to turn down the bed she would see it.

Her coming into the room awoke Timmie, her Skye terrier, sleeping on the hearthrug. He came to her fussily. She caught him up. The idea occurred to her to take him. It was something from her old life. Why not? Grahame would not mind, unlike Stephen who disliked dogs and ignored Timmie.

Calling him, she uttered the magic word "Walk!" and he frisked round her joyously. After all, Timmie would play a part very well. He added reality to her afternoon walk.

One long last glance at her beloved room, then she resolutely closed the door. Never, never, would she open that door again. Looking neither to left nor to right, she went down the stairs, out through the hall into Charles Street, with Timmie close at her heels. It was half-past three. She had time to walk through the Green Park to Victoria Station.

All the way across the Park, so lovely in its summer leafiness, she could not believe what she was doing. People were sitting on the chairs or lying on the grass. How they would stare if they knew she was the Society bride who ran away from her wedding! In twenty-four hours they would know, or something like that. What explanation would be given for public information?

She called Timmie back to her, he had found a friend over the grass. She came out across Buckingham Palace, with the red sentries on duty, the Royal Standard flying over the roof, for the old Queen was making one of her few visits to London. She had been presented three years ago, and the great little old lady had terrified her with her keen eyes watching her curtsy. Later she had sent for her, into a little drawing-room where she rested after the presentations. "Grow up as good and beautiful as your dear mother, and We shall always be glad to see you," she had said to the stammering girl. She remembered how tears had filled her eyes as she left the Presence, conscious of embodied greatness in that little old lady. After to-day the Queen would not be glad to see her.

She was in Buckingham Palace Road. She looked at her watch. It was four o'clock. She would be just in time. So far her good luck had held. She had met no one she knew. But if there were people on the boat-train who knew her, what would they think? Well, it would not matter then. The die would be cast.

As she turned into Victoria Street, where the horse buses clattered by, she entered a grocer's shop and bought some dog biscuits of the kind she knew Timmie liked. She laughed to herself as she came out of the shop. How ridiculous to be fleeing from England with a packet of dog biscuits! But Timmie's next meal was problematic.

It was ten minutes past four as she crossed Wilton Road and came to the station entrance. Cabs were rolling up, with travellers' luggage stacked up on their railed roofs. With a quickened heart she entered and looked about her. The boat-train left No. 2 platform. She walked towards it. There was no turning back now, for there were Grahame and Kitty waiting for her.

He sprang forward, his eyes lit with mingled excitement and adoration.

"Ursula!" he said, his voice trembling.

Kitty kissed her. Grahame then noticed Timmie.

"Bravo, Timmie—so you're in it, eh?" he cried, stooping down and patting the dog. Then, quickly, he whispered: "Ursula, Kitty has your ticket. Go down the platform with her. I've a reserved carriage. I'll join you there—it's better we don't parade."

She walked through the barrier with Kitty. There was a few moments delay over the dog. She would pay on the train, she said. Two minutes later they were in their carriage. There were fifteen minutes yet before the train left. Grahame appeared just before the whistle sounded. As the train moved out he leaned forward, caught her hands in his, and raising them, kissed them. "Oh, my darling!" he cried, softly. She remembered there were tears in his young eyes.

Sister Teresa looked round the café. No, the old waiter was not there—long dead, of course. The tables, the chairs, the door, everything had changed, except the room and its intense associations for her. This was the very corner where the momentous step had been planned. How frightening it had seemed at the time, how faint now were all the sensations recalled across fifty years! And it had all been a success, a very great success. Grahame had loved her to the end, a noble lovely companion through life. He had left her too early, but their happiness had been unclouded for thirty beautiful years. That communion had sealed her gratitude to God. Their children, too, had been lovely; Isabel, now a happy mother; Gerard, her brilliant son; and Ronald, the baby and the handsome one, killed at twenty-one in the attack on Messines Ridge. Grahame had died a little with him. The boy, delicate, temperamental, had caused them more anxiety than the other two; perhaps that was why he was the most beloved.

Sister Teresa looked at her watch. It was nearing twelve. The café was now almost full with smartly dressed women and a few men. It was surprising so many people were in London in August; perhaps they were going North to the moors on the

Twelfth. To Scotland. And to-morrow she was going to far Roumania where her life seemed destined to close. How strange and how short was this pilgrimage on earth, and yet how far-off momentous events grew in the retrospect of Time!

She must go now. This afternoon she must visit Isabel. The grandchildren were to be there, for this was their farewell gathering. The good Sisters would see her off at the station to-morrow afternoon.

A bill lay beside her plate. It seemed one paid now at a desk as one went out. Did they still make wonderful wedding cakes? Probably.

She rose and moved across the room towards the pay-desk. Several customers watched the passage of the tall, distinguished old nun in the cornette. As she turned from the desk, having paid the bill, an elderly man overtook her, and at the sound of her name she halted.

"Excuse me—but surely—Lady Ursula Greyne, isn't it?" asked a voice.

"Yes?" replied Sister Teresa, looking at the stranger.

He was a man of some seventy years, with a good head of white hair, an aquiline nose, and severe lines in the face. He had a legal air, and might have been a judge.

She looked at the distinguished old gentleman, a little surprised by his approach. Apparently he knew her.

"I am completely forgotten, I see—but you have not changed beyond recognition. I'm Lord Ebden."

"Lord Ebden," she repeated, smiling apologetically, for she could only dimly recall such a name.

"You knew me, Lady Ursula, as Stephen Tallard—a long time ago," he said, with a smile.

"Excuse me, yes, of course! I have been out of the world so long," said Sister Teresa.

"It's a pleasure to see you again and, if I may say so, still so beautiful," he said.

She smiled at his graceful compliment, and said:

"You have long forgiven, I hope——"

"Oh, please!" he interrupted.

"It was cruel of me. Thank you for bearing no malice. I hope you have been happy?" she asked.

"Very, thank you. My wife was a lovely woman, and my boy —my boy——"

He paused, and then she remembered. She had wanted to write when she heard the news.

"Your boy—yes, I remember, a month after my Ronnie," she said, quietly. "We have beautiful memories, Stephen."

His name slipped out. He seemed moved, but no words came. There was a pause. She held out her hand.

"Good-bye," she said.

He held her hand, and his deep grey eyes looked into her thin gentle face, as he spoke.

"Good-bye. You did right, Ursula. I could not have made you happy. I have been, I know, a hard man to live with. God bless you!"

"And you," she said, and left him.

Outside she walked for some yards, then stood a little, dizzy from this strange meeting. And in Gunter's, of all places! It was one of those incredible coincidences no story-teller could ever make probable.

He had mellowed with time. Across a silence of fifty years he had stepped after her to tell her he bore no malice. She was glad of it, for his sake, for hers. She bore no ill-will to anyone on earth. She was happy to know no one felt any towards her.

She hailed a taxi and, a little exhausted by the experiences of the morning, reached the cloistered quiet of her cell in the Convent of St. Vincent.

II

Her last day in England, a lovely last day, with a blackbird singing in the laburnum tree at the bottom of the enclosed garden, and the noisy London sparrows chirping from the rain-gutters. It was a few minutes to seven and Sister Teresa paused before the window. Already the pulse of London was beating faster in the awakened day. She joined the Sisters assembled in the hall below, and together they crossed to the Cathedral, taking their places in the reserved part, to hear Mass and receive Holy Communion.

There followed a cheerful communal breakfast, the bright gathering of these Sisters before they went to their various duties, some to teach, some to collect alms in the business offices of London and other places, where their white cornettes, tranquil faces and low voices were known.

After a quiet lunch Sister Teresa rested awhile in her cell. Her scanty belongings were packed, her farewells said. Yesterday's visit to her daughter had given her deep joy; her son Gerard and his wife, and the five grandchildren were all present, to do honour to her.

She said nothing of her visit to the specialist, nor of his verdict. Why uselessly trouble them? She kissed them all good-bye. Gerard and his wife had escorted her back to St. Vincent's.

A tap on the door wakened Sister Teresa from the half doze into which she had fallen. The door opened and one of the Sisters appeared.

"It's four o'clock—we have asked for a taxi to come," she said. "Is there anything I can carry down?"

"No, thank you. You have been very kind to me here. I love this little room."

She looked at it as she rose. It was sparsely furnished, clean and quite impersonal.

The nun waited for her, and together they went down into the hall where the Sister Superior was standing. They both insisted on going to the station with her. The taxi-man carried out her box. They got in.

They did not talk in the taxi. "This is my last sight of London," thought Sister Teresa, as she looked out of the window. "It is not likely I shall come back again." The thought in no way distressed her; on the contrary, it was rather beautiful to make this quiet farewell. She loved her life at Predeal, she was returning to a known routine, to familiar faces. *Nunc dimittis servum tuum pace.* The lovely prayer had a lovely significance to-day.

Her seat had been reserved. Yes, there was tea on the train. It was a pity if she missed her last afternoon tea in England. In her luggage there was a pound tin of Earl Grey Mixture, her favourite blend, a present from her daughter, and even at Predeal she sometimes took out the teapot, and sipped her tea accompanied with some buttered toast. It was her one luxury.

"I hope you'll have a comfortable crossing," said the Sister Superior, everything she could think of having been said.

"Your train is through from Boulogne to Bucharest?" asked Sister Frances.

"Yes—all the way."

"How wonderful! I have never been out of England. But it would frighten me to sleep on a train," said Sister Frances. She was now fifty-six. She knew she would never go out of England. She felt sorry for Sister Teresa, going to such a far-off strange country. Once she had dreamed of a pilgrimage to Rome, but that hope had long faded.

"And now, if you please, I will get into the carriage. It must be nearly time. Good-bye and God bless you," said Sister Teresa, and kissed them both.

She entered the carriage and walked down the corridor to her seat. Through the window she saw that the two Sisters had not gone. They moved towards her window and stood smiling at her.

Doors slammed. Voices called. Silently the train began to move. The Sisters waved pocket handkerchiefs, Sister Teresa waved her hand, smiling. They were gone now. The platform ended, rails, high walls, signal boxes and sidings glided by, grimy in the sunny August afternoon.

The restaurant-car attendant came to her carriage.

"Tea, madame?" he asked, briskly.

"Tea, with buttered toast, if you please," replied Sister Teresa.

The Boat Train, gathering speed, rushed on towards the English coast and the Channel.

CHAPTER IX

MR. PERCY BOWLING, OF DERBY

THERE was a pillar-box at the end of the platform in Victoria Station, and, peering at it in his short-sighted way through his spectacles, he saw that the next collection was at five o'clock. His letter, therefore, would reach Derby the next day. That was exactly what he desired. It gave him good time to get clear of England. They would not know and they could not come after him until he was safe across the Channel and on foreign soil.

For a few moments he held the letter in his hand. Once he had dropped it through the slot the die was cast. He was doing something that would be a terrible shock to all those he knew, and something they would never have believed it was possible for him to do. He had lived a blameless life for forty-five years, the soul of honour, and a man who could always be relied upon when his help was necessary.

With the posting of this letter he was committing an act which marked a complete break with his respectable past. He, Percy Bowling, with five hundred pounds in his wallet, was secretly fleeing from England. His mates in the fitting shops where he had worked, a foreman fitter now for fifteen years, with a total honourable service of twenty-four years, would have a shock in the morning when he failed to turn up. No, not in the morning. It would take some hours for his flight to become known in the manager's office, whence the news would percolate down to his mates.

148

"Well, here goes!" said Percy Bowling to himself, and pushed the letter into the box. He heard its faint plop as it struck the bottom. For another moment he gazed at the red pillar-box, with its table, and its little white disc giving the time of the next collection.

It had been a bright idea to ask for the day off, for a funeral. They would not begin to wonder what had happened to him until to-morrow, until Herbert communicated its contents, scarcely able to believe them.

He wondered how long the household in Milton Avenue would sit up for him to-night. He tried to imagine their faces when his bed was found empty, when his letter was opened and read. The singular thing was that he did not feel a bit guilty. Anyone seeing him now, in the new sports jacket and cap he had bought himself, might think he had come into a legacy. He had also a new raincoat on his arm. His portmanteau, which he had smuggled out of the house the previous evening and deposited in readiness at Derby Station for this morning's flight to London, was crammed to bursting point. All his other worldly possessions he had had to leave.

He produced his ticket and passport at the barrier. It was a lucky thing his firm had sent him to Belgium on a job last year. The passport had proved useful. He felt a little nervous about the five hundred pounds in his wallet, but he was suspicious of traveller's cheques, they seemed to offer too many clues to his movements, and he had heard it said that English five-pound notes were accepted anywhere over the earth.

He looked at his rather bulky ticket as he put it back in its folder. It took him as far as Athens. After that, advised the young man at Cook's, in the London office to which he had gone as soon as he got off the Derby train, he could book his passage to Egypt in their Athens office.

The book of tickets, with its successive leaves in green paper bearing the names of famous cities, made his flight an absolute reality. He was going to Athens first. There he might linger before the next stage, and consider his subsequent movements. Athens! And after Athens, Egypt, which meant for Percy Bowling the Pyramids only.

He took his seat in the train, and waited impatiently for it to go. He found a corner seat and sat huddled up in it, a prey to nerves now the vital moment had come. He wanted the train to start at once and get him to the boat in the shortest possible time. He had a sickly fear now that he would lack the courage to save himself.

At last. Some people scrambled on to the train, doors were slammed. The train was moving. He seemed the only person on the long train who did not have anyone to see him off. The thought occurred to him that he must be the only person among all these passengers of whom not one living soul knew he was leaving England.

"Well, you've done it," said Bowling.

An old lady in the corner opposite looked up from some papers she was sorting.

"I beg your pardon?" she asked, pleasantly.

Bowling started. He had not expected to be overheard.

"I was talking to myself, ma'am," he replied, politely.

"Ah—well, it does save one being contradicted, doesn't it?" she remarked, affably.

The other passengers in the carriage looked at him curiously.

"Would you like a paper?" asked the old lady, offering him a choice of newspapers.

He took one of them and thanked her. He opened it and hid behind it. His head was reeling a little. He was in no mood to carry on a conversation even with so friendly a soul.

He would never have believed he could do such a thing as he had done. Money, it was said, often turned people's heads. It had turned his. When the insurance man had brought him the cheque for five hundred pounds, in settlement of his paid-up Life Policy, the result of thirty years' saving, begun for him by his poor old mother when he was fifteen, he had had a blinding revelation of freedom. The stupendous idea had kept him awake all that night. The next day his head swam with the various schemes that came to him, but he knew he was a coward and once he gave voice to his ideas he would be bullied and plundered by his relations.

He was a kind man, he reflected, and therein lay all his troubles in the last twenty wretched years. Had he been ruthless or of a harder nature, how different his life would have been. It seemed to him that a number of people, like donkeys, were born to have burdens thrust upon them, which they bore with such patience that no one expected any other kind of reaction. Now, at forty-five, he was what the world so glibly termed "a selfish old bachelor."

There were two classes of persons who were always the butt of the married people, spinsters and bachelors. They were denied any virtues, and a particular abuse was reserved for the bachelor. Unlike the spinster, who generally had no choice in the matter, he was single because he was selfish or disagreeable, or both. Anyhow, he deserved and received no sympathy.

He remembered how, when the War broke out, there was a hue and cry after single men to go out and fight. The married men had to remain to look after their wives and children. No one thought of the number of landladies and widows who depended on the bachelors, whom they often overcharged.

And had any bachelor felt bold enough to ask why he should be called upon to fight for another man's wife and children, the direct result of the other man's quest for comfort or sexual pleasure, for none ventured to assert he had married for patriotism, what abuse he would have bought upon his head! Percy Bowling had gone forth and fought for his King and Country, and the other men's wives and children. He had not wanted to, particularly as it seemed very stupid to go and try to kill another unwilling bachelor fighting for another man's wife and children. But social pressure, taking on the glamour of patriotism, had carried him to the recruiting station.

A time came when the married man was called up, and, judging by the pleading before the Recruiting Tribunals, how reluctant he was to fight for his own wife and children! Not all, of course, but sufficient to reveal the hypocrisy of the women and children reason.

Actually Percy Bowling had enjoyed the War, as much of it as he now cared to remember. The blood and mud apart, he had found the discipline and the self-negation of the soldier's life a restful time. He was no longer bullied except occasionally by a sergeant-major; he slept well anywhere, at any time, he ate well and copiously, and the times of danger produced an exhilarating comradeship that warmed his blood and brought a glow of romance into his drab existence. To his surprise he had been considered a good soldier, and came out of the War with the Distinguished Conduct Medal.

He was dismayed to discover, on demobilization, that the stigma of being a bachelor was now effective in keeping him out of work. The men with women and children to keep must have preference. Percy, who had kept his mother, supported an unlucky brother, and satisfied the rapacity and whining mendacity of two sisters, had to use up his meagre savings before he was lucky enough to find work. As soon as he found it he re-

sumed his rôle, being the bachelor brother, of sole support of his
mother.

The youngest of four brothers and two sisters, he had always
been imposed upon. He remembered vividly those dismal Sunday evenings, after the family had returned from chapel, when
he had to prepare for Monday, the washing day. In the impoverished Bowling household it was impossible to send personal
and bed linen to a laundry. The housewives of the Midlands
and the North, in those pre-war, pre-laundry days, beflagged
England with washing on the line on Mondays. In somewhat
more prosperous households a charwoman came in to help, and
was entitled to a bottle of beer with her lunch, a customary per-
quisite conceded with deep distaste in the more strict Noncon-
formist households.

Washing Mondays necessitated the laying out of utensils on
the Sunday evenings, after the return from chapel. The little and
the large dolly-tubs, together with the dolly pegs, the washing-
board, the zinc wash-tub and the boards that fitted into the man-
gle, as well as the clothes-basket, line and pegs, were all kept
down in the dark cellar, as the scullery-kitchen was too small.
Percy being the youngest was called upon to fetch these things
from the cellar, for Henry and Albert came in late, having seen
their young ladies home, and Arthur, who was the intellectual
member of the family, and had the front parlour reserved for his
studies on week nights, could not be demeaned by manual labour;
he was studying to be a Post Office clerk.

So down the cellar went Percy. He hated it. He had to carry
a spluttering candle, and tread over a heap of coal slack in a
corner. Cobwebs hung from the joists, and a cold wind blew
down from the circular coal-hole grate that was just under the
front window. He had to put the guttering candle on a shelf,

pick up one of the tubs and stagger up the narrow steps to the scullery. Sometimes the cold draught blew out the candle, and he was in a horrible, coal-slack-sliding, cobwebby darkness.

These Sunday night labours, preparatory to bed, were acute misery to him. It was not the physical labour but the degradation, the injustice which distressed him. The older brothers never carried up the wash-tubs. They came in sleek, smelling of hair oil, and sometimes of their young ladies' scent, and sat down by the parlour fire, warming their feet on the fender. And there was no younger son to whom Percy could pass on his wash-tub heaving.

That servitude, he came to see, was symbolic of what awaited him. He was a mild-mannered boy, and could not bear to hurt the feelings of anyone. This was soon discovered. At fourteen he left school and went to an engineering works. He was allowed sixpence out of his five shillings wages. He had been there a year when his father died of consumption, and a financial crisis was at once felt. Henry married without delay, and three months later Albert followed suit. This further reduced the family income and left a bedroom vacant. So lodgers were resorted to and the large front bedroom was let as a bed-sitting-room.

It was first occupied by a hairdresser who came home drunk and thrashed his wife. Then one night the wife came home drunk and thrashed her husband. A week later the husband did not come home at all. He disappeared, and Mrs. Bowling learned from the tearful wife that she had no redress. She had never been married to the vanished man. Three weeks' rent was owing, and was never paid.

A bachelor was the next tenant. He was quiet and considerate, but he dropped tobacco ash all over the room. He was dubbed superior because he asked for a slop basin with his tea things, and wanted a bath twice a week instead of on Friday night. There was no bathroom, and cans of hot water had to be carried up to the lodger's room; the family always had their bath in front of the kitchen fire, the various members keeping in the front room during the washing.

Mrs. Bowling's legs were troublesome, she had her big toe-joints enlarged through excessive work on her feet, and it fell to Percy to do all the carrying. He brought up the coals from the cellar, a scuttleful night and morning, he took up the lodger's breakfast and the hot water, and on Tuesday and Friday nights the lodger's bath-water.

Mr. Spilsbury, the occupant of the upstairs front bed-sitting-room, the largest in the house, where all the young Bowlings had been born and Mr. Bowling had died, was called "a finicky old bachelor" by the family, but he had the virtue that he gave Percy sixpence a week for odd jobs. Mr. Spilsbury, who served in a haberdasher's shop in the Market Place, was very fussy about his shoes. He had three pairs, and he left them in "trees," wooden presses which the Bowlings had never seen before, and laughed at. Even Percy was not allowed to clean these shoes. Mr. Spilsbury kept his polishes and brushes in a cardboard box down by the penny-in-the-slot gas meter in the fireside recess, and polished his own boots. He also possessed a trousers' press, a thing with six thumb-screws which Percy surreptitiously used for his Sunday trousers.

"He's quite a gentleman," observed Mrs. Bowling of her lodger, when she was not feeling irritated by his 'finicky' ways. "He always carries gloves, and raises his hat to everybody."

The Bowlings often wondered if he had had a love affair. He was forty-five, but never seemed to mix much with young ladies. But on the mantelpiece he kept the portrait of a young woman dressed as Prince Aladdin, with hips like an hour-glass. On one occasion Ethel ventured to ask Mr. Spilsbury if it was his young lady or his sister.

"Neither," replied Mr. Spilsbury, curtly.

He offered no information on the subject, and the mystery was never solved.

"An actress! I can't think what he wants with an actress on the mantelpiece," commented Mrs. Bowling, who regarded theatres as wicked places.

By the time Percy was twenty his two sisters had married and gone to homes of their own. He had been an uncle for three years, for his eldest brother produced a child regularly each year, though he complained he could never make ends meet as a clerk in the Corporation Rate Office. Ethel, within seven months of her marriage, had a child, a boy.

"It's very hard on the poor girl, folk's tongues are sure to wag," said Mrs. Bowling.

Folk's tongues did wag, but the baby was bonny.

Percy was doing better now. He was clever at his work, and, his apprenticeship finished, he was earning more than his brothers, or his sisters' husbands.

"You're lucky," said Henry. "They pushed me into the Rate Office, for safety, but I'd rather be half as safe and get what you earn."

"Then why don't you leave?" asked Percy.

"Don't talk rot. Wait till you're a married man and responsible for a family!" retorted Henry.

There were now only Percy and Arthur left at home. The burden of supporting the household fell heavier upon Percy, for Arthur was studying at the University College in Nottingham and had to go there by train each day. Percy now earned thirty shillings a week, gave his mother twenty and kept ten. The home could only be kept going by increasing the number of lodgers. So the two brothers slept in the attic and lodgers lived in the three best bedrooms. Somehow they scrambled along.

Then the War came. Percy did not volunteer at first, but Arthur joined the Army at once. Percy was given plenty of hints, and the girl he was walking out with received him very coldly one Saturday evening when he called to take her to the cinema.

"Mother thinks it reflects on me to be seen walking with you in civilian clothes," she said, as they went out.

"Well, if I wasn't in civilian clothes I shouldn't be here to walk out with you," replied Percy, feeling hurt and angry. "Besides, who's going to support my mother?"

He received no answer. But when he called the next Saturday, he was told Agnes had gone out, with her cousin, who was on leave from his camp.

Percy did not call again, and three days later he received an envelope with a white feather in it. He had no doubt from whom it came. It hit him so hard that he lay on his bed and cried like a little boy. He kept the true state of affairs from his mother, who asked what had happened to Agnes. His vague answer confirmed her suspicions. She kissed her son and said, "You poor boy. When you're an old man, and I'm gone, you'll have comfort in knowing you were good to your mother. There's plenty of nice girls who'll appreciate you."

He was wanted at his works, now making aeroplane engines, so for eighteen months he bore the brunt of hints and insults. Then one day they had terrible news. Poor Arthur had been killed near Ypres. The blow was terrible for Mrs. Bowling. He was the brilliant hope of the family. She locked the lid of the piano he played, and it was never touched for the rest of the war years.

When things were not going well for the Allies, and a man-power problem arose, the pressure began to be put on the married as well as the single men. Albert, who had only one child, became nervous. Henry, who was always full of fighting spirit, felt safe with four children to support. They both agreed that Percy disgraced the family, and when a popular newspaper started an abusive campaign against what they called "Cuthberts," a term applied to single men retained in employment, Henry one day called Percy a Cuthbert to his face.

"Shame on you!" said Mrs. Bowling.

"Shame on us all to have him saving his skin when all decent men are fighting!" retorted Henry.

"I can hardly hold up my head," said Alice, whose husband had been taken.

"I think Percy ought to go," agreed Albert.

"To make less pressure on you, eh?" asked Percy, stung. "Very well, I'll go—on one condition, that you and Henry give mother five shillings a week each to make up the Army allowance."

"Don't be silly—we can hardly keep our heads above water now," said Henry.

"Then sink!" retorted Percy, with an angry flush, "I'm not going to fight for your wife and kids."

At this point poor Mrs. Bowling had to intervene, or there might have been blows in the family kitchen.

But the pressure became too great for Percy. One day he told his firm he wanted to enlist and they must release him. Two days afterwards he was in camp. He heard later that Albert had been ordered to join up by the Military Tribunal, but Henry with a family of four was still safe.

The Government proved very mean over Arthur. As he was a student who had never earned anything Mrs. Bowling was not entitled to any allowance, but she received a compassionate grant of twenty pounds.

"A cheap body," Percy wrote home on learning the news.

Somehow, with lodgers and Percy's allowance Mrs. Bowling struggled on. Then Albert was killed, and his wife went out to work and placed the child with its grandmother. When the War ended Percy came home to find he had his mother and Albert's child to keep, as his sister-in-law was working in London, and her Army allowance was insufficient. To his amazement, on applying for his former position at the works he was told that they regretted they could not for the present take him on. Army contracts were ended, part of the works was closed down, and married men were receiving preference. As a single man Percy heard that answer wherever he applied for work for the next nine months. He never had enough to eat during this time, and the struggle in the Bowling home was severe.

"Never mind, mother, we'll strike oil one day, you'll see."

"God will reward you for all your goodness to your old mother," affirmed Mrs. Bowling.

She was failing, he could see. She was now sixty-five. She could not climb the stairs to the new lodger's bed-sitting-room. Percy took over a large part of the household. Mrs. Bowling looked after the little girl. Her mother showed no sign of taking her back. She was having a struggle to live, she said. But Percy noticed it was a very well-dressed struggle. She was manageress of a tea-shop in the City. "I should lose my job if I didn't look smart," she said, when she noticed Percy's critical eye.

After nine months' unemployment Percy found a job in an engineering works at Grantham. It meant leaving home, but the money was good. He received three pounds a week. He sent one half to his mother.

Percy worked there for three years, and then he received an offer from his old firm in Derby. The wage was four pounds a week. It seemed like a gift from Heaven.

"What did I say?" asked Mrs. Bowling, prophetically.

At chapel the next Sunday she stayed on for Holy Communion, and put a shilling in the plate.

"No more lodgers," said Percy, on his return home.

The two best bedrooms were re-furnished. Percy moved into one and his mother into another. It was the first time in fifteen years that they had really possessed their own home. A little later his sister-in-law married again, and her little girl went to her. But her husband was a milk-deliverer, badly paid, and Percy assisted in clothing little Jane, of whom he was very fond.

The years passed. Ethel's boy began to show promise, and Percy volunteered the fees for a secondary school. He was already assisting Alice's boy, for her husband had become an invalid, and they had retired to the country to chicken farm. They lived on the verge of penury, so Uncle Percy bought their clothing, and when the boy had to go to the nearest town school he bought him a cycle. The lad began to win scholarships, and Alice was swift to report her son's successes. She knew there was a rival in Ethel's boy for the favours Uncle Percy bestowed.

Percy was now earning six pounds a week, and saving a little. He began to walk out with a young woman in a confectioner's shop. She was ten years younger than he, and flighty. Her one idea was to be married at once, but Percy could not see his way clear for a time. His mother was feeble and he had had to employ a housekeeper, the two boys were taking, between them, thirty pounds a year, and Jane, rapidly growing up, took ten. When his mother died, which would not be long, he feared, he could marry. He would not distress the old lady by bringing a young woman into the house.

After a year his young lady delivered an ultimatum. If he intended marrying her he must do it at once. Moreover, she wanted a home of her own. Ten shillings a week and her old age pension would be ample for the old woman. Percy felt he could not be so heartless. She broke off their engagement, and was married a month later to a railway vanman.

Mrs. Bowling lived another year. When she died Percy felt terribly lonely. He was forty, and was bewildered. Henry at once proposed he should go and live with them. In a weak moment he accepted, sold up the home and took enough furniture to furnish his room.

Within six months he felt himself trapped. Henry had purchased a motor-car on the instalment plan. He failed to keep up the payments and there was a crisis when a summons was threatened. Percy took on the payments. A year later it transpired that Henry was purchasing his house. He had got behind in the instalments, had borrowed at the bank, and was being pressed. Percy guaranteed the bank's overdraft to save the house. Moreover, Henry's second boy, an engaging lad, working in a solicitor's office, had been offered his articles free, but it meant only a nominal salary for some years. Between pride, pressure and affection Percy found himself committed to keeping young Henry in clothes.

And it seemed that every month Jane had to have something her milk-delivery stepfather could not afford, and Alice's boy and Ethel's boy would find their careers wrecked unless Uncle could kindly manage to do this, or do that. Then Henry's wife fell ill, and had to have a kidney operation. The financially embarrassed Henry shed tears and went to pieces, and to comfort him Percy offered to see the matter through. Slowly Percy awoke to the fact that of his six pounds a week, he had barely a few shillings left for himself.

He bore all this with resignation. He was happy in his work and generally popular. At times he had a suspicion that even his nephews and nieces had come to regard him as the milch cow. Henry persisted in his belief that Percy was lucky, and his sisters and their husbands agreed with him. One Christmas when they were all gathered together he looked at them and thought what a strange thing it would be if all he had done for them were snatched away. Two of his nieces and nephews would have almost no clothes left on them, Alice would be without her false teeth, as also Ethel, Henry's car and two-thirds of his house would disappear, and carpets, articles of furniture, odd pieces of jewellery would be missing from various places.

"What are you smiling at, Percy?" asked Henry's wife. But that thought he kept to himself.

One day he found himself unpopular. He had declined to pay for young Mabel's portmanteau, despite the hints that Uncle might do so. She was earning good money as a typist in an architect's office, and she was now going on holiday to Lucerne with another girl. Percy himself, an omnivorous reader, had never been abroad to see any of the places he had read about, except to the battlefields, and lately to Brussels where his firm had sent him. He never had any money to spare for foreign trips.

He was in the kitchen that evening, looking for a tumbler, when he heard Mabel talking to her mother, her voice audible through the dining-room hatch.

"Stingy old thing! I thought he'd rise to the portmanteau. That's taken twenty shillings out of my holiday," she said.

"He's just a selfish old bachelor," said her mother, at the sewing machine.

"He bought himself a new wrist-watch the other day—paid four pounds for it. Gold, if you please! Him, a mechanic. What's he want with a gold wrist-watch?" said Henry. "Can't buy Mabel a portmanteau with all he's got coming to him tomorrow!"

"Whatever do you mean, Dad?" asked Mabel.

Percy heard his brother give his pipe a tap.

"He gets five hundred pounds to-morrow on his insurance policy. Five hundred pounds!" exclaimed Henry.

"Good heavens, and the mean old thing can't buy me a portmanteau! Auntie Ethel said he refused to give anything towards Tom's motor-cycle, which he must have, as his office has been moved," said Mabel.

"I don't blame him over that. Your Aunt Ethel's always cadging something," answered her mother. "I really think, Henry, he ought to pay off the mortgage at the bank—what's a hundred pounds to him, with all that money, and a bachelor? And look what he earns!" exclaimed Mrs. Bowling, addressing her husband.

"I'm not over hopeful," said Henry. "He knows how to hold on to his money—he was growling the other day about his income-tax. I told him I'd be only too glad to pay income-tax, and what do you think he said to me? 'Your wife and children have helped you to escape that, as they helped you to escape fighting.' Brought that up, he did!"

"The impertinence of him!" exclaimed Mrs. Bowling.

"Why don't you put up his board and lodging, mum?" said Mabel.

"Why, that's an idea, blessed if it isn't!" agreed Mrs. Bowling.

"He might go," said Henry, cautiously.

"Not he! He gets full value for money here. He wouldn't find another place like it," said Mrs. Bowling, firmly.

In the kitchen Percy clutched the glass he was holding. Dismay and indignation surged in him. He restrained an impulse to fling open the hatch and cry out, "A stingy old bachelor, am I, you miserable spongers! Very well, I'll be stingy. Not a penny more of my money will any of you have!" But he had not the courage. He had always been a little overborne by Henry, ever since he was a boy, and Henry's wife he had never dared to challenge. She ran Henry and the whole house. It was she who had drawn him into this house and persuaded him to part with his own home, on his mother's death—a profound mistake.

He went stealthily out of the kitchen, back to his own room. He forgot the reason why he had fetched the glass, and sat down in his room, stunned. They begrudged him his Life Policy money, to be paid to-morrow. It was the only saving he had been able to make and there was something sacred about it. His poor mother, in all her necessity, had started the policy for him when he was fifteen. How she had scraped and made sacrifices to keep up those premiums! In her good will for him she had taken out a policy really too heavy, over-persuaded by the insurance agent, but once the premiums had been begun it became a matter of honour to keep them up. Even during the strain of his unemployment period he had refused to cash the bonuses and had kept up the premiums. And now, after thirty years, he was to reap the benefit. With "profits" the policy was worth five hundred pounds, and this sum was to be paid to him to-morrow.

He had not thought what he would do with the money. He had a vague idea of having a short holiday abroad, and of banking the rest, for although his wages were good, he had never been able to save anything owing to the needs of all the Bowlings and their affiliations. He had, indeed, dimly thought of paying off the hundred pounds Henry owed on the house.

But not now, not now. He would not pay a penny for anything, not after his niece's outrageous abuse of him, after all his kindness to her. The double-faced little hussy!

Collapsed in his chair, he buried his face in his hands. Did anybody really love him for himself? He was weak, of course, and weakness had engendered this kind of treatment. They had always battened on him because he had never had the courage to refuse them and he had disguised his weakness by persuading himself he was kind.

He knew now he could not stand up to them. He knew Henry's sullen look when he could not accede to his suggestions, he knew his sister-in-law's suave, firm ways of putting the case— "You see, Percy, if it wasn't for you——" a kind of flattery and artful mendacity. He saw how subtly Ethel and Alice, and their children, had unfailingly produced one invulnerable reason after another for his help. And it would go on. He could never escape.

Escape? A wild thought flashed through his mind. Supposing he did escape? Supposing he took his five hundred pounds and went to the colonies, to Australia or New Zealand, to Canada or South Africa? He could earn a living anywhere, he was a skilled artisan, with first-class experience. To have worked with the Rolls-Royce was a passport anywhere.

"I'm not a free man like you bachelors." How often that had been said to him! He was a bachelor, with all its penalties, but he was free. Why not live up to the reproach? He could take a holiday, first of all. Why, he could go round the world!

The thought thrilled him, and for the first time in his life Percy Bowling had a malicious pleasure in thinking of the shock to them all when they found he had fled, and they could no longer prey on him.

His flight must be absolutely secret. If he breathed one word, or betrayed himself by one action, he would be defeated. Henry or Alice or Ethel would fall dangerously ill, or one of the children would develop consumption—some irrefutable claim on his compassion would arise to tether him.

No, he must go with absolute secrecy. It would be painful to leave his firm so abruptly, though he could explain a little later, and some of his friends would feel hurt, but he had no choice save to make the break swiftly. To-day was Sunday, to-morrow

he would have the money. He had asked for it in cash, fortunately. He could leave on Wednesday and be out of England by
Wednesday night.

The thought made him a little dizzy. Five hundred pounds
would last him at least eighteen months. He would go first to see
the Pyramids, via Athens. Since a small boy he had devoured
everything he could read about those wonderful Pyramids. As an
engineer they fascinated him and he had developed his own pet
theory about their construction. He had once had an enchanting
hour's talk with a University Extension Lecturer, who had come
to Derby to lecture on Ancient Egypt, and that scholar had
thought his theory quite excellent.

Athens, the Parthenon, Cairo, the Pyramids. Then Karnak,
perhaps. He might even get eventually to Angkor Wat, the mystery of mysteries.

A little dizzy, Percy Bowling began to undress for bed. He
now felt grateful to that trio in the dining-room making their
plans for his money. What, indeed, was the use of being a
bachelor if one was not free? He would be free.

And here he was with his stupendous scheme almost completed. The train was speeding out of London, and to-night he
would be rushing through the darkness towards Athens, on the
first stage of his great adventure. He was amazed now at the ease
with which he had escaped from his relations, and how little
affected he was by the break. What a shock they would have in
the morning when they opened his letter! He wished he could be
there to see their faces. He saw Henry rushing round to tell
Alice, he heard Ethel's cry of amazement, he visualized the faces
of the nephews and nieces when they found Uncle gone beyond
their wheedling.

"Will you also please inform Mr. Farrell at the Works that I shall not be coming in again, and that I shall write to them in a few days. In keeping from you my movements I shall spare you any disappointing appeals to my selfishness. If I return in the future I shall look at my nephews and nieces with interest, to see how they have profited by exercising self-reliance. I am afraid my presence and weakness must have had a bad effect on you all in this respect."

He could hear Henry's comments when he read these passages, and see his wife's face staring at him across the breakfast-table.

He returned the paper the old lady in the corner seat had kindly lent him. When the waiter came down the train for tea orders, he asked for tea and cake.

"I think we shall have a smooth crossing," said the chatty old lady. "Besides, I am always lucky," she added, smiling.

And that was what he was, according to Henry's opinion, reflected Percy.

CHAPTER X

MR. ALEXANDER BEKIR, OF SALONICA

EVERYONE who knew Mr. Alexander Hassan Bekir, and his circle was a large one, referred to him as an "enlightened" Turk. This was not flattering to the Turkish nation, having a suggestion that as a people they were all benighted. There was a genuine desire, however, to pay tribute not only to Mr. Bekir's qualities as a gentleman but also to his domestic virtues. All who were invited to the Bekir home, a neat little place in Montpelier Square, realized at once that he was a family man, devoted to Mrs. Bekir and his three children.

Mr. Bekir had lived in London for some fifteen years, having come from Paris, and before that from Salonica. He had met and married Mrs. Bekir in Paris, where she was born and had lived for twenty-two years with her parents in Auteuil. Her father was a retired jeweller of moderate fortune. His only daughter Julie Huysman, as was then her name, had brought her husband a very reasonable "dot."

Mr. Alexander Bekir was rightly considered an excellent match for pretty, dark-eyed Julie. He was older, it is true, being then thirty-five years of age, but Julie's parents knew there were virtues in an older husband that offset the adventurousness of the young. Moreover, this marriage possessed few difficulties. Julie loved Alexander, and Alexander loved Julie. One slight difficulty arose in the beginning. Whereas Julie had been brought up a strict Catholic, Alexander, like all his countrymen, was a Mos-

168

lem. Mr. Bekir showed himself very accommodating in spirit.
He agreed to be married in church as well as in the Mairie and the
mosque, and he readily assented to the Holy Church's insistence
that the children of this marriage should be brought up as Catholics. Mrs. Bekir always smiled and made the same little joke: she
was thrice married and thrice blessed. The blessings, of course,
were her children, and no one, seeing husband and wife together,
doubted that Mrs. Bekir might have added her husband as her
greatest blessing.

Mr. Bekir, at the time of his engagement, was a junior partner
of an important and prosperous tobacco-growing company in
Asia Minor, with its headquarters in Salonica, and branch offices
in Istanbul, Samsun and Amasya. Young Bekir, his father at
that time being chairman of the company, had gone to Paris as
the European representative of the firm, and his time was equally
divided between the Salonica office and Paris. From the latter
place he made trips to the leading cities of Europe, and he was
well known, even in his thirties, in London, Berlin, Prague,
Amsterdam and other places to which his widely distributed business took him.

It was one of the trials of his prosperous life that his business
caused him to be absent so much from home. Apart from trips
of a few days at a time to various places, he had to spend three or
four months of each year at Salonica, the head office of the firm's
export business, in which Alexander had received his early training. He never failed to express his dislike of this city. After the
settlement of the quarrel between the Turkish and Greek govern-
ments he said it had become a Greek-infested place, and he was
always depressed when the time came for him to make his annual
visit to that city. Once or twice Mrs. Bekir had volunteered to
share his exile, but he would not allow her to suffer the discom-
forts of the place. Moreover, he had a dread that the children

might catch some infection. So he departed each year, usually about August, when the tobacco crops were coming in, for loathed Salonica, and always came back in time for Christmas in the bosom of his family.

The first five years of the Bekirs' married life was passed in Paris, which both of them loved. Mr. Bekir soon established and maintained the warmest relations with his father- and mother-in-law. Every Sunday they went to dine at the neat little villa in the Rue Théophile-Gautier. They dwelt, themselves, just over the Seine bridge at Suresnes, in a modern house with a large garden. It was here that Lucille was born, after one year of married life.

At the close of these five happy years, during which Mrs. Bekir lost her father, business interests began to draw Mr. Bekir more and more to London, and at last a time came when it was imperative he should live there instead of in Paris. The decision caused dismay in the household, and since much of Mrs. Bekir's distress was based on the threatened separation from her mother, Mr. Bekir, with characteristic magnanimity, invited his mother-in-law to live with them in London.

He had hoped, it must be confessed, that Madame Huysman would decline to leave her own country. She was, like many of her race, fundamentally anti-English, having been brought up on the cherished theory that Queen Victoria had caused the Prince Imperial to be slain in the Zulu War, that the British had committed every conceivable crime in the Boer War, that they owned too much of the earth, and that they had no cooks and no culture. All this, however, had not prevented Madame Huysman from being hysterically pro-British in recurrent crises in French foreign affairs. She believed in the *entente* though constitutionally incapable of feeling it should be *cordiale*.

But to England she came, and stayed, making herself a permanent member of the Bekir household in their comfortable dwelling in Montpelier Square. She learned to know the English better, but succeeded in preserving her distrust of them.

Young Mrs. Bekir rapidly acclimatized herself. It was a matter of discord between her and her mother that she liked the English so cordially. Mr. Bekir, too, after a year of discontent, settled down and soon had a circle of friends who visited him and whom he visited with real affection. Two children were born in Paris, Lucille and Dorette. His third child, a son and heir, was born in London. His pride as the father of sharp little Achille was mingled, in a vague way, with gratitude to England. The boy had an English governess, and at the age of eight was sent to an English preparatory school, greatly to old Madame Huysman's alarm. "Zey will keel him with tairreeble English puddings!" she exclaimed.

Mr. Bekir smiled and ignored the warning, and Madame Huysman, who was now accustomed to being politely ignored, said no more. But when anyone remarked on the pallor of little Achille Bekir—and he had his mother's pallid complexion, lustrous dark eyes and vermilion lips—she lost no opportunity of saying, "It ees ze dreadful English pudding he 'as to eet."

Whatever little Achille was fed on at school there was no denying he was an entrancing child. His sister Lucille, now seventeen, was already a most lovely girl, and she was rivalled by her younger sister Dorette, aged fifteen. The Bekir children were famous for their good looks, having inherited their mother's dark eyes, and their father's pleasing personality. They were never suppressed yet never presumed upon their liberty, and their good manners and graceful bearing were commended by all.

Their mother, at forty-three, was still a beautiful woman. She dressed with French chic and had a Gallic sparkle. Slight, with dark hair and eyes, her clothes were the envy of other women, though she spent only a modest sum on dress. She had the art of wearing her things with a distinguished air, and well might happy Mr. Bekir look at her with pride.

Old Madame Huysman, for all her sixty-seven years, had the gift of "carrying" her clothes, and, liberal and skilful with the cosmetics, she continued to be a not insignificant figure in a notable family. She had always been renowned for her eyes and her eyelashes, and though the eyes had yellowed somewhat, the eyelashes, cleverly blackened, were still remarkable, and gave her a slightly lascivious air. She still practised some of the wiles of the coquette, for which she had been renowned in her youth. Had not Pierre Loti once "borrowed her" for a description in one of his books? She knew the passage off by heart, and recited it on the slightest invitation. It was still obvious that Loti had been genuinely inspired.

Mr. Bekir, the head of this distinguished family of exiles, was in no way striking to observe. He retained at fifty-six an active body and an energetic nature. A rotundity proclaimed his growing stoutness, not entirely due to the pleasures of the table, and his hair had gone grey over the temples, but his zest for life had in no way diminished and his business activity seemed to wax rather than wane. He seemed likely to inherit the longevity of the Bekir family, for his father had lived to ninety-two, and his grandfather, Osman Bekir Pasha, had lived to ninety-nine, leaving behind him in Istanbul four wives, twenty-seven children, and ninety-three grandchildren. He had been financial adviser to the Sultan Abdul Hamid, and a chamberlain of the Sublime Porte.

Mr. Bekir's family was healthy and happy, his wife beautiful, his home life full of affection. He was a fortunate man. Moreover, his business was prosperous. How prosperous? That was

a thing that puzzled Madame Huysman, whose feminine curiosity never ceased to investigate the fortune of her son-in-law.
She made little progress, however. In this matter he was firmly
secretive. He rushed about, concerned with his many agencies,
but how much his company prospered neither Mrs. Bekir nor
Madame Huysman ever discovered. When challenged on the
matter he always looked serious and said, "Business gets more
and more difficult these days, with so many disturbing political
factors," which told them nothing.

He appeared, however, to be fairly prosperous. Every year
he bought a new car. The children lacked nothing, and their
birthdays were always marked by rather costly presents. On
Lucille's fifteenth birthday he had presented her with a small
rope of pearls, promising to add to them on each birthday. "It
will be a nice dowry for you, my dear, when you are a bride," he
said, smiling at his beloved daughter.

Mrs. Bekir had always sufficient money for running the household. They kept two maids and a cook, as well as a chauffeur-
handyman. Madame Huysman had brought with her from Paris
her own maid, a gaunt, hatchet-faced woman from the Midi,
who refused to learn a word of English, and insisted on having
her meals alone in her bed-sitting-room.

Mr. Bekir put up with this cantankerous creature for the sake
of domestic peace. He was attentive and kind to his mother-in-
law, but on one thing he was adamant: he would not allow her to
interfere in the slightest way with the education of his children.
She wanted Lucille to be sent to a convent school in France, to
which Mrs. Bekir would have agreed, for the lovely but wayward
Lucille was becoming somewhat difficult to manage. Mr. Bekir
would not hear of it. "I want to enjoy my family. Besides, I
don't believe in shutting up women—let them see the world and
find their feet in it." This remark, so unlike the traditional Turk-

ish attitude towards female emancipation, showed how modern and Europeanized Mr. Bekir was, though brought up strictly in the traditions of a Turkish family.

"I'm sure Alexander is a rich man," said Madame Huysman, "and I really think we should have a better car, and go about more. Why can't he take a villa at Cannes for the winter, like your father did? I know this London winter will kill me."

"But I can't leave him. He has to be away from home for three months every year," answered Mrs. Bekir.

"He should take us travelling with him. I'd like to see some of the cities he goes to. I do think, Julie, you allow yourself to be shut up too much," complained her mother.

"Well, I married a Turk!" laughed Mrs. Bekir. "But really, Mamma, it would be unreasonable and difficult. Poor Alex has to rush from one place to another, and he would be miserable if I left the children. No, perhaps later, when the girls are grown up and Achille is at Oxford, we may. It would be easy then."

"Oxford—surely he's not going to Oxford! It is dangerously damp. He should go to the Sorbonne. I can't think why Alex has become Anglicized. Achille is developing all the wrong ideas," said Madame Huysman. "I do think, also, he should do his Service Militaire."

"But Mamma, Achille isn't French—he's a Turk! If he had been born in Paris it would be different, he would be liable to serve. I can't see why he should become a French soldier—anyhow, he's still only a boy."

"Achille has French blood in his veins, the only blood that matters!" declared Madame Huysman stoutly.

"Please don't let Alex hear you say that," replied Mrs. Bekir, always alarmed by her mother's fierce patriotism.

"There are some things Alex should hear," retorted Madame Huysman. But she knew better than to give her son-in-law her advice. He had once put her in her place with unforgettable directness.

On the whole the Bekir family was a united one. They had many English friends. Members of the Turkish colony in London were not encouraged, as Mr. Bekir said there would be the inevitable political talk to which all Turks were prone. He intensely disliked such talk, and had a horror of being involved in the intrigues that seethed among the young Turks.

The children made friends with the sons and daughters of neighbours. Lucille had already created some heartaches among the youths she met at dances, and Mrs. Bekir had to keep a strict watch on the telephone. There was a time when, her rebukes being ignored, she spoke to her husband about Lucille's flirtatiousness. Like Madame Huysman, she began to wonder whether a convent school, after all, would not be the best thing for Lucille, mature beyond her years, bold, and perilously lovely. But Mr. Bekir pooh-poohed any suggestion that Lucille needed discipline. She was the apple of his eye, and he delighted so much in her presence at home that he would not agree to her going to an English boarding school. As a trial a governess was engaged. She proved a weak creature, and Lucille quickly reduced her to impotence; indeed she forced her to aid and abet in some of her rendezvous with her swains. After a year the experiment was abandoned, and Lucille went to boarding school.

August was always the month of separation. Mr. Bekir left for his annual trip to Salonica, from which he usually returned towards the end of November. In August the family went to a favourite hotel at Thurlestone, in Devon, and in September a fortnight's visit was always paid to the Huysman relations in Paris. Madame Huysman sometimes remained on until the middle of November.

The return of Mr. Bekir was always marked by a series of gay dinner-parties, dances and theatres, and also by the presents he brought home for each member of the family, including Madame Huysman, who always returned to London in time for her son-in-law's celebrations. She also received a present, generally a piece of jewellery. Her collection was already large, but her avaricious spirit caused her to await with restless excitement her son-in-law's return. He usually gave her something with diamonds. She liked diamonds, chiefly because they were the most expensive stones to possess, and they were so obviously costly when she wore them. Her collection was going to Julie, on her death, and Julie seemed to have no passion for jewellery whatever, which seemed most lamentable.

Although Mr. Bekir adhered faithfully to the undertaking to allow his children to be brought up in the Catholic faith, he remained a devout Moslem, and never neglected his weekly visit to the Mosque. For some reason this devotion excited the greatest suspicion in Madame Huysman. It seemed to her extraordinary that so civilized and worldly a man as her son-in-law should believe in Mohammed and the Seven Heavens, with the houris, promised to the Faithful in the Koran.

"How can he believe such things—besides, it's immoral," said Madame Huysman, discussing Mr. Bekir's faith with her maid, to whom she often unburdened herself.

"I've always wondered, Madame, how you ever let your daughter marry a Turk—he might take it into his head to have half a dozen wives, and put her in a harem, and where would she be then?" asked the servant, endowed with a vivid and macabre imagination.

"Don't talk nonsense—Mr. Bekir's a gentleman," said Madame Huysman, severely. "It's his religion that seems to me so singular. How can he believe that Paradise is filled with black-eyed damsels with perpetual beauty, of which he can have seventy-two, all of them with their virginity renewable at pleasure!"

"What!" exclaimed the servant, looking up from her sewing, wide-eyed at her mistress's information.

"That's what Moslems believe, or profess to believe. Did you ever hear anything like it! I've read the Koran, most of it is very boring, but some of it is really surprising. And Mr. Bekir goes to the Mosque every week, kneels down in his stockinged feet and touches the ground with his forehead. Sometimes, when I see him sitting at the head of the table, I try to picture him doing it, but I just can't," said Madame Huysman.

"But you knew he was a Turk when he married your daughter," observed the old maid.

"Of course we did! And a very happy marriage it's been. Mr. Bekir is a gentleman," replied Madame Huysman, regretting her disloyalty to her son-in-law.

"You never know a Turk, Madame. He'll surprise you one day," said the woman from the Midi, portentously.

"Nonsense! You've no right to say such a thing," snapped Madame Huysman, now angry at her maid's presumption. "Mr. Bekir is the kindest and most upright of men."

"*Cela va sans dire, Madame,*" replied her maid. "*Mais——*"

She snapped the thread between her strong teeth, and shook out the chemise she was embroidering.

"*Vous êtes une idiote!*" retorted Madame Huysman, as she left the room.

II

On the evening before Mr. Bekir left for Salonica, and when the household had just finished packing for the annual Devon holiday, Madame Huysman made a discovery that caused her to shake with excitement and indignation. Mr. Bekir, with his wife and children, had gone to the cinema, after giving them dinner at the Café Royal. It was a farewell treat, to which Madame Huysman had also been invited. But the hot August day had given her a headache and she decided to stay at home.

Shortly before retiring, a message came over the telephone from Mr. Bekir's assistant. The maids having gone to bed, Madame Huysman wrote it carefully down and placed it on her son-in-law's desk, kept in a corner of the smaller sitting-room. The desk was a roll-top one, and in the hurry of going out Mr. Bekir had neglected to snap down the shutter.

It would have been possible for Madame Huysman to leave the note on the top of the desk, which she actually did later, but on seeing the shutter unfastened she pushed it back until the desk with its pigeon-holes and papers was in view.

She looked at it a little curiously, as was her nature, although she had often seen this desk open when her son-in-law was working at it. Examining this personal domain at leisure, noting the neat pens, the pigeon-holes filled with folded papers held together with elastic bands, and the round ash-tray on which a half-smoked cigar now lay, her wandering eyes fell upon a pile of letters in a narrow tray by the writing-pad. The top letter at once attracted her attention. "The Central London Mosque" she read, in large type, and in the right-hand corner, "Office of the Imam." The letter was addressed to Mr. Bekir, typewritten, and was signed "H. A. Terofik, Imam."

Immediately Madame Huysman felt she was on the verge of a discovery. Her questing curiosity had at last alighted on some secret of her son-in-law's strange religious rites. She read the letter and found no revelation of a religious nature, but what she did learn was exciting enough. It was a letter of thanks from the Imam of the Mosque to Mr. Bekir, a faithful son of the Prophet, for his munificent gift of five thousand pounds towards the building fund.

Five thousand pounds for a Mosque. Madame Huysman was stunned. When she had recovered somewhat she read the letter a second time, noticing it was only a day old. She lifted it from the pile and looked at some other letters, which proved uninteresting, and, replacing the top letter, she closed the roller lid with a bang. She thought it prudent to leave the telephone message on the top of the closed desk. Mr. Bekir always went to his desk before retiring to see if there were any messages.

The sad thing about this astonishing discovery of Mr. Bekir's secret activity as a Moslem was that she had no one to whom she could immediately communicate it. Yet it was something she felt she must tell someone. Her maid was in bed, her daughter, when she returned, would be with her husband, and obviously could not be told then. There was nothing to be done except go to bed, nursing her news until the morning. Unfortunately, as her son-in-law was leaving for Salonica in the afternoon, he would not go to his office.

Somehow she must take Julie aside and inform her of Mr. Bekir's secret gift. For two things were now clear to Madame Huysman. Her son-in-law was a wealthy man, and he led a double life. He kept his family in ignorance of his fortune and made large gifts to the Mohammedan Church. It was easy for Madame Huysman to believe, without further reflection, that her son-in-law was wickedly depriving his family of their proper maintenance in order to make secret gifts to his monstrous religion.

There was no reason for Madame Huysman's indignation. She had lived on and with her son-in-law for the last fifteen years, never contributing a penny of her own comfortable income to the maintenance of herself and her maid in his house. But, perversely, this was Madame Huysman's reason for feeling indignation. If he could give five thousand pounds to a Mosque, of all things—and the gift began to take on the nature of an affront to her own true religion—then he could well afford to keep his wife and children, as well as herself, in greater dignity. The house was too small for the family, and it required a butler to superintend the servants and relieve Julie. More than ever she was convinced that meanness and not inability made Alex refuse to rent a villa at Cannes for the winter.

He was, as she had always suspected, a rich mean man. It was really time that Julie demanded a life more in accordance with the wife of a well-to-do, if not a rich man. At the least she should have her own town car and chauffeur, instead of having to beg for her husband's whenever she wanted to pay a call. Madame Huysman reflected how many times she herself had not gone out because it meant a taxi-fare there and back.

The clock in the hall struck eleven. Still wide awake with excitement, Madame Huysman went up to bed. Undressing, a thought sprang into her mind, increasing her agitation. Did her daughter know what was in her husband's Will? It was possible that he had left everything to the Mosque. All Moslems were fanatics. How wise her Church had been to insist that all the children should be Catholics.

Unconscious of the excitement he had unwittingly created in his mother-in-law's mind by leaving his desk unlocked the previous night, Mr. Bekir rose, a little despondent, on the morning of his departure for the Near East. It was unfortunate that the business required him to be in Salonica at the time when his son was home from his preparatory school. Lucille and Dorette he loved, but had he dared to express favouritism it would have been shown to little Achille, a sharp, pale little boy, with dark eyes and red lips, who had, more than his sisters, the vivacity of his mother.

Mr. Bekir decided to visit the girls in their bedroom. On his way there he met one of the maids carrying up breakfast to Madame Huysman, for, *grande dame,* she kept to her room until lunch, where she read the papers, wrote letters, telephoned round to her French friends in London, and received the masseuse, the chiropodist, the manicurist, and, her latest cult, the chiropractic.

Sometimes Mr. Bekir wished his wife took more control over the household, which was made to march to Madame Huysman's whims, but he was aware that controlling Madame Huysman was something no one had ever attempted. He had a begrudging admiration for the masterful, selfish old woman. And he knew that, at the approach of any conflict of wills between them, his mother-in-law had the gift of making a tactful retreat that somehow left him with an unpleasant sense of browbeating. So the peace had been kept, and one bond was strong between them, they both loved the children to the verge of idolatry.

Mrs. Bekir, fortunately, though a devoted mother, kept a firm hand on her family, and neither Mr. Bekir nor Madame Huysman had the final word when decisions affecting Achille or his sisters had to be made. Mr. Bekir had married a young woman whose physical beauty had constituted her chief appeal. He had lived with her to discover that her mental and moral qualities were equally attractive. He recalled his own mother, brought up in strict seclusion in the Turkish tradition of the old regime. She had dominated his father without the slightest acknowledgment of her influence.

Mrs. Bekir had never for a moment, from the day she became his wife, failed to express her wish and to insist upon it. Let it not be assumed that he was in any way "hen-pecked" or wife-ridden. He never felt the bonds because they were never unreasonably tight, and because his wife was always the embodiment of cheerful enterprise and shrewd foresight. He consulted her on many of the problems of his business. He always deferred to her in domestic matters. He was rewarded by the possession of a happy and very well run home, and by a wife who in her graces and her mentality never ceased to delight him, or to attract the warm admiration of all their friends.

On one matter only was there ever anything that suggested the possibility of a rift in their perfect relations. She thought he might be more accommodating to her wish for travel in his company. He had always opposed the suggestion that she should share some of his business tours, raising the objection that the children would be alone, since Madame Huysman would refuse to be left behind; and the prospect of travelling with his mother-in-law really alarmed him. Later, when the children were grown up, and, he could have added, but refrained, when Madame Huysman had made her last journey, then he would take his wife on his foreign trips. "But the Balkans are scarcely fit for a woman to travel in," he said.

Many of Mr. Bekir's autumn excursions were to remote tobacco-growing centres in Greece and Bulgaria, where the accommodation was of the most primitive order.

So Mrs. Bekir and Madame Huysman went to Devon and Paris, while Mr. Bekir travelled by train, car, horse, and sometimes donkey, through the mountainous regions of the Balkans. He had an international fame as a buyer of tobacco leaf. He was rivalled only by his brother, who attended to the business in Asia Minor. The prosperity of the Bekir organization was founded on these activities, and their annual conference in Salonica. The two brothers strictly confined themselves to their separate provinces, European and Asian. Their business had survived the competition of powerful combines and had remained resolutely independent.

Mr. Bekir, therefore, in every respect, was a happy man. A sound business, good health, a loving wife and family, these things made life good, though he was not immune from the minor worries inseparable from life.

His bath finished, he tapped on the door of the girls' room where he heard his wife talking, and, being invited in, he found Mrs. Bekir brushing young Dorette's hair, as she sat clad in a bright dressing-gown, on a chair by the window. Lucille, also in a dressing-gown, immediately flung her arms around her father's neck and kissed him on each cheek.

"Daddy, is it true we've got a bigger car? I say it is, mother says it isn't. Grandma says we ought to have one, and Dorette says I'm crazy."

"I really don't know where they've got the idea from," laughed Mrs. Bekir.

"The idea—oh, I'll tell you, mamma! Achille says a man came yesterday to measure the garage. He was a builder, and when Achille asked him why he was measuring it he said, 'To make it larger.' There!" cried Lucille, triumphantly. "We are having a new car, aren't we—a bigger and faster one?"

"Achille's getting too sharp—where is he?" asked Mr. Bekir, rubbing his head with the towel. He was in character this morning for he carried a Turkish towel and wore Turkish slippers.

"There's a terrible thing in the papers, the King of Slavonia's been assassinated," said Mrs. Bekir, not answering his question.

"What, King Peter? He's so popular. I've seen him often at Nish, walking about in the streets among the crowd," said Mr. Bekir, towelling his head. "Poor devil—it just proves that anything can happen in the Balkans."

"The poor little Crown Prince is at school here—and he didn't go home when the school broke up, in order to visit a school friend. What a terrible thing for him and his poor mother!" cried Mrs. Bekir, brushing her daughter's hair.

"Daddy, are you quite safe in the Balkans? They're always shooting someone, aren't they?" asked Dorette.

"Why do you imagine they'd want to shoot your poor old daddy, eh?" asked Mr. Bekir, putting his hand under his daughter's chin, and lifting her face to look into her clear blue eyes.

"All the girls at Roedean assure me the Turks wipe out the Armenians from time to time, so why shouldn't the Armenians wipe out the Turks, or try to?" asked Lucille, always outspoken.

"My dear, why do you talk such nonsense!" said Mrs. Bekir, reprovingly.

"Grandma says——" began Dorette.

"That's quite enough!" said Mrs. Bekir, severely.

"What does your Grandma say?" asked Mr. Bekir with a steady voice. He was a calm man, but talk of this kind to his own children stirred his anger.

"Alex—don't ask the child," protested his wife.

"I'm curious, my dear, to know just what Grandma does say about me," replied Mr. Bekir.

"Alex, don't take it so personally," pleaded Mrs. Bekir, now a little alarmed. She knew well her mother's views about the Turks, although she was always careful to say Mr. Bekir was an exception.

"Grandma says lots of things about everybody. No one takes any notice. Everyone knows she just loves talking," said Lucille, intervening. "She doesn't mean any harm."

That was true, thought Mrs. Bekir. She didn't mean any harm, but oh, how much dynamite she left lying around! Only ten minutes ago, on her way to the bathroom, meeting her mother, she had been pulled back into her bedroom to be told that she had made an astonishing discovery. Mr. Bekir had presented five thousand pounds to the Mosque!

The news had given Mrs. Bekir a shock, but she did not allow her mother to see it. "Yes, I know; why shouldn't he?" she had said at once, lying swiftly. Her husband's religious life was the one thing he kept completely apart from her. She knew he was a devout Mohammedan, but from the first day of her married life she had resolutely refrained from comment. For his part, he also never questioned her own religious observances, and in the matter of the children he had most honourably kept his bargain.

Angry with her busybody mother, Mrs. Bekir added, "Why don't you mind your own business!" to which Madame Huysman replied at once, "I think you're very foolish not to know more about Alex—he's too secretive." That had really stung Mrs. Bekir, and leaving the bedroom, with two angry red spots on her cheeks, she said, "Mamma, you've no right to make mischief between Alex and me. I trust him implicitly. Please don't ever say things like that again!" And thereupon she had walked out.

She was really alarmed now when Dorette began to report Madame Huysman's chatter.

"Daddy—are we having a new car?" asked Lucille, always diplomatic, and aware of tension in the air.

"Ah—but you have Achille's information," replied her father, cryptically.

Lucille leapt up from the chair, and took hold of her father.

"Daddy, we have—we have! And I can drive it?" she cried.

"Have you really bought one, Alex? We managed quite well with the other," asked Mrs. Bekir.

Mr. Bekir smiled.

"Yes—and no," he said. "You know, that little beggar's like

a detective," said Mr. Bekir, alluding to Achille, but with a note of pride in his voice. "I was trying to give you a surprise after I'd gone. But it's no use. We're keeping the old one for general purposes, and you're also having a new one."

"That means the old one's ours! Hooray!" shouted Lucille, jumping in front of her father. Then she kissed his bald head.

"Alex—thank you, dearest—but it's not necessary," said Mrs. Bekir, really very pleased, for she often wanted the car and found her husband had ordered it out.

"Daddy—what is it—a Rolls?" cried Dorette.

"Idiot child—a Rolls!" scoffed Lucille.

"It is a Rolls," said Mr. Bekir.

There was a yell of joy from the younger girl, a look of amazement on the faces of Mrs. Bekir and Lucille.

"I wanted you to have something really good this time," said Mr. Bekir, addressing his wife. "And now the cat's out of the bag."

"There!" cried Dorette, to her sister. "That'll show we're rich."

"Darling, don't be vulgar!" protested Mrs. Bekir. "Now do hurry up and dress."

She turned to her husband and slipped an arm through his as they left the girls' room.

"Alex, it's very extravagant—and lovely," she said.

"Oh, I can manage it. You ought to have the best, my dear," he replied, and, stopping on the landing, gave her a kiss. Then he hurried back into his bedroom to dress.

As he walked about the room, Dorette's censored report of Grandma's version of the Turks troubled him. He wished he could devise some means of keeping that mischievous old woman out of the Rolls, so admirable for her *grande dame* manner. She was the kind of old woman who should be shut up in a harem. She would then know beyond doubt what Turks could be like!

III

They all arrived early at the station, Bekir and his wife, Madame Huysman, with a bunch of flowers in her corsage, and smelling of Houbigant's *Quelques Fleurs*. She attracted the attention, as ever, and might have been going to launch a battleship instead of seeing her son-in-law off.

Excited by this annual event in their father's life, Lucille, very slim and lovely in her white frock, Dorette, dark-eyed and spry, and Achille, in the regulation school flannel shorts and coat, with straw hat displaying the vivid maroon and gold school colours, chatted and hung on the arms of their parents. Lucille had a wandering eye and saw at least three carriages in which she would have chosen to ride.

They all halted outside the Pullman saloon. Dorette and Achille had to enter and sit experimentally in their father's reserved seat. Mr. Bekir, as usual, loaded himself up with papers and magazines. The chauffeur was supervising the two porters in charge of Mr. Bekir's many bags and parcels. The moment had come when they all had nothing more to say to each other. They stood and criticized the passengers, and suddenly Madame Huysman gave a cry, and caught her daughter's arm.

"*Voilà, c'est le pauvre petit!*" she exclaimed.

Yes, there, on the crimson drugget, was the Crown Prince of Slavonia, a sad-looking little boy standing silent while three elderly gentlemen and a lady were in conversation. A middle-aged woman who was obviously a governess waited just behind.

The Bekirs watched until the little boy had gravely shaken hands and gone into the carriage.

"*Il est charmant! charmant! le petit!*" exclaimed Madame

Huysman, using her most overworked adjective. In her volatile emotion she produced tears in her eyes, and dabbed herself with a lace handkerchief. *"C'est une affaire affreuse! Le pauvre roi! La pauvre reine! Le pauvre petit!"* bleated Madame Huysman.

"I expect he's going through to Nish on my train," said Mr. Bekir, lighting a cigar. "I don't suppose anybody'll be allowed to speak to him."

"Could you, daddy? Do you know his language? Does he talk English now?" asked Lucille.

"I can speak Czech—I used to talk with his father when I went to Nish," said Mr. Bekir, modestly.

"Oh, do talk to him, daddy!" pleaded Dorette.

"Cheer him up, daddy," said Achille, hanging on his father's arm.

"The train's going—everybody's getting in!" cried Mrs. Bekir, noticing a general stir.

Mr. Bekir kissed his wife.

"Good-bye, Julie—take care of yourself, my dear," he said.

He kissed the children in turn, and then Madame Huysman. He entered the car, and they waited until he had found his seat in the saloon. They did not hear the whistle, and the train began to glide away, with Mr. Bekir smiling at them through the window. He had a brief vision of his wife, still graceful and beautiful, well dressed, with his bright-eyed children, a splendid trio. Even Madame Huysman was superbly *grande dame*. No one would doubt that she owned the Rolls-Royce when she sat in it. He could not withhold a measure of admiration from the commanding old lady.

And now for Salonica. He would be there on Friday night at half-past ten. Opening the evening paper, he looked at the quotations for tobacco shares and then turned to the gilt-edged stocks. A fraction of a point made a considerable difference, for, although no one knew it except Mr. Bekir and his brother, he was a millionaire. That would have been a shock for inquisitive Madame Huysman, but he could have given her many shocks had he wished. He put down the paper and lit a cigar.

CHAPTER XI

GENERAL ZORONOFF, OF PARIS

GENERAL PAUL VLADIMIR ZORONOFF looked at his English friends gathered around the luncheon table in the Reform Club. They were seated in the private dining-room whose long windows looked out on to Pall Mall, for this was an intimate lunch given to him to conclude his annual visit to England. For a month he had lived once more like a gentleman of fortune, with servants at his call, dignified homes, charming hosts, horses and cars and dogs, with week-end visits to country houses, with dinner-parties where agreeable conversation was exchanged between guests drawn from the Services, politics, the arts and business; in short he had been, as in happier days, General Zoronoff, one-time in command of the 3rd Guards Cavalry Division in the Army of His Imperial Majesty, Tsar Nicholas.

Seated at the table, he bore no mark of the tremendous vicissitudes of fortune through which he had passed. Dressed neatly in a dark blue reefer jacket, which now, unbuttoned, revealed a white summer waistcoat, he struck a note of effortless distinction with his trimmed white beard and moustache, his grey eyes, whose slanting lids gave him an imperious expression, and his carefully brushed grizzled hair, parted in the middle of a well-shaped head. When he smiled his face at once lost its severity, and the charm of the man became immediately visible. His voice, too, which had never lost its delightful accent when he spoke English, was pleasant to hear.

A man of sixty-five, he did not look his age, and through all
his adversity he had retained an active figure and an unimpaired
mind. There was nothing in his manner nor his conversation to
inform the world that he had been reduced from the highest
position in the great Russian Empire to obscurity in exile, from
wealth and an aristocratic atmosphere to the acutest poverty and
the humiliations it entailed.

General Zoronoff replied smilingly to his host, who had raised
his glass and wished him *bon voyage*, for he was leaving England
at four-thirty. This was the close of another memorable visit.
Thirty years ago he had been an honoured guest of the same
host, in the same place. But how changed were his circumstances! His wife, the Princess Nada Galarine, was dead, one
son had fallen fighting on the Galician front, another had perished in a Bolshevik jail. His two daughters were now teaching
in a Lausanne school, and he, himself, was—but he dismissed his
own situation from mind. Here he was, once more a gentleman
dining with old friends in an English Club.

His friend and host, Major Broad, had entertained him there
in the Tsar Nicholas and Edwardian era before the earth's foun-
dations had been shaken. He had thought then, as he had reasons
for knowing now, that in Major Broad he had sealed a friendship with the very highest type of gentleman that England could
produce. Affable, intelligent, experienced, an unfailing cour-
tesy and an inexhaustible generosity had marked the face and
bearing of this man whose friendship had been tested through
thirty years. An impeccable taste in dress had always been a
distinguishing mark of his English friend, but with this he com-
bined a distinction of manner that had its roots in the sweetness
and unselfishness of his character. Sometimes they smiled a little
at this friend, whose elegant silk handkerchiefs were permitted
to droop a little ostentatiously from the pocket, whose cuffs were

generously displayed, and who would wear a crush felt hat with a slightly Byronic air. But these lovable idiosyncrasies were the mark of a man slavish to no convention except that of politeness in every circumstance.

It was, therefore, a memorable experience to be a guest in the Broad house, or at one of the intimate luncheon parties the Major delighted in giving at his various clubs. He knew, of course, in whose brain originated this idea of giving him an annual re-visit to the London he had known and loved in the days of his distinction and affluence; for in the early years of the century he had been Military Attaché at the Russian Embassy, when that Embassy reflected the power and prestige of a great Imperial Court.

It had often been suggested that he should write his memoirs, but it would transgress too many loyalties and open too many wounds. Sometimes, at the Major's gentle promptings, he turned the pages of the past and evoked a pageantry unknown to these mean days of traditionless demagogy. Yet, whatever his present state, he had lived. The son of a famous General, descended from an ancient Baltic German nobility, he was born in lovely St. Petersburg, and trained in the Corps de Pages, that celebrated military college open only to the sons of His Imperial Majesty's highest officers. He had been drafted early to the Chevaliers Gardes, which he was destined to command later, and was on the Staff of the Grand Duke Nicholas.

When the Great War broke out he went from the Guards Cavalry Division, and, early in 1915, succeeded to the responsible position of Chief of Staff to the Seventh Army. There followed, in those eventful days, the command of the 3rd Cavalry Corps on the Galician front, with all the successes and reverses of that mobile and devastating theatre of battle, until, the Revolution breaking out at home, the Army collapsed and chaos swept over the Tsar's proud army.

The end of a regime had come, and with it was shattered everything that constituted the Russia he had known and served. From a high command he found himself a hunted creature reduced to beggary and desperate subterfuges to save his life. Betrayed, he was thrown into a foul Petrograd jail, and after fourteen terrible months, during which he had been marched out five times before the shooting squad, he succeeded in making a claim to Ukrainian citizenship. The claim was genuine for he fortunately possessed an estate near Odessa.

There was a brief interlude of security and respite from starvation, ended when the French evacuated Odessa and the Ukrainian Government fell. With the French he crossed Europe, to Paris, and was re-united to his wife. He learned there of his son's murder in a Moscow jail, and, after untiring inquiries, discovered that his two daughters had maintained themselves by teaching in a Lausanne girls' academy.

The years of exile in Paris had been endured in poverty. A small residue of his fortune, happily invested in France in pre-war years, still produced a minute income which neither supported them nor suffered them to die. A back bed-sitting-room in the Rue du Bac had been their home for the last fifteen years. It was there, after ten years of exile, the Princess Nada, his wife, at one time one of the notable beauties of the Court at St. Petersburg, had died in poverty alleviated only by the care of her friends, all in similar circumstances, but unmurmuringly brave. Providence through these last five lonely years had provided him with the oddest means of livelihood.

Slowly he had renewed, by correspondence, his contacts with old acquaintances. Major Broad, on a visit to Paris, had been shocked to find him in such straits and only the firmest demonstration of independence had restrained that noble old friend from personal financial assistance. Somehow he had survived, somehow he would continue to survive. There were thousands of his fellow countrymen in similar straits. Perhaps, when the storm in Russia had passed, perhaps . . . But he had never had any faith in the restoration of the old regime; it was all gone for ever, and a new generation was arising that had no knowledge of or affection for the Russia of the Tsars.

It must have been in an unguarded moment that he had lamented, in his old friend's hearing, the fact that he would never again see the London he had so loved, and the many friends he had made there. One morning a letter had come extending to him the warmest invitation to visit four of his old English friends. And with this letter there was enclosed a first-class return ticket to London. For the first week Major Broad claimed the honour, the second and third weeks were filled in with invitations that took him to some of the pleasant homes of England, survivals of the gracious manner of English country life. And his last week had been passed on a friend's yacht at Cowes Regatta.

So it was that, after many years, he had returned, to savour again a life of dignity and easy circumstances, to find a company of hospitable men and women, a little quicker in the tempo of life as became a new age, but no less cultured in its customs and enjoyable in its diversions.

It was, of course, the idea of Major Broad. How delicately the whole business had been organized to evade any embarrassing reminders of his present circumstances! He was tactfully steered from any situation which involved expenditure. He found tickets put on his dressing-table, theatre boxes at his service, cars at his disposal, and all the minute details attended to that smoothed his way, and created for him an illusion almost of his former affluence. He knew, throughout, whose delicate sense had planned this halcyon month for him. The touch of his friend the Major was indisguisable, and he was deeply moved to observe the competition between these good friends to make his visit so pleasurable.

General Zoronoff's own modesty did not allow him to find in his own personality the reason for his friends' attempts to give him a memorable return to the scenes he had known. His distinguished appearance, his dignity in misfortune and his smiling courage stirred their warmest affection. What, thought his hosts, would have been their reactions to such batterings of Fate?

Sir Henry Pleyden, sitting now on the old General's right, remembered the beautiful horses he and the Princess had kept at Market Harborough. She was, surely, one of the loveliest women of her time, and looking back some thirty years he could still recall the excitement with which he, a young officer in the Guards, had looked up from his stall at the Opera one evening and seen two superlatively lovely women. One was the Countess of Warwick, the other, who was she? The Princess Nada Zoronoff, wife of the Russian Military Attaché, said a friend. Within a week he had made her acquaintance. To think that that woman had trekked from Odessa to Petrograd to get her husband out of jail with proofs of his Ukrainian citizenship, to think she had died in poverty, in exile!

Some men went to pieces under prosperity, some under adversity. Men like General Zoronoff, who were bent by the storm but refused to be broken, were all the more remarkable when they came from an aristocracy notorious for its arrogance and irresponsibility. He had been a member of a Court pitiable in its subjection to superstition, he had moved in a society whose luxury could only have been supported by the economic and political suppression of millions of peasants, and his high offices were essentially based on a corrupt bureaucracy. Yet here was a man who had emerged from such conditions with a character that had never lost honour or dignity. No one ever heard him ask for a favour, no one ever heard him complain of his lot. His loyalty to the Russian people would not suffer him to indulge in the bitter denunciations with which most of his fellow exiles gave vent to their anger and despair.

Sir Henry recalled, on a former visit, how simply the General had revealed the straits to which he had been reduced, and which he had never mentioned throughout all inquiries made upon his mode of life in Paris. Sir Henry had somewhat artfully decoyed the General into a tie shop in Burlington Arcade. His keen eye had observed the holes in the gloves carried, but not worn, by the General. Inside the shop, in the course of extolling the virtues of the particular gloves he was then buying, he had suddenly said, "You must really have a pair of these excellent gloves—I always get them here. I don't think they have their equals in Paris."

Sir Henry felt he had been very adroit, but outside in the Arcade the General smiled and said, "Henry, you saw I wanted a pair of gloves, and feared I was too proud to accept them. I've accepted them—and am delighted with such expensive gloves. But it's your kindness of heart that makes my hands glow in them." It was just after this remark that the General made a magnificent bow to a lady and gentleman, Americans. He would have passed on, but they stopped him, joy on their faces at this encounter.

After a brief and cordial conversation the General said good-bye and joined Sir Henry.

"They were former clients," explained the General, apologizing for the delay.

"Clients?" queried Sir Henry.

"Yes—we went across the Alps and down through Dalmatia together. They were very nice employers," explained the General. "Very considerate, didn't want to go too fast—I'm always too slow for most of them—and they didn't keep me out late."

Sir Henry was a little mystified.

"You made a motor tour with them?" he asked, as they halted by Bond Street.

"Yes—you know, I suppose, that I sometimes get employment as a chauffeur-courier? No? Oh, hasn't Arthur told you? I'm on Cook's list in Paris, and when people want a really safe, slow chauffeur to conduct them across Europe I sometimes get the job. My six languages are my chief recommendation, though I keep the car spotless and can manage running repairs."

The traffic signal said "Go," but Sir Henry stood still, staring at his old friend.

"You mean to say you've become a professional chauffeur and you can drive a large car——"

"Forty horse-power Delage limousine," intercepted the General, a little proudly.

"——over the Alps, across Europe. God bless my soul! At your—after your life," said Sir Henry, correcting himself.

"At my age, sixty-five, yes!" replied the General. "Yes, and not too bad either. I like to go at about seventy kilometres an hour, and I'm not much good in strange towns, for I have to put on my glasses to read street names—and it's funny, but the nicest people don't like a chauffeur to wear glasses!"

He gave a laugh, and Sir Henry, who had seen many brave men, thought this was the bravest of all as he stood there and laughed at his own deficiencies as a hired chauffeur.

"But whatever made you take to this business? You could drive, of course?" asked Sir Henry.

"What makes most men find out they can do things they never knew they could before necessity taught them? Oh yes, I sometimes drove my own cars in the old days. My fiercest drive was running away from the Front!"

Again Sir Henry stared at his friend. The idea of the General running away from anything was difficult to entertain. They had now turned into St. James's Street and had reached his Club. The General was always opening strange chapters in his long, varied life.

"That time," continued the General, as they mounted the Club steps, "after the collapse of Brusilov, I was with the 9th Army under Lechitski—I motored a thousand kilometres from Czerno-witz to Odessa, through forests, swamps and snow blizzards in an old car with bad tyres, surviving for two-thirds of the journey. One poor devil with us was jolted to death—and that's where those two fingers went—frostbite at the wheel. So don't ask if I could drive!"

The General held up his hand with two mutilated fingers, and gave a chuckle at what seemed now an amusing episode.

"But how did you get into your chauffeur-guide business?" asked Sir Henry, having entered his visitor's name in the club book.

"Ah!" laughed the General. "A friend of mine, an Admiral I'd known well at Odessa, who was thrown into the sea off his own battleship and swam six kilometres to the shore, was getting a living as a taxi-driver in Paris when I got there. One day he fell ill with bronchitis and asked me to carry on with his taxi. I did, and when the poor fellow died, a week later, I kept on the job. But the weather and late hours began to knock me to bits. I heard that Cook's wanted chauffeur-couriers who were linguists, and I got a job that summer, taking Americans across Europe. And that's kept me going. Every now and then they send for me, and off I go. It's interesting, too. I see some of the old places and hotels—by the servants' entrance!" laughed the General.

Such had been part of the General's story of these last years, and here he was now, seated between Sir Henry and Major Broad, with half a dozen friends, all gathered to do him honour on this farewell occasion. This was the fourth annual gathering, and to General Zoronoff it was the event of the year. He smiled now at his dear old friend, as he raised his glass to him. And it was not to Arthur Broad alone that he made his toast, deeply as he treasured this friendship, but to the whole English tradition Broad so admirably reflected. He thought of the balls in the days when he had attended the first Edwardian Court, of the country house-parties, the messes at which he had been a guest during his military attachéship, the brilliant receptions in a London whose life still persisted in his memory, and still seemed to haunt this later city which many said had lost its pageantry and charm.

But in other countries what wreckage strewed the scene, with empires fallen, dynasties ended or exiled! And how crazy were the modern political experiments, abetted by murder, persecution, or civil war! Fortunate English people, whose nature, like their climate, avoided extremes. How steadily they were going downhill, according to their own disparaging comment! General Zoronoff often had difficulty in disguising his amusement at this consistent pessimism. Forty years ago, on his first visit, the English had really impressed him with their certainty of decay. How ludicrous his early dispatches, faithfully reflecting that mood, would read to-day, and yet, to-day, how faithfully they would again reflect current opinion.

Their host was rising. They adjourned to the gallery in the high gloomy hall for coffee, brandy and cigars. From the shadows loomed the life-size portraits of Victorian statesmen, whose names had once meant something across Europe. Dignity seemed their common asset now, though some of them in the political battle must have felt hot and dishevelled.

Francis Bowood, Arthur's bosom friend, had now provoked a lively discussion on contemporary politicians. A well-documented, witty rattle, he exulted in his iconoclastic rôle, certain to arouse opposition. Next year he would sit here, as ardent as ever in his attack on a new peril of the tottering Empire. What a sense of permanence these things gave to one whose country had been dismembered by revolution!

General Zoronoff glanced at his watch. It was half-past three. Two business men of the party had gone. He caught Arthur Broad's eye. The Major rose. Handshaking began and the General received the farewell wishes of the company.

"And you're going to Salzburg?" asked one, shaking his hand.

"Oh, to the Festival? I wish I were coming!" exclaimed a guest. "I envy you, General."

"Thank you," said General Zoronoff, gravely. But as he turned to say good-bye to another member of the party, his keen old eyes twinkled as they met those of Arthur and Henry. For they knew it was no musical festival to which he was going at Salzburg. Instead, he was resuming his duties, on the instructions of Messrs. Cook & Son, Ltd., Paris, as chauffeur-guide to two American ladies who wished to motor from Salzburg over the Grossglocknerstrasse down to Venice. In two days' time he would be respectfully waiting, in blue reefer coat and peaked cap, outside the Oesterreichischer Hof.

And now he must catch the four-thirty at Victoria.

CHAPTER XII

DR. WYFOLD, OF WARGRAVE

DR. WYFOLD was not at all happy. He sat on the first-class boat deck of the Channel steamer leaving Folkestone Harbour for Boulogne and looked gloomily at the passengers around him. There was no wind, there was a calm sea and the summer evening light filled the clear sky and was reflected in the blue-grey water. A very bad sailor, he should have felt thankful for such a halcyon passage.

He watched and wondered at the sea-gulls hovering over the ship's stern, their wings motionless, as though drawn by the suction from the smoke stack moving through the air. But his thoughts were only momentarily occupied by wonder at the gulls' flight. He could not get out of his head the extraordinary and, to his mind, preposterous mission on which he was going. He had been torn away from his garden and the rambling old house he loved, with its lawn sloping down to one of the loveliest stretches of the Thames. He was missing Wargrave Regatta, which he loved to attend, with a string of coloured paper lanterns stretched over his punt. There would be a full moon, too, and his garden was really at its best on a warm, moonlit August night. He loved to sit under the pergola, smoking his pipe and watching the moon come up over the beechwoods, and hear the owl calling in the still night. And always soon after ten o'clock, when the last light was leaving the sky, he could hear the London-Henley train draw across the level meadow into Wargrave

station, a faint familiar sound that seemed to end the pleasant
summer's day; one more pipe then, and bed, after a moment's
pause to see the white moonlight on the rose-beds, the black
shadow of the garage gable cutting a triangle on the lawn, and
the distant band of shining silver that was the Thames.

A widower of sixty, retired from medical service in West
Africa, he had fixed habits. He had always wondered at the
passion of his fellows for rushing out of England every August.
He had seen Switzerland, Germany, Austria and Italy, and having seen them once or twice his curiosity was satisfied. He liked
better *The Times* at breakfast every morning, the radio turned
on for tea—generally there was jolly music—and, after comfortably dressing in his pleasant bedroom overlooking the garden
with the flint wall he had built himself, a quiet dinner, with one
glass of port, followed by a pipe under the pergola.

He wanted nothing else. There was a time when he had
thought it nice to have children. He once wanted a couple of
sons and a daughter, but not now. When he saw what anxiety
they gave to the parents all around him he began to think he was
well out of trouble. This was, of course, a fallacy on Dr. Wyfold's part, for being a kind man, and having a reputation for
shrewdness, he was always being consulted by distressed parents. Young people liked him, moreover. A nice old boy, they
said.

Dr. Wyfold persisted, nevertheless, that he was fortunate in
having no children. His wife's death five years ago had left him
very lonely, and he felt at the time that life had come to an end.
But he was not gregarious by nature, and in a surprisingly short
time he adjusted himself to living alone and came to like it.
There were always plenty of people coming and going, for he
had two brothers and a sister, all married, all with families. He
was always hospitable to his visiting nephews and nieces. He

liked people coming to see him, but hated going away to see people. Perhaps it was selfish of him, but it was too late to change, even had he wished.

And here he was on a Channel boat, torn away from his beloved garden and plunged into a mad, scrambling mob of August holiday-makers, who were going to make the Continent resound with their *Oui oui's, Si si's* and *Ja ja's*.

His widowed sister-in-law, Janette, was the cause of his present discontent. She had come down from Rutland to see him, with an unshakable idea in her head. He was the only person who could bring home her son Reginald, whose odd conduct had filled his mother and his relations with wonder. For last Easter Reginald had gone to Austria on a walking tour and had not come back since. He was twenty-four years of age, down from Cambridge with a First in History. He had gone to the Bar and an eminent K.C. had taken him into his chambers. Clever, handsome, and with an engaging personality, the future seemed promising for young Reginald. And then had happened this extraordinary refusal to come back home after the Easter vacation. His obstinacy was made sustainable by a small private income from his deceased father's estate, to which he had become entitled at twenty-two.

"I'm certain there's a woman in it, say what you like!" declared Janette Wyfold, after she had shown her brother-in-law a dozen or so of Reginald's letters home. "Look at the address—Poste Restante, Gmunden. It tells us nothing, and it's like writing to a blank wall."

"But if there's a woman in it what do you imagine he's doing in Gmunden all this time?" asked Dr. Wyfold.

"We don't know he's in Gmunden," replied Mrs. Wyfold. "He may be entangled with her—there are such creatures, who get hold of attractive boys like Reggie."

"You mean—he's perhaps living with some woman, or married to her?" asked Dr. Wyfold.

"Not married, I hope!" cried Mrs. Wyfold.

"Then—the other thing? Dear me!" said Dr. Wyfold.

Mrs. Wyfold shuffled the letters.

"Of course he never mentions her—which makes me really suspicious. Why does he hide his address, and why is he so happy, as he declares he is?" she asked.

Dr. Wyfold did not reply. He felt her reasoning was dangerously mixed.

"I admit it's very strange," he said, at last.

"Strange! All his career's going to pieces. I seem to be of no account——"

"His letters are quite affectionate, Janette," urged Dr. Wyfold.

"Yes—but he ignores my appeals for him to come home. What can he be doing all this time? It's a mystery! He was always so hard-working—a model boy. Richard, you must fetch him back, whatever it is. If his father were living he wouldn't dare to behave like this. Up till now Reggie's never given me a moment's worry."

A handkerchief came out and Mrs. Wyfold wiped her eyes. Dr. Wyfold could not bear any woman to cry. He began to weaken.

"After all, he might tell me to mind my own business. He's a man now," said the doctor.

"You're his favourite uncle. If you can do nothing with him no one can," replied his sister-in-law. "I simply cannot go on with this anxiety. It's killing me."

"Very well," said Dr. Wyfold, after a silence, "I'll go—but it couldn't have been at a more awkward time."

Why it should be the most awkward time would have been

difficult for him to explain, but Mrs. Wyfold did not challenge the statement.

"Thank you, Richard, I knew I shouldn't ask you in vain," said Mrs. Wyfold gratefully. "Can you go at once—this suspense is unbearable."

"At once—you mean to-morrow?"

"Well, Wednesday at the latest," she replied.

"Very well—Wednesday then," agreed Dr. Wyfold.

And this was why he was travelling to Gmunden. It had all been done so quickly that he could hardly believe he was already out of England. Janette had stayed the night, and the next morning, Tuesday, he had gone to Cook's and bought his ticket. At least, the journey was simple enough, there was a through carriage, with sleepers.

It had been in his mind to send the boy a telegram, asking him to meet him, but a telegram to so vague an address as a Poste Restante was not much use; moreover, it might scare off the boy. He was on a wild goose chase anyhow, for what certainty had he of tracking down Reginald? There was one other disconcerting factor. Gmunden was crammed with Austrians taking their summer holiday, and Cook's had quite honestly warned him that there was little chance of finding a room in an hotel.

Altogether it was a dismal outlook for his peace of mind and comfort of body. He felt annoyed with himself, now, for being rushed into this unpleasant mission by his forceful sister-in-law. Janette had always been a little too downright, and he did not doubt that Reggie had reached the limit of patience. When, on leaving Cambridge, he had gone to London she had not let him go alone, like a sensible mother, and enjoy young bachelor freedom. She had taken a flat there, and the boy found himself checked in and out, with all his movements observed. There was nothing about Reggie that required this maternal vigilance, it was simply that Mrs. Wyfold was one of those mothers who could not let go. Reggie being the only child, and herself a widow, he was her whole interest.

He had borne these shackles with exemplary fortitude, thought Dr. Wyfold. If he had one criticism to make of handsome young Reginald, who took the "Met" each morning to the Temple, clad in the barrister's regulation striped trousers, black coat, and black felt hat, with Brigg umbrella, and Hawes and Curtis tie, it was that the boy was a little too docile. He had good manners, an athlete's figure, hair that was perhaps a little too "arty" for Dr. Wyfold's taste, and a few odd enthusiasms such as the ballet, collecting china—he already had two hundred china dogs—and was very Left in his political views. After one or two very heated discussions, in which Dr. Wyfold discovered that nothing in the British Constitution was sacred to the young rebel, and everybody Dr. Wyfold respected belonged to "the old Gang," he had steered off the subject, reflecting that one could not put a shrewd head on adolescent shoulders. After all, what was the good of being young if one couldn't be wrong and be tolerated?

So politics had been left alone and Reggie had been encouraged to talk about the ballet—the architectonic significance of Holst, who Dr. Wyfold discovered was a composer and not an architect, and travel, for Reginald walked about Europe whenever and wherever he could. He had been to Moscow, of course, from which he had returned a little subdued, to Berlin from which he had returned a little apprehensive but impressed, to Rome, Prague, and Stockholm. With these experiences he was ready to govern England, with a recklessness of reform that made Dr. Wyfold tremble.

So far, and it would seem only thus far, he had not rushed his boat on the feminine rocks. If he succeeded in tracking down his nephew, who was the Circe he had to combat? Whoever she was, she was formidable if she had made a young man with an excellent future defy a mother to whom he had always been dutiful, break his career by deliberate absenteeism, and, over a period of five months, defy all entreaties and break all conventions.

For, of course, there was a woman in the case. There was nothing mental in the boy's letters. He was just uninformative and firm. He was happy, he had given up all idea of a legal career, he intended to live in the Tyrol. He would come back to England, later, on a visit to see his mother, but he had no intention of resuming his former life.

The devil of it was that Reginald was now almost a man. It was not a case of spanking or of cutting off his resources. He had just enough to make him financially defiant, and not enough, reflected Dr. Wyfold, to make him financially a catch. Clearly, the lady was interested in the boy and not the bank balance.

Dr. Wyfold felt a little ashamed of himself as he thought these things. Reggie was a nice clean lad. He might be having an intense, clean love affair. There was always a lot of nonsense in the Tyrol. London had had a spate of plays and films with bare-kneed boys whooping and yodelling, and low-bodiced, aproned girls singing *Salzkammergut*. It was all very pretty, but life in a chalet was much more serious a business than slapping thighs, and leaping about like mountain goats. The Austrian peasants, as Dr. Wyfold had seen them, were a weather-beaten folk with their heads well down in a tussle with the grim soil.

The doctor looked again with disapproval at his fellow passengers sprawling in their deck-chairs. Some of them were even now sporting sham edelweiss in green Austrian felt hats, revived from former excursions. One young man, who apparently could not wait to escape from his nationality, was already walking the deck in greasy leather shorts, with heavy nailed boots and parallel leather braces banded across his chest, with an embossed device of the Austrian eagle and the legend *Im Tyrol*. *Im Tyrol*, indeed! Fancy displaying those root-like knees in such a get-up. There was a cropped-haired girl trotting after him, with a rucksack and coarse stockings. They both had New Thought written over them. What did the real Tyrolers think of these English specimens?

Dr. Wyfold relit his pipe, and admired the beautiful evening, so preferable to the human scene. He must really cultivate more tolerance. Perhaps he was getting set. It would never do to start his curious mission with a closed mind.

Although Reggie did not know it, and should not know it yet awhile, Dr. Wyfold had left a large part of his modest fortune to him. Reggie was the favourite among his dozen nephews and nieces. There was nothing yet in his conduct to lessen confidence in the boy. He was a moral man, but he had a sympathetic outlook on the temptations of youth. Years and years ago, æons ago, temperamentally feeling, he had run off with a girl and married her in defiance of his own and her parents. It had been a happy marriage also, its only flaw being their childlessness. He had run off with an English girl, of his own class, of course. She had even a little money of her own, though he had never considered that part of it—but it was useful later.

If Reggie was having an affair with a peasant girl then the matter would not be difficult, but if she happened to be a knowledgeable woman of the world then it might be difficult. Or a widow? God forbid! When a lad in the early twenties got ensnared with a widow in the late thirties the battle became desperate. She had all her experience to draw on as well as mature charm.

In any case, if he succeeded in finding Reggie, no matter in what kind of affair, Dr. Wyfold made up his mind that he would not be shocked. That would get them nowhere. Dash it all, he was probably wronging the boy, owing to his mother's unsupported suspicions. He might be in the throes of a quite honourable obsession, one, even, that he would approve. No, he would not approve. He had a great distrust of marriage between persons of different nationality.

Had Dr. Wyfold really analysed this distrust he would have found it rooted in the silent conviction that no other race was quite as meritorious as the English. Frenchwomen had chic, but there was too much *l'amour* about them. The German women were solid—too solid, perhaps. The Italians, of course, were dangerous, they were designed for grand opera, to sing magnificently while dying of consumption or stabbing their lovers. The Spanish women were haughty and devastatingly lovely till they got fat. The Austrian women were often lovely—but *temperamentvoll*—yes, that was the word, thought Dr. Wyfold, searching through his scanty German vocabulary. If one had to marry a foreign woman, then a Scandinavian was perhaps the best—they were fair, cultivated, and lived in a cold climate which made them level-headed.

There remained American women. He knew little about them except what he read in the Press of the ostentatious lives of the Six Hundred, or Six Thousand, and of the high percentage of American-born wearers of British coronets, but it seemed to Dr. Wyfold that one did not marry an American woman, she married you, and soon tired of it.

The low dunes of Boulogne came into sight. They would be in within twenty minutes. Well, there would be a good dinner on the train, it was a French dining-car, and so he would escape English cod and boiled potatoes, mutton and Queen's pudding. And there would be a decent bottle of wine procurable. Then he would retire early to his bed, and enjoy a good read before going to sleep. There were always compensations.

When would he be back? The gladiolas were just now attaining their best bloom. He had tried some new varieties this year and wanted to see them. To-day was Wednesday. If he succeeded in tracing Reginald quickly then he could be back easily within a week. Unless, of course, the boy was distressed, and needed a short time to quieten him down before the return to England. In that event, perhaps, they might go to Vienna, or even Buda-Pest.

But it was foolish to think that Reginald would be neurasthenic or have gone "peculiar." The Wyfolds were very sane stock and never had trouble of that kind. On his mother's side, too, there was good stuff. Of course you could be too sound, according to modern theories, and the psychologists had found all sorts of new horrors, the Œdipus complex, just whatever that was, the inferiority complex, the mother fixation, and all sorts of preposterous kinks to explain mental aberrations. He had once listened in to a lecture by a famous Viennese psychiatrist who had told them a rigmarole about a countess who once a week had to milk a cow, because in her girlhood she had had a liaison with a young cowherd on her father's estate, and ever after she could only be tranquillized by—really, what preposterous stuff these charlatans got away with! He had angrily switched off the radio, regretting that he could not get at the sewer-minded psychiatrist.

No, there was nothing of that about the Wyfolds. They were all soundly normal—excepting an uncle who had led an unmentionable life in pre-war Hamburg and had been found in a low quarter with his head clubbed in. And perhaps Gerard Wyfold, his cousin, was a little odd, for at forty he had gone very High Church, thrown up a solicitor's practice, put on a long black skirt and sandals, and, as Brother Gerard, was now working himself to death in a Boys' Club in Dockland. But he was rather a noble fellow, unselfish and likeable despite his oddness.

Of all the other Wyfolds there was nothing to cause comment. Reginald's own history was sound. He had been a success at Radley. He had obtained his House colours for Rugby and had rowed in the College eight. At Cambridge he had been a leading light in the Amateur Dramatic Club, having made an excellent Hamlet in one production, and he had crowned his scholastic career with a First in History. At the Bar he was notably progressing, and was under the wing of a leading K.C. Yes, everything about young Reginald was sound—until this mysterious disappearance last Easter.

One thought now occurred to Dr. Wyfold. One really knew nothing about the lives of the young and they could be astonishingly secretive even while existing in the centre of a personal revolution. Was it possible that Reginald was not in a love affair in Austria, but that he had fled from an unhappy experience in England? That would explain the flight. It should have occurred to them before. He had heard a rumour of a youthful love affair while at Cambridge—a Don's daughter who had treated him in an off-hand manner that had resulted in a "nerve-storm." Was this another unhappy experience?

"Excuse me, but aren't you Dr. Wyfold?" said a near voice.

The doctor started, his reflections abruptly broken, and looked up. It was the creature in coarse stockings, with big boots and rucksack, who was speaking to him.

"Yes, I am," he said, coldly.

"I thought so!" exclaimed the young woman affably. "Philip! Philip!" she shouted. "I want to introduce my friend Philip Sayce."

"Good evening, sir!" said Mr. Sayce, of the leather shorts and braces, cheerfully.

Dr. Wyfold felt a prisoner. They both stood over him, their ruddy faces beaming at him as if he were a long-lost rich uncle.

"But—er—do I know you?" he asked.

"Yes—I'm Lydia Sharples from Wargrave. You've been to dine with us several times. You remember Reggie———"

Good heavens, if it wasn't Brigadier-General Sharples' daughter disguised in this get-up. He melted a little.

"And where are you going—like this?" he could not resist asking, looking from one to the other.

"To Austria. We're on a walking tour. We're going to Obergurgle. The name's always fascinated us, so we're going there!" laughed Lydia Sharples.

"You seem to be used to this sort of thing," said Dr. Wyfold, looking from one to the other in their drab brown kit. "Where's your alpenstock?"

"Oh, we're not as serious as that, sir—we're just wandervogels," replied the young man whose rude health was almost aggressive.

"Oh—I thought you tied a rope round your fiancée's waist and pulled her over the peaks," said Dr. Wyfold, thawing into a joke.

"Philip's not my fiancé," exclaimed Lydia Sharples, "There's no nonsense like that, we're just good friends who like walking tours. This is our third."

"Oh—I'm sorry!" said Dr. Wyfold, holding on to his reason. "Well, you appear to have a good time."

"Rather!" grinned the young man.

"I've not seen Reggie for months, where is he?" asked Lydia, pushing back a wisp of yellow hair.

"He's in Austria—I'm going to join him."

"Oh—how splendid! We might meet. Will you give me his address?" asked Lydia, enthusiastically.

Dr. Wyfold was trapped. Whatever could he say to this remorseless young woman?

"Er—well, I really don't know—he's going to meet me in Gmunden," said Dr. Wyfold, resorting to a harmless little lie. "After that I don't quite know where we're going."

"Hello—we're getting in," said Philip, as the harbour came into view.

"We'd better get ready for the scramble. We've no seats booked—we're travelling second, so I don't expect we'll see you again. Good-bye, Dr. Wyfold," said Lydia.

"Good-bye, sir," said her companion.

And then Dr. Wyfold did the oddest thing. It wasn't in his mind, and yet he did it.

"Why don't you come and have dinner with me on the train?" he asked.

The girl's face beamed.

"That would be lovely! We can't rise to anything like that. We've only got sandwiches, but they'll do for breakfast."

"Thank you," said the young man.

"Then we'll see you again!" cried Lydia, and went off with her companion.

A strange world. Here was General Sharples' girl, looking like nothing on earth, walking about the Tyrol with a young man to whom she was not engaged. They probably slept together as part of the fun. No, he must not be a nasty-minded old man. In his day, of course, if any girl had gone off with a boy like that there would have been no doubt whatever, and she would have been finished.

But things were very different to-day. His cousin, Brother Gerard, told him that young folks to-day were really quite moral.

There were no mysteries about sex, as in the old days. Boys and girls danced and swam and hiked together, and went out swinging their legs on motor-bikes, or jammed together in little two-seaters, and proximity did not infer incontinence. There was something very frank about Lydia Sharples. There was no doubt she could look after herself, and she was highly preferable to the lip-sticked dolls with scarlet nails and smoky complexions.

The fact was he really didn't know the younger generation. Well, having that pair to dinner might educate him a little.

They were in harbour. Dr. Wyfold got up and engaged an excited French porter to carry his bag.

CHAPTER XIII

ELISE VOGEL, OF FELDKIRCH

I

ELISE VOGEL had always been told that great cities were wicked, and of these Paris was the wickedest. In all the eighteen years of her life she had never seen a great city, so she had no means of judging, and she hardly knew, indeed, what constituted wickedness, such as the great cities produced. She had never seen any place larger than her native Feldkirch at the foot of the Vorarlberg Alps, a typical small Austrian town of some forty thousand inhabitants, dominated by its high castle of Schaltenburg. Through the gorge, which opened to the Tal where Feldkirch lay at the foot of the mountains, flowed the grey Ill to join in its valley, five miles distant, the Rhine, which divided Switzerland and this western extremity of Austria.

As her mother often said, Elise was only just Austrian, for Frau Vogel had come from Buchs, eleven miles away, just over the Swiss frontier, to which Anton Vogel, a carpenter, had journeyed once a week to court her. And what a pity it was that Anton Vogel had not taken Swiss nationality, as his father-in-law had urged him, and settled down in Buchs, a partner in the family wood-joinery business, for then, as Elise's mother never failed to point out, not only would Elise have been a Swiss, but she would have possessed a father and four brothers.

For Elise's father was killed in the last weeks of the War, in the Austrian retreat from Schluderbach, and two of her brothers lay buried on Italian soil near Monte Tofana. Frau Vogel, at the close of the War, found herself a widow, with

215

two sons surviving, and a child, Elise, about to be born. How different would have been Frau Vogel's fate if she had been living across that frontier, only a few miles distant!

Elise's two brothers carried on the sawmill that Anton Vogel left behind him. For a few years they agreeably supported their mother and the infant Elise. Then one of the brothers married, and moved off to a business of his own in a near-by village. The household resources were further diminished, and Josef, who remained, was inclined to be lazy.

There was poverty in the Vogel home. At fourteen little Elise went to work in an hotel laundry. In summer she was fully employed, but in winter, when the visitors did not come, the laundry was closed. Her brother Josef always seemed to regard this as her fault, and grumbled about keeping idlers in the house. Frau Vogel defended Elise, but she was afraid of Josef, who was rough and ill-tempered. He might at any time seize the family business for himself and turn them out, so he had to be humoured.

Then, one day, he brought home a wife, who proved not unkind to Elise and her mother, but she, too, was afraid of Josef's temper. The women shrank before him, being economically dependent upon him.

When, therefore, Elise saw a way of escape she jumped at the opportunity, despite her fears. She had done some laundry work for Madame Lebrun who had stayed at the hotel where she worked. Madame Lebrun lived in Paris, and, taking a fancy to the robust country girl, offered her a position as second maid in her Paris home. She had foreseen that Elise was sturdy, a tireless worker, and could be obtained cheap. The language difficulty was not insuperable; moreover, Madame Lebrun talked German.

Elise told her mother breathlessly of this wonderful offer.

When the season ended she would again be out of work, and there would be the customary reproaches of Josef. Frau Vogel put on her best clothes and went to interview the kind French lady. It was quickly arranged that Elise should go to Paris in the first week of October.

Was it all a dream, wondered Elise in the three weeks that followed after Madame Lebrun's departure. "You'll probably never hear from her again," said her brother Josef, not able to suppress a sneer despite his own hope that she should not be a burden on the house in the coming winter.

But one morning there was an envelope with a French stamp on it, and with trembling fingers Frau Vogel opened it, while Elise stood breathless at her side. Madame Lebrun had kept her word. Elise was to leave for Paris on the fifth, and her ticket was enclosed. The chauffeur would meet her at the station. The chauffeur! Then Madame Lebrun was a great lady. She had not had an expensive room at the hotel, but anyone who kept a car with a chauffeur must be rich.

There were four hectic days during which Elise slept badly, from excitement. Her mother sewed and made extra clothes. Even Josef provided twenty schillings towards the things she needed. At last the great day arrived, and Elise, very pale, and tearful at the final moment, set off on her wonderful journey to Paris.

There were a dozen neighbours and friends to see her off. Josef actually left his work to carry the small tin trunk that held her belongings. Elise's round ruddy face shone in the crisp October air. Her blonde hair was tightly plaited in two long pigtails. She wore a black straw hat with a big black silk bow, her Sunday hat, and carried a large umbrella. Her high laced-up boots hurt her a little for they were new and squeaked. As soon as the train drew out of the station she sat back in the corner of the third-class carriage and cried. She was really frightened now, and excitement no longer sustained her.

The chauffeur, a gruff old man who had been a coachman, met her at Paris. With scarcely a word he put Elise and her trunk in the car. About half an hour later she followed him through a back gate, down some steps into the kitchen of Madame Lebrun's house in Auteuil. There she met the cook, a shrewish woman of fifty, and a maid, a woman of about thirty. Her bedroom was down in the basement, near all the domestic offices, and the rooms were so dark that the lights were on all day. Two days passed before she was sent upstairs, at Madame Lebrun's orders.

"Well, Elise, I hope you are happy?"

"Yes, Madame, thank you," whispered Elise, scarcely daring to look up at her employer in this boudoir of dazzling splendour. Never had Elise imagined such a room. It had silk curtains, thick rugs, Chinese screens, a glass chandelier, great bowls of flowers, a chaise-longue—with Madame lying on it in a blue silk kimono, a Pekinese dog huddled at her feet.

The cook had said that Madame was up to the ears in debt, and one day they would get no more meat as the butcher was tired of asking for his money. But with so much splendour around her how could such a thing be true? Madame's rings alone must be worth a fortune.

Elise lived well. The cook and the chauffeur had prodigious appetites, and, as they gorged, Elise's face burned with the dreadful things they said about their employer's meanness. For the first few weeks Elise could not follow what they said, but they took great pains to make her understand that Madame Lebrun was the meanest woman on earth, that she was grossly extravagant in regard to herself, and that she had nagged and worried her husband to death. Elise could not believe all this. The waste of food in the kitchen was terrible.

Madame Lebrun seemed to have most of her meals out. She never rose till noon, when she had coffee and rolls. At four o'clock she drove out in the Bois, at six she received friends, and at eight she usually went out, wonderfully dressed.

"She goes to the old General," said the parlourmaid.

"What old General?" asked Elise.

"What old General!" chorused the cook and chauffeur, ironi. cally.

"Her dear uncle," said the chauffeur.

Then they all laughed, and Elise was left to wonder why.

II

One day in December, Madame Lebrun's nephew, the Comte Pierre de Clarens, came to stay. He was a St. Cyr cadet, a tall, slender youth, with dark merry eyes, and a neat head and figure. Elise thought she had never seen anyone so beautiful before. His manner, voice, gestures, everything about him, were fascinating. Madame Lebrun doted on him. He came twice a year to visit her. His father was dead, and his mother, Madame's sister, lived at Étretat.

One morning, the parlourmaid having sprained her ankle, Elise was sent up to the third floor with Comte Pierre's coffee and rolls. He had a suite consisting of a bedroom and bathroom adjoining.

After tapping timidly, a drowsy voice told her to enter. The room was almost dark, the shutters being closed. Putting down the tray, Elise went to open them.

"Turn on my bath, Marie," said the Comte, his black head deep in the pillow.

Elise went into the bathroom, and turned on the water, waiting until the bath was full.

"It is ready, m'sieur," she said, coming out.

The youth in the bed turned, looked, and sat up.

"Hello, who are you?" he asked, his dark eyes examining her.

"Elise, m'sieur."

"Are you German?"

"No, Austrian, m'sieur."

"Ah, I like the Austrians. How long have you been here?"

"Two months, m'sieur."

"Where do you come from? Pass me my dressing-gown."

"Feldkirch—in Vorarlberg, m'sieur."

"I know it," said the Comte eagerly. "I've been ski-ing at Zürs. Glorious!"

He got out of bed, and wrapped a crimson dressing-gown over his blue silk pyjamas. He ran a white hand through his thick black hair. Never, thought Elise, looking at his bare throat, had she seen skin so white and lovely. Perhaps he saw the wonder in her eyes, for he looked at her keenly, and smiled.

"Come here!" he said, kindly.

"M'sieur?" asked Elise, nervously.

"*Mon Dieu,* you're pretty!" he said. With the easiest manner in the world he took hold of her with a swiftness that paralysed her, and he kissed her, soundly.

"Don't be frightened," he said, laughing, and holding her at arm's length. "Have you never been kissed?"

"No, m'sieur," answered Elise, trembling.

"No! *Mon Dieu!*" he exclaimed. Then, his face suddenly serious, he added, "Run along now."

Dismissed, she found herself outside the room, breathless, almost in tears, trembling. It was at once the most frightening and wonderful thing she had ever known.

The next morning when again she had to go up to his room she wanted to refuse, and yet was afraid to do so because a reason would have been demanded. With a thumping heart she paused outside the bedroom. It must not happen again. She would stop him, somehow.

She entered, opened the shutters, and proceeded to run the bath water. He had said no word to her, and seemed to be sleeping.

"The bath is ready, m'sieur," she said, near the door.

He looked up from the pillow, glanced at the coffee on the side-table, and sat up.

"Good morning, Elise. Come here and be kissed," he said, smiling at her.

"No, m'sieur," she replied, by the door.

"Don't be silly, Elise. I want to kiss you. I like kissing you— and you like to be kissed."

"No, m'sieur."

"Very well. You don't want to be kissed. Good-bye. *Auf Wiedersehen, meine Liebling!*" he said, laughing, and showing his beautiful white teeth.

She closed the door. Outside, on the landing, she stood still for a moment, her heart bounding. She wanted him to kiss her. His voice, his smile, his touch, made her senses reel. All yesterday she had thought of no one else. But it was wrong. He could not love her. She must not love him.

Fortunately Marie's ankle got better. Elise no more took the Count Pierre his coffee.

III

One night something awakened Elise. She opened her eyes and was surprised to find the electric light was on over her bed. She sat up, and then gave a sharp cry.

There, seated on a chair, was Count Pierre. He was eating a large piece of cake, and looking at her with an amused, mocking expression. He was in full uniform, very slim and splendid, with shining braid and buttons. He was still wearing his regimental shako with its white and red plumes, pushed slightly back over his brow. His dark blue cadet's cape, unbuttoned at the throat, rested loosely on his shoulders. As her eyes opened wide, he rose and gravely saluted, the cake in his left hand. Then he seated himself again.

"Bon soir, ma petite," he said, munching.

Elise could not speak, fear and surprise paralysing her.

"Now don't be afraid. I was very hungry, so I came down to the larder, and being down here I thought I would like to see how pretty you were in your little bed. If you make a scene, and wake anyone—which isn't necessary, for they're a long way up in the attics—I'll be in disgrace. You wouldn't do that to poor Pierre, would you?"

Elise did not answer. She could not.

"What big eyes you've got, Grandmamma!" laughed Count Pierre. "No, I'm not the Big Bad Wolf. Don't be frightened, Elise."

He ate the cake, and brushed some crumbs off his lap with his gloves.

"Now lie down, *ma petite,* and I'll kiss you good night," he said, rising, and looking down at her with smiling eyes.

She lay down, still speechless, trembling.

Count Pierre removed his hat. Very gently he tucked the sheets over her shoulders. Then, stooping, he kissed her brow. As he bent near to her she could smell the eau-de-Cologne with which he dressed his sleek black hair.

His hands picked up one of her plaits, which was outside the bedclothes, and, holding it a moment, he drew it across his throat and made a comic grimace, as if he were strangling himself. Then, kissing it as it lay across the palm of his hand, he tucked it away under the sheets. *"Bonne nuit, mon petit ange,"* he said, quietly.

Raising himself, he replaced his shako, and went to the door. There, turning and facing her, he drew himself up, saluted solemnly, and then, with a dazzling smile, blew her a kiss and switched out the light.

She heard the door close, and, above her own heartbeats, his soft steps fading down the corridor.

IV

All the next day she could think of no one except Count Pierre. Soon after noon she saw him go out with Madame Lebrun. He wore his greatcoat and, as he paused in the hall, shako in hand, while his aunt went out to the car, his eye caught Elise's and he gave her a warm smile. She watched him go down the steps into the small courtyard, and his elegant slim figure in the greatcoat and plumed shako, and his youthful handsome face had wholly captured her heart. When she had recovered from her fears last night she wondered what he thought of her, staring at him with frightened eyes, and mute. There had been nothing in his behaviour that had not been gallant, except his intrusion. And with what a captivating air he had carried off the situation!

But he must not come again. Unfortunately there was no key to the lock on her door. She thought of asking for one and then feared to lest it should provoke awkward questions. To-night she would prop a chair against the door. But to-night he would not come. He might never come again, it had been just a caprice. It was so very dangerous, for if Madame Lebrun ever came to hear of it she would be dismissed at once. And where would she go then? She could not go home, with the stigma of light behaviour on her. Josef would shout and spread the story all over the village.

If the Count came again she would have to tell Madame Lebrun. But that would get him into severe trouble.

"How long is the Comte going to stay?" she asked the cook that afternoon.

"Whatever's that got to do with you?" demanded the thin-lipped woman, snappishly.

"Oh, she's in love with him," laughed the parlourmaid. "I've hardly had a word out of her all day. I knew that would happen. He likes them young!"

Elise's cheeks burned red, and tears of indignation filled her eyes.

"Has he been kissing you?" asked the cook, looking intently at Elise across the kitchen table. "There's nothing to cry about, but don't let him come playing around. All these young swells are alike, charming until they get what they want, and then—*pouf!*"

"If he bothers you, do what I did—slap his face!" declared the parlourmaid, a woman of thirty with a long thin nose.

"I don't believe he ever did bother you," said Elise, sniffing through her tears, and unable to endure this charge against her hero.

The cook and the parlourmaid glared at her.

"You'll get what's coming to you, my fine young lady!" cried the cook. "Now, hurry up with those plates!"

But Elise, busy at the sink, collapsed into a chair, and, burying her face in her apron, sobbed bitterly.

v

He did not come to her for two nights, and then on the third night, it must have been in the early hours of the morning, she was awakened by him teasing her face with his gloves as he smiled down at her.

"*Bon soir!*" he said, softly.

"*Bon soir, m'sieur,*" she replied, a little fearfully, her nose just above the bed sheets.

He smoothed the hair back from her brow, and seating himself on the bed, facing her, began to play with her plaits.

"I've seen nothing of you for two days—can't you get Nosey to sprain her other ankle, and bring me my coffee?" he asked, laughing. "My aunt has been telling me how pretty you looked in your native dress, and I could have told her how pretty you look in bed—but that would not do, would it? Give me your hand, Elise. How old are you?"

"Eighteen, m'sieur," whispered Elise, her heart beating wildly as he held her hand in his. She noticed his finger had a ruby ring on it.

"Eighteen! *Mon Dieu*—you look like a baby. I'm twenty, and years and years older than you!"

He raised her hand, palm upwards, and kissed it.

"What a pretty little hand you have!" he said, and ran his fingers up her arm until his hand touched her neck. Then, leaning forward, he placed both hands behind her shoulders and raised her.

"Blue eyes!" he said, gazing into her eyes.

His face was so near she could smell his hair, and she noticed how white and even were the small teeth between his red lips. His eyes glowed black as he bent over her. Suddenly his mouth pressed hers, and for a long while he held her so that she could scarcely breathe. Her hands met behind his head, first in an attempt to push him away, and then, succumbing to the sensation of his lips on hers, they rested there. At last he raised his face.

"You are lovely!" he breathed, his eyes burning with ecstasy. "Don't—don't be afraid, Elise. I only want to love you, *mon ange.*"

"No—no. Go away, m'sieur," she cried, trying to withdraw herself from him. "It's very wrong."

"But why? Isn't it nice to be loved?" he asked, earnestly.

"You cannot love me. Oh, please, please go," she cried.

"Very well," he said, sitting up. "Can't you love me a little?" She did not answer. Then he saw her mouth tremble.

"My sweet child—you do love me. But you are afraid?"

She nodded, speechless. He sat a moment and gazed at her with his beautiful eyes and dark long lashes. Then, looking down on the bed, and making a pattern with his finger as he talked, he said:

"I suppose you think it's wrong of me to make love to you— a servant in my aunt's house? We're young, and you are very, very pretty, and I cannot help thinking about you—and perhaps you think of me?" he asked, pausing.

Elise nodded.

"And when I have left here——"

"Are you leaving?" asked Elise.

"The day after to-morrow, yes—I shall still think of you, for you are unlike all other girls I know, with your sweet little face, your funny little accent, your two pigtails. Bless me, don't cry, Elise!" he said, breaking off.

For something in his words had touched the fount of tears, and she began to sob.

He gathered her up and held her against him, his lips resting on her fair head while he smoothed her hair with his hand. He let her cry for a while, and then, taking a fine handkerchief from his pocket, he began to wipe her face.

"Then you do love me, Elise?"

"Yes, m'sieur," she sobbed.

"Say 'Yes, Pierre.' "

"Yes, Pierre."

She looked at him, with eyes shining through her tears. The sight of her face with its expression of adoration stirred the youth sitting on the bed, and taking her impulsively in his arms, he showered kisses on her wet cheeks, her eyes, her brow and hair.

"Elise! I love you! I love you!" he avowed, with trembling voice.

BOOK II

THEY ARRIVE

Chapter XIV

MR. FANNING'S PLOT

Soon after the Express had left Boulogne, and turned inland from the yellow sand dunes, the dining-car waiter went along the corridor tinkling his little bell announcing dinner.

Mr. Henry Fanning, who had not eaten much lunch, went forward to the dining-car. He was one of those highly strung people who cannot eat when about to set forth on a journey. In his childhood, when the great day came on which the annual holiday began, he always felt bilious with anxiety and excitement, and it was quite in vain that his mother exhorted him to make a good breakfast. He had never grown out of the mood of apprehension before journeying, although in a full life he had travelled all over the earth. Like his mother, Alice also urged him to eat well before a journey.

Now, the Channel crossing made, and the first plunge taken into the journey, he felt more tranquil and extremely hungry. Among the many disquieting features of his highly strung temperament, indigestion was not one of them. He enjoyed his food, and especially French cooking. He would eat to-night in France, breakfast in Switzerland and lunch in Austria. To-night was the most trustworthy of all times in regard to the quality of the menu. He would also have a good bottle of wine and drown his despair at being thrust out of England.

The dining-car attendant ushered him into a single seat. A young woman of about twenty-eight sat opposite. Had she been French or any other nationality but English he would have bowed, but with the Englishman's constitutional shyness in the presence of his countrymen he sat down with averted eyes, and closely studied the menu.

It was excellent, and turning to the wine list he chose a bottle of Corton to go with the filet-Châteaubriant on the menu. He ate his soup in silence. With the fish he still continued to avoid the eyes of his companion at the table. But when the wine waiter came along and opened his bottle and cleared a space for his wine glass by picking up the young lady's, he felt he ought to say something.

"These tables are rather small," he commented, smiling, when the waiter had gone.

The young woman, who had pleasant features and much character in her face, agreed on the matter.

"I wondered," she added, with a twinkle in her eyes, "if you were one of those people who can travel a thousand miles without talking to anyone."

A little startled by this statement, Fanning laughed nervously.

"On the contrary, my wife is always scolding me for making myself a nuisance by talking to everyone," he said. "I live by exercising an insatiable curiosity."

He raised his glass and sipped the wine now the steak had come.

"This Corton is really excellent—won't you drink a glass of it with me?" he asked, happy now the ice was broken.

"Oh, thank you—yes, I think I will," answered the young woman, with instant frankness.

After a little semaphoring he got the waiter to bring another wine glass, and filled it. They were now on excellent terms.

"Are you going far—the whole thousand miles of the uncommunicative Englishman?" he asked.

She laughed, revealing excellent teeth. He noticed, as she raised her glass, a wedding-ring.

"Almost the whole of the thousand," she answered. "To Vienna, actually."

"Oh—so am I," he said. "Is this your first visit?"

"No—I lived there for two years. You see, I am Austrian."

He stared at her for a moment.

"I'd have sworn you were English," he said. "You have no accent."

"I'm English by birth—I'm married to an Austrian," she answered. "You're Mr. Fanning, aren't you?"

He gave her a sharp, startled look.

"Oh, don't be afraid!" she laughed. "I'm not one of your fans. I don't read novels—so I shan't ask you for your autograph. It's singular you should come to my table."

"Why?" he asked, somewhat nettled. It wasn't her table anyhow, and he had been put there by the attendant. And although he was relieved at the thought that the young lady would not want to know how he wrote his books, he was a little hurt by the fact that she had no desire to read them. Anyhow, she was a young woman of character, and her frankness interested him.

"Well, this morning my mother made herself a nuisance by ringing you up."

"Mrs. Lessing?"

"Yes—that's my mother. She told me afterwards. What makes her think I can be of the slightest interest to you, or that I'm not capable of travelling alone, I can't think. She was so thrilled to find you were on the same train, poor dear, that she just had to speak to you."

"Aren't you a little hard on your mother—perhaps she was a little concerned about you?" asked Fanning, but without much conviction. He felt he could not let this ruthless young woman go unchallenged in her opinion.

"Oh, I know my dear mother. She loves to talk to a lion."

"Am I a lion?"

"Don't be so modest. You know you're a lion. Hundreds of women think you're *it*, Mr. Fanning."

"It?" echoed Fanning, resentfully.

"The man of genius who really understands us poor women!" she replied with a laugh.

"If you've not read my books you don't know whether I do or don't," he retorted.

"Does it matter? They all think you understand them—and that helps them."

"Oh—then you admit I'm of some use?" asked Fanning, a little annoyed.

"Don't be angry with me, Mr. Fanning. You must be a really nice man to give me a glass of this very good wine, for you know, of course, that no woman knows anything about wine, or has a palate for it. But I'm enjoying it."

He laughed with her. This frankness had a tonic quality.

"If I remember rightly your mother said you were going out to join your husband?" asked Fanning.

"Yes—I am. And you—if it's not impertinent," asked his companion. "Are you travelling for pleasure or business?"

Fanning looked hard into her alert eyes.

"You see before you, *gnädige Frau*—" he began, and paused.

"Bruck's my name—Helen Bruck," she said.

"—a very wretched man. I've been pushed out of my house by my family, and sent forth across Europe in search of a plot."

"What plot?" asked Frau Bruck. "I've been living in a hotbed of plots. I can't imagine anyone deliberately looking for one."

"Ah—that shows how little you know of a writer's life. After thirty years of fairly successful authorship the wells run dry. I can't think of a plot; and my family fear I'm now neurasthenic. They have prescribed a dose of travel. I'd much rather remain at home, but they swear it's bad for me. So now I'm going to Vienna, first, in the hope of finding a plot, though I've no idea how."

"But surely you know enough people and hear enough stories to give you a dozen plots?"

"Unfortunately it never works quite like that. The plot your friend is quite sure is so excellent proves of no use to you, for you don't see it as he does—there must be developments and sequence—a *dénouement*, unless, like Proust, you are merely concerned with psychological reactions—and I'm not that kind of writer. But don't let me bore you."

Frau Bruck smiled back at him.

"It's funny, isn't it? I fear I was rude to you just now. Do you know why?" she asked, scraping some crumbs on the cloth with her cheese knife. He noticed she had very thin, white hands, with some beautiful rings. "I thought you were a man who was completely happy, a man to whom success and every good thing had come without much effort. You see, I really know quite a lot about you. You worship your wife and your son and grandson; you have a host of friends who admire you. You've had a wonderfully varied life all over the world, you're famous and comfortably off, and not old. I hear my mother talk about you and your books, and lots of my friends rush to hear you and look at you whenever you speak—and I can't help being jealous of you!"

"Of me?" exclaimed Fanning, astonished by this frank young woman. "Why on earth should you be jealous of me? You're young, and pretty, and probably happily married, and you've——"

She interrupted him.

"You've no idea why I'm on this train, have you?" she asked. "No?"

"I'm going to see my husband, who is coming out of jail."

She uttered the sentence very simply, and only her solemn eyes showed that she had made any unusual statement.

"Yes," she went on, moving the knife backwards and forwards over the cloth. "My husband was sentenced to death for murder. The sentence was commuted to life imprisonment, and now he has been pardoned."

For a moment or so Fanning had nothing to say. In all his experience of life in many countries this was the first time that a pretty young woman had told him that her husband was a murderer.

"Was he guilty?" he asked, when at last he spoke.

The attendant came, and he ordered coffee for both of them. She accepted a cigarette and he lit it for her. There was not the slightest embarrassment in her manner. As the wife of a murderer she seemed very self-possessed.

"You remember the death of Dollfuss?" she asked.

"Of course—his assassination in the Chancellery?"

"His murder," corrected Frau Bruck.

"Yes—it was a foul business," agreed Fanning. "Poor little Dollfuss."

"My husband was one of his murderers," said Frau Bruck, unemotionally.

Fanning put down his coffee-cup and stared at his fair companion.

"Are you saying this seriously?" he asked.

Her eyes met his calmly.

"Quite seriously," she answered. "My husband has been pardoned by the Government. He imagines he is going to resume our old life when he comes out of prison next Friday. But I——"

She paused, and carefully took the ash off her cigarette.

"And—and you?" asked Fanning, breathlessly.

"I shall tell him that the idea of living with him fills me with horror. I am a Catholic. If he had been hanged I should be free, but now, in the eyes of the Church, I must remain his wife, though he is a murderer. But I will never, never live with him again. That is why I am sitting here now. I am going to tell him that. Perhaps then he will realize at last that there is someone who doesn't regard him as a patriot and hero."

There was bitterness in her voice, and Fanning wondered a little at this young woman who could follow such a resolute course. Had she ever loved him? Perhaps the question in his mind was visible to her, for, without his speaking, she went on:

"You're wondering, perhaps, if I ever loved Max? We were always very happy together, except for one thing. I always knew he was a little mad on the subject of politics. I love the Austrians, but that seems to be their disease. It probably comes from the frightful times they have passed through. The young Austrians won't leave politics alone. They work themselves up into a frenzy. You can't imagine what living in an Austrian family means. They are kind, delightful people, but at any moment a bomb may fall. Rudi joins the Schutzbund, Anton is a Socialist, Friedrich is a Heimwehr, Otto is a Nazi. They argue, they threaten, mother is in tears, the sisters plead, the father asserts his authority—and the family peace is wrecked. We've been spared that in England—so far, and when I hear some of our

would-be dictators at home I wish they could see the private
havoc as well as the public tyranny that follows. Am I wearying
you with all this?"

"On the contrary—it is all frightfully interesting to me," replied Fanning, earnestly. "May I ask how you came to marry
your husband?"

Frau Bruck looked at her hands for a while. Then, waiting
until the roar of a tunnel had subsided, she spoke. The lights of
a small town twinkled in the falling night through the dining-
car windows.

"This line has memories for me," she said, looking out of the
window. "As you know, after we leave Bâle to-morrow morning this train climbs up the valley of the Ill, and at Langen it
plunges into the Arlberg Tunnel. At Langen you get out to take
the sleigh ride over the Flexen Pass——"

"I know it—to Zürs for the ski-ing?" said Fanning, eagerly,
memories of that wonderful ride over the snow up the precipitous
mountain-side evoked by the name of Langen.

"Ah, you've been! Four years ago I went for the first time
with some friends. It was my first winter-sports holiday. You
know how it goes to your head!" said Frau Bruck. "There's
something in that air that carries all your sensations to a higher
plane—you're gods."

She paused, as if to savour the memory of that holiday. "I
met there an Austrian ski-ing instructor, he taught me to ski. He
was twenty-three, I was twenty-five. We fell in love. Everything
about us was exhilarating. I don't think that one is ever quite
normal at those high altitudes. We simply ignored the usual
obstacles. He was a Catholic and I was Protestant, he was a lawyer, just beginning, with no practice, and taught ski-ing to make
pocket money during the law vacations. Max was very handsome, in that blond sun-tanned manner that captivates my sex,

with a wonderful smile and infectious good spirits. We were deliriously happy. At the end of my holiday, prolonged from two weeks to six, we were engaged without either of us consulting our people. I'm sure no one could have been more in love than we were. When we parted I promised to take my mother out to Vienna, where he lived, to meet his people. That was in March, and in June my mother went with me, quite stunned by it all, poor soul. All her fears and doubts I swept aside, and when she met Max he completely conquered her. The whole family was charming. They were tradespeople, fairly comfortable. Max had two sisters, and a brother, a year older. The old folks were dears. I had a small income. Max was earning nothing yet, but we decided we could manage. Mother gallantly gave me a small allowance. We got married, and took a tiny flat in Augustiner-strasse."

She was interrupted by the attendant who came with the bill and his partitioned tray of money. The car was emptying.

"Oughtn't we to go?" asked Frau Bruck, looking down the car.

"No—we're not the last, and we can sit on. You can't break off and leave me with half a story," said Fanning.

Calling the attendant he ordered more coffee. "You were happy?" he asked.

"Very, very," affirmed Frau Bruck. "But, as I have told you, we were living in a ferment of politics, and the Bruck family were all up to the neck in it. None of them agreed with another. You can't imagine the scenes that took place. We would go to his home to dine with his people. Then half-way through the meal someone would mention Seipel or Fey or Starhemberg, and immediately the battle began. Father Bruck was a Christian Socialist, Hans, the brother, was a Communist, Max was a Nazi, his sister Maria and her husband were National Socialists, his other sister's fiancé was in the Heimwehr,

and later was pro-Dollfuss. I couldn't, of course, very well dis-
tinguish between all the different parties—there seemed to be a
different one each week. You can't imagine the fervour and
venom they all showed. It was simply bedlam. Max, I discovered, was a passionate disciple of Herr Schircklgruber——"

"Who's that?" interrupted Fanning.

"I'm giving Hitler his real Austrian name, before he changed
it when he went into Bavaria. I didn't guess, however, how
deeply attached Max was to the Nazi organization over the
frontier and in Munich. At the time I'm speaking of he was in
the Heimwehr. I never did get all the various cross-currents of
the parties clear. Roughly, there was a coalition of the various
Socialists, there was a block of German Nationals and Austrian
Nazis, and both these groups were equally bitter against the
Government. I was always hearing about a threatened *Putsch*,
someone was always going to wipe out someone. Max was for
ever talking of the Schutzbund, the forces of the Social Democrats, and that they would have to be tackled. He came home one
day in a Heimwehr officer's uniform.

"Well, the *Putsch* came, and the world knows how Vienna was
drenched in blood, with the Heimwehr bombarding the Socialists
in their model housing blocks. They say Italy was behind it,
that the Italian price for supporting Dollfuss against the German
Nazis was the cleaning up of the Social Democrats in Vienna, and
that Dollfuss joined up with Starhemberg's Fascist Heimwehr.
The fact remains that thousands of young men in the great blocks
of houses built by the Socialists fought a terrible battle with the
Heimwehr. I went to Floridsdorf myself, and was deafened by
the rattle of machine-gun fire. Then, as you know, the Government brought up artillery and shelled the Socialists. I saw some
of those houses afterwards. They had been splendidly built—
models of housing reform—and now they were utterly wrecked

with all the people's furniture blown to smithereens. Half the
people in that bombardment didn't know what it was all about.
It was terrible, terrible!"

"What were you doing in Floridsdorf—it's across the river,
isn't it?" asked Fanning.

Frau Bruck's mouth tightened for a moment, then she looked
straight at the novelist.

"What was I doing in Floridsdorf, you ask? I was there because I received a telephone message from an anonymous person
telling me that Max was in the block of flats the Heimwehr were
shelling!"

"But I don't understand—wasn't your husband a Heimwehr
officer? What was he doing in the Social Democrats' strong-
hold?" asked Fanning, puzzled.

Frau Bruck gave a short, bitter laugh.

"You may well ask. I didn't believe the message at first. I
went to Floridsdorf, but, of course, I could get nowhere near the
Gemeindehäuser they were shelling. The defenders were firing
up on the roof, and the troops kept us away. That night Max did
not come in at the usual hour. He was missing for two days. The
second night I was aroused by a hammering at the door. I got up,
and as soon as I opened it four Heimwehr men walked in, and
while two of them questioned me the other two searched the flat.
Max, they told me, had been among the Socialists who had
surrendered after the bombardment, and was under arrest for
treason. When they had gone I dressed and went round to his
parents. I found them in a terrible state. Hans had been arrested
that morning, Maria's husband had been killed in the fighting,
in one of the buildings. They knew nothing about Max."

Frau Bruck paused, and a sad smile came into her face.

"If only I could write, I have a plot as thick as any you could
write, Mr. Fanning," she said.

"Yes—yes, you have, please go on," he said, impatiently. "What happened to your husband? Had he betrayed the Heim-wehr?"

"No—worse."

"Worse?"

"Yes—he had betrayed me," said Frau Bruck, quietly.

She glanced round, as if apprehensive that someone might be listening. The train slowed down. All around them lights sprang up in the dark night. Crossing over a bridge they looked down upon a street, well lit, with traffic. Across the face of a cinema blazed the title, *Madame ne veut-pas d'enfants.* They began to enter a maze of railway sidings.

"Amiens," said Fanning, peering out. "He had betrayed you —how?" he asked, going back to her last remark. The restaurant car was half empty. The attendant at the far end was doing his accounts.

"On the third day after Max's disappearance I got a message from him, imploring me to go and see him in the Police Barracks where he was held a prisoner. Then I heard his extraordinary story. It seems that for two years he had had a mistress, a seam-stress, a girl of twenty-two who lived in one of those housing settlements. When he learned that the Heimwehr were going to bombard the block—which shows how deliberate it was—he rushed round to warn her. While he was there the firing began and he was trapped, and had to remain while the duel went on between the Schutzbund and the Heimwehr. He swore to me that he had seen nothing of the girl since we had been engaged. He now implored me to go and see Prince Starhemberg, whom I knew slightly, and explain to him the circumstances and get him freed from a charge of treason."

"You went?"

"Yes. I was terribly hurt, but I believed Max—I do now.

Also I was still deeply in love with him despite all his folly. I thought this would make him steer clear of political intrigue for the rest of his life. I saw the unhappy girl, she corroborated Max's story, and I took her along with me to Prince Starhemberg. He saw me at once, and was very understanding. Max was released the next morning. He cried like a baby, and his nerves seemed shaken to pieces. He couldn't get out of his mind the terrible things he had seen in that settlement during the bombardment. Some of the Socialists found him in the girl's room and took him out to shoot him, but the girl fought for his life and saved him, saying he had risked everything to warn her."

"What an astonishing story!" exclaimed Fanning.

"I haven't finished yet—worse was to follow," said Frau Bruck. She paused as a rather extraordinary-looking couple walked down the car, followed by an elderly man. The couple were in hiking kit, untidy, and bursting with good health. They banged along between the tables, noisily talking over their shoulders to the man behind as they left the car.

"How do people like that get the money to travel—why don't they use it for going to the hairdresser and the dressmaker?" asked Frau Bruck, petulantly. "They're probably going to walk across Austria—we see a good many like that and it doesn't make me proud of my compatriots."

Fanning laughed, and lit another cigarette.

"Oh, I don't mind—they're young and enjoying themselves. Probably quite intelligent when you come to know them—they're passing through the Chelsea stage, that's all," he said, a little surprised at her intolerance. "But please go on with your story. You said worse was to follow—I can't imagine what it is."

"All that I've told you happened in February. The Government wiped out the Socialists, in fulfilment of Italian orders, the Government settled down again and little Dollfuss resumed his flirtation with Italy—for which I can't blame him. Italy was the only card he could play against the Nazis, who stopped at nothing. They poured propaganda over us, they spied on Austria, tapped its telephones, bribed its officials, and planted emissaries everywhere. They had a marvellous underground organization, they had imported thousands of tons of explosives for blowing up railways, offices and houses. Nazi terrorist gangs were operating all over Austria. We weren't really touched by all this in Vienna, although we were drenched by Nazi propaganda from the German frontier, by radio, and pamphlets dropped from aeroplanes. We knew Dollfuss and the Government were putting up a desperate fight for independence. The Nazi Government had done its best to ruin us economically by banning German tourist traffic. Fortunately the English took up the Austrian vogue and kept the holiday places going.

"I didn't take much notice of this turmoil, and like most of the Austrians I'd no idea of a plot being carefully hatched to kill Dollfuss and seize the Government. We were all very proud of our little 'Millimetternich' as we dubbed him, although we were not very happy about his Mussolini connection, but he was doing his best for Austria.

"After his release Max was very quiet for a time. He resigned or was forced from the Heimwehr. He didn't talk politics so much. But I noticed he was often very late, and there were notes constantly being left for him at the flat, as well as messages over the telephone. I challenged him once about these notes and asked him if he was getting mixed up with a political party, but he assured me the communications were all connected with his business.

"On the morning of July 25th I went out to lunch with a Viennese friend, Frau Sturm, at her flat in Herrengasse. Her husband is a doctor, and his consulting-room is in the flat. We were all having lunch, when he received a telephone call asking him to go urgently to the Ballhausplatz. The Ballhausplatz is the Austrian Foreign Office and the Chancellor's headquarters——"

"I know it well, I once interviewed Count Berchtold there, when he was Foreign Minister to the old Emperor," said Fanning.

"Then you know just where it is, and what it's like," continued Frau Bruck. "Dr. Sturm was surprised to be called there—it was like being suddenly called to Downing Street, and he was not practising in high official circles, but he went at once. He came back in about a quarter of an hour, and told us that something was wrong. He had been refused admittance to the Ballhausplatz, and an armed guard had talked to him through a grating in the door. The police had surrounded the building.

"Dr. Sturm had scarcely told us this when over the radio came the news that Chancellor Dollfuss had resigned and Dr. Rintelen had taken over the Government. 'That's a *Putsch*. I wonder if they've captured Dollfuss,' said Dr. Sturm at once. A few minutes later another radio message contradicted the other. We didn't know what to think. We all decided to go round to the Ballhausplatz. When we got there, there was a crowd outside the building, and a cordon of armed police and soldiers. Then we learned what had happened. At one o'clock the Nazis, disguised in Government uniforms—they had chosen the time when the guard was changed—had driven into the courtyard, overpowered the guard, closed the gates, and were holding all the inmates, including Dollfuss and Major Fey, as prisoners. You know the rest of the story, how they shot the Chancellor, refused him a doctor or a priest, made him believe they had seized power, and let him lie for two and a half hours on a couch while all his blood dripped away. At half-past seven the Nazis had to surrender. It was then that the poor little Chancellor was found shrunken and dead on a couch, with bullet holes through his neck and shoulder.

"You can imagine the sensation in Vienna that evening. I went back to the flat and waited for Max to come in to dinner. He did not come at his usual time. At eight o'clock I ate alone, and sat reading the papers. I waited until half-past eleven, and then rang up his people. They had not seen him. I went to bed. He did not come in that night at all. I was wondering what to do when there was a ring. I went to the door and two men informed me they were detectives, that I was under arrest, and that the flat would be searched. I then learned that Max was confined in the Marokkaner Barracks with a hundred and fifty-four of the Nazi rebels who had surrendered in the Ballhausplatz. They took me away, and I was locked up for four days, when my lawyer got me released."

"Good heavens, what an experience!" said Fanning.

"I had to endure much more than that," said Frau Bruck, nervously folding one hand over the other. "The nightmare was only beginning. As a result of their bargaining the rebels had been given the promise of safe transit to the German frontier. But when it was discovered that Dollfuss had been murdered the authorities naturally revoked their promise and put the rebels on trial. Six of them who had invaded the Chancellor's room, from which he had attempted to escape into the Corner Room, were charged with his murder. My husband Max was one of these six. A wretch called Otto Planetta confessed to firing the bullets. He was hanged—and is now a Hitlerite hero. My husband's death sentence was commuted to a life one. Last week he was pardoned, following the rapprochement with Germany, and on Friday he is to be released from jail. That's why I'm on the train. I'm going to meet him. I shall give him back this ring."

She moved the thin gold band on one of her fingers.

"Does he know?"

"No. He killed my love for him very soon. Now, I despise him. He is a liar, a mass of vanity, and dangerous. They should have hanged him," said Frau Brock, bitterly.

Her words shocked Fanning. They seemed strange coming from a young woman of her appearance.

"He must have been blinded by politics," said Fanning.

Frau Brock picked up her handbag, preparatory to rising.

"I've tried to think that, but it's no use," she said. "He was unfaithful, he never told me the truth, and he was impossible to live with. You wonder perhaps why I'm going to see him. It will give me great satisfaction to tell him that I despise him and that I will not live with a murderer. He is so vain, so mad, it may make no impression on him, but I want to see. You may think that terrible of me. Perhaps I am terrible. So you see, Mr. Fanning, my mother hadn't really a very pleasant companion for you."

She smiled bitterly, and rose to go.

"Anyhow—perhaps there's a plot for you?" she asked.

Fanning shook his head, as he followed her.

"No—no, I couldn't use that—it's too terrible," he said, following down the swaying car.

Back in his wagon-lit he was astonished to find it was half-past ten. The lights of a town began to twinkle in the darkness. They were approaching Lion. He decided to turn in. One of the pleasures of travelling by wagon-lit was reading in bed.

While he undressed, Fanning ruminated over the story Frau Brock had told him. He was still a little horrified by the implacable spirit of that young woman. Max was a bad lot undoubtedly, but to travel a thousand miles to enjoy the spectacle

of his discomfiture seemed vindictive to Fanning. Obviously
Frau Bruck could not forgive him for having wrecked their
happiness, and wounded pride lingered from the revelation of
the mistress in the Gemeindehaus. Most women in love would
have survived these shocks, they might have clung even more
devotedly to their man, and in this case would have denied indignantly the accusation of complicity in the murder of the
Chancellor.

Supposing Frau Bruck were still passionately in love with her
husband and she were going to meet him on his release, supposing she were still afraid, after pleading for him with
Starhemberg, that his mistress might have an attraction for him,
and——

Fanning stood still, gazing into the little mirror over the basin,
while the train roared on over the moonlit plateau of Laon.
Heavens, here was his plot! What a story—the winter sports,
the handsome Austrian ski-instructor, the fighting in Vienna, the
discovery of the husband arrested as a traitor, the revelation of
the mistress whom he had gone to warn, the desperate wife's
interview with the romantic Prince Starhemberg, the growing of
the Nazi plot, the participation of the husband, under compul-
sion preferably, the murder scene in the Ballhausplatz, the trial,
the wife's terrible ordeal, the reprieve and the long wait for his
release, re-union, the return to England, peace. . . .

He saw it all, saw the possibilities, the scope of the drama, the
richness of the characterization, the swift movement of the story,
a panorama of love, politics and contrasted nationalities.

Fanning could hardly button his pyjama jacket for growing
excitement. He opened his writing-case and took out the note-
book he always carried. Then he got into bed and switched on the
headlight. In half an hour he had the first synopsis sketched out.
The opening chapter was already formulated in his head. He

would create a young, impressionable girl enjoying her first winter sports, show her brother's alarm at her growing infatuation
with the ski-ing instructor . . . the love scene in the snow. . . .

He must begin at once while the ideas were in spate. To-morrow evening he would be in Vienna; there he would begin writing. But why go on to Vienna? He wanted to get down to work
at once. Why not get off the train at Bâle early in the morning,
and go straight back home? But the double journey would be
tiresome, and Alice would worry him for the reason.

Then, in a flash, he had an inspiration. Of course! Hastily
taking down his Continental time-table, he looked up his route.
Yes. They arrived at Kitzbühel soon after noon to-morrow. He
knew there were good hotels there. Moreover, the place was renowned as a ski-ing centre. Nothing could be better. He would
set his opening chapter there, with a scene on the snowy slopes of
the Hannenkamm.

For over an hour he lay in his bed thinking, while the express
roared through the night towards the Swiss frontier. Then,
finally, the whole new novel roughly shaped out to his satisfaction, he switched off the light, and fell asleep.

CHAPTER XV

NIGHT JOURNEY

YOUNG Mr. and Mrs. Derek Blake, having finished a pleasant dinner, went back to their adjoining wagon-lit. The train halted in Laon for a few minutes and they took the opportunity to step out and stretch their legs on the platform. A rather stout gentleman had the same idea, and he drew aside at the end of the corridor to let them pass. Pulling out a watch, he observed, affably, "We are in goot time to-night!"

They agreed, and stepped down on to the platform very pleased at having been spoken to by the famous Herr Gollwitzer.

"We must run over to Salzburg and hear him conduct, it's only a couple of hours by car," said Derek.

"I wonder how many times a year he makes this journey—did you notice he said we were in good time *to-night!* Does he ever get tired of travelling all over the world? I don't think I ever should!"

"Darling, I'm sure you're tired now—you've had a long day."

"The most exciting and lovely day of all my life!"

"What time were you up, exactly, this morning?" asked Derek.

"About seven—I couldn't sleep, Derek. I saw the milk-cart come up the Square for the first time for years!"

"I woke at five. What kids we are!" laughed Derek. "Will you sleep to-night, on the train?"

"Oh, yes—oh, I think so, I——"

She could not finish the sentence, and became dumb with

250

embarrassment. Looking at her, he saw her cheeks had reddened. He laughed, and pressed her arm.

"You must sleep, darling, or you'll feel worn out," he said. "Funny to be walking here, with my wife!"

"Why here?" asked Dorothy.

"I never come through Laon without thinking of my Uncle Dick. I worshipped him as a kid. He used to come up and tuck me in bed, and tell me stories; he was a grand chap."

"He's dead?"

"Yes. He was badly wounded in the fighting on the Chemin des Dames in May, 1918, when the German Army broke through. He was taken prisoner and died in a casualty clearing station here. Somehow he scribbled me a note just before he died, and I got it six months later. He was only twenty-five and a captain with the M.C.—a grand chap," said Derek, earnestly.

A whistle blew. The passengers hurried into the train.

Mr. and Mrs. Blake went back to their wagon-lit and found that during their absence the beds had been made up.

"They think we ought to go to bed," said Derek, looking at his wrist-watch. "Jove, it's almost eleven."

He walked through the communicating door to his own compartment and glanced around. Then he pulled down one of his portmanteaux from the rack.

"Shall we turn in?" he called through the open door. "You must be tired."

No answer came, and he walked into his wife's compartment.

"I think I'm too excited to sleep," she said, not looking at him, and bending over her dressing-case.

"My dear girl, you'll be a wreck if you don't get some sleep. Let me do that," he said, unbuckling the straps round her case. "It's almost an acrobatic feat undressing in these boxes—but you should try an upper berth on an American train: if you can manage that you can manage anything."

He stood for a moment. There was an awkward pause.

"Well, I'll get undressed," he said, and went into his own compartment. The door closed with a snap.

Dorothy did not do anything for a few seconds. She stood opposite the little mirror and looked at herself. She was Mrs. Blake and for the first time in her life there was a man who had the right to walk into her room. She could walk into his, of course, but that was somehow unthinkable.

She took off her coat. She looked at the door, and wondered whether to slip the catch. No, she must not do that. He was undressing. He might come in later. Would he come in, or, knowing what a long and exciting day she had had, would he leave her to herself?

He would, of course, say good night. And surely to say good night he would come in, in his dressing-gown. Then after a few words he could go to bed. Or would he stay?

She unfastened her skirt, slipped out of it and hung it up. Then, sitting on the bedside she took off her shoes and stockings, removing the blue rosette garters she had put on in Chester Square. In a few minutes she was undressed and in her satin nightdress. On the top of this she wore her blue silk kimono, a present from Gladys.

There were sounds in Derek's compartment. He was actually whistling. Was he whistling because he was nervous also? Surely he would knock if he came in, he mustn't see her like this, with her hair all untidy. Opening a small lizard-leather dressing-case she took out an ivory hand-brush. Then she spread several gold-topped bottles on the little table. The whole set was a present from her aunt. She took off a diamond wrist-watch, Derek's present, and began to brush her hair.

For the next twenty minutes she was busy with her toilet, but
at last she had finished. There was nothing to do but get into
bed. How quiet Derek was, there was not a sound. He had
ceased to whistle.

Dorothy knelt and said her prayers, a habit of childhood that
had never been broken. It was a little uncomfortable on the
swaying train, and she could not really concentrate on what she
was doing. Rising, she looked across the little compartment,
then, switching on the light over the bed, she turned out the
other. She slipped off the kimono and slippers, picked up a book,
and got into bed. It was comfortable, but she was so wide awake
that sleep was quite impossible. And, of course, she could not
read. How the train roared through the night, and how her own
heart beat within her!

Was Derek coming in to her? Surely he would come in to kiss
her good night, even if not to stay awhile. Perhaps, like her, he
was feeling—well, just how was she feeling? She had no clear
emotion. She was happy and a little frightened, and expectant
and panicky. It was so very silly of her. Darling Derek was
probably feeling much the same.

Was he coming in? Men surely didn't take as long as women
to undress? Perhaps out of sheer niceness, thinking she was tired,
he would not come in to-night. He was always considerate. But
if he didn't come in, then wouldn't it be a little strange, considering this was their first night together as man and wife? Of course
they were on a train, which made it all rather different.

A knock? Her ears strained. No, there was only the rumble
of the train. She lay back again and stared at the roof of the
compartment, at the ventilator, at the alarm handle, with a lead-
sealed band and *Avis* and *Bekanntmachung* over the warning
concerning its use. Her silk knickers and Princess slip swung on
the hooks. Where was she now? How strange to be here in bed,

no longer Dorothy Sewell, but Dorothy Blake, with her husband on the other side of that door!

She looked at her watch, which she had replaced on her wrist after washing. It was half-past eleven. Her father was asleep in Chester Square. The street lamps would be shining on the plane trees in the Square. St. Michael's spire would rise black against the moonlight, and here she was being carried across France, on her honeymoon!

Dorothy reached up for the little bag of lavender she had placed under her pillow. She always slept with it. It was a sort of talisman. Its contents were gathered each year from the lavender bushes in her aunt's garden.

There was a tap. Her heart jumped.

"Come in!" she called, with a controlled voice, restoring the lavender bag to its place under the pillow.

The door opened and Derek stood there, smiling at her. He seemed not in any way embarrassed.

"Comfy?" he said, coming in, and closing the door behind him.

"Very," she answered, looking at him as he stood over her.

He was wearing a red silk dressing-gown. His pyjama jacket, open at the throat, was crimson. His hair was exceedingly glossy, and as he sat himself down on the bedside she detected a pleasant odour of hair oil. Her hand lay on the coverlet, and he held it and played with her fingers.

"Sleepy, darling?" he asked.

"Not very, Derek."

"Well, it's been a great day."

"Wonderful."

He ran his hand over her arm, smoothing the white flesh as she smiled at him.

"I can't believe it's you, darling, all mine, here," he said, and then, bending over her, he kissed her lips, and her bare throat.

She slipped one hand over the glossy black head as he leaned over her, his face just above her, with all his love shining in his eyes as he gazed at her. She felt his lips on her brow, and then on her mouth, and closed her eyes, savouring his nearness. His arms slipped around her, and she felt enveloped by his male strength as he held her and looked at her with eyes that worshipped.

"I shall always love you, Dot," he said, in a low voice of passion. "Always and always, my darling."

Her hands spoke for her, caressing his smooth neck and shoulders under the open jacket. Withdrawing one hand he pushed back her hair, talking softly the while. In delicate love-play the minutes slipped by. Then she held up his wrist, strong and square against her own, with fine black hair covering the white flesh, and looked at his watch with the broad strap binding it.

"Twelve o'clock! Where are we, Derek?" she asked.

"In heaven, my darling," he said, smiling down at her.

She closed her eyes.

"Sleepy?"

"No—only very, very happy," she murmured.

He kissed her again.

"I'll leave you now, you must sleep, my pet," he said, gently.

"Yes."

A long kiss. The train swayed and roared in the night. Then he rose.

"Good night, my dearest."

"Good night, darling Derek."

A smile, another kiss, and then he was gone, the door closing between them.

She lay there, not moving, not thinking, her eyes closed as if to conserve the emotions that surged through her. Derek was gone. He had been very, very sweet. He knew she was tired, that she had had a long day of wonderful excitement. So he had left her, to sleep. It was gentle of him to discipline his passion in this manner. Her future happiness was safe with a man so considerate, so tender.

She turned out the light. The perfume of his presence and the warmth of his kisses still enveloped her as she lay in the darkness. Derek, darling Derek. The train seemed to be saying that also. Derek, darling Derek, Derek, darling Derek.

The refrain of the express beating its way through the night mingled with her own fading thoughts as she lay in the darkness, and then she heard it no more as she fell into a tranquil sleep.

II

Herr Gollwitzer woke up with a start. *Gott in Himmel,* whatever was that?

Again he heard it, above the noise of the train. It was someone moaning, someone in pain. Herr Gollwitzer listened. There it was again. The sounds came from the compartment next door. This time the moaning mounted to something like a cry. The passenger next door was obviously in agony. The voice, a shrill one, rose and fell, whimpered and moaned.

Herr Gollwitzer was wide awake now. It was not a nightmare. He switched on the light, and heard again the moaning of his neighbour, clear above the noise of the train. Hastily finding his slippers and dressing-gown, Herr Gollwitzer unfastened his door and peered out into the dim corridor. There was no one about.

For a few moments he hesitated. Should he tap on the next door and ask what was the matter? There was quiet now, or at least he could not hear anything. Suddenly, even as he paused, there was another series of moans and cries, and this time Herr Gollwitzer had no doubt that it was a woman's voice.

His mind rapidly sought an explanation. Violence, murder? No, not murder assuredly. Things like that happened in books. It was hardly possible for such a thing to take place on a train, next door to him. Appendicitis? Yes, more probably. The poor woman was in great agony.

Dashing back into his compartment he pressed the bell long and hard for the attendant, wondering briefly whether he shouldn't pull the chain and stop the express. Then, having rung hard, he peered out into the corridor.

There was no one. Another outburst next door filled him with agitation. Should he knock and go in, if the door were unfastened? Girding himself round the waist with his dressing-gown rope, he was about to bang on the door when it opened and a little man in glasses, without a coat and with his shirt sleeves rolled up, appeared in the doorway. He seemed very excited, glared at Herr Gollwitzer and, pushing him aside, stepped into the corridor, closing the door behind him.

"I heard someone—" began Herr Gollwitzer, in French.

But just then, hurrying from the end of the corridor, the car attendant appeared. He carried what looked like a blanket, and the moment the little man in his shirt sleeves saw it he grabbed it and disappeared again into the compartment behind him, but not before he had cried to Herr Gollwitzer, in German: "Go away! Go away!"

The door closed with a bang. Perplexed, Herr Gollwitzer, now feeling angry, stared at the door, and then turned to the attendant.

"What the devil's the matter here! Is someone dying?" he demanded.

The attendant, a man almost as stout as Herr Gollwitzer, with the round, red face and dark eyes of a French son of the soil, shrugged his shoulders and spread his hands vigorously.

"No, m'sieur. Worse, someone's being born," he said, with an air of aggrieved protest.

"Born! Whatever do you mean?" exclaimed Herr Gollwitzer.

"*C'est vrai, m'sieur,*" said the attendant. "They discovered a stowaway in the mail-van from Paris—it joined us at Chaumont —a young girl, hidden behind the mail-bags. She looked like death and said she was in great pain. She seemed to be dying. We went all through the train till we found a doctor. I knew there was one here, by his baggage labels. So we found him and he went down to the mail-van to see her. He saw at once what it was and said we must find the girl a bed——"

"A girl?"

"Just a slip of a girl, m'sieur. The poor little thing looked terrible. There isn't a bed free, so the doctor's put her in his—in there, m'sieur! *C'est incroyable, n'est-ce pas?*"

The attendant looked at Herr Gollwitzer like a man who had been affronted and sought sympathy.

"So that's what I heard. I thought it was murder!" exclaimed Herr Gollwitzer. "You never heard such a noise, poor girl!"

"I must go, m'sieur. He wants hot water," said the attendant, and disappeared down the corridor.

Herr Gollwitzer retreated into his own compartment. He rubbed his hands through his hair, took off his dressing-gown and glanced at his travelling clock. It was half-past three. For a moment he stood pondering, then he got back into bed. After all, he was a musician, not a midwife, and there was nothing he could do, though he felt sorry for the poor little girl. But why ever did she get on the train in that condition, and a stowaway! It looked as if the girl was in want and was trying to get home for the event. Was he going to hear more of this business? His sleep was broken anyhow.

Herr Gollwitzer drew the sheets over him and was about to switch out the light when the moaning was renewed, but this time it was louder and seemed to be mounting to a climax. What a terrible ordeal this birth-giving was! Herr Gollwitzer broke out into a sympathetic sweat.

It was no use—how could he sleep knowing what was going on? He switched on the light and sat up. There was silence again next door. But not for long. He heard the low murmur of voices, groans, and then, high above the noises of the train as it tore through the night, a thin prolonged wailing.

There was no mistaking that sound. It was a new voice crying in the world, an infant's tremulous complaint to life as it began its pilgrimage.

Herr Gollwitzer found a handkerchief and mopped his brow. The crying continued, but pulsated, and after a while ceased. He wondered about the girl-mother next door. Was she safely through the ordeal? Was it a boy or a girl? And somewhere there was a father who was without a twinge of pain for his share in nature's business!

The conductor mopped his brow again, and tucked the sheets around his large stomach. How strange life was! He had always longed for a son, and life, so good to him in many ways, had defeated him in this. His marriage had been a failure from the beginning. He had married an opera singer. He had married her for a home, and she had married him for a career. After ten wretched years of quarrels and reconciliations they had parted, dead to each other. But he had been so wounded that, when he was freed by her death, four years later, he had not dared a second venture. By then he was forty-five and dashing all over the world. He felt cheated of something. He loved children. He wanted a son, above all. And the years had drifted away, and he was now sixty-two, famous and childless and dependent upon his faithful Hans for all the comforts of his life.

Strange, mused Herr Gollwitzer, sitting up in his bed, how capricious life was. It seemed as if every man, no matter how successful, found dregs in his cup. He had felt mocked yesterday by the happiness of that young man in Cook's London office, who proudly announced the birth of his son. And here was a poor girl hiding away on a train and presenting some fellow, perhaps a quite heartless wretch, with a child of his blood.

The world thought he was a great success. In his profession he had no serious rivals. And he loved his work passionately. But it was not enough to triumph, and be lonely, when any office clerk could go home to his wife and children.

So gloomily pondering his fate, Herr Gollwitzer sat up in the night. Then, his thoughts reverting to the accouchement next door, he began to wonder how it fared with the mother and child. Should he ring for the attendant and inquire? All the commotion had died down. No, he would wait. He was now wide awake and sleep was impossible. He reached across for the score of *Don Juan,* which he would be rehearsing at Salzburg to-morrow morning. Slowly he went through it, and was soon engrossed. Half an hour must have elapsed, when he was startled by a tap on his door.

The door slowly opened and, turning, Herr Gollwitzer saw it was the doctor who had peremptorily told him to go away. He now advanced hesitatingly into the compartment, peering through his large glasses at the occupant.

"I want to apologize for all the disturbance you have suffered," said the doctor, still collarless and coatless. "I was called out to a girl in the mail-van, and found she was in birth-throes. The only thing to do was to get her into bed, and so I put her in mine.

I'm afraid it's spoilt your sleep. I am Dr. Herman Hirsch, of Innsbruck. I believe I have the honour of speaking to Herr Gollwitzer?"

"Yes, I'm Gollwitzer. My dear doctor, there's nothing whatever to apologize for. I'm only too glad to know that that poor young woman had a doctor to attend to her, and one so kind. Tell me, how is she?" he asked.

"She's come extremely well through the ordeal—the baby's a splendid boy, exceptionally fine. But these peasant girls do it easily," said Dr. Hirsch.

"Do you know anything about her, where she's going? Can I help her?"

"That's kind of you, Herr Gollwitzer. I don't know much yet. She got on the train at Paris, hiding in the mail-van. She'd no money and her one thought was to get home to Feldkirch before the birth. She was a servant in Paris."

"The child's illegitimate?"

"That I don't know, but it's probable. It's the usual story, I expect. Well, what a night! I'm wondering now whether to wire for an ambulance at Feldkirch, if they've got one, and put her off the train there. I could put her out at Bâle, where we'll be soon after five, but it's a little risky so soon, and it's Swiss. The girl's Austrian and I think it would be better to put her off at Feldkirch, where her people can look after her. She can get the birth certificate there and keep the boy Austrian."

"Doctor," said Herr Gollwitzer, having blown his nose loudly and pushed back his untidy hair, "will you find out for me from the girl whether the boy's illegitimate, and if so whether she knows who is and where is the father? I might be able to do something for her. Anyhow, take her on to Feldkirch, and if it's a matter of expense, call on me. I'll see the poor creature through."

"That's very kind of you, Herr Gollwitzer," responded Dr. Hirsch.

"But will you get me that information first?" said Herr Goll-witzer. "Can you question her yet?"

"Oh, yes."

There was the sound of a baby lustily crying in the next com-partment. The two men looked at each other and smiled.

"That sounds healthy," commented Herr Gollwitzer.

"Yes, he's full of life all right. I've a request to make of you. I wonder if you'd let me bring my clothes in here and dress? I can't get any sleep now, and I rushed into only a few things when they woke me up. Perhaps I'll get a doze in a first-class compart-ment."

"Certainly—use this place," replied Herr Gollwitzer.

"Thank you. I'll go along now and talk to the girl. We must settle what's to be done," said Dr. Hirsch, and left the compart-ment.

Herr Gollwitzer did not attempt to sleep. He picked up the score of *Don Juan* and tried to study it again. But it was useless. He had an idea in his head, and it excited him. When, half an hour later, Dr. Hirsch came back, he turned to him eagerly.

"Well—have you learned anything?" he asked.

Dr. Hirsch spread out his hands and raised them in a gesture of despair, after he had deposited his clothes.

"What a story! It's much as I imagined," he said. "She left her home last October. She lived with a widowed mother, in her married brother's house, at Feldkirch. Pretty rough, I gath-ered, and the girl was bullied by her brother when she fell out of work. She was at an hotel there in the busy season, and one of the visitors, a Frenchwoman, offered her a job as undermaid in her Paris house. So she went. Her name's Elise Vogel, she's nineteen. She was happy there. In December the woman's nephew, a St. Cyr cadet, came on a visit. He appears to have been a gay young spark, very dashing. He soon began to make love to the girl and you can imagine what an easy prey she was, dazzled with his uniform and his assured manner. When trouble came he seems to have faced up to it pretty well. He got her out of the household before anything was noticed, and installed her in a *garçonnière* in Paris, where he went to see her when he was free. The girl was very frightened and lonely, but he doesn't appear to have neglected her. Then in June, after his passing out examination, he joined the Aviation Corps and was sent to a school at Le Bourget. He visited and wrote to the girl regularly, for he appears to have been fond of her, and, knowing that she dreaded it, he dissuaded her from going home until after the child was born, which he said he'd provide for. Then, for a whole week he neither came nor wrote. She got worried, and her money was running out. Finally, a fortnight having passed, she went out to Le Bourget, found the school and asked for him. Then she learned that he had been killed ten days before in a crash."

"Poor girl—what a blow for her. You think the story's true, he was killed?" asked Herr Gollwitzer.

"Oh yes, he was killed all right. They told her where he was buried. She fainted, and one of the orderlies went with her and put her on the bus. So there she was, alone in a *garçonnière* with the rent paid to the end of July, and no money, and her advanced condition. Finally, in desperation, she went round to the boy's aunt, her old employer. She was literally thrown out of the house, in five minutes. The woman raved, called her a liar, and worse. She was turned out of her *garçonnière* last Saturday. For four nights she hired a cheap room. Then her money was ended. She ate almost nothing yesterday, and in desperation she had the idea of getting on this train. She went to the station, found it went to Feldkirch, and, seizing the opportunity, jumped into the mail-van and hid among the mails. That's the whole story. It's pretty terrible, but I suppose it's not the first nor the last of its kind. There's nothing bad about the girl, she's just a simple peasant girl who was dazzled by a suave young blade. He used to go down to her room at night, quite platonically at first."

"Who was he—a St. Cyr cadet?" asked Herr Gollwitzer.

"That I've noticed the girl doesn't say, beyond the fact that he was at St. Cyr and at Le Bourget. She carefully keeps his name out of it, so I didn't press her," answered Dr. Hirsch, putting on a collar and tie.

There was silence for a few moments.

"Tell me, doctor," said Herr Gollwitzer, looking at him keenly. "Do you think she'd part with the child?"

Dr. Hirsch reflected for a few moments.

"Yes, I think she would. She's not very happy at home, I gather, and there's likely to be a scene. It's possible the brother might refuse to have her back. Certainly, they won't want the child. And if she goes out to service again, something's got to be done with it. Are you thinking of an orphanage?"

"No, of adoption."

"Adoption! You know of someone who might take the child? He's a fine boy."

"Yes. I'll adopt the child," said Herr Gollwitzer.

"You, Herr Gollwitzer!" exclaimed the astonished doctor, staring at him. "For yourself?"

"For myself. I've always wanted a son. This may be Fate trying to serve me at last. Now, will you go to the girl—but keep my name out of it, I mustn't see her—and say you know someone who will take the child, and that it will have everything it can possibly require. If she agrees to complete surrender, and only then, say that two thousand schillings will be placed to her account at a bank. I shall want you to do something else for me, doctor. I want you to look after this girl and her child until the time that she is well. Then you must find me a nurse and send the infant to me in Vienna. Can you do that?"

"Yes—it's quite possible. I live in Innsbruck. I suggest that I take her off the train at Innsbruck, for several reasons. I can put her into hospital there, where she'll have every care. I can find a good nurse for you. But what I'm really thinking of is the girl," continued Dr. Hirsch. "There's no reason why her people at home should know anything, unless she wishes. She can possibly find a place in Innsbruck. I might help her. What do you think?"

"Excellent!" replied Herr Gollwitzer, heartily. "Nothing could be better."

Dr. Hirsch put on his waistcoat and coat, and folded up his dressing-gown.

"I'll go and make the proposition to her, if she's not too drowsy. By the way, I've got an assistant now," said Dr. Hirsch smiling.

"Who?"

"They've unearthed an old nun on the train. An English woman. She's a wonderful old thing. She's looking after them now."

The train began to slow down. Daylight was coming through the chinks of the blind. Dr. Hirsch raised it and looked out.

"Why, it's Bâle already!" he exclaimed. "I shall go and get some coffee in the station restaurant, we've fifteen minutes here."

The doctor went out. Herr Gollwitzer looked at his watch. It was five o'clock.

At half-past eight, while he was dressing, there was a tap on the door and Dr. Hirsch entered.

"Well, I've had a talk with her," he said. "She's lying there with her baby, looking fine. She's quite willing to part with the child and she realizes it's a wonderful opportunity. She dreads going home, and she's anxious for her family to know nothing of this. So it's arranged that I take her off the train at Innsbruck and look after her. She asked whether she could see the child occasionally. I said no, it was impossible. It seems hard-hearted, but it's really the best, both for the child and her, if you're going to adopt it."

"I must make that condition. The boy'll be like my own son," said Herr Gollwitzer.

"It's much better than an orphanage. She does know he'll be all right. I said you were a well-to-do Viennese gentleman, and that you and your wife always wanted a child."

Herr Gollwitzer looked a little dismayed.

"But I haven't a wife. I want the boy for myself," he said.

"Oh," exclaimed Dr. Hirsch, a little surprised. "No wife? Well, we'll let it go at that, we needn't say anything more. But aren't you tackling rather a job?"

"Yes. That's why I want a really trustworthy nurse. I travel a lot, as you know, so she'll be left in charge. Get me the very best, doctor. Spare no expense. And now, won't you come and have some breakfast with me? We must be near the Austrian frontier. Yes! There's the Rhine!" cried Herr Gollwitzer, looking out of his window.

Together they went along to the breakfast car. Dr. Hirsch, it transpired, had a flourishing practice in Innsbruck. He was on his way home from a Medical Congress at Edinburgh.

"I suppose you know we've got the Crown Prince of Slavonia on the train? That was a terrible business!" commented Dr. Hirsch. "I saw him, when I was stretching my legs at Buchs just

now—he looked miserable, poor little chap. I was glad to see
they've let him have a rabbit!"

"A rabbit?" repeated Herr Gollwitzer.

"Yes, I saw it through the window, squatted on the table,
munching lettuce."

"It would be very interesting to know the life history of everybody on this train—why we are travelling on it, what's going
to happen to us when we get off it," observed Herr Gollwitzer.
"Take that infant just born, for instance."

"It would be very terrifying, I think. Mercifully we don't
know," replied Dr. Hirsch. "But I would like to see what the
future holds for one passenger!"

"You shall, since you're at the very beginning of this experiment—and can keep the secret. Will you be a godfather?" asked
Herr Gollwitzer.

"With pleasure."

Herr Gollwitzer sat back, as he buttered a roll.

"I think the young man's begun life very well," he said, beaming through his glasses. *"Ach,* why here's Feldkirch, his
mother's place. I wonder if she knows."

"When I saw her a little while ago she was soundly sleeping,"
said Dr. Hirsch.

III

When the train reached Kitzbühel a little before one o'clock,
after its winding journey up through the Tyrolean valleys, about
a dozen people descended to the platform. Fanning, following
his resolution overnight, was among the passengers who left
the train. He had hoped before leaving it to see Frau Bruck
again, if only to thank her for the great service she had unwittingly done him. He reflected, however, as he sat in the ancient

landau, which he deliberately chartered in preference to a motor-car, that perhaps it would not have been wise to tell her that her life story was going into a novel. She might have been alarmed, though, of course, by the time he had completed work upon it she would find it almost unrecognizable.

He leaned back in the seat, feeling very happy. The place looked delightful in the midday sun, with its background of mountains beyond the long valley. He had not decided where he would stay. He would choose what seemed to him the most attractive hotel. He wanted quiet above all and a room with a pleasant view in which he could write. For the story was shaping itself all the time and the first three chapters were already clear in his head.

The horse and carriage clattered up past the church and came to the Hauptplatz, with its high gabled houses, and their bright yellow, green and red painted shutters and balconies. The popularity of the place was denoted by the number of hotels and cafés under whose canopied tables, set out on terraces, the visitors were now lunching.

The driver turned, a little puzzled by his fare, who seemed to have nowhere to go. They had come to what looked like the old walled gate of the town. It was a Pied Piper sort of place, with its overhanging houses and wooden balconies blazing with geraniums and petunias. The young women wore their traditional costume of short-sleeved bodices, pleated skirts and embroidered aprons, the young men sported gay cutaway jackets, leather shorts and white stockings. Were they natives or visitors from South Kensington, dressing the part? Anyway, the fancy costumes went well with the slightly musical comedy atmosphere.

They drove through the gateway, and the newer town sprawled across the valley. A bright new hotel, with tiers of balconies, suggested efficiency by its smart exterior. It had a pleasant terrace for dining, and a splendid view of the mountains. Fanning told the man to drive there.

Fortunately they were not full. He selected an excellent room on the third floor, with a little iron balcony of its own. A youth in *Lederhosen,* with a green apron and embroidered stockings, carried up his luggage. He threw open the French window on to the balcony.

"Schöne Aussicht!" he exclaimed, with a grin that showed splendid teeth.

Fanning laughed. It was so true to the innkeeping formula. In Italy they always went to the shutters, threw them open and declared, dramatically, *"Bella vista!"* Here it was, without any exaggeration, *schöne Aussicht!*—a beautiful view.

"Ja, danke," responded Fanning, tipping the stocky youth a schilling.

He grinned again, shaking back a mass of blond hair, and pointing across the valley, exclaimed, *"Kitzbühler Horn!"* and then, pointing to something round the corner of the balcony, said, *"Sprungschanze wunderbar!"* and, with a scoop of his hand, went *"Pssss!"* to indicate its exhilarating ski run.

Fanning again thanked him, but the youth had not finished his repertoire. He took out of his pocket a carefully folded paper, and, opening it, presented it to him.

"Heute Abend, Platzmusik und Schuhplattl!" he announced, pointing to the paper, and, thinking the visitor might not understand, he swung his green apron aside, hopped, and soundly slapped each leather-covered thigh. *"Ich!"* he said, proudly, to denote he was one of the performers in this Tyrolean dance. Then, instantly solemn again, he bowed, and withdrew.

Fanning looked round the room. Then he tried the small table by the wall. No, it did not wobble as he feared. It now remained to discover if the food was good. So far the hotel seemed excellent.

Whistling to himself, Fanning closed the door and went to the lift. Life was not too bad after all, when you had a plot.

IV

Mr. and Mrs. Blake retired early to bed that night, but not before they had been in the town to hear *Platzmusik,* played by the town band, dressed in their Pied Piper coats, knee-breeches, white stockings, and hats with enormous feathers stuck jauntily in them, as they marched behind flaring torches. And the Blakes had also seen *Schuhplattl,* danced by the village youths and maidens. Mrs. Blake, who had never seen this before, believed the lads actually did give each other such sounding smacks on the face, and she was quite carried away by the boisterous rhythm of the dance with its thigh-slapping accompaniments, and the finger twirling with the pigtailed, tight-bodiced maidens.

And when she walked home, arm in arm with Derek, past the brightly lit cafés, out of which flowed the sound of zithern music and happy voices, along in the shadow of the balconied houses, and through the solid tower gate into the quiet of the moonlit valley, with the grey shapes of the mountains like sleeping mammoths, she was excited and tired and almost deliriously happy. What years and years away seemed that old life in Chester Square! Was her father just going out with a letter to the pillar-box on the corner, to catch the last collection, and were all the old ladies giving their dogs a final run before locking up?

"Happy, Mrs. Blake?" asked Derek, as they walked down the valley towards their hotel.

She looked at him with shining eyes, and pressed his arm.

"I shall wake up and find it's all a dream," she said.

He laughed, stopped, put his arm round her waist, and kissed her warm cheek.

"You will wake up and find your loving husband at your side, Mrs. Blake," he said.

He was the first to wake. The room was light and a ray of vivid sunshine lay across a strip of the floor. For a second he wondered at this unfamiliar room, with its slatted wooden shutters. Then full consciousness told him where he was. He turned at once towards the twin bed, and, raising himself on one elbow, looked at his wife's face deep in the white pillow. She was fast asleep and looked singularly child-like in her natural beauty. One hand lay out on the coverlet, with the ring on one finger which he had placed there less than two days ago. Should he wake her?

He turned and glanced at the travelling clock on the bedside table. It was half-past eight. It looked as if it was a fine morning. What day was it? Friday, August the——

Whatever was that noise? Derek listened. There was a clicking somewhere outside. At first he thought it must be a bird, but the sound was too regular. He listened intently.

"Good morning!" said a voice at his side.

It was his wife's voice. Her eyes were open and she lay smiling at him.

"Good morning, darling!" he said, turning towards her, and, reaching over, he picked up the thin white hand on the coverlet and kissed it. "Slept well?"

"Very—and you?"

He did not answer but laughed, and leaning out of his bed, over her, he bent down and kissed her.

She wriggled a little and playfully pushed his face away.

"Oh darling, you've got a beard!" she exclaimed.

He rubbed his chin with her hand.

"Sorry! Men have beards in the morning. I'll get up and shave. I wonder if that hot water functions in the bathroom."

She did not answer, but putting her hand up to his neck, pulled the dark head down to her, and kissed him.

"I love your funny rough face, and your tousled hair," she said, running her fingers through it.

He kissed her hair, and catching hold of her hand, squeezed the thin ringed fingers.

"Who gave you this?" he asked, with mock seriousness, indicating the plain gold ring.

"A young man named Derek Beddington Blake who, when asked whether he would marry me, said 'I will' and put this ring on my finger," she answered. "Wasn't he bold?"

"Wasn't he lucky!"

Dorothy raised her head and listened.

"What's that?" she asked.

The clatter still persisted outside, sharp in the still morning.

"I don't know—it was on when I woke. I thought at first it was a bird of some kind."

They listened. There it was again, a quick rattle beyond the shutters.

"Why—it's someone typewriting!" said Dorothy.

"So it is!" exclaimed Derek, the mystery solved. "Whoever wants to be typewriting here, at this time?"

He sprang out of bed, walked across the bedroom and threw back the shutters on the balcony. The dazzling sunshine of a perfect August morning flooded the room. Dorothy sat up with a cry of delight. Beyond the window, across the valley, the fleecy mists were rolling up the mountain-side. The grey roofs and flower-laden balconies of the chalets on the lower slopes were in full sunshine. Above them a belt of dense pines lost their heads in the white blanket of mist. Then, higher up, the mountain again emerged, its vivid emerald-green slopes shining in the morning sun.

"Jove! This is glorious—come and look at it, darling," said Derek, stepping bare-footed out on to the balcony.

Hastily slipping on her dressing-gown, Dorothy ran across the room to join her husband. Kitzbühel and its long valley, surrounded by the morning mountains, lay out in the clear sunshine. The white road stretched from the old gate in the ancient walls, through which they had come last night, across the valley towards St. Johann. Somewhere from the mountain slopes came the sound of cowbells.

"Oh!" said Dorothy, taking her husband's arm, and then was silent in wonder at the scene before them.

Tap-arap-tat-tat-tat-a rap-tat.

The sharp clatter broke out again. It was just below them. They leaned over the balcony, and below, quite unconscious that he was being observed, sat a man in front of a typewriter which he had placed on a small table pushed right up against the balcony. Evidently he had already breakfasted out in the sunshine, for a tray with a cup and coffee-pot had been pushed aside. A plate held down some sheets of paper.

The man at the typewriter was writing at great speed, bent slightly over the machine, which he seemed to handle expertly. Presently, coming to the bottom of a sheet, he pulled it out from the roller and added it to the pile under the plate. Then he picked up a tin of cigarettes, took one and lit it. Taking up another sheet, he was about to insert it when he happened to look up, to find two young faces intently watching him from above.

For a moment he was startled, then his rather serious face broke into a smile.

"Good morning!" he called. "I hope I'm not a nuisance with this typewriter—I haven't woke you up?"

"Oh no, sir!" replied Derek, as Dorothy darted out of sight. "It's rather funny to hear typewriters and cowbells going together."

The man below laughed, pulled at his cigarette, inserted the new sheet, and looking up, said:

"Yes—I'm afraid I'm a blot on the landscape. But I must work, and I couldn't keep in."

"Rather not!" agreed Derek. "Good-bye, sir."

"Good-bye."

The typewriter clattered on.

"What a funny thing," said Dorothy, "to find a man typewriting here. Do you know, I'm certain I've seen his face before. I wonder who he is. I'm sure he's somebody famous."

"Why?"

"I don't know. His face is familiar somehow."

"Well, we can soon find out. Shall we have a pyjama breakfast on the balcony?" asked Derek.

"Oh, splendid!" cried Dorothy. "Let's!"

Picking up the telephone, Derek ordered breakfast.

"And, I say, can you tell us the name of the gentleman immediately under us?" he asked.

There was a pause, while the concierge sought the name of the occupant.

"Oh, Derek, ought we to?" asked Dorothy, at the mirror.

"Why not? Hello, yes?" cried Derek, listening.

Then he put down the receiver.

"Well, we're no wiser, darling. It's a Mr. Henry Fanning, of London."

"Henry Fanning! Of course! Oh, how exciting!" exclaimed Dorothy, putting on satin slippers.

"Why, who is Mr. Fanning, anyhow?"

"Derek, you've heard of Henry Fanning, the famous novelist? His books are wonderful! To think he's here, under us—perhaps writing a new novel."

Derek lit a cigarette and began to take shaving things from his dressing-case.

"No—never heard of him. I can't read novels. Perhaps he's writing to his wife, or his creditors. He seems hard pressed," he said, laconically.

"Oh, Derek, don't be cynical. I love his books," remonstrated Dorothy, combing her hair as she sat before the mirror.

He stood behind her for a few moments watching her, entranced by the intimacy of the scene, and then, just as she lifted up her hair from the nape of her neck to brush it, he stooped and placed a kiss on the cool white flesh. She turned with a laugh and pressed his cheek against hers.

"Then I love Mr. Fanning," he said, quietly. "Love me, love my novelist. But, darling, don't ask me to read the wonderful Mr. Fanning. I'm stupid that way. I'm only good at starting broken-down motor-cars!"

"But Derek, you didn't, you know! You couldn't make it work!" said Dorothy.

"No—I couldn't. But I did take a certain very charming young lady to a house where I knew I would find her again," he replied.

"Was that a good thing?" asked Dorothy, still holding the dark head against hers.

"The best day's work I ever did," he said, his arms encircling her from behind.

For a long moment they did not move or speak. Through the open window came the hurried clatter of Mr. Fanning's typewriter.

CHAPTER XVI

DINNER AT HEILIGENBLUT

I

HERR GOLLWITZER said *Auf Wiedersehen* to Dr. Hirsch, who got off the train at Innsbruck with his charge. For the rest of the journey to Salzburg he spent the time musing on his impulsive undertaking. Whatever would Hans think when he was told? Would he scold him or enter into the adventure? For it was a great adventure to take a young life and mould it. As yet Herr Gollwitzer had no idea of what he intended doing. But there was plenty of time to make plans for his adopted son. He had agreed with Dr. Hirsch that the baby and its nurse should be kept in Innsbruck for the next six months, during which time the doctor would supervise its welfare. If, however, the mother found service in Innsbruck, then the baby must be nursed elsewhere. Dr. Hirsch was emphatic on the point that the parting of mother and child should be irrevocable.

Herr Gollwitzer felt a little unhappy about that poor little servant girl. He had made a private undertaking with Dr. Hirsch that until she found a good position he would make her an allowance. The doctor agreed to act as the agent in this matter but was certain the girl would find a new position quickly.

"Don't worry yourself. I've known dozens of cases like this and after a month or two the girl becomes quite indifferent to the fate of the child."

"I feel very inhuman," murmured Herr Gollwitzer.

"Inhuman! Why, you're a fairy godfather, a veritable *deus ex machina!*" exclaimed the doctor.

"*Deus ex wagon-lit,*" corrected Herr Gollwitzer, with a faint smile.

"You could get a thousand babies to-morrow on far less generous terms."

"*Himmel*—what a prospect!"

So on the way to Salzburg Herr Gollwitzer persuaded himself that he was not a heartless villain. The boy's future was assured. He would have everything a boy could want. There was one sad thought underlying Herr Gollwitzer's excitement. He could hardly expect to live long enough to see the boy grow up. Well, the process of growing up would be very interesting, and there would be young laughter in his house.

When the train arrived at Salzburg in the afternoon Herr Gollwitzer was met by Herr Geicher, of the Salzburg Musical Festival Committee. A great number of the passengers left the train, and were greeted by their friends.

"Salzburg is more crowded this season than ever. There's not been a seat available for *Don Juan* for over a fortnight," said Herr Geicher, as they drove through the streets to the hotel in the Dollfuss Platz.

The town was thronged with visitors. The English seemed in the majority, for Herr Gollwitzer's experienced eye detected them all in their disguise of native costume. These charming girls in figured bodices and pleated skirts, with dainty aprons, and jaunty little hats, were not simple *Mädchen*. When they opened their mouths they spoke English, sometimes with American as well as Oxford accents.

As for the young gallants, so dashing in their embroidered

leather shorts, with tasselled *Strümpfe* decorating their brown legs, and cutaway jackets with brilliant lapels and silver buttons, they had stepped out of the chorus of *The White Horse Inn* rather than out of the mountain chalet, where the native youth boasted only a very greasy pair of ancestral leather shorts, and a white shirt washed in a running stream.

All these fancily dressed visitors added such gaiety to the lovely little town on the grey Salzach that it always seemed to Herr Gollwitzer rather futile to play Mozart in the Festspielhaus. Salzburg itself was a stage, with a thousand puppets dancing to the staccato music of her native genius.

Arriving at the Bristol, he was warmly welcomed by the manager and the concierge, old friends. He had his favourite corner suite of rooms. When Geicher had left him, having fixed all details for a rehearsal in the morning, Herr Gollwitzer closed the windows of his bedroom, took off his shoes and lay upon the bed. It was four o'clock, and a stuffy August afternoon, in a town that was either baked with sunshine, or drenched in rain. The excitement of last night's journey, and his broken sleep, had greatly tired him. He lay on the bed and in a few minutes was sound asleep.

It was nearly six o'clock when he woke, much refreshed. This was the hour he most loved in Salzburg. The crowd was moving across the bridge, a congested happy mob, in bright Tyrolean costumes. The natives hung about the quay and watched the fashionable world. These Festival weeks filled the little town with feverish life. After August it would settle down into a year-long slumber again, but now it made money out of its cosmopolitan visitors.

At this hour some of the actors in the festive scene had changed their rôles. They were no longer Tyroleans in *Lederhosen* or

Dirndl costume, they were very serious musical enthusiasts attired in dinner jackets and evening frocks, hurrying to take a snack before the performance in the Festspielhaus. When the opera was ended they would jam themselves into restaurants and, amid a clatter of dishes and a medley of cries for frantic waiters exhibiting a peculiarly Austrian facility for industrious disorder, they would fiercely debate the merits of the performance they had heard.

It was singular how little pleasure they seemed to derive from their prostration before the goddess of music. What acute pain Fräulein Schultz's demi-semi-tone flat in the *Aria* had given them. What rage was theirs at Signor Locavelli's monstrous impertinence in taking that *pizzicato* passage *troppo presto* when all the world knew it should be *allegro ma non troppo*. True, the great Toscanini——

And then all tongues stopped, for the passing of the Most High. Yes, there was the Festival Director, and Signor Locavelli, and Trotheim the tenor, and the famous Baroness Blowitz, who financed the Blowitz Quartette, all coming in to eat like ordinary mortals! A few moments of awe, and the babel would break out again, with *"Zahlen, Zahlen, bitte!* Oh really—how frightful! Herr Ober, do please—" from customers beseeching to pay and get out into the cool night, where the fountains splashed silver over the horses of Atlas, and the moonlight fell on baroque façades and touched with caricature the faces of apostles and bishops, cherubs and devils, all the fantastic embellishments of those eighteenth-century sculptors who played with stone as conjurers play with plates and balls.

But at six o'clock Herr Gollwitzer did not go towards the bridge, to be caught up in the human stream flowing over the slaty Salzach. He turned his steps towards the calmer scene of

Schloss Mirabell, in whose strictly patterned garden the slanting sun enhanced the colours of the gaudy parterres. He sought a favourite seat, his back to the old palace built by a prince-archbishop for his mistress, where he could view the Festung, that fairy-tale fortress high on its rock. This evening, touched with gold against the violet clouds, the grim old place with its massive bastions seemed to float in the heavens. In whatever light Herr Gollwitzer saw it he loved it, a memorial of medieval tyranny, of Salzburg's venal prince-archbishops.

And now, as the sun fell, the wall of the Bavarian mountains seemed to rise about the plain. The conductor got up and took one turn around the gardens. Those who saw him, and recognized him, thought that he was deep in contemplation of the opera over which he was to wave his enchanted baton on the morrow. But they were wrong. The great man was not engrossed in *Don Juan,* but in the drama of the Arlberg-Orient express in which he had played so singular a part.

Had he been *troppo presto* when he should have been more *tranquillamente?* No. He had picked up a baton for the opening movement of a life-symphony, and he was not going to fumble with the score, however full of crotchets and quavers. And as his feet turned towards the exit of the gardens, with the golden evening lengthening the shadows of its walls and burnishing the many windowed façades of Schloss Mirabell, he was not engrossed in a composition of Mozart, but in the composition of a telegram that should inform, without alarming, the faithful Hans of the momentous task on which he had embarked.

By the time he reached the hotel he had sketched out the message, and, taking a form, he wrote it out. Then he gave it to the concierge for dispatch, in order to enjoy the expression on that good fellow's face when he counted the words.

*Arrived safely. Bought a boy born on train for adoption.
Get well soon. Your help urgently needed. Gollwitzer.*

The concierge counted the address and the message.

"Twenty-four words—five schillings, sixty groschen, Herr
Gollwitzer—shall I put it to your account?" asked the concierge,
without the slightest note of curiosity.

"Yes, please," said the conductor, and left the reception desk,
making his way to the lift.

"Gott in Himmel! Are babies born and adopted on the train
every day? I suppose the fellow's taught his face never to register shock," murmured Herr Gollwitzer to himself, as he waited
for the lift.

II

Among those who had recognized the famous conductor as he
walked through the Mirabell gardens were two ladies who sat
on a seat by the central pond, watching the passers by, and embroidering as they talked.

"Why, look, Ethel," said Mrs. Cora Cressington, "there's
Gollwitzer!"

Mrs. Silving looked up from her embroidery, which she ac-
complished without glasses despite her seventy-seven years, and
looked across the ornamental pond. There, on the other side,
was the unmistakable world-famous figure, his broad felt hat
carried in one hand, the golden sunlight playing over his round
face and massive brow.

"You know, I regret leaving in the morning. I do think we
should have stayed and heard *Don Juan* to-morrow," said Mrs.
Silving, watching the receding form of the conductor.

"Well, my dear, let's stay," answered Mrs. Cressington,
threading a needle.

"No, I'm afraid we must go, we can't keep Nita and her husband waiting any longer in Venice, and I definitely told Captain Pym we'd sail on Sunday morning. Besides," added Mrs. Silving, "we've insisted on Cook's sending that chauffeur out at once. We're a week behind our schedule now."

"One of the joys of owning your own yacht is that you can sail when you like," observed Mrs. Cressington. "But I agree that we shouldn't keep Nita waiting any longer. I do hope that chauffeur has come. He should be there when we get in."

Mrs. Silving paused in her work to observe some pretty Tyrolean dresses worn by two peasant girls who walked by. She sat with her back to the sun, with the long façade of the Schloss golden in the level light of evening. They had been here for a whole week, on their way through to Italy, held up by the illness of their hired chauffeur, who had toured with them for a month since leaving Paris. And now Mrs. Silving was due to join her yacht, waiting for her in Venice, with Mrs. Cressington's former secretary, Nita and her husband, on board. The week had passed very pleasantly with concerts in the morning and opera in the evening.

"What did they say was the name of the new chauffeur?—it sounded very peculiar," asked Mrs. Silving. "I hope he talks intelligible English and knows the route to Venice. A lady in the hotel told me last night that the turns on the Grossglocknerstrasse are just terrifying, but you know what some women are like—they enjoy screaming on any excuse," said Mrs. Silving, her robust mind contemptuous of feminine weakness.

Mrs. Cressington laid aside her work, opened a small bag, and unfolded a telegraph form.

"I have it here," she said. "*Relief chauffeur Vladimir Zoronoff arrives Friday fifteen-twenty. Cooks.* The name's Russian, I hope he is a steady driver."

"He sounds most unsteady," commented Mrs. Silving, embroidering again. "He may decide to commit suicide in a way the Russians have as soon as he sees a really alluring precipice. Well, I'm not really alarmed. When I think how in the last two years I've survived storms, hurricanes, rides up mountains on cables, down them on donkeys, volcanoes, hard beds, and Italian church guides, a precipice is not out of keeping as an exit from this exciting world. Don't you think it's time we went, Cora dear? We've those people coming to dinner."

They collected their things and put them in a hold-all. Then they walked slowly through the gardens towards their hotel, Mrs. Cressington, the younger, tall and sedate, Mrs. Silving, smaller, silver-haired and sharp-eyed, missing nothing.

At the Oesterreichischer Hof, their hotel, they found a message waiting for them to say that M'sieur Zoronoff had been, and would call again at seven o'clock for instructions.

Promptly at seven the Russian chauffeur was shown up into their room. He was not a bit like what they expected. He was not young and strong, with a brisk manner. He was distinctly elderly, with a rather delicate face, and a trim beard. His grey hair was white at the temples.

"I'm surprised they've sent one so old," said Mrs. Cressington, when he had gone. "I hope he's safe."

"Well, we wanted him steady. I don't think he's going to rush us over the Alps. I shouldn't be surprised if he's sixty—poor old man," commented Mrs. Silving, forgetful of her seventy-seven years.

III

They started on Friday morning at ten o'clock. The car was at the hotel door, the luggage was stacked on the rack. Promptly at the hour, largesse distributed, Mrs. Silving and Mrs. Cressington, two American widows who had made Europe their playground, emerged, smiled at the bowing concierge, tipped the door porter, shook hands with the manager, and took their seat in the Delage coupé.

A small crowd of Salzburgians watched their departure, bronzed youths, round-faced girls with mottled aprons, a few visitors, touts and newspaper venders. They looked enviously but affably at the two ladies with their large car and chauffeur, with peaked cap, dust-coat and goggles.

The car moved off through the streets, already gay with visitors out shopping. They passed the town villas, burrowed through the Mönchsberg, part of the rock on which Hohensalzburg and its fortress were built, and came to the flat plain at whose extremity rose the Bavarian Alps, faintly blue in the morning light.

The day was perfect. There was a fresh cumulus-laden sky with great depths of sunlit blue. As they came to Bad Reichenhall the mountain scenery closed in around them.

Mrs. Silving, whose passion for travel not even her seventy-seven years could abate, sat back at her friend's side, a smile on her face, masked with sun-glasses and a travel veil.

"He seems very steady," she said, referring to the chauffeur in front.

The head before them, with its grey hair emerging from beneath the peaked cap, was that of an elderly man. Mrs. Silving from her side could just see the chauffeur, quarter-face, and she noticed how straight was the nose and well trimmed the beard and moustache.

"You know, Cora, he looks like an admiral—he only wants gold epaulettes, and I should feel like saluting," said Mrs. Silving.

"Have you noticed his hands?" asked Mrs. Cressington.

Mrs. Silving looked at them as they lay on the wheel. They

were slender, with oval, well-kept nails. On one finger there was an engraved ruby ring.

"You know, I wonder if I shall dare to call him Vladimir," said Mrs. Silving. "I once heard a Russian Grand Duke lecture in Detroit. He was the ex-Tsar's cousin, a giant of a man, and of all subjects to lecture on he chose—Earthly and Heavenly Love! My, how those women queued up to get the Russian version! I felt really sorry for the poor man, being pole-led by the Dame President of the Club. He looked just like an amiable bear on a chain. Somehow Vladimir reminds me of him."

"Perhaps he is a Grand Duke," said Mrs. Cressington, smiling.

"Well, that wouldn't surprise me—there seem to be dozens of them about, looking for homes. Anyhow, I'd like to know Vladimir's history."

Unconscious of the speculation concerning him, General Zoronoff was enjoying the morning's drive up into the Bavarian Alps, across a spur of which they were now running towards the ravine that led again into Austria and towards Zell-am-See. They left Bad Reichenhall, and above rose the peak of Predigstuhl, with its cable railway for the ski-ers. How strange to be on this road again. Thirty-six years ago he had driven along it, one February day, in a sleigh with his German host, Baron Falhausen, of whose house-party he was a member. And here he was, a chauffeur from Cook's, driving two American ladies over the once uncrossable Grossglockner range to Venice.

By lunch-time they were at Zell-am-See, which greatly excited old Mrs. Silving, for it had long been the home of Salzenthal, the famous pianist, who had owned Fort San Antonio, the fortress-pension on the Venetian lagoon, where she often stayed. And in this Schloss, where Salzenthal had died, now lived his old manager, Herr Teller.

They found the Schloss, swept along a rising drive and presently came to a terrace with a magnificent view of the lake. Below them lay the little town with its baroque church and old tower. The town ran down to the edge of the See, and around it rose the snowy monarchs of the Tauern range. There in the brilliant sunshine shone the white crest of the Imbachorn and heaven-piercing Hocktenn and a stupendous panorama southwards of the great Grossglockner range over which they were to climb that afternoon.

A joyous welcome awaited them from Herr Teller, his daughter Kathi, and the irrepressible Anton, a volatile, handsome young man who had sailed Mrs. Silving about the Venetian lagoon. Herr Teller would have kept them, but firmly adhering to their schedule, Mrs. Silving and Mrs. Cressington departed.

"Had you a good lunch in the town, Vladimir?" asked Mrs. Silving as they descended the drive.

"Very good, Madame, thank you, at a place on the side of the lake."

Mrs. Silving looked at her friend. Well, she had called him Vladimir.

"Your turn!" she said, nudging her companion.

"I hope the car will manage the Grossglockner, Vladimir?" said Mrs. Cressington, not to be outdone.

"I think so, Madame, the salients are not as steep as on the Simplon, I hear."

"Then you've done it before?" asked Mrs. Silving.

"Oh no, Madame—it's a new road from Italy into Austria."

An hour later they began to climb the Fuscher Tal, past Ferleiten, a cold lonely outpost at the foot of this northern precipitous arête.

"Why, it's like climbing the side of a house, to go over the roof," exclaimed Mrs. Cressington.

The valley sank down and down. Across the valley, on the

opposite mountain-side, waterfalls made silver streaks on the wall of the dark rocks. They turned and turned.

"Vladimir's very careful!" said Mrs. Silving, gratefully. "But I don't like this—it's forbidding."

They were now in a cold, grim world. A mist began to envelop them. Nothing seemed to live in this rarefied air. They crossed a barren plateau.

· "The first tunnel," called the chauffeur. "Over seven thousand feet in altitude."

They plunged into deep gloom, and later emerged into a white fog. The car crawled along the road. They were still climbing. Another tunnel loomed up.

"The Hochtor tunnel, eight thousand feet," said the chauffeur, proceeding out of the white fog into a cavern. Along the low arched roof electric lights dimly burned. Mrs. Silving and Mrs. Cressington wrapped rugs about them and shivered.

They came to the end of the tunnel and, as if a curtain had suddenly lifted, they were in a blaze of sunshine, the whole world bright below them. Afar, a vast snow-covered range lay under the crystalline air. They began to descend, then in about twenty minutes they took a right-angle bend, and all they had heard, or anticipated, was fulfilled a thousandfold. For there, immense and magnificent, lay the giant glacier mounting the vast slope to those peerless heights where the virgin snowfields of the Grossglockner shone in their eternal solitude.

"Oh!" exclaimed the two ladies, and General Zoronoff, himself awestruck by this majestic spectacle, brought the car to a standstill on the broad rock platform made for a car park. *"Franz-Josephs-Hohe,"* said a notice.

The two ladies got out of the car and went to the rail, whence they looked down to the ice river below. The crevices were like wrinkles on the white face of the glacier. Far above, a towering lonely monarch, the Grossglockner lifted its dazzling peak into the blue sky.

"You have driven beautifully, Vladimir!" said Mrs. Silving, a little giddy in this sharp, rarefied air.

"Very carefully!" added Mrs. Cressington.

The chauffeur raised his peaked cap.

"Thank you, Mesdames," he said, with a slight bow.

"Most gentlemanly," observed Mrs. Cressington, when he had turned away.

"But he is a gentleman, I'm sure—we must find out his history, Cora," said Mrs. Silving. "Are we going down there?"

"I think so," replied her companion, looking at the far-off dim valley that seemed on another planet. "I wonder how long he's been a chauffeur. I'm certain he's a Russian refugee."

Mrs. Silving laughed a little.

"Why do you laugh?" demanded Mrs. Cressington.

"Well—we're only guessing that he's Russian from his name. He may be a respectable bourgeois Frenchman down on his luck. We must find out. I'm consumed with curiosity. He's so aristocratic in his bearing. No, Cora, he's an admiral, I'm sure," asserted Mrs. Silving.

"Or a Grand Duke."

"Even that. Cora, we'll ask him to dinner to-night."

"But Edith! Our chauffeur—don't you think—won't the other people in the hotel——" she asked hesitatingly.

"I don't care a rap," said Mrs. Silving. "I'm going to ask him to dinner. He's sure to have a plain suit. I'm getting cold, we must go."

A little before seven o'clock, after a thrilling journey down the mountainous slopes, round breath-taking hair-pin bends, they came to lovely Heiligenblut, the Alpine village built on a ledge at the head of the valley, with the Grossglockner and its glacier for a background. Most prominent of all, on its jutting rock platform, the church lifted its slender spire to heaven, a symbol of man's faith under the shadow of nature's fortress.

The narrow high street, overhung with the balconies of the local inns and chalets, was thronged with tourists, for this once lovely outpost of the alpinist tackling the Grossglockner had now become a popular halt for the motor traffic negotiating the Alpine highway connecting Austria and Italy.

The ladies were delighted with their hotel, an enlarged chalet with a balcony commanding the long valley, falling below. The boots brought in their luggage. The chauffeur, doffing his hat, approached them.

"I hope you are not too tired," asked Mrs. Silving.

"It must have been most wearing to your nerves," added Mrs. Cressington, smiling at the grave, bearded man before her.

"Thank you, I am not at all fatigued," he answered. "What time would you like to start in the morning, Madame? We should not be later than ten to reach Venice by sunset."

"Oh, we'll be ready at nine," said Mrs. Silving. "Earlier, if you think wise."

"Then nine, I think, Madame, to be safe. Thank you. Will that be all?" he asked.

Mrs. Cressington looked at Mrs. Silving. The moment had come.

"We hope you will give us the pleasure of dining with us this evening, M'sieur Zoronoff," said Mrs. Silving, using his surname for the first time.

The chauffeur looked at the ladies a moment or two before replying.

"It's most kind of you—with very great pleasure, Madame Silving," he replied, bowing slightly.

"Then—at eight?" said Mrs. Silving.

The chauffeur withdrew.

"You know, Cora," observed Mrs. Silving, as she watched the dignity with which he went from them, after a courtly bow, "he's not an admiral in disguise, he's an ambassador. He makes me feel a queen!"

But at eight o'clock when the ladies came down into the simple reception-room they felt rather nervous about what they had done. Supposing he hadn't a spare suit, and came in with his blue reefer jacket?

"It had black buttons—so no one would know," said Mrs. Cressington.

"I could wish they were bright brass!" declared Mrs. Silving, with stout bravado.

The hotel seemed to have grown into a de-luxe one in the last half-hour. There were people actually in evening dress, proceeding to the dining-room. Waiters with white shirt fronts appeared. It had seemed only a simple chalet hotel when they arrived.

"Do you think we should have a corner table?" asked Mrs. Cressington. "Most of the people seem to have gone in."

"Why, Cora, that would be almost insulting. I shall ask him to give me his arm and walk right down the room. He might be my husband for all they'll know. I don't look my years."

Mrs. Cressington had to laugh, but just at that moment the expression of her friend's face changed, as she stared over her shoulder.

"Good evening," said a voice.

Mrs. Cressington, turning and beholding their guest who had come in, struggled hard not to show her astonishment. For there before them, magnificent in a uniform jacket, stood Vladimir

Zoronoff. The jacket, tight-fitting and squared at the shoulders, was of light blue cloth, with two rows of silver buttons. Epaulettes of scarlet, matching the chevroned wrist-bands, had braid and fringes of gold. A low black velvet collar carried twin gold stars at the fastening. Over the left breast-pocket ran a coloured strip of decorations.

Mrs. Silving was the first to recover her breath.

"Then we are both wrong. We said you were an admiral or an ambassador," she cried, laughingly.

"We knew you must be something," added Mrs. Cressington.

"May we know your correct title?" asked Mrs. Silving.

"Certainly. I am General Zoronoff, late of the Russian Chevaliers Gardes, and one time Chief of Staff to the Grand Duke Nicholas," he said.

"And we wondered whether we could ask you to dinner!" exclaimed Mrs. Silving, with her engaging frankness. "General, what an amazing story you must have!"

He smiled at his hostesses.

"Well, I have lived—and have great memories," he said, quietly.

"If you have no objection, we would like to hear some of them," said Mrs. Cressington. "Unless they are too painful."

"One achieves a philosophy," replied the General. "There are compensations always, I believe."

"And now, General, let us go in to dinner," said Mrs. Silving. "Will you give me your arm? These board floors are so slippery."

She took the proffered arm, and with the General on her left, a resplendent figure with his light blue jacket, and trim beard, and Mrs. Cressington on her right, she advanced towards the dining-room.

The boots and the concierge held open the glass doors, and

with all eyes in the long room watching them, the General and the ladies, escorted by the head waiter, walked to a table at the far end.

And it was there, at dinner in Heiligenblut, that Mrs. Silving and her friend found entertainment in General Zoronoff's story beyond anything they could have imagined.

CHAPTER XVII

DR. WYFOLD'S QUEST

I

ATTNANG is the junction for passengers proceeding from the Vienna main line to Gmunden. Dr. Wyfold, descending at Attnang, found that he must wait half an hour for the local train, or that he could hire a car and reach Gmunden in a few minutes. He decided to take a car and he proceeded some eight miles through a smiling valley down towards the famous holiday resort on the Traunsee. He had been recommended to the Hotel Bellevue and when he arrived there its situation greatly pleased him. It faced the lake and a long esplanade of plane trees. To his relief he was given an excellent room on the third floor, with a balcony. *"Schöne Aussicht!"* said the concierge, throwing open the shutters.

He did not lie. Below lay the Traunsee, shimmering in the late afternoon, with a dozen white-sailed yachts gliding across the blue water. On the other side of the lake, here at its head perhaps a couple of miles wide, rose the thickly wooded Grünberg, and beyond it came the great Traunstein, sweeping upwards from the lake. Farther down the lake rose a superb vista of mountains shutting in the long expanse of water, the Erlakogel, the Wilde Kogel, and the Sonnstein, grey-blue walls cutting the sky with their serrated edges in the clear, early evening.

When Dr. Wyfold had washed and unpacked he again stood on his balcony, high above the road and the well-trimmed treetops lining the esplanade. Away on the left an orchestra was playing, hidden among the trees. To the right, on a small island connected to the shore by a wooden bridge, stood a castle, with an onion-shaped cupola on its tower, an edifice of romantic baroque architecture. Dr. Wyfold learned later it was Schloss Ort, with a strange history, for it had been the home of an eccentric Archduke, who left it one day with his bride, the daughter of a blacksmith, to set forth on a new life in America. The Archduke's yacht left Europe to cross the Atlantic, and was never heard of again, Archduke, bride and crew disappearing into the void.

Well, thought Dr. Wyfold, as he strolled along the enchanting esplanade by the lake, after hearing the story of Schloss Ort from the concierge, this attractive town seemed to be a place of mysterious disappearances. Somewhere he had to find a hidden nephew. It should not prove difficult, for the place was small.

Presently he came to a pleasant little park on the lakeside, with a Kurhaus and a café, on whose terrace a band was playing lilting Strauss waltzes. He selected a table, ordered coffee, and surveyed the company at the surrounding tables.

It was a happy holiday scene under the pruned plane trees. The café had grown out on to a small lakeside terrace, with the Esplanade between, and as the band played and the visitors drank and talked, watching the dancers, or the sailing boats now crimsoned in the sinking sun, the town seemed to be taking its evening promenade. They were mostly visitors in bright holiday attire, with a sprinkling of natives enjoying the animated scene.

It was quite possible, since this was the place and time of Gmunden's *conversazione*, that he might see his own nephew come strolling along. Evidently all the world and his wife came to drink *Kaffee mit Schlagsahne* at the Kurhaus.

Dr. Wyfold was happy. He lit a cigar. Now he was here he felt it was a good thing for him to have got away from home.

He was becoming a hermit, and his garden had begun to exercise a tyranny over him, so hard and ceaselessly did he work in it. Gmunden was a delightful place, with its background of mountains, its placid lake, and the long Esplanade with its promenade in the green tunnel of the plane trees. To-morrow he must begin his task, if his alertness this evening went unrewarded.

In the brief talk with the concierge he had received an excellent tip. The police received the names of all foreign tourists visiting the town, from the returns made by the hotel proprietors. He might trace Reginald in this manner.

The police, to whom he went early on the morrow, could not help Dr. Wyfold. They were very polite but plainly their affairs were in a state of chaos. The heavy influx of visitors quite overwhelmed the administrative department. It was true that returns were made, with passport particulars, by the hotels, but they were not kept in alphabetical order. They produced an enormous sheaf of returns which went back for two months. After that the papers seemed to have disappeared.

Dr. Wyfold saw it was quite impossible to wade through all those papers. With much politeness he was referred to the Verkehrs Bureau in the Rathaus, with no result. He went to the Post Office, and battling with an incomplete knowledge of German he discovered that they had no idea whether there was a Mr. Reginald Wyfold, nor when he came for his letters.

In despair Dr. Wyfold left a note addressed to his nephew saying he was at the Bellevue, and departed. His whole morning had been completely wasted. Obviously he could not sit down on the doorstep of the Post Office, from opening to closing time, for a whole week on the chance that Reginald might call for letters.

What now? That was the question in Dr. Wyfold's mind as he

sat at lunch in the crowded dining-room of the hotel. He decided he would make a round of all the places where the visitors went, the cafés, the tennis-courts, the Strandbad, the *thés dansants* in the hope that his nephew might frequent one of them. He was an excellent swimmer and it seemed probable that he would turn up on the pleasant plage, with its terrace restaurant built out over the lake.

Three days passed, without the discovery of a single clue. Dr. Wyfold spent his mornings at the swimming place. The weather was hot and sunny. The doctor put on a costume, hired a deck-chair, and sunned himself while reading *The Times,* two days old, which now came to him by post. Often he wandered along to the end of the wooden pier and watched slim youths, their bodies golden-brown, perform amazing diving feats; some of the girls were just as expert.

It was a happy scene. Sometimes these young Austrians practised their English on him, and he developed the habit of inviting them to have ices with him on the café terrace. In four days he had become a popular figure with these Austrian Adonises and Venuses. The "Herr Doktor," they all called him, and somehow it became known that he was looking for a nephew. Half a dozen golden youths volunteered to become his nephews. They all had a passion to go to England. They were convinced they had only to live there to become rich.

By Wednesday of the following week Dr. Wyfold began to feel that he was making a fool of himself. That morning he had had to write to his sister-in-law and confess that, so far, he had failed, and was without a single clue. Each day he had gone to the Post Office to inquire if Mr. Wyfold had taken his note. No, it was still there. The young woman behind the counter said there were now three letters for Mr. Reginald Wyfold.

Surely soon he would call for his letters! And what then, Dr. Wyfold asked himself. It rested wholly with his nephew as to whether he called at the Bellevue, or communicated.

On Thursday morning, towards noon, as Dr. Wyfold dozed in his chair, he was awakened by a voice exclaiming, "Why, it is!" Starting out of his light sleep, he saw that the speaker was the Sharples girl, accompanied by her hiking friend, Philip Sayce. They were both in swimming costumes and were burned black. Lydia Sharples' face had peeled and she was a formidable object, but her cheerfulness was unabated.

"Oh, Dr. Wyfold—what a strange thing we should run into you just now! We walked from Bad Ischl yesterday, and who do you think was the first person we ran into when we got here —Reggie!"

Dr. Wyfold stared at Lydia Sharples' pickled face, and at the grinning youth beside her.

"Of course, we felt certain you were with him," rattled on Lydia, "and he was astonished when we told him you were here."

"When we told him you said you were coming here," corrected young Sayce. "For, of course, we didn't know for sure what had happened to you."

"No—for you see you said you were joining Reggie," said Lydia, relentlessly.

"Where did you see him, what time?" demanded Dr. Wyfold, ignoring the inference.

"Well, it must have been about eight o'clock, opposite the big hotel with the balconies," said Lydia, pointing towards the Esplanade.

"What!" exclaimed the doctor. "Outside the Bellevue! But I'm staying there! This—this is ridiculous! I've been here for a week looking for Reggie. The young fool gave me nothing but a Poste Restante address—and I can't find him. Did he say where he was?"

"No—and he was really rather strange, wasn't he, Philip?" said Lydia.

"Frightfully standoffish. We didn't seem at all welcome," observed Philip.

"Yes—and when we asked where he was staying, with the idea of meeting again, it was quite plain he'd no desire to see us," said Lydia. "I thought, perhaps, he didn't want to be seen with a couple of rather battered hikers."

Lydia Sharples laughed at her own remark.

"You know, Dr. Wyfold, Reggie was always a little odd," she added.

"Odd?" he queried.

"Well, perhaps I shouldn't say it, but I always had that impression," said Lydia, candidly. "Still, you're bound to run into him, like we did, aren't you?"

"But am I?" exclaimed Dr. Wyfold irritably. "I've been on a fool's errand for a week now——"

It was a slip, and the sharp Lydia saw it in a moment.

"Oh—is he hiding, Dr. Wyfold?" she asked. "That would explain why he was so peculiar with us."

The doctor picked up his towel and his *Times*. He glanced at the tower clock. The lunch place was filling up.

"Look here, my dear girl, you and Sayce come and have lunch with me in the restaurant. You've guessed some of the story. I'm going to tell you why I'm here, and what a mess it all is, just because of that idiotic boy. But you must promise to keep your mouth shut."

"Oh, we will!" affirmed Lydia.

At lunch he explained his reason for being in Gmunden. It

was a great relief to talk to someone, for the business was beginning to prey on his nerves. Lydia and Philip were sympathetic, but they could make no suggestions. They were leaving the next day. Reginald had looked well. He was wearing nothing but a white vest and a pair of leather shorts. He had no hat, no stockings, and wore sandals. He looked magnificently fit and bronzed.

II

By Friday Dr. Wyfold was beginning to work up a temper. He would have gone home, but mounting anger made him obstinate. He would find that young devil, somehow. But on Friday afternoon when he made his daily call at the Post Office, where the young woman now smiled at him as though he was an eccentric who should be humoured, his temper broke out. The letters awaiting Herr Reginald Wyfold had been called for!

Whatever it was Dr. Wyfold had said, the young lady fortunately did not understand. Outside the Post Office, angry and baffled, Dr. Wyfold suddenly saw a ray of hope. Reginald knew now where he was staying. He might call at the Bellevue.

That evening when Dr. Wyfold went out after dinner, to take his coffee at the Kurhaus, he left word saying he would be back at half-past nine.

"You are expecting someone?" asked the concierge.

"Yes, my nephew may call," answered Dr. Wyfold.

"Very good, sir," said the concierge, always obliging.

But Reginald did not call that evening, nor all Saturday, nor all Sunday. Dr. Wyfold felt both angry and hurt. It was too plain now that Reginald was deliberately avoiding him. Why? That question now filled Dr. Wyfold with determination not to be defeated. There must be some way of finding his extraordinary nephew. Find him, he would.

Dr. Wyfold as a tourist had one weakness. He could never see a mountain without wishing to go to the top of it. Every morning on opening his shutters and stepping out on to the balcony with its magnificent prospect, he looked southwards at the towering Traunstein, the monarch of the district. The ascent, he learned, took four hours. One went first by boat down the lake to Lainaustiege, from which village the ascent, not difficult, began.

So on Monday morning, taking a day off from his quest, Dr. Wyfold set forth, equipped with a light rucksack in which he carried his lunch. He was a sturdy walker, and had a sound heart.

The morning, slightly misty at first, soon cleared, and the day promised to be hot. The chugging paddle-steamer drew off from Gmunden and beat its way down the lake. The boat was fairly full. A man on deck played a zithern, sang Tyrolean songs and yodelled. It was all very musical comedy. Even the doctor felt an impulse to wear *Lederhosen* and leather braces. Indeed, he had almost succumbed to a green felt hat with a badger tuft like a shaving brush at the back.

He found himself talking to two pretty Austrian children and this presently led to a conversation with their parents. The family came from Vienna. The little boy and his sister, bright-eyed and vivacious, chirped like birds. Along the blue lake shone the villages, with their baroque towered churches. The mist, rising in white banks up the mountain sides, revealed chestnut and pine woods and shining upland meadows dotted with wooden chalets. So bright and smooth were these pastoral settlements that it seemed as if the mountain sides had been shaven.

Dr. Wyfold was sorry to part from little Franz and Sonia. He had taken their photographs and promised to send them. The family shook hands and bowed when they said *Auf Wiedersehen,* and they stood waving to him as the steamer drew away from the pier.

The ascent, after leaving the village, followed a wide stony road. Later, he passed through a belt of pine-woods. The lake and village began to fall below, with an ever-widening prospect. It grew hotter and the doctor removed his coat and opened his shirt. The exhilarating air made him want to sing, but he had no breath to spare. It was twelve o'clock. In another half-hour he would have his lunch. Up above, on higher ledges of the slope he could see chalets dotted about. For some time yet there would be these human outposts. The higher chalets were simple huts to which the cowherds moved for the summer pastures.

After half an hour, choosing a place with a particularly fine view, the doctor sat down and opened his rucksack for lunch. He was hungry and ready for a rest. There was not a cloud in the sky, and the view was clear. In the silence of this rarefied air he could hear the humming of insects over the grass.

His meal finished, he lit one of the light Austrian cigars, so cheap to buy in this country, and smoked it in great serenity of spirit. Life was very good, despite preposterous nephews and forceful sisters-in-law. He wondered what the weather was like at Wargrave, and whether they had fixed that new boiler without knocking down too much plaster.

The sound of distant cowbells broke the silence. It served to remind the doctor that he was thirsty and a drink of cold milk would be very welcome. Being a tidy and methodical man he gathered up the remains of his meal, wondering why hotels always provided twice as much bread and hard-boiled eggs as was necessary. He screwed up the pieces of paper, and put everything back into the rucksack, and then started off again.

It proved a long way to the next chalet, a low wooden one-story structure made of logs, with a built-out balcony. The roof was made of heavy flat stones. It was evidently summer quarters for these upper pastures on which a herd of cows were now browsing. There was a rough cart track to what appeared to be a milking-shed. There were gay flower-pots along the balcony, and, rather surprisingly, the two ground windows had pretty curtains.

Dr. Wyfold followed a rough footpath up to the chalet which had a magnificent prospect, with the Traunsee shining far below. He mounted four steps up on to the balcony, approached the open door and rapped with his stick.

No one answered. Dr. Wyfold looked in through the open door. For a mountain chalet it was well furnished, with a large stove in one corner, and two easy-chairs. The boarded floor had a couple of sheepskin rugs on it. A Tyrolean clock with weights and a long pendulum ticked solemnly on the wall. It was the only sound in that still living-room.

Dr. Wyfold turned back to the balcony. There was a round metal table with a couple of chairs, a row of flower-pots in the long wooden trough that fronted the balcony, and in one corner, a low string hammock. An enamel tobacco jar stood on one of the window-sills, with a pipe at the side of it. Some used plates were still on the table, with the remains of a meal. Evidently the family lived on the balcony.

Dr. Wyfold wondered whether it was worth while waiting, for no one responded to a second knocking. They were all out, and visitors were so rare and honest, apparently, that the chalet had been left open. Looking into the second room opening on to the balcony, the doctor saw two low truckle-beds and a man's clothing lying about.

He was still looking through the window when footsteps made him turn. Coming towards the chalet, with a dog at his heels, was a man, a peasant, almost naked except for his leather shorts.

He was an astonishing figure of a man, of medium height, with very broad shoulders, and muscular arms and legs. He looked about twenty-eight, and the mountain sun had burned his skin to a deep bronze. He had masses of brown hair, bleached to a light honey colour, which swept back from a broad brow. He wore heavy native shoes, and no stockings. His *Lederhosen* were girded about his muscular belly by a wide leather belt on which an elaborate design had been embroidered with wire. He bore on his shoulders a yoke from which hung two wooden buckets containing milk.

He paused on seeing the doctor, with no surprise on his tanned face, looked at him steadily, and after a pause he said *"Grüss' Gott!"* the native greeting.

"Grüss' Gott," replied Dr. Wyfold. "I came to see if you could give me a glass of milk," he added, slowing choosing his German words.   .

"Yes. A moment," said the young man.

Without saying anything more, he walked on, carrying the bucket, and disappeared round the back of the house.

Several minutes elapsed. When he appeared again he had a small pail of milk, and a drinking-cup, which he placed on the table, where Dr. Wyfold seated himself.

"This is a wonderful view," said the doctor, thanking him and filling his glass.

"Yes."

The doctor drank. The young man stood on the balcony watching him, but not speaking.

"Ah, that's good!" exclaimed the doctor, filling the glass again. "It's a lonely life here?"

"I like it," said the young man.

'You are only up here in the summer?"

"Yes."

"And in winter—where do you live?"

"Anywhere."

"Anywhere?" repeated Dr. Wyfold.

"I teach ski-ing—whenever I get a job."

"Oh," said Dr. Wyfold. So the man was not exactly a peasant. He had an intelligent face. Never had he seen a fitter human being. His bronzed body rippled with muscles when he moved, the skin had the satin sheen of perfect health.

"It must be a healthy life," commented Dr. Wyfold, his eyes running over the young man's body with professional appraisement.

"Yes," answered the Austrian, and for the first time he smiled, revealing strong white teeth.

The doctor pulled out a packet of cigars and offered his host one.

"*Danke, nein.* I do not smoke."

"No?" exclaimed the doctor, surprised. He looked at the pipe and tobacco jar in the window.

"It's not mine," said the young man, reading his thoughts.

"Oh—I see. You're not alone. I should think one can't live alone here?" asked the doctor, agreeably.

"Yes, I can. But not now."

Dr. Wyfold, having finished his second glass, lit his cigar. His host watched him. He had an animal passivity and stood there, without moving or speaking, a breathing statue of perfect manhood. Dr. Wyfold was sorry he was hampered by his scanty German. He would have liked to talk to him about his life on these uplands.

"Well," said the doctor, rising, "that was very good. How much, please?"

"Nothing—you are very welcome."

"Oh, but I would like to pay," he urged.

"No, it is little," said the young man, with a graceful gesture and a smile.

"Then *Auf Wiedersehen*," said the doctor.

"*Auf Wiedersehen*," answered the young Austrian.

Dr. Wyfold walked across the balcony and shook hands as he turned to go. His own was grasped by a big strong hand, roughened with toil. Then, just as he went down the steps, his glance fell on a book that had been balanced on the ledge of the balcony. Its title gave him a slight shock.

He walked on. How reserved and dignified the young peasant was, a magnificent animal, with a certain suspicion in his attitude; living this lonely life in the mountains made a man slow to accept the presence of strangers.

But when Dr. Wyfold had gone a hundred yards a sudden thought made him turn. The young man was still on the balcony, watching him. The doctor's suspicion became a conviction. The fellow wanted him to go, he was nervous about something. Deliberately, Dr. Wyfold turned and walked back to the chalet. The Austrian smiled as he came up the steps, but the expression was an uneasy one.

"Do you speak English?" asked Dr. Wyfold.

"A leetle, please?" replied the young man.

"Who's reading Gibbon's *Decline and Fall of the Roman Empire?* It is difficult English."

The Tyrolean did not answer for a moment or two, his clear blue eyes regarding the Englishman.

"It is my friend's."

"Who smokes the pipe and lives here?"

"*Ja.*"

"He is English?"

"*Ja.*"

"Is his name Wyfold?"

"Ja."

The two men looked at each other in silence for a time. There was no hostility in the younger man's face, he just calmly looked at his questioner.

"I would like to see him—I am Dr. Wyfold, his uncle," he said.

Again there was no change of expression on the young man's face.

"He is out," he said, quietly jerking his head to indicate that his friend was somewhere up on the slopes.

"Then I'll wait for him," said Dr. Wyfold, firmly. "I see you are not surprised to learn I'm his uncle. You knew I was here?"

"He told me."

"What is he doing here?"

"He works with me—with the cattle."

"How long has he been here?"

"Please, you sound angry," said the young man. "Why?"

The question was so childlike in its frankness that Dr. Wyfold regretted his manner at once.

"I'm sorry. You see, my nephew has given us a lot of worry. He's almost disappeared," explained the doctor, struggling with his German.

"He is very happy here," volunteered the young man.

"Doubtless—but he's been away six months, his mother is very distressed and has asked me to find him. Can't you go and fetch him—I must see him."

The young man looked at the doctor and hesitated a moment. Then he said, "Please, will you sit down? I will go for him."

"Thank you," said Dr. Wyfold, sitting down.

The young man went down the steps, whistled his dog, and disappeared round the chalet. Dr. Wyfold waited. So he had found Reginald at last. Whatever the mystery, there seemed to be no woman in it. This was an Eve-less Eden. His task was that much easier. It now resolved itself into practical Socialism, or some odd philosophy of life.

In about ten minutes he saw two figures coming across the pasture towards him. One was that of the Austrian, the other——

For a moment or so Dr. Wyfold could not recognize his nephew. Like his companion, he was naked from the waist up, with only a pair of leather shorts girded at his hips, and heavy shoes. Then recognizing Reginald in this young god with the golden skin, he saw how completely transformed he was. Every movement expressed supreme physical well-being, and as he came up the steps the poise of his head and shoulders, the clear frank expression of his eyes, his whole bearing was that of a man in whom health and mental happiness were visibly expressed. For a space Dr. Wyfold, rising, could find no word of greeting in his astonishment.

There was not the slightest embarrassment in his nephew's manner.

"Hello, Uncle Dick!" he said, holding out his hand.

"Reggie—what is all this about? You knew I was here? Why are you hiding yourself?" asked Dr. Wyford, unable to keep a note of protest out of his voice.

Reginald did not answer, but glanced at his companion, and then, addressing his uncle, "This is my friend, Max Schuler," he said.

Max Schuler bowed.

"I will go, please, and you will talk," he said, and left them.

"Now, Reggie," said Dr. Wyfold, as soon as he was gone, "what is the meaning of all this—why have you been dodging me?"

Reginald looked frankly at his uncle.

"I've not dodged you. You've been tracking me down, uncle, at mother's request."

"Well, naturally. We can none of us make head or tail of what's come over you. Frankly, we thought it was a woman—it's not, I assume?"

Reginald sat down opposite the doctor. What limbs the lad's got, thought Dr. Wyfold, running his eye over the figure before him. He could understand any woman falling in love with this golden Apollo.

"Well—you've seen no Circe here?" laughed Reginald.

"What are you doing here?" asked Dr. Wyfold, irritably. "Why haven't you come home? Your whole career is going to pieces. We can't keep on apologizing for your absence for ever."

"My dear uncle, don't. I haven't asked you to come here. I didn't call to see you because I know that nothing I can say will make my mother, or you, able to understand my reason for not going home."

"What is your reason, Reginald?"

The young man did not answer for a few moments, and sat rubbing his hands up and down his thighs.

"Uncle," he said, looking at him earnestly, "I can't give you a reason—not a reason you or mother will understand. That's why I did not want to see you. I've told my mother—and you know how fond of her I am—that I will not go back to the old life. Not on any account!"

"Why not?"

Reginald smiled at his uncle.

"You see, uncle, you are now asking me the very question the answer to which won't satisfy you. I'm not going back to London, and the Law Courts, to white shirt fronts and patent slippers, to eight o'clock dinner and R.S.V.P. invitations to dances and cocktail parties, because all the time I was living that round I had a sense of frustration. When I came out to the Tyrol last Easter, it was as if something had snapped in me. I tore off my old clothes and I walked and talked with real people, people whose feet and hearts aren't hardened on pavements, people whose eyes aren't blinded with arc lights and electric advertisements, whose ears aren't filled with crooners and jazz music and——"

"You mean you've gone back to Nature," interrupted Dr. Wyfold, and then checked himself. He must not lose patience. The young went through complaints of this kind, some of them. Others suffered from extreme sophistication. "I can appreciate all that," he added, "but you know, Reggie, one can get very tired of Nature, even of this."

He waved his hand to indicate his surroundings.

"It's not Nature, it's something in me, deeper," said Reginald.

The two men looked at each other.

"What, precisely?" asked the doctor.

"I was never really happy, either as a boy or a youth. I've not been happy all the time since I came down from Cambridge," said his nephew.

"But didn't you choose to go to the Bar?"

"Yes—it isn't that. It's something I wanted, deep within me, a completion of my instinct. I've found it, here," said Reginald, quietly.

Dr. Wyfold looked at his nephew. The boy was deadly serious. He detected, to his surprise, a note of fanaticism. This was going to be more difficult than he had imagined.

"Are you suggesting a—a religious—a mystical reason?" he asked, as sympathetically as he could.

"No, uncle," said Reginald, hesitatingly.

"Then what, exactly?"

"Exactly, I can't tell you."

"My dear boy, if you have a reason surely you can express it, somehow!" expostulated Dr. Wyfold.

"Not in any way you would understand," replied his nephew.

Dr. Wyfold jerked back his head, then he smiled.

"Do you mean I'm not intelligent enough?" he asked.

"I mean nothing offensive at all, Uncle Dick. I can only ask you to respect my convictions."

"But my dear Reggie, what are your convictions? What is all the mystery about? Why are you hiding yourself away in this cowman's hut——"

"I'm not hiding away—you've insisted on coming here," retorted the young man.

"I've found you, wholly by accident. Why all this Poste Restante business, why did you ignore my note, why won't you come home, why are you jeopardizing all future prospects? Really, Reggie—can't you see how strangely you're behaving?"

Reginald rubbed his neck, and then looked out across the valley below them.

"Strange to you, to my mother, yes. But I am happy as I have never been happy in my life before," he said, quietly.

"I can see you're well—it's a healthy life, I don't deny. But you can't live all your life in a peasant's chalet, looking after cows!" exclaimed Dr. Wyfold.

"Why not?"

"Why not!" reiterated Dr. Wyfold. "Really, my boy, you don't mean to tell me——"

"Uncle, don't let us quarrel," said Reginald, interrupting. "It is my life, and I'm old enough to make my own choice. I'm very fond of mother, and of you, Uncle Dick, but I have no intention whatever of going back to London, to that old life, to all the— to all the——"

He threw out his hands expressively, leaving the sentence unfinished.

"I can't say more, uncle. I warned you I couldn't say more," he cried, earnestly.

"Then, Reggie, what do you propose doing?" asked Dr. Wyfold, patiently. "Are you going to stay here all your days, with a cowherd for a companion, or marry some peasant girl? Your own income's very small."

"It's more than I need here. Max is not a cowherd. He was a physical instructor in the Theresianum at Vienna," said Reginald, spiritedly.

"I'm sorry—but what is he doing here, with cows?"

"He inherited a dairy business from a relation in Gmunden. In the winter he lives here, when he hasn't a job teaching ski-ing. In summer he comes here among his cattle. We've entered into a partnership. For the first time in my life I am completely happy. I'll go home to see mother, occasionally, but that old life's dead— completely dead. It doesn't matter whether mother or anyone understands or not. I've made up my mind, Uncle Dick."

Dr. Wyfold saw that he had made up his mind. This was a mental thing, and he was baffled.

"Well, I don't know what I'm going to tell your mother," he said, after a silence. "She thought, of course, you'd got tied up with some girl. I wasn't sure. I wondered if there'd been any love affair at home that had gone wrong. We feel these things acutely when we're young. But your mother said not. There's just one thing, Reggie, and I say it without being offensive to your good mother. Did you want to live alone more—had she got a little on your nerves? If so, I think after a talk with her——"

"Uncle, it's nothing of that at all," interrupted Reginald. "Mother was rather trying at times—but we got on all right."

"Then—there's nothing I can do?"

"Nothing, Uncle Dick."

"I really don't know what I'm going to say to your mother, how I'm going to explain your conduct," said Dr. Wyfold.

"I know that. It's why I didn't want you to come. I can't explain," answered his nephew, earnestly.

There was silence broken only by the cowbells.

"Very well, my boy," said Dr. Wyfold. "I'd better be going. I'll have to give up the idea of climbing to the top. I'll go back to Lainaustiege and get an earlier boat."

"I'll come with you to the village—I'll pop on a shirt."

He looked like a young savage standing there, with springy loins and square, muscular shoulders. His hair had bleached in the sun, like his companion's.

He went indoors, in the bedroom next to the living-room. Looking in, the doctor saw that the Austrian was cooking at the stove.

"Max, I'm going with my uncle down to Lainaustiege," said Reginald, having put on his shirt. "Anything we want?" he asked in German.

"*Nein, danke,*" replied his companion. Putting down the frying-pan, he followed Reginald out on to the balcony.

"Good-bye," said Dr. Wyfold, holding out his hand.

It was grasped firmly by the young man's rough hand. He brought his heels together and bowed.

"*Auf Wiedersehen,* Herr Doktor," he said, his blue eyes gravely resting on the older man. "You go to England?"

"Yes."

"One day I hope much to come," he said, with a gentle smile.

He stood watching them from the balcony as they went down by the path, until they had turned from view.

All the way down to Lainaustiege they did not allude again to the subject of the doctor's visit. Reginald told him much about the lives of the peasants, their incessant toil and frugal living. Max was an expert folk dancer, and had coached a *Schuhplatt-lertanz* team in Gmunden which had won the championship at the annual festival at Prien on the Chiemsee, where he was born. Reginald was a member of the team. Max was the oldest of a family of nine children. His father was a peasant farmer. His second sister was a successful singer at the State Opera in Vienna. There was a vein of histrionic talent in his family.

They had half an hour to wait for the steamer at Lainaustiege. Dr. Wyfold asked Reginald if he would like to come to Gmunden on the morrow, to dine with him. Somewhat to his surprise, Reginald accepted at once.

"Would you like to bring your friend?" asked the doctor, feeling an extension of the invitation was compulsory.

"Oh no, thanks. One of us always has to stay and look after the cattle. And Max doesn't care much for the social stuff," said Reginald.

The steamer came in. They said good-bye until the morrow. Reginald stood waving until the boat was well out into the lake.

Two days later Dr. Wyfold said a farewell to Gmunden. He was going home. His mission had completely failed. He had written to Janette, and the letter he posted was his third attempt. He was completely baffled. There was nothing in the boy's conversation or manner to suggest that he was mental. He propagated no odd political doctrines, or religious theories. In his talk he was completely normal. But on the subject of his return to England, and to his professional work, he was adamant. Baffled and irritated, Dr. Wyfold could not withhold a measure of admiration from his obstreperous nephew. The lad knew what he wanted and had found it, apparently. And that could be said of only a few people in this world.

Well, he had made a fool of himself, reflected Dr. Wyfold, sitting back in his seat in the Vienna-Boulogne express. And now he would have to face his sister-in-law, who would be certain she could have done the business better.

Let Janette try. She would come up against something in her son's character that would greatly surprise her. He was no longer the charming boy, amenable to her wishes. Whatever influence now dominated him, causing him to reject all the old standards of life, Dr. Wyfold had been made conscious of one thing; it had called forth the assertion of Reginald's manhood. He had seemed like a young lion, magnificently virile, in that mountain fold of the Traunstein.

Chapter XVIII

GOOD NIGHT, VIENNA

Now that the train was drawing into Vienna after its twenty-four hours' journey from the French port, Emil Gerhardt's weariness was dispelled by the growing excitement of his arrival in a city he liked. The journey had had its diversities. There was an old nun sitting opposite to him, a charming old Englishwoman, obviously of good class, with whom he had got into conversation. She was returning to her convent at Predeal, in the Transylvanian mountains, after visiting her relations in London.

In the early hours of the morning, as they were all dozing, a man had come into the carriage and had explained, addressing her somewhat excitedly in German, that he was a doctor, and a baby had been born on the train. Could she give any assistance in nursing it?

Thereupon the old nun and the doctor had disappeared, and all the carriage, awake now, sat speculating on this odd event. The nun did not appear again until the train had left Innsbruck. She said very little, except that the baby was a bonny boy, and the young mother and child had been taken to a hospital in Innsbruck.

"When do you get to Predeal, Sister?" asked Emil.

"To-morrow afternoon," she replied.

He marvelled at this old nun who undertook such a long journey. Why hadn't she a wagon-lit? Was she too poor, or did a vow of poverty make it impossible? Last night he had made

316

her a footrest with some of his baggage, and he had procured her
a bottle of Vichy water and some biscuits in the early stop at
Buchs.

The train arrived in Vienna on time. Saying good-bye to the
nun and his fellow travellers, three of whom were going on,
Emil descended to the platform. He had a slight hope that his
friend Rudolf Steyer might be there to meet him. But there was
no one. He knew Rudolf's hours at the hospital were very
irregular.

He took a taxi and gave the driver the address of the flat in
Lerchenfelderstrasse. It was just eight o'clock and the light of
the summer evening was beginning to fade. The tourists in
Vienna would be dining now at the restaurants along the Ringstrasse. Of old he had loved dining there, in the shade of the
trees. There was a favourite restaurant of his, Hartmann's, in
Kärntnerstrasse, almost opposite the Hotel Bristol. One dined
out there on the terrace, and saw all the cosmopolitan life of
Vienna flow by. Just now, in August, many tourists passed
through the city, coming from all the countries of Europe, with
English and Americans predominating.

Well, there was no dining on the Ringstrasse for him, these
days, not until his luck changed. He sat back in the taxi and fell
into a reverie. How nice it would be to take Daphne out to lunch
in the Stadt Park, with the flower-beds all in bloom, and the
orchestra playing on the terrace where one dined, overlooking
the parterres and the leafy promenade. She had the kind of *chic*
that was particularly Viennese. She would love the music,
Strauss's lilting tunes, frothy but exhilarating, which they played
so well. He would see her dark eyes sparkling with excitement as
they clinked their glasses in this gay city of *Der liebe Augustin.*

Ach du lieber Augustin, alles ist hin, Geld ist hin.

The old jingle rang in his head. It was prophetic. Like Augustin, his money was gone, his sweetheart was gone, and there was no money for feasting. Daphne must wait for better days.

He gave an unhappy laugh at his foolishness. Wait, indeed. What reason had he for thinking that Daphne would wait for a change of his fortunes? Why should she wait? How much did she care for him? How much of her kindness had been pity for him? He had never dared to express his love for her, in these days of disaster, thrown off by his fiancée, and exiled from his country. In that unbearable moment of parting on the platform he had almost blurted out his feelings, but the moving train had spared him that exhibition.

He shut his eyes. He could see Daphne now, coming up to his bedroom as he was packing. She had given him a travelling alarm clock, her own. "Oh, do take it, Emil, and perhaps you will think of me when it wakes you in the morning!" What exactly had she meant by that? For she seemed embarrassed the moment she had said it, and, thrusting it in his hand, had hurried away.

The taxi stopped. It had arrived at the block of flats in Lerchenfelderstrasse. He paid it off and stood for a moment on the pavement. Rudolf's flat was on the top floor, up a long flight of stone steps. A hungry-looking youth came up and offered to carry his bags. He let him take two of them and, carrying the third himself, led the way up. The stone-vaulted corridor was dimly lit. At last they arrived, and Emil's fears that he might find the door locked were dispelled by the immediate appearance of an old woman, who must have been listening for him.

"Herr Gerhardt?" she asked, smiling.

He paid the youth and entered the tiny flat. He knew it of old. He had stayed there with Rudolf, who made up an extra bed in the living-room, for it was a two-roomed flat with a tiny kitchen-bathroom.

A dachshund, Rudolf's Tita, came and welcomed him fussily. Emil deposited his baggage and looked round the cheerful little sitting-room.

"Herr Steyer—when will he be in?" he asked the old woman, as she closed the door in the lobby.

"Herr Steyer has gone to Gratz, this morning. He had to go very suddenly. I'm Frau Toder. I 'do' for him. He was very excited—it all happened yesterday. He's got a post. He had to go at once. He told me you were coming, and I'm to look after you. There's a note for you, Herr Gerhardt."

She took a note off a bureau. He opened it.

"DEAR EMIL,

"Welcome to Vienna, but, alas, I shall not be here when you arrive. The most wonderful thing has happened. I have got a place as junior house surgeon in the Military Hospital at Gratz. It has all happened in twenty-four hours. I shall be back in ten days. My tenancy ends then and I must move my things. Make yourself at home. Old Frau Toder will look after you. Will you keep an eye on Tita? I hate leaving her, but don't know yet if dogs are allowed in my new quarters. Send me a line when you get here.

"RUDI."

Rudolf's address was at the bottom of the letter, which Emil read with increasing depression. He had looked forward to Rudolf's bright company.

"And there's another letter," said the old woman, giving it to him. "It came this morning. Will you be wanting me now, Herr Gerhardt? I'm expecting my husband home."

"Oh no—I'll be quite all right. Have you fed Tita?"

"Yes—she's been home with me since Herr Steyer went, but I thought you'd like her for company," said the old woman, smiling. "What time will you want breakfast? Herr Steyer had it at eight."

"That'll suit me splendidly, Frau Toder, thank you," replied Emil, opening one of his bags.

"Then I'll say good night, Herr Gerhardt. I've made up Herr Steyer's bed for you."

"Thank you. Good night!"

The old woman went out. He heard the lobby door shut.

"Well, Tita, my dear—so you've lost your master, eh?" said Emil, laying out his things, preparatory to having a bath in the kitchen-bathroom.

Tita, long and sleek, jumped up on to the lounge and wagged her tail, pleased with male company.

As Emil turned, looking for a hook to hang his coat, his eye caught the letter he had put down unopened, when Frau Toder was talking to him. He picked it up. There was a local post-mark. He tore open the envelope, and looked at the printed heading. It was from the Austrian film company with which his old Berlin friend was now connected. He eagerly ran his eye over the typescript and then suddenly his heart seemed to stop.

". . . as Herr Waldstein had not arrived five days after he was due to return from Berlin, we made inquiries and learned that he had been arrested and sent to a concentration camp. So far we have been unable to establish contact with him, or even to find where he is interned. In the circumstances we have had to abandon the proposed picture for which he had cast you.

"We fear there is nothing for the present that we could offer you, and you will readily understand that Herr Waldstein's detention will involve us in considerable loss. While we shall be glad to see you when you arrive, we feel, in fairness to all parties, we must make it clear we can hold out no definite hope of any contract. We have only just succeeded in finding in Herr Waldstein's correspondence your proposed Viennese address, to which we are sending this letter."

Emil stared at the sheet of paper in his hand. Numb, he read it again. All his hopes toppled into ruin. He stood, shaking, too hurt to cry out. Then he collapsed into a chair, and sat there, unconscious of Tita, who came up and licked his hand. The first thing of which he was conscious was a public clock somewhere, striking the half-hour.

A few minutes ago he had felt hungry, and had decided, in a mood of recklessness—now that Rudolf was not with him—to go and dine at Hartmann's, and toast his new life in Vienna. But he had no hunger now. Rising, he looked round the flat, then he picked up his hat.

"No!" he said, kindly, to Tita, who rushed towards the door. The dog slunk away, disappointed. Emil picked up the key Frau Toder had left him, and went out.

In Lerchenfelderstrasse he paused. A tramcar rattled by. Then he began to walk. But he saw no one, nor knew in what direction he went. They had taken Louis Waldstein, they had thrust him into one of their foul camps where they were probably beating the life out of him, as they had beaten the life out of many. Perhaps he was dead now, had committed "suicide" as they cynically announced. One Jew less to contaminate noble Aryan blood, one more "eliminated" to enhance the prestige of Nazi thuggery.

Then he laughed so loud that passers-by turned and looked at him curiously. He increased his pace. Presently he emerged in the gardens beside the Palace of Justice. The very name of the place mocked him. He hurried on down the tree-lined Burgring until he came to the Opera House. But the lights and the traffic and the gay crowds were not for his dark mood, and he struck off behind the Burg Garten. Later, he found himself looking up at the Chancellery in Ballhausplatz. Above him were the windows behind which another Nazi murder had been committed. Why didn't they paint it red, symbolic of the blood they had allowed to drip from Dollfuss in those long hours of agony!

He marched on. He was in narrower and darker streets now. Then he crossed the Schottenring and, later, came to the large public hospital where Rudolf had studied. He turned homewards, but, suddenly, as he came into a side street, the light of a lamp fell on something that pulled him up. There on a hoarding, confronting him, was his own face.

It was an old poster, dirty and weather-beaten, advertising a film called *The Youth Patrol.* It was one of his old films, flamboyant propaganda for the new Germany, in which he had played the heroic rôle of a young standard-bearer. There he was now, with a military cap cocked jauntily over his brow. The wind had torn the poster, someone had made a blotch of mud over one eye, but oh, how he grinned there, *Gott in Himmel,* how he grinned!

Fury seized him as he looked at it. He felt degraded by the use they had made of him, by his smiling, lying endorsement of their schemes. And as he looked the face leered at him, so that a wild hatred of that handsome, tan-faced, twenty-toothed, uniformed dupe possessed him and provoked him to a frenzy of remonstrance. He looked around and chance supplied him with something fitting. Mud, washed down from the floor of a garage, lay in the gutter. He bent down and scooped it up, and with handful after handful plastered that grinning face on the hoarding.

"Hey! Hey! What's the game? What's he done to you?" cried a chauffeur, coming out of the garage, and seeing a young man, his hair fallen over his eyes, muttering frenziedly and plastering the advertisement with dirt.

Emil turned savagely on the man.

"They've killed him! Do you hear, they've killed him as they killed your Dollfuss!"

The chauffeur stared into the agitated face of the hatless young man.

"Hey, my lad, what's———"

But the wild figure had rushed away before his words were completed.

Late, how late he did not know, Emil arrived back at the flat in Lerchenfelderstrasse. He had walked off his fury, he had walked off his despair. He had grown very calm, for it was all clear now. Rudolf's absence in Gratz became an act of Providence.

He unlocked the door and stepped into the flat, switching on the light. Tita came running towards him. He stooped and patted her, then picked her up and talked to her. He walked through into the kitchen-bathroom, and stood there for a few moments. Then he returned to the sitting-room, put down the dog, and lowered the lid of the writing bureau. He wrote three letters, one to Rudolf, one to Rex, and one to Daphne. But the one to Daphne, after he had sealed the envelope, he tore up. Why cause her distress?

He got up, and carried a small arm-chair into the kitchen. The dog followed him.

"No, Tita! Back to your bed. Go on, back, Tita!"

He pointed to the dog-basket. Puzzled but obedient, the dog crept into its basket, and sat there wagging its tail. He walked across and patted it.

"Good dog!" he said, and switched out the sitting-room light.

He entered the kitchen and closed the door. Rolling up a towel, he placed it along the bottom, and then plugged the key-hole with paper. There was no fireplace, but the bath geyser had a ventilation pipe. He found the trap and stuffed in a dishcloth. The window was close-fitting. He opened the door of the gas oven and placed the chair between it and the geyser, facing the window, whose blind was not drawn. Across the darkness of the sky shone the illuminated face of a clock in a tower.

Emil turned on the taps of the gas oven and the geyser, switched out the light and sat down in the chair. The smell of gas soon filled the small kitchen. He began to feel drowsy.

Later, he heard faint chimes. Opening his eyes he saw, dimly, the round white face of a clock, its black hands pointing to twelve.

He gazed at it, with blurred vision, and then, murmuring "Good night, Vienna!" sank back, overcome.

Chapter XIX

MIDNIGHT AT BUDA-PEST

I

PERCY BOWLING was enjoying his long railway journey across Europe, but after leaving Vienna he began to feel a little weary and he was glad when his companion suggested they should go into the dining-car.

"There's nothing whatever to see, except the Danube, for the country's flat almost all the way between here and Buda-Pest," said Madame Balaton.

The journey had been made very pleasant by this most agreeable little Hungarian widow. She spoke English well, she was chatty, and, despite her fifty years, she was attractive, with a pretty round face and lovely grey Magyar eyes. In her day, reflected Bowling, she must have been a great beauty. Her hair was still dark, her skin white and unwrinkled. Slightly stout, she moved quickly, and she was well dressed.

He had first noticed her in his carriage after they had left Boulogne the previous evening. He had pulled up the window when they entered a tunnel and she had thanked him with a winning smile. For a time they did not speak, and then, going into the dining-car, he had followed behind, and was placed next to her at a table holding four persons. They began a conversation and he learned she was an Hungarian, Magyar by birth, who lived in Buda-Pest. She had been in London on business, her first visit since the War. She had often been there before, visiting an aunt who had married an Englishman.

The acquaintanceship thus made in the dining-car was strengthened further when Mr. Bowling, in the course of the night journey insisted on standing out in the corridor for a time, in order that Madame Balaton might rest her legs on his seat opposite, for the carriage was full, and the occupants were dozing perpendicularly.

At Bâle they went to the station restaurant together to get coffee, Madame Balaton leading the way, for she knew the station well. It was in the large dining-hall, as they hurriedly drank their coffee, that he learned a little more of his engaging companion's history. Her husband, who had died five years previously, had been a bank clerk. With the little money he left she had opened a *pension* in Buda, on the right bank of the Danube.

During the War Madame Balaton's aunt, a widow, living in South Kensington, had died, and she received news, via Switzerland, for Austria-Hungary and England were then at war, that her aunt had left her one-third of her estate, a sum of about five thousand pounds.

But since Madame Balaton was the subject of an enemy nation, she could not receive her legacy, all property and funds being sequestrated and administered by the British Crown. At the end of the War enemy claims were in suspension until the signing of the Treaty of Versailles. At last she had hopes of receiving her legacy, only to learn that all enemy funds were retained pending an international clearing-house settlement. Finally, after futile appeals and much correspondence, she had gone to London to make a claim in person.

"And what do you think they told me?" asked Madame Balaton. "I could only get the money by becoming English, and that meant marrying an Englishman! I said to them, 'Do you think an Englishman's worth five thousand pounds?' Oh, how they laughed at that! They were very polite, but they're holding fast to my money. Now is that honest?"

"It's shamefully dishonest," said Mr. Bowling, with real indignation. "Do you mean to say our Government's behaving in that way, when we're all at peace?"

"Yes—it's mine and it isn't mine," said Madame Balaton. "That's the funny thing about it—they're not taking it for themselves, they're even paying interest, and my money's grown to about eight thousand pounds—but I can't get it without marrying an Englishman!"

Madame Balaton laughed merrily, showing her pretty teeth. She did not seem at all depressed by the injustice of it. Evidently her *pension* was a thriving one. She was well dressed and had some good rings.

At dinner that evening she ordered a bottle of wine and insisted on Percy Bowling drinking with her.

"You'll love Buda-Pest. Everyone does. It is *schöne, schöne,*" she said. "Oh, the Danube, the lights along the quays at night, the cafés with zigeuner orchestras!——"

"But I shan't see Buda-Pest," interrupted Bowling. "I'm going on to Athens."

Madame Balaton opened wide her Magyar eyes.

"No! It is not possible! No one who has not seen Buda-Pest can pass through it! It is the gayest city in all the world," she cried. "You must stay!"

"I'd like to—but I don't know a word of the language, and I wouldn't know where to go," replied Bowling.

His companion raised her glass. He raised his.

"To your stay in lovely Buda-Pest!" she said, clinking their glasses.

"Thank you—if only I could," he replied.

"Of course you can—you must! I shall be really hurt if you

go through it. Listen. It is very simple. You come to my *pension*, yes? I give you a room very, very cheap. In the morning if Buda-Pest doesn't please you, you go. Why stay on this train two nights?"

Percy Bowling began to hesitate. The thought of a bed was as tempting as the thought of Buda-Pest, with its renowned gaiety. Why rush through to Athens? He had no one to meet there. He was his own master for the first time in his life.

"It would be rather a good idea," he said, hesitatingly.

"Ah, you come, eh? You will never want to go. And when you see the women—the most beautiful women in all the world —walking along the Corso, you will never, never leave our wonderful city! No, never, never!"

Madame Balaton filled their glasses again, and raised hers, laughing at her companion across the table. She was a little flushed with her excitement and Mr. Bowling was rather nervous about what their neighbours at the table would think. But either they did not know English, or they did not seem at all surprised.

When Mr. Bowling accompanied little Madame Balaton back to their carriage it was settled that he broke his journey at Buda-Pest when they arrived there at midnight.

II

Madame Balaton took charge of him from that time onwards. She saw that his bag went with hers, commanded the porter, ordered the taxi. They left the station and, to Bowling's surprise, all the streets seemed ablaze with lights, although it was midnight: they crossed a long suspension bridge which she told him had been built by English engineers, and he had a brief vision of a broad and dark river rimmed, up-stream and down, with myriad lights.

The taxi turned to the right when over the bridge, and entered a dark street. Presently it began to ascend a steep incline. Old houses with gabled windows seemed to be built up one over another. They bumped over rough cobbles and came to a halt at the foot of an immense flight of steps, lit by a sequence of lamps that seemed to disappear into the sky itself.

"Wait here!" cried Madame Balaton, quickly getting out.

She rang a bell in a wide nail-studded door. It opened instantly, as if they were expected, and Bowling followed her into a cobbled archway. A door opened in a dark wall. A girl in a white apron excitedly greeted Madame Balaton in an incomprehensible tongue. Another girl appeared and helped with the luggage.

Madame Balaton led the way up a wooden staircase, dimly lit. Bowling had a sensation of great adventure touched with a little fear. It was like a scene in a Continental film; an apache might dash out of a doorway.

On the first landing Madame Balaton opened a door and switched on lights. Before him was a long room with two windows, a large bed, a table and wardrobe, a couch and several chairs. To his surprise there was a fitted washbowl. This was his room.

"I'll charge you three pengoes a day. Look!" said Madame Balaton. She crossed to a window, opened the shutters and stood aside for Bowling.

The view made him catch his breath. Buda-Pest lay below him, a fairyland of lights gemming the darkness and the sweeping curve of the Danube with its slender bridges. Across the river there was about a mile of embankment blazing with lights. It was the Franz Joseph Quai, with the Corso, explained his hostess.

"Will you be ready in ten minutes?" she asked.

"In ten minutes?" he repeated, wondering what she meant.

"We'll go out to some of the cafés—no one goes to bed here until two o'clock," she explained. "It's just reaching its best over there."

"Certainly," said Bowling. He was tired, but the excitement of this new city stirred his senses.

Mr. Percy Bowling had read about life in novels. He knew there was night life on the Continent, with beautiful but light ladies, wicked counts, champagne, music and dancing. But all these things had really belonged to fiction and Hollywood for him. Now, before his amazed eyes, fiction became fact. If all these people were destined for Hell, as he had been assured in his home town, they certainly looked happy and were going there with zest.

Madame Balaton no sooner plunged him into the noisy vortex of one place than she pulled him out and plunged him into another. They had visited three cafés; this, the fourth and largest, quite bewildered him. It blazed with light. Hundreds of people were crammed at small tables laden with glasses. A buzzing of conversation was drowned in the music of an orchestra mounted high on a platform rising tier on tier to the ceiling.

Bowling had never seen or heard such an orchestra. It consisted of about forty small gipsy boys, swarthy and black-haired, their ages ranging from ten to sixteen. They were dressed in Hungarian costume, with red waistcoats frogged with gold braid, embroidered blue trousers and white linen sleeves, ballooned and gathered in at the wrists. It seemed probable that they had been born with violins under their chins. They played without a scrap of music, continuously and with inexhaustible vivacity. They made their violins scream, weep and wail. They drew out of them heart-rending laments, sad legends, wild dances, and worked themselves into a frenzy of incitement. The conductor, a child of ten, pale and perspiring, led his cohort to the verge of dementia. Each performance ended in a storm of applause. Glasses clinked, voices rose, the windows steamed.

Madame Balaton rose, and said something to Bowling. He followed her out. The cool air was refreshing. They got into a taxi. But Bowling discovered he was not going home, they were going to the Blue Barrel, high up on the hillside of Buda, where the immense Royal Palace lay like a mountain under the moon.

The Blue Barrel had a portico and a dance floor. The floor was bordered with small tables, in festooned alcoves lit with lanterns, under the open sky. It had a sad wailing orchestra with a wandering conductor who seemed to keep a tortured spirit under the bridge of his violin. He called at each table and played close to the patron's ear tragic folk-songs, melodies that evoked the melancholy of the vast plains of the Puszta. He made his violin sob out the love story of a forsaken maiden, the despair of a lover, or voice the abandon of horsemen rounding up the wild herd.

"What is that?" asked Bowling, when the violinist had played close to his companion. Tears seemed to have fallen from the bow.

"That is the story of a youth who went to fight because his sweetheart commanded him. He is dead. His sweetheart walks proudly, his mother stumbles broken-hearted. 'It is to the earth I come, Lázló, my son, to join you. She goes to another,'" interpreted Madame Balaton.

The orchestra broke into a passionate zigeuner dance. The floor filled up. Percy Bowling raised his glass of Tokay and toasted his laughing companion, then he led her to the floor and they were lost in the swirling throng.

It was nearly three o'clock when their taxi drove them home. They should have been exhausted, but the music and the wine, the dancing, the shining boulevards, the chains of lamps, the bright cafés, the gaiety of this sleepless city of music, stirred the blood.

"What a place! What a place!" reiterated Percy Bowling, flushed and excited, as he looked out of the taxi window.

"So! You love Buda-Pest?" asked Madame Balaton. "Did I not say you would? *Die Schöne Stadt!*"

"*Die Schöne Stadt!*" repeated Bowling, mimicking her German.

She laughed and slipped her arm through his.

No, he would not go to-morrow. He was not compelled to go anywhere. He was free. The world was a wonderful place. He was living at last. The future? Why worry? Events shaped themselves, as now. Here he sat with his charming new friend, driving through gay Buda-Pest.

And suddenly, struck by a romanticism he could never have believed possible, he did a thing no Englishman ever did. Like a demonstrative foreigner he raised Madame Balaton's hand to his lips and kissed it.

"*Ach, mein Lieber!*" sighed Madame Balaton, and leaned towards him with shining eyes.

CHAPTER XX

NOON AT NISH

WHEN the express was divided at Buda-Pest, one part going east towards Brasso for Bucharest, the other south for Belgrade and Nish, branching thence for Salonica and Athens, or Sofia and Constantinople, little Prince Sixpenny was fast asleep, for it was midnight. He had gone to bed almost immediately after dinner, served in their private compartment, and eaten in the presence of M'sieur Stanovich and Colonel Tetrovich. The meal finished, Miss Wilson had appeared and put him to bed. He was train-weary and had scarcely eaten all day. He had got the truth at last from M'sieur Stanovich. His father had been killed by a bomb thrown under his horse as he had ridden out from the Palace to attend some Army manœuvres. He had been killed instantly. So he was now the King of Slavonia.

"But I don't want to be King," he cried.

"Ssh! You must not say such a thing!" reproved Colonel Tetrovich. "It is your duty and your privilege to serve Slavonia. Remember the example of your father. The people are devoted to you."

"But they've killed my daddy!" cried Paul.

"It was a Communist," replied Colonel Tetrovich.

He looked at M'sieur Stanovich. Both knew the bomb had been thrown by the party to which the Colonel actually belonged, a military party eager to seize power on the pretence of a revolution.

"Don't worry your head, Your Majesty," said M'sieur Stano-vich, kindly. "The whole country loves you and grieves for your father. You'll have many friends."

"Is mother safe?" asked Paul of Miss Wilson when he was undressing. He liked M'sieur Stanovich, who had let him have his rabbit in the carriage, despite Colonel Tetrovich, who wanted it sent away and said it smelt, which was quite untrue. Very rudely Paul had said, "It's you who smell!" a remark that for once silenced the overbearing Colonel.

Miss Wilson assured him the Queen was quite safe, though she had no idea what the state of affairs was. Her heart ached for her charge. She knew well what lay before him. The happiness and freedom of his boyhood had gone for ever. That night, as she had often done in the Palace at Nish, she read him to sleep. Then she turned out the light and left the wagon-lit. The rabbit in its box was down on the floor. It also slept.

Paul was awake the next morning at seven. He raised the blind and looked out of the window. They were on a bridge crossing a broad, dun-coloured river. It was the Save, and ahead, beyond innumerable small islands, at the confluence with the Danube, was the citadel of Belgrade.

Paul hopped out of bed. The rabbit was already awake and turning in his box. Opening the wire cover, he lifted him by his long ears and got back into bed, nursing the rabbit on the quilt. There was one leaf of lettuce, and a little bran in the bottom of the paper bag on the shelf. Paul emptied it into the lid of a cardboard box. At this moment Miss Wilson hurriedly came.

"Paul, dear, we must keep down the blind!" she said, going to the window and drawing it.

"Why?" he asked.

"We're drawing into Belgrade. There'll be a deputation, and

Colonel Tetrovich is going to say you're fast asleep and can't be disturbed."

"How long are we in Belgrade?"

"About half an hour."

"Oh, splendid! Then we can get a lettuce for Gerry."

"Gerry?" queried Miss Wilson.

"I'm calling him Gerry in memory of Gerry Hamilton. Miss Wilson, he must be awfully hungry, he's only had this one lettuce since we left London. I know! Tell Colonel Tetrovich he must get me a lettuce."

"Darling, you mustn't be naughty. You can't ask Colonel Tetrovich to do a thing like that," exclaimed Miss Wilson.

"I detest him. I'd like to make him fetch a lettuce for Gerry, and salute him when he brings it."

"Now, Paul, we're in the station. Keep your blind down. I'll fetch the lettuce," she said.

"Oh, thank you, Miss Wilson," he cried, and lay back in bed while Gerry sniffed at his face.

At noon they arrived at Nish. His mother, in deep mourning, was at the station. There were ministers and soldiers, and, far back, a crowd behind a cordon of armed police. His uncle Prince Peter, two aunts, M. Javonovic, the fat Prime Minister, who used to play chess with his father, and the Mayor of Nish, were grouped behind his mother. There was a Guard of Honour, which Paul scarcely saw. Walking at his mother's side he went out of the station, into a closed car. He heard a voice giving commands, a clatter of feet, a rattle of musketry. He saw a dark crowd, hatless and sad, watching him silently as he drove past; the broad, well-paved streets were flooded with the noonday sunshine. The cafés were spread out under the trees, the villas in their leafy gardens had their coloured awnings drawn. The car traversed the bank of the river Nishava, and then turned in at the Palace gates. He had arrived home.

II

Paul slept that night in his familiar bed, in the corner room overlooking the courtyard, with its central fountain, and the grey Nishava, sweeping under the bridge and the walls of the Citadel.

Actually, Paul could not sleep. His mind was full of the varied impressions of this strange day. There had been the meeting with his dear mother. She had not cried when she met him, but the moment they were in the Palace she broke down and hugged him to her. When he asked to see his father, he was told it was not possible yet. A catafalque had been erected in the ballroom. All day the people had been filing past their dead king.

Paul sat up. He heard the clock over the stables strike one. Then he must have slept. His room was quite light, with an almost full moon looking in through the window. He sat and listened. Everything was quiet. As of old, Miss Wilson was sleeping next door.

He was now wide awake. He got out of bed and went to the long French window, which was open. He stepped on to the balcony. The night was warm. Immediately below him there was a striped sentry box. The moonlight glinted on the helmet of the guard standing by it. Nish lay soft as a crayon drawing in the white light. The grim Citadel frowned over the river and the Turkish quarter opposite, whose minarets still bore witness to the Turkish occupation up to 1877. The city where Constantine the Great was born looked beautiful in the summer night, spread over the hillside, with its tree-lined promenades and bright villas set amid luxurious gardens.

Standing there, for no reason at all, Prince Sixpenny suddenly thought of the house in Surrey, and the kind Hamiltons. What ages back it seemed since Gerry had come out to call him down from the dovecote, and it was only sixty hours ago! It all seemed years and years, and now he was home again it was all a rather faint dream.

At the thought of England and Gerry, he suddenly remembered the rabbit. How had he come to forget it? He had not seen it since they left the train. The fear that it might have been left in the train smote him. In the excitement of arrival, and all the subsequent bustle, he had forgotten Gerry. And Gerry, now, was the symbol of that happy time in England, of his school friends, of the Hamiltons, and the house with the lovely meadow, and freedom to roam about with his friends, wearing only a cricket shirt and a pair of flannel shorts.

There was a room by the bottom of the grand staircase in which boxes and parcels were stored before the Palace marshal distributed them. Was Gerry's box there? How terribly hungry and thirsty he must be! The thought agitated him. He would go and see.

Putting on his slippers, Paul opened the door and stepped out into the long corridor. It was deserted. One light burned halfway down it. Paul went noiselessly along until he came to the staircase. He was on the second floor. He went down the broad staircase, with its bronze gilt rail, its alcoves with statues and palms. His feet sank in the thick scarlet carpet. He came to the first-floor landing, a point of danger, for there before him were the high, closed doors leading into the ballroom. He thought soldiers might be on guard outside them, but there was no one in sight.

He reached the ground floor, tiptoed across the wide marble hall, and peered in through a small glass window. The night porter was fast asleep in a chair. Moving on, Paul gained the door of the cloak-room, opened it, stepped in and switched on the light.

It was in a state of disorder. There were boxes everywhere. Swords and uniform coats, and rolls of drugget for the entrance steps, chauffeurs' greatcoats, the major-domo's silver-braided tail-coat; it was a general dumping ground. Paul quickly surveyed it all, and then his heart jumped. There, on a table, was the wire-covered box, with *Best New Zealand Butter* in bold black letters on the side. And, under the wire, alert at once, was Gerry.

Paul picked up the box, switched off the light and left the room. He moved to the staircase, and mounted until he came to the ballroom landing. He paused, with his heart beating quicker. His father lay in state in there. Dare he have one look?

With his free hand Paul turned the handle. The great mahogany door swung back noiselessly. He stepped inside on to the polished floor, and then he stood, awestruck by the scene before him. Three immense crystal chandeliers hung from the high ceiling of the ballroom. The far one reflected the light of the six tall candles that burned on the black catafalque. Between the giant candlesticks, draped with the flag of Slavonia, lay the coffin. At each corner stood a motionless figure, with bent helmeted head. There were four of them, soldiers of the King's Bodyguard, in their blue coats, white trousers and polished Wellington boots. Paul was their honorary colonel. It was the first military uniform he had worn.

For a long time he did not move, staring at the solemn spectacle before him. Then, impelled by an overwhelming desire, he moved noiselessly in his slippers down the long floor until he reached the catafalque.

He knew the guard had seen him. He saw one of them sway slightly over his reversed musket. But they kept up the pretence of an unseeing vigil.

Paul stood still. The catafalque was banked up with large wreaths and great clusters of white lilies and scarlet cannas. The coffin was too high for him to see in it. Paul put down his box.

"Please lift me up," he said, to one of the guards.

The young soldier gave him a startled look, glanced at his companion at the opposite corner, as if seeking advice, and then put down his musket on the dais and came to Paul, lifted him up, and mounted the first step of the dais.

Paul could see his father lying in the coffin. He was in a uniform coat, a ribbon and orders across his breast. His hands were folded over a small jewelled crucifix. The face was calm and white.

For a long moment Paul looked at his father. Then the tears began to fall down his cheeks and his slim pyjama-clad body shook in the arms of the soldier.

"If you please, Your Majesty, you must go back to bed," said the young soldier. Despite himself, tears welled in his eyes.

"Yes," said Paul, between sobs.

Still carrying him, the soldier stooped and picked up the box. Then he walked down the ballroom, his heavy boots breaking the silence. They reached the door.

"I can go now—thank you," said Paul, his arms about the soldier's neck. Looking into his face, he saw he was only a lad of about nineteen.

"Let me take Your Majesty to your room," said the young soldier. "Please, where is it?"

"The next floor," said Paul, choking back his tears.

The soldier mounted the stairs. He was strong and did not

feel his burden. He came to Paul's room, and there, first depositing the box with the rabbit, he set Paul down on his feet.

"That's my rabbit from England," said Paul, removing the wire covering, as he knelt beside the box.

The young soldier removed his helmet and knelt down with him, stroking the rabbit.

"I think he'd like some water—he must be thirsty," said Paul. He got up, went to a wash-stand and poured some water from a carafe into a soap dish, and brought it to the rabbit.

"Perhaps he feels too strange," said Paul, when the animal refused to drink.

The soldier watched, on his knees beside the boy. The rabbit was lifted back into the box and the wire netting was replaced. They both stood up.

"Your Majesty must go to bed now. I must go, too. If the officer comes—" the soldier began to explain.

"Tell him you brought me back to bed," said Paul, getting into his bed. "What is your name?"

"Mischa Kusac, Your Majesty," said the soldier, holding his helmet under his left arm, and standing stiffly again. He had crisp hair and a peasant's round blue eyes.

"Where do you come from?"

"Stalatz, Your Majesty."

"Oh, with the castle. I've seen it," he cried. He pulled up the counterpane over him. "Good night, Mischa. Thank you for being so kind."

"Good night, Your Majesty."

The young soldier drew himself up, replaced his helmet, and saluted before leaving.

When the door had closed Paul turned out the light and lay thinking. His father had not been disfigured, as he imagined when they would not let him see him. On the bedside table he could hear the ticking of the watch his father had given him on their last day together in the Palace. The thought made him choke. Burying his face, he had to cry a little. Kings did not cry, but he could not help it. He had not let Miss Wilson see him cry since leaving London. Only Mischa Kusac, the soldier boy, had seen that.

He heard a steady marching of feet on the gravel in the courtyard. He knew that sound. They were changing the guard. He listened until their feet had died away. Then the clock in the stables struck the half-hour. He slept.

CHAPTER XXI

EVENING AT SALONICA

I

WHEN he had finished lunch, after the train had left Nish, Mr. Alexander Bekir dozed most of the afternoon. It was very hot as the train crept up the valley alongside the torrent of the Morava, and proceeded to enter several tunnels as it penetrated the mountainous barrier. He knew the route well, and the last few hours of this long journey to Salonica always found him impatient. So, with the aid of an excellent bottle of wine which had induced sleep in the hot afternoon, he did not wake until the train had reached Skoplje, whose many mosques and minarets bore witness to its former Turkish character.

There followed a long rocky defile amid barren mountains, then more tunnels, and a wide, monotonous valley. It was five o'clock. Mr. Bekir opened a novel he had bought at the bookstall in Belgrade, but his mind wandered. Was Madame Huysman monopolizing his present to Julie? He could see her sitting back in the Rolls-Royce, superbly *grande dame*. But no, to-day was Friday, and they would be down at Thurlestone. At this very moment they were all probably on the beach. He could almost hear the cries of Achille, Lucille and Dorette as they splashed in the water, while Julie sat and embroidered. One August he had spent a happy week there with them, before departing on his annual visit to Salonica.

The train chugged on through the mountain passes. They be-

342

gan to follow the course of the Vardar. They were nearing the Greek frontier. Once upon a time all this had been Turkish territory, and he had heard his grandfather tell of how he had been Governor of a vilayet in this country. Mr. Bekir looked on it with an envious eye.

Towards evening they came to the Greek frontier and customs station at Djerdejelija in the plain. They were now only eighty kilometers from Salonica. The sun began to set. Mr. Bekir always regretted this train did not arrive in time for him to see the last light of day over the peaks of the Chalcedonian mountains, and, to the south, the mountains of Thessaly dominated by venerable Mount Olympus, seat of the ancient gods.

For the last half-hour the train travelled through the wide plain north of the estuary of the Vardar. At half-past ten they entered the station. Mr. Bekir's long journey had ended.

A few minutes later, seated in a taxi, he was driving through the town, along the wide Rue Egnatia which crossed the lower town, now mostly rebuilt since the disastrous fire in 1917. Then, beginning to rise from the town bordering the Gulf, they came to the older part of the city, with narrow streets and overhanging houses. Higher and higher they mounted, and as they penetrated this labyrinth of streets, the ancient Turkish character of the city began to reveal itself. Many of the mosques survived, converted to churches, but their minarets had all disappeared.

The taxi bumped over the rough cobbles. Unsavoury smells pervaded the hot August night. The moon gave enchantment to what by day stood revealed as a quarter of ruinous old houses. Their windows were grilled and latticed. Villas that had known more prosperous days stood secretively behind high walls hiding inner courtyards.

Under one of these walls, before a heavily studded gate, in a dark winding street in the shadow of the monastery of Vlatéôn high on its rock, Mr. Bekir's taxi stopped.

He got out, and pulled an iron chain. The clanging of the bell broke the heavy silence. In a few seconds footsteps were heard crossing the cobbled courtyard, and a small wicket gate opened. A man looked out, his face almost invisible in the darkness.

As soon as he saw Mr. Bekir standing there, he broke out into a torrent of excited Turkish. Mr. Bekir, greeting him, passed through the wicket gate, while the man, an old negro in green Turkish trousers, brought in the luggage.

The inside of the courtyard provided a surprising spectacle. It was very large, with a central fountain around which grew some carob trees. Three sides of a house with white walls glimmered in the moonlight. Its upper floor had long open balconies.

Mr. Bekir crossed the courtyard to an open-air staircase in the corner. He slowly mounted it, passed though a door on the balcony, and was greeted by an old woman, who, talking all the time, followed him down a long corridor.

He entered a low room, dimly lit by a hanging lantern, gave his hat and coat to the woman, put on a long silk gown, fastened by a sash, and sat down while she took off his shoes and placed heelless slippers on his feet. All the time she talked to him in Turkish, laughing and shaking her fat body. The old negro eunuch now appeared. Yes, Madame expected him and was waiting in the haremlik, he replied in answer to his master's question.

Alexander Hassan Bekir, placing a tasselled fez on his head, rose from the chair, and passed through a small doorway with a bead curtain. A leather-padded door confronted him. He pushed it open, and crossed the threshold of his harem.

He was in a long, low room decorated with Persian faïence tiles. There was a slight perfume in the air. It was softly lit. At the far end, on a low couch, sat a very stout woman of about sixty. At her back, on the upper part of the wall, were draperies of old silk, embroidered with Arabic inscriptions.

"Hassan!" cried the fat woman, delightedly, clapping her hands with excitement. "Oh, Hassan—you have come! Allah be praised!"

She made no attempt to rise, and Hassan Bekir, answering to the name by which his wife greeted him, stooped and kissed her brow, and seated himself at her side, patting her white soft hand.

"Zaideh and Medil—where are they, Casima?" he asked, looking round the harem. "Not in bed?"

"Oh no, they are up, but so tired with excitement, and trying to keep Zilla good."

As she spoke a young woman, in loose silk trousers, came into the room. With a cry she ran towards Hassan Bekir, and stood while he rose to kiss her. She was the youngest of his three wives, a girl of twenty-five, of high birth, a true daughter of the house of Osmanli. She was of the new Turkey of Kemal Pasha, but scorned it. Her father had been exiled and had died in Cairo, but not before she had passed the threshold of Hassan Bekir's house. Last year she had given him a son, Ali, the only male child of the house, for Casima had given him three daughters, all of them married, and Zaideh two daughters, one dead, and one Zilla, aged ten, here in the harem.

"I will tell Zaideh," she said. "She is playing with Zilla in the nursery. The child is terribly sleepy, but said she must sit up for you."

"Go to her, Hassan," said Casima, who was so stout that she never walked anywhere. "And you will see how Ali grows, the darling!"

She picked up her embroidery, an "ayet" for her bedhead, with a text in Arabic from the Koran stitched in gold thread on a ground of rose velvet. She had always treated her husband like a small boy, and, dismissed, he followed Medil obediently.

In the nursery Zaideh rose from a divan to greet him, full of questions concerning his health and his journey. His second wife was a woman of forty, with dark sad eyes. Much of her beauty still remained, but she had been saddened by her failure to give her husband a son, and by his marriage of Medil, and her success in this respect. But the two women got on well together. They were both greatly in awe of Casima, who ruled them firmly.

Hassan stooped and kissed his little daughter Zilla, black-haired and black-eyed. The child always reminded him of Achille. She had the same dark face and vivacious manner. He sat and talked with her. Yes, he had brought her a present from England. He had brought them all presents.

"Oh, what are they? Please! Please!" exclaimed Medil excitedly.

"To-morrow morning you shall see them, my dears," said Hassan Bekir.

"But we shan't sleep for wondering!" said Zaideh.

"Daddy, is it a wrist-watch?" asked little Zilla breathlessly.

"In the morning you will see. And now good night, darling," he said, bending over the child in her bed.

She put her thin little arms around his neck, and kissed him.

"Oh, daddy, I'm so happy you've come," she said.

Hassan tucked the coverlet over her, smiled at her mother, and turned to Medil.

"Ali?" he said.

"Fast asleep! Come!" said Medil, softly.

He followed her into a small room, with two beds, one for Medil, one for her son. A small dark head lay on a pillow. The baby was fast asleep. One pink naked foot protruded from the coverlet. Hassan looked down on his son in the cot. When he had last seen him he was only three months old. The boy was growing rapidly. Hassan gazed at him with a grateful heart. He had Bekir and Osmanli blood, he would grow up a true son of the Prophet.

II

Hassan Bekir rose early the next morning and went up on to the flat roof of his house. It was six o'clock and the risen sun already warmed the air. The view from the roof of his house, high up on this foothill of Mount Khortialis, was magnificent. Around him lay the old part of the city, an amphitheatre that sloped down to the Bay, with its large harbour and shipping. Behind him the old walls, which had once enclosed the city, were still intact, crenellated, and flanked with crumbling towers. The Eski-Delik gate, with its high arch, was unbroken in the north side of the old ramparts. Down by the long quay on which the popular cafés were found, rose the great White Tower, at the eastern extremity, with its memory of Sultan Mahmoud's massacre of the imprisoned Janissaries. At the western extremity of the long promenade lay the harbour and the jetty, with the tobacco leaf store-sheds and offices of Messrs. Bekir & Co.

Hassan Bekir loved this city. He loved it for many reasons, chiefly for its beauty, situated thus at the foot of the mountains, with the blue bay and the great Gulf for its highway to the East. Of all the cities of the Orient, excepting Constantinople, it had a greater number of monuments of antiquity and, above all, of the Middle Ages, than any other. Was it not here, to visit his beloved Thessalonians, the Apostle Paul had come? A devout Moslem, Hassan Bekir, nevertheless, treasured these associations with history. He lamented bitterly the disappearance of all the minarets, the conversion by the Greeks of all mosques into churches. It had always been a city of refuge: for the ancient

Greeks, when Athens was in ruin; for exiled Cicero and Pompey; for the twenty thousand Spanish Jews evicted in 1492 by the Alhambra edict. It had been a Turkish dominion until 1910, when the disastrous Balkan War had resulted in the Greeks regaining possession of the old capital of Macedonia. Those wretched Greeks had despoiled the beautiful old place. Not a minaret remained from which the muezzin could make the call to prayer for the thirty thousand Moslems who still lived in this city.

But there was a great compensation. In these degenerate days, when Turkey had lost her prestige, when her dictator, Kemal Pasha, obsessed with modernizing, had decreed the abolition of the ancient traditions of Turkish life, the faithful Moslem could still preserve here his customary life. Here he might wear the fez, here his women could go forth enveloped in the black *tchar-chaf* and *yashmak*, attended by their negro eunuch. Here, safe from official interference by hectic reformers, the harem was inviolate. Behind the high walls of his house no edict of a crazy dictator took effect. The easy-going Greeks left him in peace. It was here that ancient Turkey still lingered.

Hassan Bekir looked out over this city of liberty, beautiful in the morning sun, with its terrace houses, flat roofs, ancient walls and splendid harbour. Allah be praised, a man might still live in dignity and faith, as his forefathers had lived.

He turned towards Mecca, unrolled the prayer rug, and removed his slippers. Then, on his knees, he bent low, touching the ground with his forehead three times.

"Allah il Allah! Allah il Allah! *Allahu akbar!*" he cried, throwing his arms upwards, and again touching the ground with his brow.

CHAPTER XXII

MORNING AT PREDEAL

THE sun, whose rising over the Chalcedonian mountains had found Hassan Bekir at prayer on the flat roof of his house in Salonica, came slowly through the early mist that clothed the mountain-side where Predeal lay, high up in the pass. The great range of the Transylvanian mountains was still enveloped in mist, but the villagers were astir.

Sister Teresa was awake soon after six, despite her long journey concluded the previous evening. She had been met by two of the Sisters, who greeted her as soon as she had descended from the train that continued its journey down the Prahova Valley to Bucharest, a hundred miles distant. They had driven from the station in an old closed horse carriage, through Predeal, its high street full of summer visitors from Bucharest, out to the Convent set amid pinewoods looking southwards down the valley.

What a welcome the Sisters and the children had given her! How lovely the country was, with the autumn tints and the harvest already advanced, for autumn came early here, high up in the mountains.

She had borne the journey wonderfully, and now, as she rose in the sharp morning and dressed in time for early Mass in the convent chapel, she opened the window of her cell and gazed out. Down on the road that led by the convent to the fields where they were gathering the wheat, an ox-wagon slowly passed, its wheels squeaking in the still morning. Then a small boy drove a herd of buffaloes and cows along to new pastures. More oxen, straining under their yoke, drew a farm cart, their breath steaming in the cold air. Then, suddenly, a shaft of sunlight filtered through the mist and struck the top of the dense pine forest.

A bell tolled for the early service in the chapel. Sister Teresa dressed in her dark blue habit, with white cornette, and a rosary and crucifix swinging from her waist. The Sisters had suggested she should rest this morning, after her long journey, and she had half consented. But now, when she woke, she felt well rested and alert. The mountain air was like a tonic. Surely that doctor in Wimpole Street did not know what the air of Predeal could do!

A few minutes later, down in the hall, the Sisters, collecting for chapel, were surprised to see their Mother Superior descending the stairs. She greeted them all by name, and led the way into the convent chapel.

After an early breakfast Sister Teresa returned to her cell for an hour's devotional reading. She repeated the Little Office of Our Lady, and the special prayers. Then rising from her *priedieu*, set in an alcove, with a crucifix hung on the wall above, she went to a chair by the window and read the book whose pages she knew by heart, Thomas à Kempis' *Imitatio Cristi*.

But, strange to say, her mind wandered this morning. She began to think of her fellow passengers in the Arlberg-Orient express. There was that poor little peasant girl from Feldkirch. The doctor was taking her to a hospital in Innsbruck. How did it fare with her and the baby, she wondered. She had nursed the tiny infant while the mother had had a short sleep after the train had left Bâle. It was strange to be thus holding a newly born infant again after forty years, and she had experienced a brief sense of having slipped back to the hour when she had held her own babe, Ronnie, the last born and most beloved.

Was this child destined, after many years of care, to be sacrificed on the altar of Moloch, to lie mangled in his prime on a battlefield? All Europe was seething with unrest, strange and dreadful doctrines of force were being propounded and the nobility of patriotism degraded for political ends.

It was not her province to think of these things, but she could not ignore them. The world seemed to be slipping into organized evil and intolerance. There was the story told to her by that delightful young German, who had been so kind to her on the train. He had begun talking to her about music, when they had seen Gollwitzer pass down the carriage to the dining-car. The young man had then revealed the fact that he was a film actor and had worked in Berlin, Hollywood and London. Then, later, he told her the story of his exile, bitterly, she thought.

"I hope you'll be very happy and successful in Vienna," she had said to him, after he had gathered his things together as the train drew into that city. She had confessed, with a smile, that she had never seen a film. "There were few such things before I took the veil, and now, of course, I do not go. But I wish you success."

He looked at her in great astonishment, his blue eyes wide open at her confession.

"How difficult it is to realize there's anyone who hasn't seen a film!" he exclaimed. "And you never will?"

"Never," she said, with a quiet smile.

"Do you know, Sister, I've never talked with a nun before," he said. "But you're not like a nun, if I may say so."

"Why not?" she asked, much amused.

"I don't know—you're so human. I should like to know more about your life—what you think of; if you ever regret leaving the world."

"Of course we're human!" she said. "Our thoughts are of God and His purpose with us."

"You will be shocked when I tell you I've lost faith in God—in one with a personal interest in human beings," he said very seriously, but shyly.

"I am not shocked. I am sorry," she replied. "There is nothing will take the place of faith. Without faith in human will we can scarcely do anything. We have faith in the driver of this train, in the signalman to whom our lives are entrusted. How then can we live eternally without faith in God? But I must not preach to you," she said, checking herself.

His beautiful face had smiled at her, sadly she thought. He was young and sensitive, and suffered as only the young can suffer.

"I am sorry I must say good-bye. It is comforting to talk to you. I'm unhappy and becoming afraid of life," he said. "You see, I've had so much, and it came so easily. I've never willingly done anyone harm, and after what has happened to me recently, I'm rather like a frightened dog with a tin can tied to its tail—I work myself up into a panic."

He talked freely and introspectively, as only a young German would talk. She saw how deeply moved he was. The train drew into Vienna station. He passed his luggage out through the window to the porter down on the platform. Then, pushing back his blond locks, almost silver, so fair was he, he held out his hand.

"Good-bye, Sister. You have made my journey very pleasant. I like to talk English. Thank you."

"Good-bye, and God be with you," she had replied.

He looked at her, smiled a little sadly, bowed and left the carriage.

He was a mere boy, and she saw by his quick expression and restless hands how worn were his nerves. For some reason he was in her thoughts this morning, his fair face very clear before her.

Sister Teresa looked at her watch. It was half-past nine, she had much work to do. There had been an accumulation of things during her absence. She had to appoint a new teacher in the orphanage. The convent farm was not prospering. John Nicolai had not been the same man since his only child Marina had run away to Bucharest with Stefan, the good-for-nothing Magyar violinist. Nevertheless, he should not drink, and beat his wife and neglect the farm. She must warn him. And at ten the Mayor of Predeal was coming to her office. Three times, reported the bailiff, had the town's roadmenders fired the convent's woods with their camp-fires, and now the Mayor disputed the compensation claimed. His own niece was in the orphanage. He was a Russian by descent, obstinate and crafty.

There was a tap on the door.

"Come in!" she called.

The little Sister Monica, who had just taken her vows, stood in the doorway, shyly. She was a happy little soul, the daughter of an official in the Royal château at Sinaia. She worked in the convent bakery. But this morning her face was sad.

"If you please, *Ma Sœur,* may I go home to Sinaia? Yesterday morning my grandmother died. She is buried to-morrow. The motor-bus leaves in the morning at ten and I can be back at six," said Sister Monica, in reply to the Mother Superior's query.

Sister Teresa gave her the permission. The little nun gravely thanked her and retired.

The morning mist had now risen from the pine forest and the sunlight came flooding in through the eastern window of the cell. Sister Teresa went to it and stood for a time looking at the beauty of the early autumn morning. She could see, down the mountain-side, the peasant women, their heads bound in bright kerchiefs, gleaning the harvest field. Many of them had been away all the summer, working with their men in the re-foresting nurseries that the Government maintained in these Carpathian Mountains. During that time they lived in cabins, sleeping on beds of pine needles. It was considered great good fortune to get employment in these nurseries.

How lovely the earth was, thought Sister Teresa, as she looked out over the golden morning. Her heart beat quicker at the familiar scene. Someone was felling a tree in the woods, the chop-chop of the axe came clearly across in the sharp air. Some of the children were having a singing lesson in the school-room. Right up the mountain-side, set in a clearing of the dense forest, the windows of a summer chalet, belonging to a Bucharest magnate, caught the sun and flashed their reflections, like fire in the dark wall of forest trees. In the singular way that thought is provoked by associations, she was reminded of how, years ago, the windows of Kensington Palace used to burn with the morning sun. She used to take Ronnie to the round pond to sail his boat, and as they came across Kensington Gardens the windows of the palace shone dazzlingly. "Does the Queen make them shine, mummy?" she remembered he had once asked.

Sister Teresa looked at her watch. It was nearly ten o'clock. She must go down to her office. Strange, but that young German was in her mind again. He was unhappy and anxious, she felt. His charm still lay upon her, curiously.

Kneeling at the *prie-dieu*, she began a prayer for him, beseeching holy comfort and guidance for his troubled boy's heart.

II

The Mayor of Predeal arrived at ten o'clock and was shown into the room where public business was transacted by the Mother Superior. A demure nun invited him to sit down, and left the room. He was a butcher by trade and his coarse clothes smelt of the slaughterhouse in which he had been working since seven o'clock. Any other man visiting the convent would have changed into his best clothes. But not Boris Tortcher, fortified by a quart of rachiu, swallowed at the inn on the way up. He was not afraid of a lot of nuns. He resented having to come to see the Mother Superior. He was the new Mayor, and she should come to see him. And she was going to get nothing out of him. He knew these crafty Catholics, always wheedling money out of people.

He sat and waited, shuffling his heavy feet. He looked at his watch. Why, it was five minutes past ten! He was the Mayor of Predeal, and he was being kept waiting by an old nun, one of those proud Englishwomen.

Stamping out of the room, he startled a nun in the corridor by shouting at her.

"Hey you! Tell the Mother Superior I'm waiting for her, and I'm a busy man," he said, and went back into the room.

A nun knocked at the door of Sister Teresa's cell to inform her the Mayor had arrived. There was no response. She knocked again, and, no answer coming, she opened the door and peered in. Sister Teresa was on her knees praying, her head bent over her folded hands. The nun quietly entered, shut the door, and stood waiting in silence. After a time she coughed discreetly, to inform the Mother Superior of her presence, but without effect. Then, a little puzzled by the statuesque quietude of the kneeling figure, she approached nearer. Something in the attitude of Sister Teresa seemed a little strange.

"*Ma Sœur!*" she whispered, and again louder, "*Ma Sœur! Ma Sœur!*"

She bent closer to the unresponding figure of the Mother Superior, and then, suddenly aware of Death's presence, she fled from the room, calling for the Sisters.

CHAPTER XXIII

ATHENS, FULL STOP

I

THE Arlberg-Orient express was completing the last stage of its long journey across Europe. All night, after leaving Salonica, it chuffed along southwards, hugging the flat plain by the Gulf. It passed the foot of Mount Olympus and, turning inland, went down the Vale of Tempe, sung of the poets of ancient Greece. But in the darkness nothing of its famed loveliness could be seen. Nor was Nikolas Metaxa concerned with the classic scenery of his beloved Greece. Having secured a place for his feet to rest, he slept soundly, snoring in concert with three Levantines and a fat Greek who had entered the carriage at Salonica.

During the stop at Lamia he woke and looked at his watch. The dawn was coming over the mountains. He was now only a hundred and forty miles from Athens. The train resumed its journey. He stared out of the window thinking of odd things. M. Gregoropoulos would just be going to the early fruit market at Covent Garden. Xenia would be fast asleep in her bedroom over her father's shop. Why had she not written this last week? A stupid fear that she might have jilted him, tired of waiting, came into his head. He dismissed it. Her letters were always full of love for him. Had she changed much in appearance during these five years? He was no longer a slim youth himself, he had thickened with good living at the Restaurant Phaleron.

He found himself thinking about the little King of Slavonia.

256

Nikolas had got out of the train and joined the crowd in the station at Nish to see the official reception. The poor little boy looked very frightened among all those grandees saluting and bowing. The Queen was quite overcome. He felt sorry for them, although he had no sympathy with Royalty and all the rest of the top-dog gang. But they were human. There was a miserable little anarchist working in the Phaleron kitchen. He wanted equality for everybody, but he was a shirker at his work, and a mean liar when found out. "Not so much of your 'we,' " Nikolas had said to him one day, during one of his voluble diatribes, "I don't want to be classed with you. You're not a man, you're a mess of envy. You can't do your job, so why want to take on others?" That had shut him up for a few hours.

It was full day now, the heat was quickly growing, although it was not yet eight o'clock. The train arrived at Thebes. Nikolas got out and bought himself a bottle of water and some grapes. A boy calling *"Seeka freska!"* suddenly brought back the ghost of another boy who had gone out into the streets of Athens selling figs.

The whistle blew, the train started. They crossed a plain, and came again to a rocky defile. The countryside was Greece in all its beauty, vivid in sunlight, with bare outcrops of rocks, and ranges of mountains with mauve and violet hues in a shadowed patchwork of colour under the blazing blue canopy of heaven. They passed Tanagra. The Levantines in the carriage opened a basket and shared a meal of sausages smelling strongly of garlic. It was a smell Nikolas now hated. He had never forgotten his shame when, that evening in the Englishman's flat in Athens, reference had been made to the nickname Mr. Teddy had given him and to his smelling of garlic. He had never touched it since.

Nikolas's eyes ached with insufficient sleep, with the glare of the light, but he watched every mile of the way through Attica.

The train, coming out of a gorge, turned and crossed the dried-up bed of a torrent. Nikolas's eyes opened wider, his heart gave a bound. There, in the distance, was Athens, with the Acropolis and its temple cutting the sky, and green-girdled Mount Lyca-bettus rising nobly from the plain in which the city lay! And at the sight of these landmarks of his beloved Athens his eyes filled with tears.

They were moving through the suburbs now, sidings and fac-tories hemmed them in. Nikolas took down his bowler hat and dusted it. The train slowly drew in, halted, so that he wanted to get out and run along the track, and crawled on again into the Larissa station. Was Xenia there? He leaned far out of the carriage. Then he hurried with his bag down the corridor to the door.

She was not on the platform. She was not in the station. He looked everywhere. The train was on time. Saturday, ten-thirty, he had said in his letter. Surely she had not mistaken the date? His elation had vanished, and he felt tired, and full of appre-hension. All the people of the express had now gone. He picked up his bag and slowly walked to the entrance. He felt ridiculous in his hot clothes and his bowler hat. He took the hat off and carried it. Crossing the booking-hall, someone waved an arm and came hurrying out of the vivid sunlight.

"Nikolas! Nikolas!" cried a man, excitedly.

Nikolas could not see his face, black against the light. He stared, then, all at once, his heart thumped. It was Menelas Argyros, the cobbler, Xenia's father. He cried out to Nikolas, mopped his perspiring forehead, and then embraced him ecstat-ically, kissing him on each cheek.

"Nikolas, my boy! Nikolas! The tram was blocked!" he panted, patting Nikolas's back, his beaming face beaded with sweat. His loose shirt was open at the collar, he had not shaved.

"Xenia, where's Xenia? She knew I was coming?" demanded Nikolas.

"Yes—yes, I'll tell you, in the tram," answered the breathless Menelas.

"No—a taxi," said Nikolas, recklessly. There was bad news: Xenia had jilted him.

They got into a taxi. Menelas gave the address.

"Where is Xenia?" demanded Nikolas the moment they were seated.

"Oh, my poor boy!" said Menelas, putting a hand on his knee. "We are in great trouble."

"Trouble?" echoed Nikolas.

"Xenia has been nearly killed. Ten days ago she was knocked down by a motor outside the Post Office, where she'd gone to post a letter to you. She was so excited that morning when your letter came, saying you were coming home, that she had to go straight away with her reply to the General Post Office, to be sure it went at once. Well, getting off the tram, she ran round the back to cross the road, and didn't see the motor coming along. It went over her—it wasn't the driver's fault. They took her to the hospital, and sent for us. We didn't see her then. We saw her two days later. They told us—they told us, Nikolas—oh, my boy—" broke off the little man, tears streaming down his hot, fat face.

"Yes—yes—they told you—what?" cried Nikolas, in a trembling voice.

"Nikolas—she'll never walk again. Our poor lovely Xenia!" sobbed the old cobbler.

Nikolas felt his heart stop still. They entered the busy Rue Constantine, but he scarcely heeded where they were going. The sun seemed to have gone out of the sky.

"Her spine is injured—she's paralysed in the legs," went on the old man, wiping his eyes.

"But they can do something—the doctors can do something!" repeated Nikolas.

"Nothing, Nikolas, nothing. It's a miracle her legs are spared."

"She knows?"

"Yes. She's quite calm, poor child. It's you she thinks of," answered the cobbler.

The taxi came to the University, past Korai Street, where once Nikolas dreamed of opening his restaurant. But he did not notice where they were. There was a weight dragging at his heart, and he was too dazed to see the bright city of his youth.

II

At five o'clock that afternoon they admitted Nikolas to the ward in which Xenia lay. She had changed little in the five years of separation, and he noticed how lovely were her eyes and skin as she lay half propped up on the white pillows. They could hardly talk to each other at first, and he sat holding her hand, while they smiled bravely at each other. But after a while she began to ask him about his life in London. Presently she spoke of herself.

"I'm sorry for you, Nikolas. I wanted them to stop you coming, but they wouldn't. I'm no use to you. I could never bear you children, or work in the restaurant. You must go back to London, Nikolas, you are getting on so well there," she said, forcing a smile to her face.

"Xenia! Xenia!" was all he could say, his eyes brimming, his hand pressing hers.

She talked then of other things. She was glad he was staying with her parents.

It was time for the visit to end. Nikolas leaned over and kissed her. He would come the same time to-morrow, he said.

Her eyes followed him all the way down the ward. Then she turned her face to the pillow, and cried until she could cry no more.

Out in the street, Nikolas stood bewildered. He did not know where to go now. He hardly knew what he was doing. All the wonderful plans he had made for this day and other days now meant nothing to him.

It was nearly six o'clock, the hour when the Athenians began to take their promenade in the National Garden. He walked on towards Constitution Square and, coming to the Royal Palace, looked at the monument to the Unknown Soldier, and watched the two evzones parading in their white frilled fustanellas and shoes tipped with red pompons. The familiar sight would have thrilled him at any other time. He passed on into the shady Garden, and, coming to a seat with a view of Mount Hymettus, sat down and fell into a melancholy reverie.

What now, he asked himself. His world had crashed into ruin. His heart ached for Xenia. She was so lovely even now, condemned for ever to a kind of half-life. In a month, the doctors had told her, she would be able to sit up. She would be able to work with her hands, and to propel herself about in a wheeled chair, but never to walk, unless a miracle happened.

It was impossible to imagine Xenia crippled. She was always so light on her feet. She loved dancing, and no matter how tired, after her work in the café, she had often got him to take her to a dance-hall. He remembered also how swift she was when he had chased her down the hillside and through the pinewoods that last day at Daphni. Afterwards, they had lain in the shadow and had sleepily heard a shepherd playing on his pipe as he went by with his sheep.

Why was he torturing himself with these memories? He got up, walked to the curving terrace of the Zappeion, and emerged on the boulevard that led by the high bastions of the Acropolis. Still walking, he mounted to the iron gates before the Propylæa and, seating himself there, watched the city below, reddening in the light of the falling sun. The voice of its life rose faintly from the plain. It was here he had first come with Xenia, on a warm spring night. They had been a little shy of each other then, until, in his youthful ardour, he had suddenly taken her in his arms and kissed her.

She would never come here again, unless carried by someone. Always there must be someone now to look after her. The dream of their restaurant was dead. He could go back to London now, she said. He had not answered that statement. He knew she had said it to release him, that she had faced the fact of her uselessness as a wife and mother.

He could go back to London. They would readily take him back at the Phaleron. He would not now be going to a strange and frightening city. He had grown to love London, for all its greyness. He had friends there, and more than friends. There was Maria, in love with him, with her three hundred pounds and a desire to go into a nice little business in Soho.

He dismissed the idea indignantly, ashamed of thinking such a thing while poor Xenia lay there, crippled from the waist down. How different it might all have been but for that accident! If he had married Xenia, and the accident had happened afterwards, what a responsibility would have been his!

The thought gave him a shock. Supposing that had been the case, he could not then have fled to England. He would have made the best of it in his love for her.

He stood up suddenly, as if a revelation had struck him. Surely he should act now as he would have acted had Xenia been his wife? He loved her, he had asked her to wait for him, which she had, in her strong faith in him.

The sweat broke out on his brow and he trembled as he stood there in the warm evening. For a while he looked out over the wide city, now under the violet pall of Athens' evening light. Then he started downwards, his mind made up, his heart lighter.

At the back of the cobbler's shop in Hadrien Street there was a small pergola built out from the wall, with a vine growing over it. It was under this, in the cooling evening, that Nikolas found Menelas Argyros and his wife sitting. He joined them, carrying out a chair from the kitchen. For a time they carefully avoided any allusion to his visit to the hospital. He was the first to speak of it, and presently they all talked freely. He heard a full account of those terrible ten days, of Xenia's urgent plea that he should be told before he started his journey.

"I would have come even sooner," said Nikolas, quietly.

The old woman looked at him. The cobbler smoked. There was a silence.

"Xenia said in her last letter that old Kamenos was wanting to sell his restaurant in Hermes Street. Has he still got it?" asked Nikolas.

"I don't know, Nikolas—why?" asked the cobbler, taking the cigar out of his mouth.

"I think I could make something of it, if the price isn't too high," he answered.

"But won't you go back to London, Nikolas, now that—that——" faltered the old man.

"Of course not," said Nikolas, briskly. "Why should I? Xenia's got her brains and her hands. She can give change, and keep bills, and sit at the desk, as well as keep an eye on things when I'm marketing. And with a wheeled chair she'll be able to get around all right. Oh, we'll make money, you'll see! And who knows, one day she may find she can walk again. Miracles do happen. Surgeons to-day——''

He stopped. The old woman had burst into tears. He looked at her, then he got up and went over to her, and put an arm across her shoulder.

"Now, mother, don't be so upset," he said, cheerfully. "Xenia'll be all right, you'll see!"

The old woman caught at his hand and, sobbing, pressed it against her cheek.

Nikolas looked across at Menelas, and Menelas, smoking, looked at Nikolas. Then, taking the cigar out of his mouth:

"Yes, mother. Xenia'll be all right with Nikolas," he said.

THE END